KING
OF COINS

Also by Nicholas Carter:

KING
OF COINS

Nicholas Carter

ORION

Copyright © Nicholas Carter 1999
All rights reserved

The right of Nicholas Carter to be identified
as the author of this work has been
asserted by him in accordance with the
Copyright, Designs and Patents Act 1988.

First published in Great Britain in 1999 by
Orion
An imprint of Orion Books Ltd
Orion House, 5 Upper St Martin's Lane
London WC2H 9EA

A CIP catalogue record for this book
is available from the British Library

ISBN 0 75281 008 1

Typeset at The Spartan Press Ltd,
25 New Street, Lymington, Hants
Printed in Great Britain by
Clays Ltd, St Ives plc

DRAMATIS PERSONAE
The Bloody Score

✦

HOUSE HOWATH

- JOHN GULLIVER, LORD HOWATH *Warden of the English Middle March upon the Scots border*
- MIRANDA *his daughter*
- JAMES ELDRITCH *Howath's Captain of Horse*
- MERRON *James' younger sister*
- JEREMIAH HOBBY *sergeant of archers*
- WILLIAM HACKER, GEOFFREY ELVER, CLEMENT TEAGUE *serving in Howath's retinue*
- EDWARD NAILER *Howath's clerk*
- LONG LIZZIE FAITHFUL *Howath's favourite whore*
- RUTH MALAHIDE *herbswoman*

HOUSE GUELDRES

- CHARLES, DUC DE GUELDRES *rebellious nobleman*
- ABELARD, VICOMTE D'TOINUEILL *'The Bastard Geldray', his illegitimate son, commander of the Landsknecht Black Legion*
- FRANCESCO SAVVI *Lieutenant Colonel of the Black Legion*
- CONSTANTIN MUHLBERG *Savvi's Locotenent and assassin*

HOUSE TARSI

- ALBERTO TARSI, SEIGNEUR OF MONT GALLIARD *a gentleman of war*
- ANGELICA *his daughter*
- CONSTANZIA *her maid*
- CESAR ALLESSANDRO SCARALATCHI *his court composer*
- FABRIZIO AMBOLINI *former choirboy and Scaralatchi's catamite*

ADDITIONAL CHARACTERS

- KING HENRY VIII OF ENGLAND
- KING FRANCIS I OF FRANCE
- THE CHEVALIER BAYARD *knight*
- CARDINAL AMERIGO RUNCINI *head of Papal delegation to Aosta*
- EDWARD KRAVEN *a merchant, Howath's confidante*
- EUSEBIUS DELLA STROMA *Count of Lunigiana, an ally of the Gueldres clan*
- ALEXANDER KERR *reiver chief and Laird of Tullymallock upon the Scots border*
- ANGUS *his son*
- ABBOT HERVE ODO *of the Abbey D'Eleron in Southern France*
- ABANDANDO BRICONET *Papal Legate to Avignon and agent of the Holy Inquisition*
- WILFRED STITCHWORT *fireworker*

PROLOGUE

✦

'Some princes flourish one day and
come to grief the next, without
appearing to have changed in
character in any other way,'

Machiavelli, *The Prince*

Beside the Castello Villefranco,
in the Maritime Alps

✦

Every living thing in the fortress had been turned to stone by grief. Even the rushlights, glimmering on cast-iron stands in every alcove, seemed unnaturally subdued, the feeble illumination barely lifting the all-pervading gloom. Priests chanted their litanies while helpless surgeons conversed in whispers, waiting for the inevitable end. Duke Lodovico lay dying, and the rumour-mongers who teemed in the bowels of the castle reckoned his precious Duchy wouldn't last long without him – not with his wastrel of a son set to inherit.

The Mounier domain was one of a number of tiny duchies, counties, principalities and marquisates clustered about the foot of the Alps, hemmed in by towering mountains, treacherous seas – and all-powerful enemies. To the west, France. To the east the grasping Republic of Genoa, to the north, the sprawling Marquisate of Saluzzo. Between these conglomerations there were any number of smaller outposts, parcels of territory which owed their allegiance to a larger host state – ekeing out an existence like ticks on a bull.

The resourceful Mounier clan was typical of the breed.

They had ruled their clifftop eyrie for seven generations, walking a precarious tightrope between France, the rising–falling Italian states and the ever-present Empire. They had earned independence of a sort in the barren no-man's-land between the mighty adversaries. Their stronghold had endured siege and famine, blizzards and battering, but the canny old Duke's days were shortening fast. The patient, grey-green seas swelled around the standing rocks and subsided once more, the creeks and crannies running with foaming water. White spume fell away from the piled foundations of the castle, standing bleak and proud above the waves.

Even the choughs and crows which wheeled about the

3

seaweed-racked towers had been silenced, mourning the old Duke's passing as they flew majestic caracoles beneath his shrouded balcony.

The watcher dropped the heavy velvet drape back into place, plunging the lofty platform into darkness – natural habitat of Signors Vitt and Belatavicci, senior stewards to the Grand House of Mounier.

The courtiers had been watching the stormcrows gather from their ill-lit gallery above the sea wall, fascinated by the carrion birds' endless manoeuvres. They had watched them with silent foreboding as they glided by on stilled wings, soulless eyes scanning the rocky pile as if searching for some sign the old man had gone.

A puff of smoke from the twisted chimney stack, the lowering of the Mounier banners, the mournful toll of a bell.

The dank passage was still as a morgue, fragrant torches dimmed. Long shadows reached out over the bare slabs of crudely-dressed stone, pierced here and there by the sightless stare of ancient embroideries, the long-dead ancestors Duke Lodovico would shortly be joining.

The two men hidden in the alcove spoke in undertones, the minute movement of their lips testimony to their skilful and well-practised confidentiality. Nobody would have known they were conversing at all, save for the occasional plume of vapour which escaped their narrow mouths.

'There's no use in denying any longer, sir. The French will hear of it before he's cold!'

The cowled man grimaced at his companion's frank assessment.

'They've enough on their plates with the war and all, do you imagine they will spare troops for an insignificant backwater such as this?'

His companion took a shallow breath – all he needed to maintain his fragile shadow-life. 'They would spare troops to try for Villefranco, even if the Emperor Elect himself was camped before the Louvre! Baldassare is the lesser of the two evils, I say.'

'*Il Sghero*? That tyrant? You know what that would mean for young Gerhard.' The speaker ran his forefinger across his throat. 'And we wouldn't be far behind him!'

'None of us will live forever, Master Vitt!'

'Indeed not, *Signor* Belatavicci, but I rather fancy seeing out

4

the month, if you don't mind,' the other man hissed, giving his companion a withering glance. Igon Vitt – the old Duke's chancellor – shrugged his shoulders, the cold wind working its way through the lancet and piercing his thinly-fleshed bones.

'Baldassare's not as bad as all that, for a soldier.'

'For a whoring mercenary! He's no more than a bandit, if you want the truth!'

'Duke Lodovico was a soldier, in his youth.'

'His brother's a thug and a killer. He and the Duke are as different as black knight and white bishop. If you call him here, you're signing Gerhard's death warrant.'

'He wouldn't dare. His own nephew?'

'Come now sir,' Belatavicci whispered. 'He'd crush him like a bedlouse.'

Vitt pondered this in silence. His companion raised his eyebrows. 'You think we'd outlive Gerhard, eh?'

'He could be persuaded to abdicate, times being what they are. His father has raised a student, not a soldier.'

That was true enough. Lodovico had brought up his son by the strictest platonic principles, sending for the finest tutors from all over Italy to complete his classical education. Gerhard could speak six languages, play the clavichord, sing, act and could even turn his delicate hand to writing passable poetry in the French style. Fine attributes for a stoic, for a renaissance scholar, but feeble qualifications for a new Duke, surrounded by a sea of greedy, grasping, ruthless enemies. A cracked walnut trapped by slowly shifting boulders. The entire Duchy, their entire existence, could be swatted away in an afternoon and nobody would raise a whisper of protest.

'But he will be *de jure* Duke of Villefranco, no matter what bloodthirsty oaf takes over the reins. Baldassare couldn't afford to leave him alive, not even if he was locked up in some damned monastery.'

'We could hide him.'

'He'd have his whereabouts out of us in half an hour.'

'We could send him overseas.'

'And . . .' the chancellor held up his hand, his acute hearing detecting the softest movement on the staircase at the end of the passage.

'Here he comes!'

The two men seemed to melt back into the walls, their tired robes matching the bruised and mouldy stone. They watched the

5

feeble glimmer of a candle illuminate the stairwell, cast a giant shadow over the mildewed hangings.

The pale wraith swept down the passage, holding the dim lamp before him. The lurid yellow light cast a sickly pallor over his pinched features, turned his unkempt hair to spiderweb strands. The intruder stared straight ahead, his watery blue eyes mistier than his lightly woven robe.

'My lords, are you so terrified of my father's death you cower in alcoves and pretend it cannot be?'

The courtiers glanced at one another, horribly bemused by the watchful lordling. Gerhard paused, a shimmering apparition in the candlelight.

'My lord, we feared to discuss matters of such import in your father's bedchamber: the surgeons, the servants . . .' Belatavicci explained, well aware any denial would be futile.

This prince was a weakling, but no fool. Why the damned youth seemed to flit about the castle like an anaemic bat!

'He is failing then?'

The courtiers bowed their heads.

'And I shall soon be Duke of Villefranco.'

'As God wills, my lord.'

Gerhard nodded, smiled wanly and passed on down the corridor.

Belatavicci sighed with relief. Vitt snorted. 'We'd best get after him. But mark me, if we don't send word to Baldassare, we'll have the French breathing down our necks by the end of the week!'

'We must think things through. Baldassare . . .'

'It's either the devil we know or some prick of a Vicomte from Paris or Orleans. Believe me Belatavicci, I know these French. We'd be better off selling our souls to the Turks!'

The servants crossed the room on tiptoe, barely disturbing the dust in the stuffy bedchamber. Old Lodovico was lying out on his sweat-damp pillows, his carefully combed hair and fine silver beard lovingly arranged over the soiled bedding. The surgeons had bled and leeched him, as much to ensure they earned their fee as through any medical necessity. They stood by now, wringing their hands as if willpower alone could save the doomed Duke.

Gerhard closed the heavy door with a quiet click, and regarded his father from the end of the bed. The old man's chest rose, the piled bedding betraying his feeble breath.

Still not dead then. What was he waiting for, a handwritten invitation from St Peter himself?

He smiled beatifically, crossed the room on his slippered feet.

'Father dear. You look so much brighter than this morning,' he lied. Lies came easily to young Gerhard. They ought to, he'd lived a lie these last sixteen years. Gerhard allowed himself a tiny smile of satisfaction.

Very soon now, and he could stop pretending.

'Perhaps some broth? A little tonic?'

Lodovico clutched feeble as his son's underdeveloped arm. He had long since lost power of speech, thank Christ.

'You see father dear, your grip is as strong as ever! You will quite bend me in two, clasping my poor wrist so!'

Belatavicci and Vitt, who had crept into the room after their prince, glanced significantly at one another. Belatavicci leaned closer to his companion.

'You're right. I'll send word to Baldassare. Better the devil you know than a limp-wrist milksop.'

By St Mary's Wharf, Calais, in the English Pale

◆

'Sweet wife, my lambkin Miranda,' the merchant crooned, running his crooked finger beneath the girl's chin. He raised her head a notch, admiring her fresh-faced beauty as if he were pondering whether to buy a piece of classical sculpture. Howath's daughter was without doubt the finest catch in the English Pale, the whole of France for that matter.

And he had caught her, trapped her fluttering heart as if he were spinning for larks on a summer down back home.

'There really is no need for you to go bothering yourself with these wearisome details,' he explained, endlessly patient. 'Who serves who, what, where and when? Your father – God rest his good soul – and I, have more than enough clerks and solicitors to see to everything.'

God knew he was paying them enough to settle the old man's estate. He smiled winningly, clasping the girl with gentle familiarity. The truth was the merchant could hardly keep his hands off her.

She had captivated him during their procession through the Pale the previous summer, the tedious journey which had culminated in their eventful visit to the legendary Field of the Cloth of God. Miranda Howath's ravishing beauty had made the finest knight in armour look tired and tarnished. She had attracted more admiring glances than the fairest pavilion or the sleekest, most sure-footed destrier. Neither the ambitious Henry VIII nor his magnificent guest Francis I could have boasted such a fabulous filly. Edward Kraven had never imagined the girl would have fallen for his rather mature charms.

He was, after all, a friend of her father Lord Howath and almost thirty years her senior. He was coolly intelligent, kindly enough but careworn – prone to worry-fits which thickened his blood and thinned his hair. Tall and stooped, he would hold his

8

head at an angle as if he were afraid of missing some titbit or rumour.

Kraven had joined the massive pilgrimage to Guisnes to witness the long-awaited meeting between the great kings. To marvel at the splendour of their respective courts, bask in their reflected glory – and seek out a few mercantile agreements of his own.

What he had not anticipated was prospecting for a bride – not with hotspurs like James Eldritch around. The young rogue was typical of the conceited swordsmen who had flocked to Guisnes, bent on showing off their prowess before two of the most prestigious courts in all Europe. Eldritch had been captain at arms to Miranda's father, an enigmatic, unevenly-tempered upstart with ambitions far above his lowly station. He had, in his overweening arrogance, completely neglected to secure the virgin prize he had apparently imagined to be his by right. Had he shown the girl the slightest consideration he could have counted on inheriting Lord Howath's castles, possessions and warband the moment the wedding banns were read.

But he had made an appalling miscalculation, his petulant scheming ending in shameful failure and personal disgrace. He had attempted to win Howath's warband for himself, tricking his master out of his men while he was crazy in his cups.

His punishment? To wander the wastes of Northern Italy for a year and a day, a black-hearted mercenary in the service of strangers. Eldritch and his hard-riding warband had become the property of a thrice-damned whoremaster called the Vicomte D'Toinueill – known as the Bastard Gueldres to the tongue-tied English.

The two were made for one another, Kraven thought darkly. The canny merchant, older and so much wiser than the impetuous captain, hadn't let the girl out of his sight ever after. He had remained at her side, as kind and considerate as a man could be, while her poor deceived father sickened with shame and took to his bed at the merchant's splendid townhouse about Calais' wharves. Kraven was a wealthy and successful merchant, vice-chairman of Bristol's prestigious Society of Merchant Venturers. He owned seven ships as well as substantial properties in Bristol and Calais. He had established a complex network of contacts all over the Mediterranean and was well known in Crete and Cadiz. He could draw on several lines of credit in most of the major ports – which was a sight more than his old friend Howath could claim. Nobody could have accused him of ingratiating himself into the sickly warden's household – he could have bought and sold the old fool a dozen times over.

The late Lord Howath's only asset – Miranda – was just seventeen years old. She was tall and slim, her complexion as fresh as a bluebell in a Spring glade. Her dark hair cascaded down her back, the curling tips just brushing her swelling hurdies.

Kraven closed his eyes and pictured her as she had been on their wedding night, blushing in the ripe heat given off by the banked fireplace. Her nipples had stood out against the light calico like frosted cherries, the dark dimple of her belly button and her neatly trimmed pubic hair showing clearly through the deliciously opaque material. He thought he had died and gone to heaven, to have brought off such a stunning coup. To have wedded one of the most eligible girls in the entire Pale, made this angel his chattel.

Not that Miranda had a great deal of competition in the bleak streets of backwater Calais, Kraven remembered with a sour frown. The governor's girls looked like warthogs shipped in from the desert heart of Africa. The harbourmaster's hitherto favoured fillies wouldn't have brought him a handful of shekels at the Algiers slave market!

No, Kraven knew he had stumbled on a prize, a fantastic, uncut jewel, full of her own bewildered innocence. He knew Miranda had never been noted for her stunning intellect – God rarely bestowed so many gifts in one mortal. But he hadn't paid court to her in order to corner her intelligence, nor did he intend her to sit up all hours balancing his ledgers. She did her service between the sheets, where she could bring his ripest fantasy to sweet, sticky life.

Miranda raised her brown eyes from her needlepoint, tongue protruding between her lips, at once knowing woman and innocent child. By Jesu! The simple-hearted girl would drive him to distraction.

'But I can't help wondering what you will gain by calling poor father's retinue home. A few hundred rapscallion soldiers! They were always making such a mess at Crow Hole, with their filthy boots and stinky clothes! Where would we keep them, husband dear? Surely not here in Calais? It's so cramped and gloomy for them!' Miranda looked about the sumptuously-appointed room, the lapis lazuli about the fireplace, the expensive, watered silk hangings, the fine paintings Kraven had acquired during his speculative missions around the courts of Europe. Kraven tilted his head fondly, indulged her with a smile.

'Miranda, Miranda,' he began, smoothing his beard as if he were a patient schoolmaster overseeing an unruly student. 'If you insist on wearying yourself with the dreary details of our business, so be it.' He took a deep, contemplative breath. Miranda tried to concentrate, acutely aware she knew next to nothing about the peace talks her husband had been so diligently attending the previous weeks.

'The truth of the matter, my dear, is that the discussions which have kept me away from you for so long are on the brink of a complete and irretrievable breakdown.'

Wolsey was playing Fabian as only he could, intending as always to avoid, or at best, delay, committing England to any damaging alliance. But not even Wolsey was man enough to master Charles' envoy Gattinara. He summarised the position as simply as he could:

'The Empire is putting increasing pressure on us to alter our present, pro-French policies.'

Miranda bit her lip, wishing she hadn't asked.

'We will be at war with the French before the year is out,' he concluded. Here at least was something she could grasp. The girl's angelic features crumpled with concern.

'More fighting? But I thought everyone had made friends at Guisnes! Those lovely tents, the chapel they dedicated! I thought Henry and Francis parted as brothers, promising everlasting peace,' the naive child responded petulantly.

'So they did my dear; so they did. But twelve months is a long time in international politics. And it is now politic for Henry to seek closer ties with the Emperor-Elect, Charles.'

'Kings, Dukes, Constables, Emperors! They are no more than village bullies fighting one another outside the ale house,' Miranda decided, scowling. The merchant indulged her pitiful grasp of European affairs.

'Well said my dear, although I wouldn't go broadcasting those views in the warehouse or upon the wharves,' he added cautiously. 'But Henry's decision obliges me to take . . . certain precautions, as regards our own fortunes.'

'Our fortunes? What fortune have I brought you, a poor, silly girl?'

Kraven licked his lips, smiled graciously. 'It's simply not worth bothering your head about, my sweet.'

'I know my dowry wasn't as large as it might have been . . .'

Dowry? Kraven would have paid Howath his daughter's weight in gold, to win her hand. A dowry had been the least of his considerations, when he had approached the poor warden the previous Christmas. They had settled the entire business in half an hour, Howath nodding like some dotard from his piled pillows. Kraven winced at the memory.

'Miranda, light of my life. I would never dream of picking over the details of your dowry, behaving like some wretched Venetian trying to squeeze a few more shillings from my in-laws. I was more than content with the bargain I made, even if the sums involved were . . .' Kraven shrugged, as if he were hideously embarrassed to dwell on such mercenary concerns.

Miranda threw down her needlepoint, her eyes bright.

'There! You admit it! Even though the sums were not so large as you had cause to expect, you were about to say so yourself!'

Kraven shook his head. 'I assure you, my little sweetbread, I was more than satisfied with the arrangement made by your late father and I. Crow Hole, Mountjoy Castle, your mother's jewels, all your father's weapons, bag and baggage.'

Draughty ruins, cheap paste, a selection of rusting swords he could barely lift and half a dozen wagonloads of assorted trash and kindling, Kraven thought sourly.

Miranda pouted. 'There! And all the time you pretended you were more than satisfied with the settlement!'

She was on the verge of tears, precisely where Kraven wanted her.

'There is not a man on this Earth more satisfied with his settlement, my precious gift from heaven,' he crooned, placing his hands over her shoulders and holding her into the seat beside the fire. 'But with things the way they are, I have no choice but to call the Ride back from this Italian adventure Eldritch has taken them off on. They might certainly prove useful, if Francis invades the Pale,' Kraven admitted with silky understatement.

'Invades?'

'Why of course my dear. We live on a frontier every inch as exposed as your poor father's Middle March. The French could sweep us all into the sea, should they choose,' he said warningly.

Miranda picked up her needlepoint and wished for the hundredth time Merron was there to guide her. James had taken his energetic younger sister with him, leaving her to try and make sense of this complicated world by herself.

Merron always knew exactly what to say and when to say it. She never had to be reminded which fork to use or which glass to sup from, and was never troubled to remember people's names. She knew some Latin, a little Greek, and could read poems in French that sounded quite divine (even though Miranda had no idea what the delightful verses actually meant). Merron knew algebra and could recite the capital cities of every state in Europe – even if she did occasionally forget to hold her tongue before her elders.

'And the last thing I desire is to insult your father's memory by failing to ensure that his beloved daughter, the sole fruit of his loins, is adequately protected,' Kraven said heavily.

Miranda felt a prickle of pride. Edward might be old and slightly grey around the temples, but he was always *so* thoughtful. He had treated her as an adult, rather than as a spoilt child. Her smile slipped a little. She looked guiltily at her embroidery. Kraven noticed her momentary concern, and wondered if his gentle manoeuvring had upset her more than he had anticipated. The warden was barely cold in his tomb, and it might not be meet to invoke his memory quite so frequently.

But Miranda wasn't thinking about her father. She might not be the wisest woman in the world, but she was acute enough to recognise that the high regard she felt for Kraven bore no relation to the love, the rash excitement she felt when she remembered James, far away in Italy.

In truth, Miranda had been transfixed by Eldritch's awkward attentions, delighted by his gruff enquiries into her health and well-being. He could strap on a sword and charge about the Highlands after Scots bandits, but he had always been comically unsure of himself when he had found himself alone before Miranda's heaving breastworks. The girl stifled a giggle, glanced up at her now bewildered husband. Kraven wondered what strange mood swing had wrested her mind from his control.

She sighed.

'As you wish, husband.'

The merchant paused. 'Then you are quite content for me to send word to Eldritch and the rest to return to Calais forthwith, to collect the warband's contract of indentures in my . . . I should say our, name?'

'Quite content.' She seemed deliberately careless, suddenly agreeing with all he had to say when moments before she had been ready to question his motives. Kraven prickled.

Eldritch!

She wanted to see him!

'Of course, this business with the abbey, the trial, one wonders what state of mind they will be in, if indeed they ever return to the Pale.'

He watched Miranda's hazel eyes flicker over her needlework.

'The last word we had from Aosta was before Christmas.' He shrugged, as if he would not vouchsafe the warband's continued existence. 'From this Tarsi character we have heard so much about.'

From the little Kraven had been able to glean from Merron's letters and his own network of agents about the North of Italy, Eldritch had thrown in his lot with an Italian soldier of fortune called Tarsi, in order to defeat the scurrilous charges brought against them by the Vicomte D'Toinueill. Kraven had met the sinister count back in Guisnes. He had known him to be the worst sort of scoundrel and cheat the moment he had set eyes on him.

'Thank God the Vicomte's lies were proved false,' Miranda said with a vehemence Kraven had rarely marked before.

His heart lurched, his acute mind racing with angry accusation, indignation . . . and appalling realisation.

Could it be true?

Despite his trying to trick her own father out of his warband, despite his careless conceit and foolish posturing, his wife loved James Eldritch, that arrogant, upstart ingrate! The fiend had ridden off into the unknown without a moment's thought for her or the father he had wronged. Instead of detesting him for eternity and cursing his wretched memory, she loved him harder than before, worshipped him with all her gentle heart – the heart she should have kept for him!

Miranda rarely mentioned Eldritch by name, and only ever in connection with some fondly remembered doing of his sister Merron. The artful girl had been Miranda's maid back at home on the Scots border, and had travelled to France as her friend and confidante. Sometimes, Kraven thought hotly, Miranda would invent some memory, some piece of girlish fun she had shared with her former maid, just to give herself an excuse for mentioning that detested name.

Eldritch!

To think he had given the boy a start, when his drunkard of a father had finally quaffed himself to death! He could have let the boy and his skinny-shanked sister starve on Bristol's wharves, but he had taken pity, arranged his posting to Crow Hole, and service with Lord Howath, King's Warden of the English Middle March.

The wretched boy had never thanked him for that Christian service, and here he was – or rather, there he was – gallivanting about Italy dangling his own wife's heart from a string!

'Thank God indeed,' Kraven murmured. Perhaps it would have been better if the cunning Vicomte's attempts to incriminate his enemies had succeeded. Eldritch would have certainly joined Tarsi on the scaffold. Miranda might have wept for days, but she would have forgotten him, given time. And yet here he was proposing to fetch the young spark back to Calais, to parade Miranda's lost lover before her all over again. He could just imagine the show the young buck would make, the devilish hero returned from unknown perils! His simple-souled wife would be captivated once more, entranced by his black-eyed stare.

Kraven tugged his beard in distraction.

But on the other hand, the warband was by far the most valuable commodity in Miranda's hastily-arranged dowry. With the war between France, England and the Empire about to erupt once more, a troop of seasoned horse soldiers would be worth their weight in gold. He could rent them out to some warlord and sit at home while they went campaigning. He could then fill the holes in the ranks with ragged-arsed farmboys and begin the process all over again. Running a pack of mercenaries was the second-oldest profession, and could be just as lucrative as its illustrious predecessor. So long as one used one's brain rather than one's heart, Kraven thought grimly.

'I was concerned young James might have been hornswoggled by this Tarsi character, tricked into signing over his men just as Gueldres had alleged.'

'Merron said no such thing,' Miranda said with spirit. 'Tarsi had *assumed* James would be so grateful for his acquittal that he would volunteer the Ride's services. But James refused,' she said haughtily.

James, James, James! Kraven thought hotly. Why, if she mentioned his cursed name once more he would strike her, so help him!

'Merron is a simple serving girl, my sweet. You cannot set too much store by her explanations. It seems to me this Tarsi detected some element in Eldritch's make-up he found objectionable. Either way,' he said before the girl could even think of contradicting him, 'it would not have been meet for James Eldritch to pledge the warband's service. Your father held his indentures, not him.'

Miranda stared into her lap, the needlepoint forgotten. She realised she had angered her husband and was anxious not to upset him further. He might even guess at her attachment to James, if she was not very careful.

'Gueldres tricked your father into handing the warband over to him, but the moment he was found guilty of that despicable attack on the abbey, the contract was made null and void. In other words,' he said, his temper flaring, 'the ownership of the Ride reverted to your father, and now it belongs . . .' he paused, squeezed her shoulders reassuringly.

Miranda froze. In other words, the Ride belonged to Edward Kraven, along with the crumbling ruins, the costume jewellery, the rusting swords.

And her.

'There my dear! The very thought of that beast Gueldres, making sport with our dear friends so, it makes my blood boil!' Kraven lied, shamefaced. The girl must have stolen his wits, to expose his feelings so easily.

'I will send my man Salt to Italy at once, and bring them home safe and well.' All of them apart from Eldritch, perhaps. 'There, now. What do you say to that?' he asked, heart in his mouth.

'I shall be delighted. To see my dear Merron again.'

For the first time in three months of marriage, they understood one another perfectly.

PART ONE

✦

'Harsh necessity and the newness
of my kingdom force me to do such things
and guard my frontiers everywhere,'

Aeneid, quoted Machiavelli, *The Prince*

By the Château Celestine, on the outskirts of Marseille

✦

The intruder crouched in the overgrown flowerbed, the tangled vegetation helping to disguise his unauthorised reconnaissance of the tumbledown château. The extensive grounds must once have been magnificent – but the fine lawns and gardens had gone to rack and ruin, and the wild undergrowth had concealed him all the way from the copse where they had left the horses. The shadowy figure waited amongst the creepers, alert for any signal he had been detected. But the merrymakers were too busy drinking and whoring to mark his presence. He had heard them a hundred yards off, bellowing and howling like night beasts accompanied by the discordant music of pipe and drum.

Brazen whistles and cheap trumpets hooted as if he had stumbled upon a nursery of spoilt children. He despised their farmyard antics, the crude lusts which had no doubt accelerated the ruin he saw all about him. His self-righteous contempt steeled his heart, convinced him he would be safe enough, here in the heartland of his enemies.

The Duc de Milhaud might be a long-lost cousin, but he was still a member of the detested Gueldres clan, the scattered family which had come within an ace of encompassing his extinction back in Aosta.

The intruder bristled with hatred.

He crept forward, parting the trailing brambles and ivy which hung about the sorry structure. The cankerous vines reminded him sharply of illustrations of the Tower of Babel, the hothouse weeds which had infested its sordid platforms.

The hellish orchestra played on. Surely not even the French could listen to a racket like that, he thought hotly. The wretched screech of poorly-tuned fiddles drowned out the noise as he ducked down and crawled beneath a window. He reached up and held on to the carelessly swinging shutter, raised his head to peer into the interior of the garishly-lit castle. His eyes, accustomed to the dark, were dazzled by the sudden illumination, and he ducked back down again with a curse.

He could hear them clearly now, shouting and huzzahing as the party-goers spewed on towards the small hours. The guttural laughs of the men mingled with the chattering, shriekingly insistent women.

What a nest of fornicating vipers!

By God, Lillith would never have allowed herself to be kept in such perverted squalor! They must have chained her against her will, tied her to the battered furniture to prevent her from hurling herself from the nearest window. The intruder closed his eyes. She would surely be locked up in some dungeon, further complicating his hazy rescue plans.

James Eldritch clenched his fists and tried to restrain himself from hurling the shutter open and slaughtering the entire pack. He breathed deeply, a silver plume in the chill air.

The captain blinked quickly and raised his head again. He focused slowly, as if his brain could not quite comprehend what he saw. The room was large – far grander even in its present extremity than Lord Howath's cramped apartments back at Crow Hole. A long table had been unceremoniously rammed up against one wine-splattered wall as an impromptu serving bar. The table was bedecked with bottles and pitchers, half of them rolling about spilling the last of their contents over the floor. Every other surface in the room had been stacked with goblets and glasses, great drinking horns and ornate punch bowls. The bizarre orchestra had clustered about one end of the table, attacking their instruments with panic-stricken precision. There were three fiddle players, a viol, two recorders and a flute. A woman in a red and gold striped cloak sat at the virginal, her thin hands glued to the ornately carved keys. Every now and then she looked over her shoulder, as if she were encouraging the miserable village band to play on. Every single musician had been blindfolded, presumably to ensure the beggarly neighbours could not actually see what was going on around the ring of couches set out just behind them.

The pink shapes he had at first taken to be carelessly bundled drapes were human bodies, writhing, crawling and bucking in ghastly ecstasy. There must have been fifty of them at least, all shapes and sizes. Slim, elegant ladies being pawed by grossly misshapen men with leering mouths and blooming bellies. Obese dames impaling themselves on stripling boys, their faces contorted into masks of hatefully exaggerated pleasure.

Little children – boys and girls – scampered and played among the entwined couples, as if their parents had brought them to a summer picnic by the river. Eldritch lowered his head, nauseated with dread. To think his elder sister had been kidnapped by these rogues, these slaves of Sodom! He dragged his sword from its scabbard, held the heavy blade in his fist. The deadly weight felt good, the shining steel would cleanse them, exorcise their beastly possessions!

There was a sudden crash and a curse behind him. Eldritch peered into the shadows, watched a naked man attempt to hold himself upright against a garden cane while simultaneously urinating over a bush. The rogue looked in danger of doing himself a mischief, entangling his anatomy in the trailing vines and brambles. He was chattering away to himself in French, clearly disadvantaged by his semi-erect penis. Eldritch froze, watched the dark-haired Frenchman raise his eyes heavenwards, stepping from one foot to the other as he waited for his erection to subside.

Eldritch stared, startled by the sudden movement about the man's round belly. Another set of hands had emerged from beneath his arms, circling his waist and groping towards the man's over-active member. The owner cursed, glanced over his shoulder as a young girl let him go, danced out behind him with her hands twined above her head.

Eldritch swallowed, captivated by the girl's elfin figure. Despite her slight build, her breasts were large and well-shaped, her nipples hard as buttons in the cold air. She performed a perfect pirouette, and then curtsied towards the house, no doubt giving the rogue a handsome view of her shapely buttocks. The naked man's intermittent flow spluttered to a halt once more. He glared at the dancing girl, grinning coquettishly as she danced out of his reach.

'Missing your mark, Claude? That's not like you!'

Eldritch's sword flickered in the lurid glare pouring out of the window. He had to concentrate to follow their flowery southern accents, the Langue Doc which still flourished in backward Provence.

'I'll piss straight enough, if you don't watch out!'

'Not even the mighty Milhaud could perform such a feat, from there!'

21

'How much do you wager, dumpling?'

Dumpling? There wasn't more than an ounce of meat on the girl, Eldritch thought distractedly. Perhaps he had misunderstood the expression.

'Never mind me you stallion, hit the wall from there, and I'll let you keep my serving girl!'

'The one with the squint? She's blonde above and brunette below, you know how much I loathe such pretence.'

'Your White Rabbit has quite spoilt you, my dear Claude. The blonde and the black page. He's supposed to be a prince of the blood, in Africa!'

'You didn't buy him for his regal lineage, my dear Countess!'

'Nevertheless. The pair of them are yours, if you can piss on the wall from where . . . No no! Stand where you are, cheat!'

'From here? Do I sleep in a stable?'

'You might just as well, Monsieur! Why do you think she left you to your own devices?'

'Hah! She'll be back, tail between her legs!'

They both laughed crazily.

Eldritch peered between the shrubs, watched his noble quarry concentrate on holding his penis at the correct angle. He frowned. If he did find the correct range, the rogue would be pissing all over him!

'No no, Charlotte, no tricks or I'll take another step closer! Stop it, can't you see the barrel's too long for the shot?'

'Damp powder, my dear Duke?'

A duke, pissing on a wall like some back-alley urchin, Eldritch thought, scandalised by their repulsive antics. If he dashed out now, he'd have to silence the whore of a countess as well as her ape of a lover.

'Damn this cold!'

'You offer me nothing but excuses! There now, I demand a forfeit!'

'Whatever you see, you're welcome to,' the Duke growled, glaring down at his dysfunctional tackle.

'I'll take the White Rabbit, if she ever returns from her jaunt to Villefranco.'

'She'll be back I say! Do you think little Gerhard will satisfy a she-devil like her?'

'She's after his gold, not his dirty water!'

'Well she went through mine quick enough, damn her to hell!

But I still say she'll be back, the moment she claps eyes on that celery-munching monk!'

Eldritch peered around the vegetation, watched the agitated Duke fiddling with his crotch. His companion must have gone back into the house.

'Wait! Charlotte, come back, there! I told you!'

The sudden arc of urine splattered the bushes, a filthy shower for the long-neglected flower beds. Eldritch grimaced, rising from his cover as the Duke turned the stream in his direction. He strode through the lashing vines, his lean features contorted with rage. The Frenchman blinked, trying to remember which one of his guests had remained clothed. He spotted the drawn sword and the golden stream stopped abruptly. Eldritch was on him before he could raise the alarm, thrusting the weeds aside to close in on his victim. Milhaud dropped his penis and turned to run for the sanctuary of the house, but the intruder was too quick for him, cracking him over the back of the head with the pommel of his sword. The Duke cried out, dropping to his knees in the shining white gravel. Eldritch sheathed his sword, hooked his hand under the man's armpit and began to drag him off towards the overgrown rhododendrons. His victim's heels left parallel tracks in the rough gravel as Eldritch struggled to escape with the dead-weight Duke.

'Claude! Where are you?'

Damn! It was the wretched Countess, come to see what the commotion was. Eldritch glanced over his shoulder, realised he was precious yards short of cover. The Countess was standing on tiptoe, peering over the wild lawn at the scowling intruder and his groaning charge.

Eldritch grinned feebly and waved his free hand. 'My master the Duke has taken too much drink,' he said haltingly. The girl folded her hands over her fine breasts with belated modesty, squinting at the stranger's dark features as if she were trying to place his scarred face.

'Where are you taking him?' she called sharply.

'To the summerhouse, my lady. He likes to dry out now, so he can return a little while later and enjoy your company into the small hours,' Eldritch explained, favouring the young beauty with an ingratiating smile. Thank God he and his sergeant, Jeremiah Hobby, had noticed the ramshackle pavilion on their way towards the house. The girl raised her chin imperiously, as if she knew the layout of the grounds as well as any of the Duke's guests.

23

'I'll come with him. I could do with some air.'

Eldritch cursed under his breath.

'As you wish, my lady.' He watched her spring across the gravel on tiptoe, the neat triangle between her legs stretched in all directions by her exaggerated steps. She reached the long grass, giggled with delight as the dew cooled her feet. She gave Eldritch a long look.

'How is it I haven't seen you about the house? Are you a Scotsman? Your accent . . .'

'I am English,' Eldritch replied stiffly, trying to drag his eyes from the girl's chest. His mouth was as dry as the gravel. 'I generally serve the master's kinsman, the Vicomte D'Toinueill.' The Countess frowned.

'Cousin Abelard? We haven't seen hide nor hair of him since that terrible business in Italy. How is the randy goat?'

Eldritch blinked, trying to concentrate on her staccato questions. The girl seemed unconcerned by her complete nudity, certainly less concerned than the awkwardly glancing Englishman.

His sisters had always called him priggish (as well as a host of other, less flattering, epithets) but what manner of woman would stand before a complete stranger, as bare as a babe? And look him directly in the eye as if he were a thief in the night! He was no thief, but his motives this night were not exactly charitable.

He wished the pretty minx would skip off back to the main house with the rest of her debauched friends. She had clearly been utterly corrupted by their vile antics, shorn of any idea of decency. It was hardly surprising she felt no shame, given their uncompromising tastes in entertainment.

The Duke groaned.

'Why don't you put him down? He's not going anywhere, snoring like that.'

'He will catch his death of cold, my lady, left out in the night air.'

The Countess smiled. 'It doesn't seem to have cooled his ardour just yet.'

She poked him with her toe.

'I'd best get him indoors, let him sleep it off.'

'You are a most excellent and particular steward, for an Englishman,' the Countess said slyly. Eldritch eyed the summerhouse, the glimmering framework just visible in a band of trees

24

not twenty paces off. Hobby was waiting in the trees, some way beyond the flimsy structure.

He'd lose his eyes, when he caught sight of this sweetmeat.

'I am bound by oath to serve the master's clan,' Eldritch said, gritting his teeth. His own painful erection threatened to cut off the flow of blood to his legs at any moment, constricted within his codpiece in a most uncomfortable manner. He leaned the swooning Duke against his knee and changed holds, adjusting the tightly-fitting garment as he did so. The Countess smiled, her light eyes shining in the suddenly bright starlight.

'And what do I call you, um?'

Eldritch hoisted the Duke up and began to drag him off once more. 'Selby, my lady.'

'Selby! Selby the Steward!' She bent down, easing her hand beneath the Duke's armpit and helping to boost him through the long grass. They left a silver trail in the dew which must have been visible from the moon!

Eldritch's agitation lent him extra strength, and a moment later the unconscious Duke was lying amongst the litter of dead plants and broken pots on the floor of the summerhouse. The glass panels were smashed or covered in mildew, and it was barely any warmer inside than out. The Countess tiptoed through the debris, nosing into the little nooks and crannies, examining the few books which hadn't been torn up as kindling. Eldritch unclasped his cloak and offered it towards the curious girl. She turned her back to him, arched her neck as he slipped the heavy fabric over her finely boned shoulders.

Eldritch took a deep breath.

'You seem somewhat perturbed by my nakedness, Selby.'

The Englishman grinned feebly, the livid scar on his cheek stretching pink. He had work to do with this viper of a duke, without having to pass the time of day with his inquisitive house guests. The girl opened her eyes wide and then frowned in exasperation.

'By God, Englishman, what have I got to do, draw you a picture?'

Eldritch's eyes flickered, unwilling to contest her bold stare.

'I didn't come all the way out here to trample on flower pots!'

Eldritch's entire body was twitching, living an impatient life of its own beneath his closely-buttoned clothing.

'By the saints, you English!' She took a quick step forward, slipped her hand behind his head and wrenched his mouth down to hers. Eldritch closed his eyes, relishing her touch. Her fingers twined in his long hair as she stood on tiptoe to receive him. He wound his arms about her waist, dragged her closer, clasping her buttocks through the rough fabric of his cloak.

'Ouch! What is this damned thing made of? Dog hair?'

'Take it off,' he croaked, hardly able to master his voice for the fierce thumping in his chest. He dared not imagine how long it had been since he had held a woman. Not since his early days at Crow Hole, not since . . .

She fiddled with the heavy clasp. Eldritch lost patience, eager to explore the body she had paraded before him with such devastating effect.

Eldritch trod on the Duke's outstretched hand, completely forgetting his miserable existence – and his own pressing mission. He had no time to dally about with wenches, with his poor sister imprisoned within, subjected to lecherous tortures which would have disgusted the most debauched Persian satrap. He tried to pull away from her, but the Countess clung to his lean body, her hands busy inside his doublet, under his shirt front, over his uncomfortably bunched hose.

Lillith would have to wait.

Marie-Charlotte Armonde, Comtesse du Lac, leaned sideways and extracted a piece of broken pottery from beneath her right buttock. She tossed the fragment aside and eased herself from the broken-down couch where they had lain – balanced precariously amongst the flower pots – for the past hour and more.

The sudden movement dislodged a leaning leg, depositing the dozing Englishman into the litter on the floor. Eldritch gave a start, groping for his sword. It lay tangled in his clothing beside their draughty bower.

The Countess lifted his doublet from the floor and shrugged the sweaty coat about her, shivering with cold. She smiled at his bewildered expression, the slow realisation it was practically dawn. Eldritch seemed as electrified by the few pale streaks across the sky as he had been by the soft golden down between her legs. He leapt to his feet, buckling up his belt and tugging his hose together. His shirt was still smeared with dirt where they had rolled over the piled sacks by the door, locked together like serpents shedding their skins.

The Duke was where they had left him, several shades paler than he had been. His remarkably adaptable penis had shrunk back into its crown of dark hair, a hermit crab retreating into its rockpool lair. Eldritch knelt beside the cold Duke, holding one finger to his neck as he fastened himself up. The Countess was hugging herself, their passionate loveplay more than exhausting her surplus energy.

Her crotch chafed where he had thrust himself at her, rampant and rigid as the prancing unicorn on her family arms. She could tell the handsome stranger hadn't been near a woman in a very long time, but hadn't imagined his surly good looks disguised such an intensity, a vacuum of sheer longing. He had craved her touch, craved every inch of her like no man before. He had seemed utterly inflamed by passion – once he had finally put aside the little-boy-lost act and given in to it. Having surrendered to his baser instincts, her deranged lover had lost himself, drowning between her legs as if he had been swallowed up by a ferocious, gold-fringed whirlpool.

She couldn't remember anything quite like it, in all her highly precocious seventeen years.

The Countess had been spending too much time with tired old men, jowly hogs who needed a twelve-year-old to sit on their faces before they could manage to get it up. Milhaud's parties – once the delighted talk of all Provence – had become desperately shabby. Lonely nobles no longer prayed for an invite, they played tennis instead. It was hardly surprising. Even the most hair-raising escapades hadn't sparked their jaded appetites. And the further he went, the more Marie-Charlotte felt she needed air. To escape their rheumy-eyed lusts.

Fornicating amidst the sorry grandeur of the old ruin, no wonder the legendary White Rabbit had sought other, fresher, pastures. The Duke himself, well, he had always found time for her, detached himself from his latest girl (or boy) to renew the acquaintanceship he had established when she was barely old enough to understand what he had been about, greeting his little favourite in the most intimate manner, whether or not they were in respectable company. He had fucked her once, hanging over their box at the opera! How the orchestra had missed their notes, glancing up at the hooting Duke and his blushing accomplice. He had been one of the best lovers she had ever had – until his favourite bedmate had left him for another prince, left him to stew in his own juice while she had drained another fortune. Now, Milhaud moped about the rambling wreck of his home, fuelling his excesses with ever-increasing quantities of wine. He barely knew who he was groping these days, staggering about in a torment, obsessed by his bacchanalian extravaganzas.

'Whatever is the matter? Is he quite cold?' she asked over the stranger's shoulder. The Englishman swallowed, nodding his head in distraction. He was cursing himself in English.

The alarmed Countess knelt beside him, peering down at Milhaud's yellowing features in panic. 'He's not dead? The cold!'

'I only hit him once,' Eldritch whispered, gingerly reaching out to touch the almost invisible wound. It hadn't even bled.

The Countess was looking at him, aghast.

'I knew by your manner you were no serving man, but I didn't imagine you were his assassin!' she cried. Her suddenly sharp tone reminded Eldritch where he was and what he was supposed to be about. He cursed his own stupidity and clasped the girl's outstretched arm. The Countess arched away from him, propelling herself towards the summerhouse door in sudden, terrorised realisation. He clung to her wrist, dragged her around and threw his free hand over her mouth before she could attempt anything more than a half-strangled yelp.

'Quiet! I didn't come here to kill him, you fool! He had information I needed!' Her eyes were bulging above his interlocked fingers. Eldritch modified his grip, peering out over the grey grounds beyond the screens. 'Don't scream, I mean you no harm.'

She blinked, frantic with fright.

'I can't be taken here, don't you understand? I came here to ask him questions, to find my sister! If you scream, I'll never find her. So you won't scream, will you?'

The Countess understood his chilling threat well enough. She nodded.

He lowered his hand a notch.

'You killed him for your sister?' she enquired, swallowing with difficulty.

'I didn't mean to kill him! What good is he to me now?'

Eldritch cursed. Could it be his disgust for their repulsive behaviour had soured his long-repressed anger, turned the knockout blow into a fatal strike? He was paralysed with indecision, crouching in a summerhouse beside the corpse of a French nobleman, within hailing distance of a houseful of his damned friends. The girl was staring at him, studying his grimly-scarred features in the feeble light of dawn.

'Le lapin blanc,' she murmured. Eldritch bristled.

28

'What about it?'

'She's not your sister, Lady Lillith, the White Rabbit?'

Eldritch glared so hard tears of anguish sprouted from the corners of her eyes. She knew who the devilish intruder was now, recognised the resemblance in his challenging eyes. They were filled with hunger, just like his sister's. A different kind of hunger maybe, but hunger nevertheless.

'Lillith's my sister,' he agreed, sick at heart. The snippets of conversation he had overheard earlier fell into place like some fiendishly complex lock, imprisoning him with the brutal truth.

'She's gone. She's left the Duke, travelled to Villefranco in Milhaud's best coach,' the Countess sobbed. Eldritch was still trying to remember how they had referred to her, this mysterious White Rabbit the Duke had missed so much. Only a fool could have misinterpreted such a nickname. His sister was a whore, she had been a whore all the while: only he had refused to acknowledge the fact.

'The White Rabbit,' he breathed.

The girl averted her eyes, terrified by his manic leer.

'She's gone to the new Duke . . . she wasn't happy here!'

Eldritch felt an overwhelming urge to smash the beautiful girl's head into the wall. He fought to govern his terrible temper, the righteous rage which had blazed like a meteor across the French skies and left Milhaud lying cold as stone at their feet.

'What are you going to do, cut my throat?'

'I meant him no harm. I mean you no harm,' he explained earnestly, his jawline contorted in bitter recrimination.

So Lillith had left another corpse in her damned wake? Hadn't she done enough damage, breaking their poor father's heart and obliging him to earn a crust as a soldier up on the borders? It was Lillith he should blame, not this poor, misguided girl.

'Explain that to the magistrate, to his brothers and friends!' the Countess exclaimed, sensing the murderous impulses she had seen flex behind his hooded eyes had subsided once more.

She had never been so scared in all her life.

But then, neither had Eldritch.

Thirty leagues from the sea, sixty and more from the border? By God, a few days in France and he was already an outcast, a desperate fugitive just like his exiled rival Gueldres!

Eldritch licked his lips, remembering the corpse before them was a close kinsman of his bitterest enemy. The enemy who had tried so hard to bring about his own execution. Gueldres hadn't hesitated to bear false witness against him and his friend Tarsi, to lay a trail of incriminating evidence all the way to Tarsi's stronghold of Mont Galliard.

But Gueldres had tricked and teased him with his knowledge of Lillith's whereabouts, blackmailing Eldritch to assist in his dastardly escape. He had been forced to help the vile traitor slip the net, to speed his getaway over the rice fields. Gueldres had turned him into a traitor. Now the burning anger he had carried ever since had swamped his senses, turned him into a murderer into the bargain. He looked at the terrified girl, his racing mind made up.

'We're leaving.'

'Leaving? We won't get out of the grounds, once his people realise he's missing!'

'They'll be abed a while yet, I wager. The horses aren't far.'

The girl regarded him coolly.

'So you mean to kidnap me. Have you any idea who I am?'

'Have you any idea who I am?' he asked, taking her by the elbow and lifting her to her bare feet. 'You'd best grab one of those sacks. We've a long ride ahead of us.'

'Damn you!'

'Aye,' he murmured. 'Damn me.'

By the Castello Villefranco, in the Maritime Alps

✦

The old Duke had kept detailed records of his incomes and expenditures, assembled complete profiles of every courtier, clerk and servant who had ever earned as much as a sou at the Castello Villefranco. The voluminous documents made for fascinating reading, and had diverted young Gerhard for hours. The two whores who had arrived – highly recommended – from Marseille that morning, had long since fallen into a grateful sleep. Their long legs were entwined beneath the soiled sheets, tangled up with sheaves of vellum the new Duke had already digested. The crisp papers rose and fell, rustling like a bedful of crickets as the women snored on, apparently exhausted by their extended loveplay. Their lover was lying on his belly, propped up on his elbows in a rumpled nightshirt. He was reading by the light of a guttering candle, tipping the document towards the flickering illumination to decipher some of the awkwardly compressed passages. A shapely foot twitched beneath his nostrils as he turned the pages, rifled through his dead father's files for interesting titbits.

Gerhard had learned of his servants' petty dealings, marvelling at their narrow horizons and half-cocked ambition. He was quite tickled to discover so many references to himself. It was really quite humbling to read of their worries about his health, his manhood and the very great likelihood of his being assassinated in his bed. He was invariably described as 'the poor boy' or the 'innocent dreamer'. Some made him the 'candle-wasting scholar' or the 'kindlie yonge gentleman in companie with hys astrolabe'.

The Duke shook his head and selected another bundle from the opened chest beside the bed. Gerhard scanned the copied message, noting that it had only been dated a few weeks earlier, when his poor father had yet been on his deathbed. Lodovico's principal advisors must have been getting cold feet at the prospect of life without him. Gerhard whistled softly. It was a copy of a note which had been penned by his father's chancellor, Igon Vitt. It urged his uncle Baldassare to return from the wars in Italy as soon as possible, to offer succour to the poor orphaned boy. The youth in question looked up, trying to estimate how long the message would have taken to reach the old soldier. A week at most? And if Baldassare was minded to respond to the heartfelt appeal, he could be expected to arrive within days.

Gerhard scratched his nose with his quill. He would certainly have to be on his toes, alert and ready to receive his notorious uncle. He thought for a moment, laid the note aside and reached back under the covers. Where were those damned warrants?

He groped under the sheets, hoicked a fragrant foot aside and found what he was looking for. A list of prisoners currently detained at the old Duke's pleasure in the castle's cavernous dungeons. He picked the scroll up, dipped his quill in the ink balanced on the dresser, and began to read.

'"Cosimo Farantini, forger." I despise forgery.' He ran the loaded nib through the name.

'"Angelo Baggoni. Adulterer." A married man carrying on like some lovesick student,' Gerhard sighed, deleting the name from the list. He carried on, crossing out every name until he arrived at the foot of the page.

That ought to save a little money. Vitt had already accosted him about the household accounts. All those useless mouths taking up valuable room in his castle. The Duke's wandering eye fell on the last-named prisoner.

'Mantisso Montalban.' The name rang a vague bell somewhere. Gerhard's quick eye scanned the attached indictment. Five charges of arson resulting in three deaths and countless hundreds of livres of damage. The accused, an alchemist and amateur engineer, had been investigating the properties of various inflammatory agents and had uttered threats of an arcane nature against the ruling house of Mounier. More than enough to see him burned at the stake for his trouble, Gerhard would have thought. He had been seized in possession of various explosive devices: bombs, mortars and exploding rockets. He had shot one of his father's guards with a 'fireworking engine of elaborate and dastardly design' and spent two months in the *oubliette* for his trouble.

A fireworking engine. Gerhard wondered if the rogue had survived his appalling sentence. The *oubliette* was no more than a shallow grave with bars on top. Food, if you were lucky enough to get it, was dropped in from above by fellow prisoners struggling over the few scraps they were allowed. Water, well there was plenty running down the walls. Perhaps this Mantisso would prove useful, if and when his notorious uncle came calling. Gerhard reached over the dresser and rang the bell rope. The whores started, groaning in their sleep and turning over under the piled correspondence. His counsellor swept into the noisome chamber before the subdued echo had quite died away.

Belatavicci bowed low, trying to avert his eyes from the tangled papers and the slumbering whores. Their legs and arms protruded from the rumpled bedding as if the new Duke had taken his first tentative steps into the adult world by chopping the unfortunate women into pieces to see how they worked.

Oh, they had worked well enough, and been well paid for their efforts. The women were notorious courtesans, eagerly sought out by half the houses in France. It had taken months of tricky correspondence and an outrageous down-payment to tempt them up to chilly Villefranco.

Duke Gerhard had taken to his new role like a duck to water, turned from blushing virgin to dissolute rake in a week. He had rogered half of the household before he had taken the trouble to learn their names, as if limbering up for his accomplished visitors. He ought to have turned his mind towards a treaty with his all-powerful neighbours, instead, he had set himself up as the goat of Villefranco. He would be suffering from the French disease before the month was out, if he didn't mend his fornicating ways.

The wily courtier looked closer, realised with some relief the stains blossoming over the counterpane had been caused by spilled wine rather than amateur surgery.

'You rang for me, my Duke?'

'I did. Take this list to the dungeon master. I want the buggers out by lunchtime.'

Belatavicci smiled graciously. 'My lord's clemency will be celebrated throughout the Duchy, warming the hearts of his devoted subjects. But if I might be permitted to sound a slight note of caution . . .'

Gerhard waved his quill in irritation. 'I don't want them freed. Execute them! Forgers and thieves, adulterers and cattle rustlers? We've mouths enough without feeding up a pack of damned criminals!'

Belatavicci frowned. 'Your father's keen sense of jurispru-
dence . . .'

'My father is lying in his tomb beside the chapel. I intend to run
this duchy on a rather tighter rein than he did. See to it,
Belatavicci.'

The young pup had certainly honed his voice for his new
role. The courtier had always found his nervous whining fist-
clenchingly irritating, but it was certainly preferable to his
imperious barking.

Gerhard held his counsellor's eye for a moment.

'You might as well clear those musicians out as well. We can't
afford a damned orchestra. Also that lousy Greek. I've no use for
his fairyland observations any more.'

Gerhard made himself comfortable on the bed.

'Things will be changing here, in case you haven't the wit to
work that out for yourself. If you and Monsieur Vitt don't like it,
you can of course pack your bags and clear out with the rest of
the arseholes.'

Belatavicci bit his pendulous lip.

'*Au contraire*, my Duke. A stronger, more forceful approach
might well be meet, in the trying days ahead.'

He wouldn't be around long enough to find out, one way or
another, the courtier thought hotly. Baldassare would pull the
little shit's arsehole over his ears for him, that was for certain. His
quick eye darted over the list of names Gerhard had passed him.

'The prisoner Montalban, my lord. I imagine you ring his
name with the intention of making an example of the madman.'

'Indeed. This fireworking engine of his.'

'A deadly tool, my lord. No more than a rifled steel tube
mounted on a simple wooden stock, and filled with gunpowder.
The most horrendous of weapons, in the wrong hands.'

'Bring it up here, and have the prisoner transferred to the
gatehouse tower, on half rations.'

'I . . . er . . . As you wish my lord.'

What did he intend to do, try out his masterly powers of
persuasion to probe the fiery pit of Montalban's mind? The one
rogue who had actually deserved to die spared for future
reference?

He watched the new Duke lift another portfolio from the chest
beside the bed. He hadn't wasted any time investigating his late
father's papers, the courtier noted grimly. He and Vitt had spent
long hours assembling that library, poring over files, cataloguing

the documents to ensure old Lodovico was never at a loss to find some snippet of information. Gerhard seemed to have taken a perverse delight in ruining their system, deliberately mislaying every article, tearing the numbered corners from each bundle. The counsellor suppressed a groan of irritation as he broke open another scroll with callous amusement.

'You have certainly spent enough of your time trying to marry me off. I never realised the efforts you made on my behalf.'

'It proved an impossible task, to locate a suitable bride for the prince of such a distinguished house.'

One of the whores giggled, disguising her amusement by coughing violently and turning over. Gerhard glanced over his shoulder, wondering if the bitches were merely pretending to be asleep. Impossible! They had assured him he was the finest lover they had ever had. The noise they had made would have drowned out a cellar full of starving cats!

'They couldn't come up with a decent dowry, you mean,' he corrected modestly. 'Vitt's left a note here about some horse called Tarsi. At Mont Galliard. That's away over the border isn't it? Up beyond Saluzzo.'

'I regret the precise whereabouts presently escape me,' Belatavicci explained cautiously.

'Surely not. You were there yourself, just last summer. I seem to recall you being delayed by some siege.'

'Ah yes. That Mont Galliard. An enclave located within the Duchy of Savoy. A trying little place. The girl in question spent her entire day directing the resistance from the walls, a most unsuitable prospect for a gentleman of the blood.'

'She sounds as if she possessed considerable spirit, if nothing else,' he said, reaching out to grab one of the sleeping women by her ankle. 'I like a woman with spunk!'

There was another fit of giggles from beneath the sheets. Gerhard frowned for a moment, and then turned back to the iron-faced counsellor.

'But then she would be – Alberto Tarsi's daughter. I hear they have fallen on hard times since losing their home to those scoundrel mercenaries. Hasn't he accepted a command with Uncle Baldassare?'

Belatavicci shrugged nonchalantly. 'I have not heard from his honour the knight-general for some weeks.'

'But surely you wrote informing him of his brother's ill-health.'

'Your father had been ill for some time, but yes, indeed, my lord Duke.'

'Of course.' Gerhard tossed the bundle aside and hauled a heavier portmanteau up onto the soiled counterpane.

'And what do we have here?'

'I believe, my lord, they are various doodlings your father acquired during his service with His Majesty Francis I.'

The Duke opened the leather case and drew out a sheaf of variously-sized diagrams. The faded drawings and musty water-colours seemed to feature different views of any number of strange contraptions.

'Worthless relics, I fear, my Duke. Your father met the artist at Amboise. The Florentine, Leonardo da Vinci. A boastful brag-gart, but gifted by God with pen and ink, your father told me.'

'He must be as mad as our friend Montalban. What are these supposed to be?'

Gerhard held the offending design up. Belatavicci glanced at the sketch, brow furrowed.

'Some kind of cooking pot, I imagine. Duke Lodovico was always a keen patron of the arts . . .' The courtier paused, unwilling to raise the spectre of the Duke's recently dead parent. 'They say Francis attended him when he died.'

'Died?'

'Two years ago, my lord. I'll dispose of them forthwith.'

Gerhard held up his hand. He turned the design the other way up. An iron pot, full of holes, trailing a fiery comet.

'It's some manner of bomb, a mortar round or something similar.'

'Then why the holes, my Duke?'

Gerhard shrugged, flicking through the rest of the file. There were all sorts of complicated devices. A set of wings the size of a house with a man suspended from some kind of central apparatus. A long tube rather like a sealed canoe, with a cutaway section revealing a man lying out full length. From the accom-panying mermaids and fishes, Gerhard presumed the engine was supposed to sail under the water.

The very idea!

One design featured a large cart, rigged up with an immense corkscrew attached to several sets of bat-like wings. What was it supposed to do, fly through the sky?

Each plan had been scribbled out and revised, altered and amended. Rambling notes spidered off into the margins.

'The man Leonardo, is better known as an architect. A man of some talent, even if he said so himself.'

Gerhard mumbled something under his breath.

'I'll keep the designs for now, Belatavicci. Leave us.'

The courtier bowed low and backed out of the room. Insolent shit, he thought. He wondered how long Baldassare would take to reach them. He smiled to himself as he wandered off down the passage to find the dungeon master.

By the Imperialist Camp, Nus, in the Lower Aosta Valley

✦

The Imperial delegation had arrived out of the blue that noon, riding into the ill-kept camp and catching its caretaker commander – Alberto Tarsi – completely by surprise. The officers had been appalled at the state of the place. General Von Huff maintained a shabby camp made for shoddy soldiers.

Tarsi had apologised profusely, mortified to think he had been left in temporary command of such a shambles. His chief, that sour-tempered bandit Baldassare Mounier, had absented himself on domestic business of his own – leaving his understudy to lick the discontented force into shape.

And Mounier wasn't the only absentee, not by a long chalk. As well as missing its senior officer, the regiment had been left short of at least half its junior captains. The rogues had taken advantage of the prolonged inactivity to slip off to their sweethearts or mistresses, or taken themselves off hunting in the hills. The master gunner had already gone over to the higher-paying French, and the baggage master – responsible for the quarrelsome rabble known as the whores and knaves – had been stabbed in a drunken brawl over a bowl of stolen eggs!

Men were deserting by the dozen. The multinational warband he had been left to command was dissolving for lack of pay and opportunity.

The officers crowded into the command tent were too weary to pay full attention to their exasperated ally's litany of woe. Their new commander, Franz Von Huff, had only received official word of his promotion earlier that week. He had not had time to count his guns, let alone get to know his widely dispersed regimental commanders – distributed like a string of paste pearls along the north-western flanks of the Alps.

Earlier that summer it had seemed the Emperor Elect's fortunes

38

were in the ascendant. Mouzon had fallen to the Imperialist general Nassau. Mezieres seemed certain to surrender soon, despite the heroic efforts of its commander, the legendary Chevalier Bayard, to hold the town for his master Francis. It seemed to many as if Almighty God had taken up the double-headed eagle banner of the Empire. Had he not hurled lightning bolts out of the sky, blowing up the French magazine in Milan and sparking a titanic explosion in which three hundred of the Seigneur de Lescun's troops had perished?

But as the summer wore on French fortunes had begun to recover. Bayard had held on the Mezieres, defying all efforts to dislodge him. De Lescun's brother Lautrec had relieved Parma, and Fuenterrabia – key to Spain – was under close siege by the French General Bonnivet. The bloody manoeuvrings had sharpened the rival commanders' appetites for invasion, fuelled belligerent designs for further conquests. Now, with the summer fast wearing thin, the Imperial forces in Italy were husbanding their strength for an attack on Milan – the key to the fruitful but war-weary Lombard plain. The French were holding on for now, but their cruel rule was bitterly resented by the long-suffering population and without powerful reinforcement the Imperialist armies would surely sweep the invaders back over the Alps.

Von Huff had been assigned a flanking role, his object to prevent French reinforcements reaching the city from the west. Simple enough on paper, but rather more problematical on the ground. For a start, there were half a dozen routes the French might take. He would be obliged to juggle his forces, cover as many of the high passes over the Alps as possible, trusting to God and his grievously outnumbered soldiers. Their cosy, backwater billets were about to become battlefields once more.

Von Huff was a hugely experienced soldier, a wily, wrinkled little gnome in black lacquered armour and an outsize, ostrich-plumed helmet. He rarely joked, drank little, and always made a point of sharing the soldiers' hard tack and cheese. He had learned his trade the hard way, lugging a pike in the Burgundian wars before graduating to command a company and finally a regiment of the hard-fighting but fiercely militant mercenaries known throughout Europe as *Landsknechts*.

It was an odd word meaning Servant of the Country, though it was generally agreed that Scum of the Earth might be nearer the mark.

Von Huff made himself as comfortable as he could on the battered stool, crouched in the windswept pavilion like some peasant taking a shit in a ditch. The surrounding camp was seething with discontent. He could sense the furious muttering behind every yawning canvas, seeping out of every lantern-lit wagon. The rabble-rousing clamour reverberated about the camp like the clatter of the crickets.

Caesar would have thrown a fit, to see such a shambles. The guns and limbers had been scattered about like decrepit carts in some Tuscan farmyard instead of being properly lined up in the artillery park. Horses and mules had been roped up outside their owners' tents instead of being properly tethered away on the perimeter of the camp, where their dung could be collected by the roving horseboys. The troops he had spotted during his rapid tour of inspection had turned out to be surly, filthy-faced fellows, ganged up about a dice game or idling away their time with some camp-following whore. Half of them, decked out in rotting lambswool jerkins or lengths of rusty-coloured plaid, were babbling away in their heathen tongues, gesticulating at their officers as if they were itinerant brush sellers. English.

He hadn't imagined he'd be taking over many of them. Worse than the English, a squadron of Scots horsemen, red-haired barbarians who talked their own mad dialect and rolled their eyes at everyone who came near. Von Huff had never seen anything like them – not since he had campaigned along the coastline of Albania during the distant days of his youth, at any rate.

The disgusted general knew he was wasting his breath berating the soldiers in the field. He remembered their colonel from the old days. Baldassare Mounier had always been a lousy, dissolute fellow, more of a bandit than a soldier. The brute hadn't even had the decency to meet him in person, sending this whining Italian in his place. He knew Tarsi was an able enough field commander, but he hadn't stopped moaning since they had arrived an hour and a half before.

'Gold! They won't budge an inch unless they're paid, and soon! Some of them are claiming backpay dating back to Ravenna!' Tarsi complained. Von Huff wiped his creased brow, examined the film of grease on his dark fingertips. He was fast tiring of the mercenary chief's endless laments.

'I've Germans, Burgundians, Italians, Hungarians as well as a pack of mad-dog Scots and English. But they're all saying the same. Pay up or they'll pack up.' Tarsi looked earnestly at the weary general.

Von Huff shrugged his shoulders, his old armour creaking on its worn leather straps. 'That's all very well and good, Seigneur. But I assure you we have heard the same story a dozen times this week. Your men will be paid, the moment the Imperial exchequer can collect the necessary bullion. You understand the Emperor Elect has taken the main field armies into Northern France. We are to support him by attacking Milan, drawing the enemy south.'

'I see that. But if the men aren't paid it might well be too late, my lord. They need coin, and soon, if you expect to find them at their posts this time next week.'

Von Huff glanced at his companions, experienced campaigners well used to the fickle mood of their mercenary troops. Tarsi paused, wondering how far he dare press his penniless Imperial paymasters. In his experience, there wasn't a great deal to choose between Charles V and Francis I when it came to paying for a soldier's service. Both would make elaborate promises about the fortunes waiting to be earned, but they were notoriously forgetful when it came to fulfilling their end of the bargain. The soldiers who made war and death their living never trusted their commanders. Their first loyalty was always to thaler or livre, shilling or guilder. They had learned a simple rhyme from their Swiss comrades, the mountain pikemen who had turned the art of war on its head with their flamboyant tactics, their irresistible phalanx of eighteen-foot pikes.

'No rattle no battle.'

They had stuck by the simple catechism – or numerous local variations thereof – as if it were the most pious prayer their barely-remembered mothers had ever taught them. Mercenary troops had been known to halt a battle halfway through, enter into open negotiations with the enemy, discussing their pay and conditions with hair-raising frankness while their commanders looked on aghast. Opposing forces could be bought off and bribed, just so long as a king or commander had the resources at his immediate disposal. It appeared to the canny Italian that Charles had marched without ensuring the forces on the outer fringes of his Empire had been adequately primed. Did the lantern-jawed dotard expect them to die in his name for nothing?

Alberto Tarsi certainly wasn't intending to risk his neck without adequate recompense. He had been forced to return to the Imperial colours, to take up arms he had once hoped to have laid aside for good, through sheer necessity. It was either fight for the Empire or see his rapidly shrinking household return to ekeing out a living as lousy peasants. His recent calamities – the ruinous siege of Mont Galliard and the consequent court case brought by his enemies in House Gueldres, had come within an ace of losing him his honour. He might have escaped with his head and name intact, but the dreadful ordeal had left him precious little else.

He had lost his home, the castle of Mont Gilbert Le Galliard, the key to the high pass. He had been robbed of his able major domo and his best field officer, and his daughter Angelica – accused of a series of preposterous crimes – had been forced to endure the terrible attentions of the Inquisition, an ordeal which would blight her mind for the rest of her life.

Worst of all, the man who had stood beside him through those terrible days, the soldier he had hoped to set up in his dead captain's place . . . well. Tarsi wasn't even sure he could trust the mercurial Englishman. James Eldritch had taken off on a desperate venture of his own, pledging he would return the moment he had located his missing sister, whom he had received word of living in Marseille. Eldritch had left his younger sister Merron and the bulk of his hard-fighting warband behind as a guarantee of his goodwill and eventual return. They had agreed that during the younger man's absence Tarsi would assume command of his company.

Tarsi was happy enough with the bargain – he had seen the rascals in action, learned to respect their almost supernatural abilities with the dreaded longbow. Tarsi knew the *Transmarini* – the five hundred survivors of Lord Howath's original retinue – had no real choice but to remain with the colours. Without a properly articled commander to supply them with pay and provisions, they would be unable to support themselves on the long journey home.

They were desperate men – and that made the foreigners the only troops he could rely on.

The general seemed to sense Tarsi's anxiety, waving his captains out of the stuffy tent. He took a refreshing draught from the looted wine Tarsi had offered by way of hospitality and watched the Italian pace the headquarters tent.

'I have come on a matter of some delicacy, Seigneur Tarsi,' the little man sighed, lowering his voice to a confidential rasp. 'We believe one of your old enemies, Count Stroma of Luningiana, has already held secret negotiations with the French, intending to open the Aosta valley to Francis and his fornicating Swiss.'

Tarsi checked, turned on his heel at the alarming intelligence. His own agents had brought word of an extraordinary buildup of communications between Stroma's palace in Aosta and his outposts at the northern end of the valley. But Tarsi had supposed the traffic related to domestic matters, evidence perhaps of the Count's drive to establish new alliances following his damaging involvement with Gueldres' most recent plot.

It was well known the length of Italy that Stroma and his manipulative protector Gueldres had been as thick as thieves for years. It was inevitable that the latter's disgrace would affect his old crony. For the second time in a decade, the Count's fortunes had been turned on their head by his perilous friendship with the conniving Vicomte. It would have been natural for Stroma to seek out new friends in the valley – allies who had already cocked a snook at Imperial interference. And Stroma would certainly have found such friends at Mont Galliard.

Tarsi hadn't been surprised to hear that some of the first visitors to Mont Galliard had been Stroma's slippery ambassadors, anxious to sign a treaty between the Count and the castle's new owners. Between them, they would control the pass and share the precious road toll revenues. His spies had monitored the ever-increasing traffic with some interest, but he had not possessed the means or money to do much about it. He certainly hadn't anticipated the unlikely bedfellows would have sold out to the French, that the hard-pressed Stroma might make himself a new deal with the invaders from over the Alps.

'He always was a conniving little shit, just like his turd of a master, Gueldres. They would have signed pacts with the Devil himself, if they thought it might harm me.'

Von Huff studied the burly knight as he paced back and forth before him. He knew Tarsi's reputation, the bloody victories he had won for his mistress Margaret of Savoy a decade before. The grateful Duchess had rewarded him with the keys of Mont Galliard, but his rapid advancement had created as many enemies as his brave campaigns had routed. There had been no shortage of conspirators eager to see him thrown out on his arse.

43

It was typical of the boastful Italian to imagine the entire war was being fought solely to deprive him of his precious castle.

'There are bigger issues at stake, Seigneur. If Stroma has signed a pact with the French, then we can expect an army of Swiss in the high pass, in days, perhaps hours. If these reinforcements are allowed to reach Milan, our offensive might well end in abject failure.'

Tarsi scowled at the general's workmanlike assessment. He knew the Imperialist cause needed a big coup, an astounding victory to draw the fickle Italian states into the war on the Emperor's side.

'I trust you and my lord of Mounier are up to the task of holding them,' Von Huff enquired.

'His affairs in Villefranco might keep him some weeks,' Tarsi pointed out.

'Then you, Seigneur, most hold the Swiss away from the main army, with the men you command here.'

'But if what you say proves true we might well be facing ten times our number,' Tarsi said sharply. Von Huff nodded, a white-capped bird in his black-lacquered plumage.

'You must hold them, all the same.'

'And in return? You know the price of my service?'

'Imperial headquarters is well aware of the settlement you seek.'

Tarsi raised his eyebrows, determined to ensure the little tyrant knew exactly what he was fighting for.

'In return for holding the pass through the winter, Imperial headquarters will allow me the use of a full field army, plus all artillery, pioneers and specialist troops necessary to re-take Mont Gallliard from the parasiticial crew who took it from me.'

The little general accepted the terms with a small shrug of his shoulders. 'Hold the pass while we take Milan and I pledge to you, Tarsi, I will be first through the breach.'

His heartfelt promise might have sounded as hollow as a drunkard's codpiece – if it had been made by a younger man. Tarsi accepted it as it had been meant – as a solid-gold statement of intent.

'The first through the breach after me, my lord,' the Italian soldier of fortune corrected.

By the Castello Villefranco in the Maritime Alps

✦

The chancellor watched the knot of riders materialise out of the early morning mists. He gave an involuntary shiver as he estimated their numbers, cast his cowl back over his closely shaven head.

'He is come,' he whispered.

'Ah, you'll give yourself a squint, Monsieur, staring so,' his colleague scolded half-heartedly. Belatavicci had shielded his eyes as he tried to identify the horsemen clattering along the high road, trying to pick out the smudged device on the windblown gonfalon which snapped above their heads. 'We still have time to shut the gates in his face, if it's him.'

The smaller man shrugged. 'The garrison wouldn't stand above an hour. You know the lily-livered scuts Duke Lodovico insisted on employing.'

The two men had taken up a new eyrie in the long gallery above the gatehouse, where they could converse without fear of being overhead. The passage was open to the elements and was considered the worst posting in the entire castle. A few silver pennies usually sufficed to persuade the frozen sentinel who had drawn the duty to rejoin his comrades about the brazier back in the guardhouse. The grey-cloaked counsellors had a superb view of the craggy approaches and the lonely crossroads beyond. The ancient Via Aurelia which had brought the dead Duke's long-lost brother from his wars in Italy.

'And in any case, Monsieur, it was your letter which brought him here.'

'My letter? Is he a monk? Is he some hermit living out his years on a remote isle? Baldassare would have come calling sooner or later. Our only hope is that he allows us to continue in our present duties.'

'Whatever befalls the boy.'

Igon Vitt tensed at the mention of their youthful chief. He had certainly confounded their expectations so far, turning his tutors out of the castle the moment his poor father had expired. The new Duke had gone through the household like a dose of salts, sent a whole pack of well-fed artists, jugglers, dancers, musicians and mathematicians packing. In their place he had brought in gamblers and whores, card sharps and magicians. His spartan quarters had been transformed into a harlot's boudoir, hung with tasteless red and gold banners and hangings brought up from the teeming Marseille bazaar.

He had hung his chamber with wind chimes and cheap bead curtains, the sort of gear one would have expected to find in a Saracen's tent. The pious counsellors had been scandalised by the vice-ridden doppleganger who had usurped the gentle Gerhard's body. Instead of the finely-educated Renaissance prince Duke Lodovico had set his heart on, Gerhard had grown up into a boorish whoremonger, a childish whippersnapper. The gossips below stairs reckoned he had already impregnated three of the serving wenches. Two more had run off after refusing his carnal attentions, preferring to starve on the mountain rather than submit to his beastly habits.

'He's cleverer than I would have anticipated, given that he's been stuffing his head with that head-in-the-clouds Greek mumbo-jumbo. I fear we have seriously underestimated his abilities.'

'Nobody could have anticipated such a bizarre transformation. But the very fact he has already exposed his true colours to you and me demonstrates his lack of experience. So he's developed a taste for whores and knaves? Baldassare will still eat him for breakfast.'

'What about that damned assassin, that Montalban character he's been so chummy with? All that kit and caboodle he's had carried into his workshop?'

'Ah, he might burn him in his bed or set fire to the stables, but I can't see him going up against Baldassare with a knife, can you?'

Belatavicci sighed. Both men fell silent as the portcullis shuddered and creaked below them.

'Well it's too late to worry now. They have just opened the gate.'

Baldassare Mounier ducked his head under the rusty grille and turned his warhorse around in the formidable courtyard of the

Castello Villefranco. He hadn't been back in six years and more, but the old place hadn't changed much. The fortress had grown out of living rock, the original medieval tower surrounded by curtain walls and laboriously excavated ditches. The wall ran around the mountaintop, reinforcing nature's own handiwork. The old soldier took a quick look around the inner walls, noting the guns which had been placed to cover the gate had been positioned too high. They would be unable to depress the barrels sufficiently to fire upon any enemy who had managed to force a way in through the gate. The courtyard walls would shield the intruders they were intended to contain.

Baldassare shook his head and swung himself out of the saddle. His bodyguards had already drawn up about him, the feeble gatekeepers remaining in the alcoves as if they were afraid of being caught out in a draught. What a set of sprats! No wonder his dolt of a brother had tried so hard to steer a course between the various warring powers. He wouldn't have survived a month if he had been forced to fight for his right to govern the tiny Alpine Duchy.

Well maybe it was time to alter Villefranco's role, to put this fortress on the maps of the mighty.

The main doors swung open and a squad of spearmen trotted down the steps to form an impromptu honour guard. They were followed by a couple of toadies in grey cloaks, who bowed and scraped before him as he strode towards the staircase.

'My lord of Mounier, we welcome you to the Castello Villefranco, in the name of our chief, the former prince, your sweet nephew Gerhard.' Mounier gave the shaven-headed aco-lyte a rapid examination. The mealy-mouthed courtier had subtly distanced himself from his chief, referring to him as his 'former prince' rather than the rightful duke, as if his elastic loyalty had not yet been fixed.

The soldier nodded. 'I trust my brother didn't suffer.'

'He was attended by the finest Florentine doctors and surgeons. He died as peacefully as he had lived.'

Baldassare managed to contain a shout of derisive laughter. 'God be praised,' he growled, modifying his amusement into a cough. 'Well there's no use in hanging it out, meeting my poor nephew I mean.'

'The young man awaits you in his quarters. He sends word he is studying the stars.'

He'd be seeing them soon enough, Baldassare thought blackly.

He raised an eyebrow, glanced at the square of deep blue sky magnificently framed by the surrounding courtyard walls. He was not a connoisseur of murder, but it was obvious to the most righteous commentator that Gerhard was not up to running his beleaguered Duchy. He would have to go, and Baldassare would send him on his way quicker and quieter than most.

'Alone in his grief?' he enquired.

'Alone indeed my lord. As alone as any human ever was,' the counsellor said tragically. Baldassare nodded. These dogs were clearly realists, hoping to secure their positions under a rather more formidable master. He could not blame them. As a soldier he would prefer to deal with the most loathsome realist than some honest-to-goodness dreamer with his head up his arse.

Gerhard could hear the brute clattering up the steep staircase, his steel carapace, sword and spurs ringing off the mouldy brick-work like a peal of brazen bells. The youth had stepped out onto the balcony despite the vicious crosswinds, to be alone with the crows and choughs which wheeled and cawed about the high tower. He could feel his heart beating hard beneath his fur mantle, and he noticed his long, tapering fingers were trembling slightly – just as they had when he bedded his first wench the month before. Seventeen in four weeks, not bad for a beginner, he mused.

Gerhard had decided to face his uncle alone, rather than try and hide half a dozen guards around the lonely tower. Baldassare was well used to the cut and thrust of Italian power politics and would surely spot such a trap. He could hack any of Villefranco's potential assassins into dog meat without raising a sweat. And besides, Gerhard knew his uncle wouldn't make any kind of move in front of potential witnesses.

The Duke stood beside his elaborately mounted telescope, swung the heavy barrel this way and that. This was it. Turn your back on him!

Gerhard bent down and placed his eye to the black barrel of the telescope, trusting his fortunes to the gods above. His senses stretched, straining for clues as to his uncle's dreadful approach. His nerves soared as the heavy door swung open. He felt his uncle's heavy footfalls through the stone floor.

'Gerhard, my lad! My Duke I should say! You've grown a bit, since the last time I clapped eyes on you!' Gerhard willed himself to remain stooped, his unprotected back exposed to a veteran killer who had surely come to finish him! To cull the puny boy as if he was the runt of the litter, no use to man nor beast.

He sensed Baldassare's eyes flashing back and forth along the open balcony, seeking out the hidden corners where he had expected to see Gerhard's guardians. There were none. Gerhard was utterly alone on the narrow ledge. A seventeen-year-old boy and a soldier of forty and more harsh winters. A killer who might break him in two with his bare hands! 'Do you make a study of the stars, uncle?' He had willed himself to remain calm, and was gratified to find his voice had remained melodiously impassive. 'They say we can find our destinies, mapped out across the heavens.'

'I can't say as I do, my Duke.' Gerhard sensed his uncle had moved around him. He could almost feel his bristling shadow as the soldier took a cautious peek over the balcony to the hungry anonymity of the crags below.

'Ah, there it is! My astrologers predicted a shooting star, a comet to mark the passage of my dead father's soul!' Gerhard straightened for the first time, momentarily disconcerted by his uncle's armoured bulk, the fierce, boorish features twisted up with contemptuous malice. He had stepped closer to the platform, closer than Gerhard had imagined. The boy smiled.

'Perhaps it is a token of war – the cataclysm which awaits us all?'

'Pah! The French haven't shifted their arses in a twelvemonth. They're holed up in Milan, murdering the leading citizens for blowing their noses without handkerchiefs,' Baldassare grunted.

Gerhard simpered, fluttered his limp fingers at the telescope. 'Do take a look for yourself, uncle dearest.'

Baldassare's fierce grin slipped a notch. Nobody had called him dearest in a very long time. The boy had stepped away from his apparatus and was warming his hands over the brazier one of his thoughtful servants had provided for him. The puny rabbit.

Baldassare drew a draught of air through his pug nose and bent down. Gerhard raised a fuming taper from the brazier.

'Is the apparatus the right way round? I can't see a damned thing!'

The boy raised the glowing tip to the small steel touch-hole, cunningly concealed in the stock of the telescope/gun.

'Then you must look harder, uncle dear,' Gerhard said, touching the burning taper to the tiny bowl of finely milled

49

gunpowder which Montalban had used to prime his cunningly disguised invention.

The heavy apparatus leapt on its wooden frame, wreathed in a sudden dragon-plume of acrid smoke. The sudden report was horrifyingly loud on the enclosed balcony. Baldassare leapt back in alarm, a fraction of a second too late to dodge the lead slug which caught him on the side of his forehead. The big man staggered backwards as the report echoed over the mountain, knocking the crows from their graceful caracoles.

Gerhard drew his dagger, the thin blade sparkling in the blue smoke, terrified the old soldier had ducked the treacherous shot. Baldassare staggered back, a red paw clamped to his temple. His teeth were bared, his left hand about his catgutter. The ball had missed his eye but cracked his skull, spilling his lifeblood in great vivid gouts over the stone.

Montalban, hidden out of sight down the stairway, heard the shattering explosion and came racing out onto the balcony. He was bent double, struggling to hold his arquebus level.

Baldassare reeled about, face to face with the sooty-faced rogue who had accomplished his doom.

The deranged engineer raised the heavy barrel as far as his undernourished arms would allow, and tugged the crude trigger back with a grunt of effort. The ornate mechanism cracked shut, plunging a spluttering matchcord into the pan. The force of the blast hurled the grinning assassin into the wall, knocking him cold. The clumsy weapon clattered over his outstretched legs, tearing the skin from his shins.

Mounier caught the blast square in the groin. A fistful of lead pellets tore through his well-worn codpiece, lacerating his lower belly and turning his genitals to ribbons of red gristle. The stunned warrior was carried backwards, lifted from his dead feet by the tremendous blast. Gerhard held on to the disguised gun as his uncle's body sailed over the balcony and turned half dozen somersaults into the sharp crags two hundred feet below.

Gerhard swore he heard the sickening splatter as the massive body impacted with million-year-old limestone. He had been stupefied by the colossal blast, blinking like an owl through a faceful of hot soot. His ears popped as he gulped clean air. He could just make out the dim shrieks from the staircase as Baldassare's careless bodyguards ran into another of Montalban's devices. They had parked a simple wooden cart in a corner of the courtyard, partly concealed under a mass of fresh straw. A couple of grubby peasants had shoved the load to one side, uncovering a rack of dull grey pipes which looked to the bewildered bodyguards like a church organ tipped on its flank. The cunningly disguised gunners stood back, holding a flaming linstock to the peculiar lead troughs welded over the ends of the pipes.

Montalban called it Leonardo's Engine, after the artist whose fanciful sketch he had used as a basis for his design. The twelve barrels had been stacked in two tiers, held together with steel bands and bolted into the hull of the wagon. He had warned the gunners the recoil might be ferocious, but nobody could have anticipated the tremendous force with which his deadly engine erupted into life. A dozen fist-sized barrels spewed flame, hurling a deadly hail of nails, lead slugs and fowling pellets at the dismounted horsemen taking their ease under the lee of the wall. The vicious arc of steel fragments lashed the startled guards, flaying the very armour from their arms and legs as they cowered before the punishing storm. Shrapnel catapulted from the stone walls, rebounding into the few fortunates who had been standing behind their ragged comrades, shielded from the full-frontal blast. A dozen and more of Baldassare's best troops were reduced to bleeding sacks, shredded by the flesh-gobbling firestorm.

The cart had been lifted two feet and more from the ground, a ton and more of wood and steel hurtling through the air like a child's kite caught up in a tornado. The equally startled gunners didn't stand a chance. The wagon pulped the pair of them, obliterating their bodies against the six-foot-thick gatehouse wall. The heavy pipes had burst asunder, twisted and smoking in a bed of warped bands. The hull of the wagon had been knocked out, the heavy timbers turned to matchwood by the devastating blast.

The enormous report bounded around the enclosed courtyard, such guards as were left standing clapping their hands over their ears to stop their brains from exploding.

Gerhard felt the convulsions rattle the very foundations of the castle, loosen the mountain from its deeply buried bed. He held on to the deadly telescope, ears popping as his deranged engineer picked himself up from the doorway, grinning with ghoulish delight.

Montalban was opening and closing his toothless mouth, but the Duke couldn't hear anything over the angry shrieks of the stormcrows wheeling around the tower, soot-bellied harbingers of a new doom.

By the Château Celestine,
near Marseille

✦

It was nothing short of scandalous.

A high-ranking nobleman stripped naked and left for dead in his own summerhouse, his cold corpse discovered by an intoxicated groundsman out after rabbits. A princess of the blood dragged off like some dirty-arsed serf, thrown over the back of a horse and carried off into the forest.

And nobody had seen a thing.

Abandando Briconet, Papal Legate, agent of the Holy Inquisition, and newly appointed chief of the south-eastern department of Francis I's sophisticated intelligence network, could hardly credit what he was hearing. He had been summoned from his base in Avignon by an urgent dispatch direct from army headquarters, authorising him to set aside his current assignment and launch an immediate investigation into the bloody murder of the French officer.

Claude Pohl, Duc de Milhaud, might have been a rather nondescript regimental commander – his troops were no more than rejects from the fleet and sweepings from the local waterfront – but he had been about to join them to the immensely powerful forces Francis had ordered north of the Alps ready for the descent into Italy.

Briconet had reviewed what he knew of the murdered man as his dreaded black and red coach rumbled up the coast road from Avignon. The Duc de Milhaud was forty years old, a notorious rake whose self-destructive tastes had already eaten through the greater portion of his family fortune. Briconet had discovered that the Duke had taken up his commission in order to clear some of his more pressing debts with the local vintners, rather than through any desire to exercise his almost non-existent military abilities.

But the dissolute Duke had not met a violent end on some

glorious field of battle – he had been bludgeoned to death in his own backyard. Briconet's superiors – the vastly experienced soldiers trusted with every detail of the coming invasion – wanted to know why. They clearly felt the murder was important enough to warrant Briconet's full attention and had suspended his current duties.

Up until his urgent new appointment Briconet had been working as an *agent provocateur*, using a small fortune in gold and silver as well as his awesome powers of persuasion to advance His Majesty's Alpine ambitions. The legendarily incorruptible cleric had been entrusted with a subtle and demanding role: persuading the frontier nobility – a notoriously independent breed – to assist the French war effort. He was free to beg, bribe or blackmail as necessary: any means so long as the shrewd border fiefdoms aided France and denied the Empire.

It was just the sort of role on which Briconet thrived. Shadowy, underhand and devious. He had, after all, sniffed out heretics from Lisbon to Hamburg, uncovered witch covens and foreign plots, accused treacherous nobles and exposed double agents. But he was also a master detective, able to sense a lie before it had left the fearful prisoner's mouth. He had sent as many men to the stake as his hero, the fanatical Bernardo Guy himself. A fact which he never hesitated to remind his listeners of in the most hair-raising detail imaginable. His diabolical descriptions of previous torture sessions worked like a charm. Most prisoners confessed before he had even taken his gloves off. Woe betide the Duke's killers, if they ever fell into Abandando Briconet's bloody hands.

A series of fearful household servants had already been dragged before him, their bloodied features and splattered clothing eloquent testimony to the rigorous persuasion his assistants had already administered.

Briconet had been sorely tempted to subject such house guests as remained to the same brutal investigation. He had been outraged by their carefree answers, their surly denial of any involvement in untoward behaviour. He had barely been able to recognise the sorry wretches for what they were, mistaking drunken dukes for footmen, red-eyed ladies for scullery maids. Their clothing had been dishevelled, smeared and stained with spilled food and slurped wine. The once-proud Château Celestine was virtually derelict, the grounds wrecked, the plantations overgrown. The filthy rooms smelt like a Turkish harem. He had noticed various items of clothing had been stuffed behind cushions, odd shoes lying forgotten beneath overturned chairs. A great hoard of empty bottles had been deposited in the vermin-infested kitchens.

Briconet might have been a pious servant of God, but he had seen enough of the foul world to know an orgy when he saw one. Men and women disporting themselves about the floor like beasts of the forest, their lewd limbs twined like mating snakes. The very idea made him shudder.

They had tried to compose themselves of course, to cover up the evidence of their hideous debaucheries, but Briconet could see the hellfire glint of guilt in every bleary eye. They had all told the same story – that this drunkard of a Duke had not even mentioned he was due to report to army headquarters. The news that Milhaud had been appointed to command a regiment of troops had come as a complete surprise to many of them.

'Claude? Soldiering? Who for?'

'He would have used up all his soldiers as fast as he goes through whores, begging your pardon, your reverence.'

'It might have been wise to let him serve the Empire instead. You could rely on Milhaud to f . . . foul things up well and truly!'

It appeared the reluctant warrior was in the habit of dismissing all but a chosen few servants while he entertained his house guests. The only staff permitted to attend the debauched parties were dark-skinned eunuchs, dumb beasts fetched over the seas for the express purpose of silently servicing their fornicating master.

Briconet waved his wrist in irritation. Two blank-faced soldiers hauled the semi-conscious gardener away, leaving a trail of blood spots on the greasy floor. His assistant Maître Sourris finished scratching the flimsy details the groundsman had provided into his bulky, ink smeared ledger and looked up expectantly.

'He says the same as the rest. We have no clear detail as to what was taken,' the fat clerk complained. 'Without some sort of inventory we will not even know what and therefore who we are looking for.'

'There might not be any need of an inventory. The dog could not say whether the Duke was carrying a purse. Hardly surprising in the circumstances,' Briconet fumed. He drummed his fingers against his jutting chin.

'What sort of bandit strips a man of his braes? A doublet, yes. A shirt, perhaps. But all his underlinen?' Sourris shook his head, making his fleshy throat wobble.

Briconet grimaced, already weary from his long and arduous journey from Avignon. They had arrived late that evening, ten hours or so after the fiendish deeds had first been reported. The badly kempt ground and summerhouse floor bore clear scars of the perplexing struggles.

'Fool! Did you not mark the abrasions on Milhaud's heels, the marks over the lawn? He was dragged over from the house as the intruder had found him. Stark naked.'

Maître Sourris blinked in bewilderment, wondering why on earth a high-ranking nobleman would have been out on a chill night without his clothes. 'An intruder would have been visible to anybody at any of the rearward windows,' he pointed out.

'I very much doubt there were many here in any condition to stand.' Sourris looked suitably shocked. 'There is no need to make a note of that in your report,' Briconet said testily. 'Let us consider the facts we have found, rather than the assumptions passed on by army headquarters. Milhaud was found in the summerhouse, two hundred paces from the rear of the house where the attack took place. One blow from a heavy instrument, a club, the pommel of a sword, and his skull is broken.'

Sourris nodded eagerly.

'Knocked over the head and dragged off towards the woods,' Sourris agreed. Briconet's habitual scowl resolved itself into a mask of fierce contempt.

'Why drag a dead man two hundred paces, across a lawn visible to anyone who had cared to look out of the window?' His obese assistant tugged at his nose.

'To rob him in peace?'

'I have just told you, I consider the Duke was completely naked when the attack took place. Unless he was in the habit of hiding the family silver where the sun doesn't shine.'

Sourris' widely spaced eyes opened in alarm at this unholy prospect.

'No, my dear Maître, I believe the blow administered outside the house was intended to stun our victim, not kill him. I cannot imagine any other reason why the intruder or intruders should have gone to such lengths to carry him to the summerhouse.'

Sourris coughed. 'Is it at all possible the lady in question was acting in league with the intruder? From the marks on the lawn it would appear she lent the man a hand, hauling the body off.'

'A good point, Maître. But we have been given four conflicting reports of the costume the Comtesse du Lac was wearing at the time. I don't trust any of them. I believe the girl went out into the garden after her lover, the Duke, unclothed.'

Sourris whistled with disbelief. 'A countess, without her clothes?'

'Indeed. Once again, there is no need to report my every observation on this matter. But one look at the ground will surely show you all you need to know. The tracks of the Duke's heels, dragging along the ground like this. Hauled along backwards, presumably by his assailant. A large man in heavy, iron-shod boots. The girl's feet were bare, but the prints she left behind are deeper than one would have expected, given her height and estimated weight. I believe she was ordered to lend a hand, hauling the Duke's body to the summerhouse.'

'How appalling for her!'

Briconet wagged his crooked finger. 'But wait Maître. She might have imagined the Duke to be swooning, just like our mysterious assailant. It is my guess the intruder had dragged the Duke off, intending to interrogate him in private!'

'A spy, just as Monsieur La Palice believes!'

Briconet's gaunt features resolved themselves once again. His thin lips curled back from his streaked teeth.

'If I were the intruder, I would have hesitated to take such risks for such a minor prize. The Duke was a penniless rake; he would have found himself in command of every latrine detail in Italy! No spy worth his salt would have bothered with such a waster.'

Sourris looked suitably scandalised by his master's insights, but knew well when to hold his tongue.

'This has little to do with spying and wars. It is my belief this was a personal quarrel. Given the Duke's character, I would suggest a matter of honour might have been about to be settled. Once again, the blow on the head was not intended to kill.'

'But kill it did. And what would the intruder want with the Comtesse?'

Briconet shrugged. 'Perhaps he had no taste for cold-blooded murder, and preferred to take the witness with him?'

'Stark naked?'

'Perhaps. Our groundsman found tracks beneath a large oak in the grounds. Two horses, two sets of large, iron-soled boots. If he had come intending to escape with a prisoner, I would have imagined they would have brought a spare horse or two, eh?'

Sourris shook his head, marvelling at his master's almost supernatural powers of observation.

'But even so. We will go over the guest list once again, re-examine any links with our current military operations. I want to know of every damned foreigner, every shaveling lieutenant, every boastful captain who might have been at the party. Send riders to every inn within ten leagues. It is possible our intruders spent some time reconnoitring the grounds before they struck. Have our agents put aboard every ship on the Marseille water-front, and send word to the border guards to double their watch. Two men, travelling incognito with a hostile young woman.'

Sourris made himself a quick note, nodding furiously. Briconet clicked his fingers.

'If the Countess was naked,' he theorised, 'then she would have required clothing from somewhere if she wasn't to stand out on the road. Get in touch with the magistrates in a ten-league radius, I want to know of every minor theft in the last two days, no matter how insignificant it appeared. Chickens from a barn, a skirt from a washline. You know the sort of detail we require.'

Sourris straightened his back, nodded eagerly.

It was a pleasure to work for the old man, when his blood was up.

Briconet's diligence was rewarded within two hours. A rider brought word from the Seigneur of Roquevaire, half a dozen leagues north of the château. The village laundress had reported several items stolen from her washlines in the early hours. Well-worn country gear which she had been in two minds about washing at all. What sort of a rogue would steal such rags from a poor village washerwoman?

The inquisitor had allowed himself a thin smile of self-satisfaction at the news.

'Roquevaire, I know it well. It lies on the coast road, the most direct route to Saluzzo, Tenda, Monaco, Villefranco, the *Alpes Maritimes*. And, of course, to Italy.'

Sourris beamed. 'Well then, my guess would be Villefranco! According to one of the cooks, Milhaud's mistress had just left him, taken up with the new Duke out there. Marnier?'

'Mounier,' Briconet corrected, his acute mind sensing another important clue. 'What name?'

Sourris winced. 'No name. Not a proper name anyway. She says the girl was known as the White Rabbit. Because she liked to . . . you know.'

'The White Rabbit? What kind of name is that?'

'The only other thing she remembers, might be significant.'

'What?'

'She was English. She was supposed to have worked her way up from the waterfront.'

'English?' Briconet exclaimed. 'Well well well.'

James Eldritch woke with a start, squinting through his sleep-haze at the unfamiliar surroundings. The cheap boarding house was typical of the region. It was built like a fortress and smelt like a bear pit. The ruckled bed was moist with their sweat and loveplay. He flung the covers back, alarmed by the bright sunlight shafting through the cracks in the shutters.

The girl squawked and clung to the stained counterpane, muttering oaths in her impenetrable Langue Doc dialect. Eldritch crossed the floor, his cold feet tangling in their discarded clothing. He wrenched his sword from the litter and pressed his ear to the door. He could hear Hobby snoring, the resonant gusts rattling the windowpanes in the narrow hallway he had been detailed to guard.

Eldritch picked his way to the shutters and peeped down into the busy street. Market traders were already doing brisk business, offering fragrant game, baskets of vegetables and great steaming platters of fresh fish. The Englishman's nose twitched as he sampled the delicious aromas sidling up the wall.

'Come back to bed,' the woman invited huskily, holding the counterpane open to reveal her slim, golden body.

Eldritch cursed his own miserable willpowers. Finding time for haughmaganding instead of continuing his escape eastward.

Their escape, he reminded himself.

The three of them had arrived after dark in the village of Roquevaire, the captain passing over a handful of coin to an indifferent landlord wearing the filthiest apron Eldritch had ever set eyes on. The brute had bitten on each coin, his stained teeth the colour of old anchor chain. He had barely glanced at the tall stranger, his small eyes glinting as he reckoned the value of the silver livre he had handed over. One livre was worth 20 sous, one sou 12 dernier. More than enough for a night's bed and board in this shite-pit.

'Put your horses in the lean-to round the back,' the rogue had invited in his gurgling southern accent. Hobby had sorted the animals while Eldritch swept into the inn with the girl half hidden beneath his cloak. The landlord had shrugged, unwilling to spoil his bargain by making any undue enquiries into the stranger's business.

'We've tarried too long already,' Eldritch told her, hurling the damp skirt and stained shift over the bed. He had stolen the clothing from a washline behind a row of cottages a few leagues back. The ragged garments had helped disguise the girl's natural grace, turned the Countess into a common polecat. Her auburn hair was a wild tangle, her eyes ringed with fatigue.

She certainly looked the part now.

Eldritch knocked gently on the door and peered down at the blinking sergeant. Hobby seemed to fill the hall, his broad shoulders brushing against the mouldy plasterwork on either side of the passage. The huge archer rubbed his knuckles in his eyes, blinking against the sunlight filtered by the studded door.

'Get the horses saddled, we'll be down directly.'

Hobby rubbed his vast barrel of a belly. 'Staying for breakfast are we?' he enquired hopefully.

'It's damn near noon man, why didn't you wake me?'

'Wake you? I didn't get to sleep for hours, listening to you two banging the boards to wake the dead!' Hobby exclaimed.

'Never mind all that,' Eldritch replied hotly, wishing he could follow his own advice. He had ventured everything to find his damned slattern of a sister, and here he was behaving with the same utter disregard for his dignity or name. The Countess had unstoppered his senses, releasing a tornado of pent-up passions. Only a fool would have dallied with a woman, lain backwards next to the corpse of one of the most powerful nobles in the region. Only a madman would have postponed his escape, halted his flight to freedom in order to reacquaint himself with her earthy charms.

But he hadn't been able to help himself. She was as effervescent as a cloud of sparks, throwing her head back to laugh and cry out in her passion. He could still smell her enticing aroma, her sweet sweat smeared over his skin. Eldritch felt himself blushing as he fought into his hastily divested clothing.

'Get up, I mean it. We should have been away before dawn. Now we'll have to push our way past that lot,' he said, jerking his thumb at the shuttered window. The girl sat up in bed, tugging the covers over her breasts.

'Where are you intending taking me, anyway? I gave you my word I would not say a thing.'

Eldritch snorted with laughter. 'I am supposed to believe that, am I? Get up and into those rags or I'll carry you out as you are,' he snarled.

The girl flushed with anger, utterly unused to being addressed in such an offhand manner. But one look in her lover's smouldering eyes warned her from further protests. She swung her legs out of the warm covers and picked at her new wardrobe, sulkily tugging the shift over her tousled hair.

Hobby had saddled their horses and stood by as Eldritch purchased a third animal from the rogue of a landlord. The captain had parted with another two livres for the knock-kneed nosebag, a work-weary grey with a hanging head and a mass of wet mucus at its snout. It might get them another few miles though, Eldritch thought grimly. The Countess closed her eyes in shame when she saw the big sergeant lead the beast from its stable. He looked far more capable of carrying the horse than the poor beast did him.

'First you kidnap me, then you rape me, then you wrap me in rags and expect me to sit upon this sorry specimen,' the girl exclaimed, her slim cheekbones flushing. Eldritch gripped her forearm tightly, steered the furious Countess towards the wretched animal. The milling villagers didn't seem overly concerned by her plight, pushing past on their way along the narrow street.

'Hold your tongue! I don't intend to swing on a French scaffold just yet.' The girl seemed torn between fierce hatred and raging excitement. Nothing like this had ever happened to her, and some small part of her was enjoying every breathless moment of the adventure.

But he wasn't going to get away with talking down to her as if she was some farmyard trollop. She tugged away from the brutal Englishman, felt the steel slide across her midriff. The bastard had laid a blade on her!

'Hurry up my sweet, or I'll cut you another one!' he rasped, forcing her through a gang of shrieking fishwives. The Countess glared at him, outraged by his callous threats.

'Captain!'

Hobby's shout echoed over their heads, bounded between the closely built hovels which stood either side of the street like so many over-cooked cakes. The crowd was silenced by his sudden bellow, turning their heads to see what the commotion was about. The giant sergeant had mounted his horse, his elevated platform giving him an uninterrupted view of the main road through the village. A pack of horsemen had just spurred into sight, kicking up a stormcloud of grit as the puzzled locals leapt out of their path.

Eldritch was electrified with anger and astonishment, cursing himself as he bundled the girl towards the grey. Charlotte, freshly invigorated by his beastly insults, threw her head back and yelled her alarm.

'Quiet!' Eldritch bawled, shouldering the girl against the worn saddle and boosting her from the ground. Charlotte kicked out, catching him a glancing blow on his elbow. Hobby had spurred forward, bringing Eldritch's charger broadside to the main street. The bewildered peasants melted away from the sudden alarm, anxious not to be caught between the barbarous strangers and the blackguards galloping down the street after them. Hobby reached over, grasping the struggling girl by the scruff of the neck. He held her straight by main force as Eldritch slipped under the grey's chest and hauled himself into his own saddle.

A trumpet blared. The riders had drawn swords, lances levelled as they kicked a path through the logjam of loaded carts and hand-barrows.

'Ride!' Eldritch yelled, turning his prancing stallion in a tight circle and grasping at the grey's reins. The famished beast seemed to discover some hidden reserves of energy, matching the larger horses as they hurtled out of the narrow village as if they had been fired from a gun. Charlotte held on to the beast's filthy mane, terrified she would be thrown clear and brained by her fall. The three of them swept around a bend and cantered through the village pond, scattering a squadron of white ducks. Eldritch risked a quick look over his shoulder, saw the pursuing troops force their way through the stall-choked street and gallop after them.

His mind was reeling, stupefied by their perilous escape. How had the French authorities known where to look for them? What rogue had marked their confused route through the trees? He hardly dared think who had betrayed them. Was it possible the fiendish girl had left some message while he snored?

Old Howath had been right all along. Never trust a woman!

Beside the Castello Villefranco,
in the Maritime Alps

✦

Duke Gerhard peeked out into the smoky courtyard as if his dead uncle's troops had hidden themselves in every corner, sworn to avenge their master's treacherous death on the tower above. The youngster could hardly believe the shambles Montalban's fanciful engine had left behind. More than a dozen men at arms lay in splattered steel heaps beside the wall to his left. The mouldy stone had been splashed with blood and gouts of slippery grey brains, deeply scored by the rasping shards which had cut the unfortunate guards to ribbons. Gerhard picked his way over the hideously mutilated corpses, careful to avoid stepping in their remarkably vivid blood. He held the hem of his gown to his mouth, lips compressed at the appalling, coppery reek of blood and the hot fox stink of spilled guts. The men at arms looked as if they had fallen into a vast threshing machine, diced and sliced by death-dealing blades. The wall was pocked and scarred with odd lumps of metal, the musket balls, pellets and nails Montalban had stuffed down the barrels of his awesome weapon of war. The dizzy engineer had tottered down the staircase after the Duke, eager to see the results of his deranged handiwork. He left the nauseated Gerhard picking over the corpses while he made his way straight to the engine itself.

Or rather, what was left of it.

Montalban could have wept. The strongly-built wagon he had used as a base for his unlikely contraption had collapsed, the timbers burnt black by the ferocious blast. Most of the barrels had split down the middle or buckled completely, their sooty mouths curled over like dying fish in the bottom of a boat. The complex bands and buckles he had worked through the night to perfect had split apart; the powder troughs were fused together like grey jam. The straps which had held the complex arrangement of barrels had been twisted beyond repair. Leonardo's

Engine was nothing more than a heap of scrap metal surrounded by sooty heaps of its own kindling.

The poor crew members were little more than smears of red paste and broken bone. They had been crushed beyond recognition when the vast engine had hurtled backwards, squashing the human cockroaches against the pitiless wall. The impact had sent such a shiver through the old stone that several balconies had been loosened from their mortar beds. A dozen tiles had been dislodged from the bell tower, with fatal consequences for several of Gerhard's dumstruck guardsmen. Montalban ran his filthy sleeve over his nose, trying to think of some way of harnessing the destructive recoil. More ballast in the bottom of the wagon, perhaps? He would have snapped the axles if he had piled on any more stones. The genius Leonardo – whose designs he had adapted – had clearly intended the war-wagon to be mobile and manoeuvrable. His sketches showed the contraption being wheeled to and fro by no more than a couple of lightly-armed gunners. It would be no good if it was too heavy to push about the battlefield, he thought hotly. Montalban couldn't imagine many troops would be foolish or obliging enough to charge straight at an immobile, multi-barrelled gun.

His master harboured no such reservations as to the weapon's worth. He trotted over the courtyard, mesmerised by the appalling destruction. 'Fifteen, fifteen fully armed knights cut down like new corn!' Gerhard exclaimed. His fearful troops were just beginning to emerge from their hidey-holes, terrified by the ear-splitting explosions and sickened by the brutal slaughter of the strangers – not to mention the accidental braining of their own comrades.

Igon Vitt and his colleague Giacomo Belatavicci had made themselves scarce during the bloody confrontation, only emerging when the dust had begun to settle over their cowled heads. They had hurried down to the courtyard expecting to find Baldassare stalking about a ring of corpses, and were somewhat taken aback to find their precious prince had not been thrown from the tower like a bucketful of slops.

'A miracle! Thank God you are safe!' Belatavicci cried, blinking in disbelief as he surveyed the carnage in the courtyard.

'A thousand mercies you survived, my Duke!' Vitt seconded, brushing the powdery mortar from Gerhard's stooped shoulders. 'Rebelling against his own liege lord! Who could have imagined your own uncle would have arrived with such murderous intentions!'

'Who indeed?' Gerhard asked waspishly. 'Where were you when he arrived? Skulking in the boggard? Hiding out in your lonely passage?'

Vitt looked suitably crestfallen.

'We had hurried to the gatehouse to instruct the gatekeepers to lower the portcullis! The cowardly dogs had already abandoned their posts, my Duke!' Belatavicci shrilled. 'Such is the stamp of soldier your poor father saw fit to employ!'

Gerhard shook his head. He knew full well the rogues had been sitting quietly, waiting for Baldassare to climb the steps and choke his life out before they emerged to re-negotiate their contracts with the new master.

'You spotted hounds! Do you imagine I spent fifteen years in my chambers tutored by the finest classicists in Italy to become fluent in stupidity?' Gerhard snarled, his righteous soldiers stepping out of the shadows to support him with somewhat belated menace.

'My lord, I cannot . . .'

'Riders on the high road!'

The sudden shout from the battlements turned them all to stone, pale statues amongst the steaming shambles.

Gerhard recovered his wits first.

'Lower the damned gate!' he screamed, gripped by twisting vines of panic. His foot soldiers clattered across the courtyard. One tripped over a severed hand and measured his length on the slick cobbles. The guards raced back to their warm alcove, clasped the heavy capstan to lower the portcullis. They bent their backs, heaving with all their might, but the gate remained where it was, ten feet above the cobbled gateway. A chance deflection from the exploding carriage had sent one of Montalban's steel braces hurtling across the courtyard to lodge in the gear mechanism. The monstrous chain grated on the buckled band, grinding the sooty fragment flat, but the wedge held and the chain stuck fast.

Gerhard was paralysed with fear, staring open-mouthed as the portcullis quivered above the open gateway. His troops – lily-livered rascals that they were – ran for the main door or scuttled up the staircase to the battlements. A helmeted guard leaned out of one of the lancets in the fortified gatehouse tower, gauntlet cupped about his mouth.

'A score of men at arms with black banners, coming this way!' he bawled.

Black banners? What fiends were these? Another squadron of Baldassare's bastard bodyguards, hurrying to the sound of the dreadfully destructive gun?

Gerhard stepped from one outrageously curled slipper to the other, beside himself with uncertainty. Montalban grinned feebly.

'We'd best get inside, barricade the inner keep,' he suggested, glancing around the slaughterpen courtyard. 'It's the best we can hope for now Leonardo's Engine is wrecked.'

'I believe Signor Montalban's suggestion might be sound, my Duke,' Vitt stammered, clutching the youth by the arm and hoisting him towards the main tower with an awkward mixture of excessive deference and brute force.

For once, the waspish youth held his tongue and did as he was bid.

Abandando Briconet's bodyguard cantered up the steep track and lowered their banners to ride beneath the stuck portcullis. The riders reined in, turning their warhorses in the bloody courtyard as they awaited their master. The knights gazed about the shambles, wondering what devilry they had interrupted. They were all coated in dust, their faces red with the long chase along the coast road. The horses stood shivering amidst the pools of congealing blood, their drooping muzzles smothered in sticky foam.

Briconet's great black wagon rumbled over the cobbles, a squad of panting spearmen helping to propel the vast hull up the slope. The foot soldiers fell back, presented arms as Briconet lifted the leather curtain flap and peered out at the unexpected carnage.

Was it possible the English assassins they were pursuing had somehow arrived before them, massacring the feeble inhabitants as if they were fresh-faced novices running about in their underthings? The assassins had given them the slip outside Roquevaire, losing themselves in the steep, fir-choked hillsides which overlooked the coast. By the time his convoy had forced a passage through the crowded market, the fleet-footed rogues had disappeared down one of the deer tracks which radiated out into the vast woodlands. Briconet had detached dozens of men to guard the crossroads and had in the meantime pressed on for Villefranco, hoping to catch up with the mysterious White Rabbit he had heard so much about.

The captain at arms strode forward and saluted. He didn't seem at all put out by the shambles he had found in the corner. 'They've locked themselves up in the main tower, my lord. Do you want me to knock them up?'

Briconet glanced about the walls, noticed the fearful faces peering down at the unannounced visitors. They certainly seemed shocked by their insolent approach and hardly looked capable of the sort of piggeries evidenced by the mutilated bodies he could see piled against the wall. On the other hand, Briconet reasoned, it wouldn't be the first time the arrival of a caravan belonging to the Holy Inquisition had put the fear of God into some scrawny-shanked lordling in his sty. His black wagons had been this way before. He had left dozens of filthy heretics blazing at the stake to remind the population of the terrible wrath of heaven.

'Of course not!' Briconet snapped. 'This castle belongs to the Duke of Villefranco. Correct me if I am wrong, Captain Druchet, but His Majesty Francis I has yet to declare war on his own vassals.'

'No my lord,' the captain said, stepping back as Briconet climbed down from the stifling compartment. The little man walked over to the wall, made a cursory examination of the bodies.

He had come investigating the murder of the Duc de Milhaud. The drunken wretch had been dispatched by a single blow to the head, a small discoloured bump on his temple the only evidence of any mischief. The men lying on the cobbles had met a rather bloodier end, their heads and limbs torn off by some terrific blast, bellies riddled with flying shards and shot. Their modern armour had been pocked and pounded by a fearsome hail of metal. Briconet frowned. He had thought at first they might be the victims of a firing squad, lined up before a company of arquebusiers and shot to pieces. But these men had been armed as well as armoured, bunched beneath the wall as if they had been awaiting the order to ride out. The inquisitor turned, squinted at the wrecked carriage in the opposite corner. It seemed to have been caught up in the same fiercely destructive explosion.

Druchet followed him across the cobbles as the agent examined the burnt-out wreckage and its peculiar load. A dozen or more steel tubes, the size of organ pipes, had been stacked in the wagon's oaken hull. He leaned closer, noticed the barrels had split up the middle, the crude trough which had fed them fused and twisted by the tremendous heat.

Interesting, Briconet thought.

Druchet looked over his shoulder, his black brows furrowed.

'What manner of device is this?' Briconet asked.

'Some sort of multi-barrelled gun my lord . . . I believe the English use a device called the shrimp . . .'

The captain's discourse was interrupted by a flurry of trumpets from the main tower. Briconet looked up as the great doors were swung open, and a squad of soldiers in Mounier livery trotted out to form a double rank either side of the entrance.

'It appears Duke Villefranco has decided to come and greet us after all,' Briconet sighed. He straightened up and made his way towards the youth who had appeared in the doorway flanked by a pair of fawning advisors. They were skulking on his threshold as if reluctant to come any further into their own yard.

Briconet's bodyguards formed up with commendable skill and precision, lining up opposite the Duke's nervous household troops as if they were black-harnessed chessmen. The courtiers detached themselves from the Duke's shadow and hurried down the steps towards the scowling visitor.

Briconet smiled as he recognised their pale faces. He could not bring their names to mind, but he remembered them well enough from one of his previous progresses about the region. Bloody expeditions which had silenced the bells in every village, left hundreds of those poor, deluded servants of the anti-Christ roasting at the stake for their hellish treacheries.

Briconet narrowed his eyes, recalling that the aged Duke of Villefranco had died recently, leaving a beardless boy to oversee his tiny, mountain duchy. It appeared his passover had not been without contest.

The old Duke's fawning henchmen dropped to their knees, lifting the inquisitor's cloak to kiss the dirt-trailed hem.

'My dear lord Briconet, hammer of all heretics, devoted champion of the Holy Inquisition!' the shaven headed counsellor trilled, abasing himself before the distracted agent. Briconet frowned, tugged his hem back.

'May Almighty God bless this day of deliverance!' the other chimed in, his long hands splayed on the bloody cobbles as if he were worshipping some filthy icon. Briconet gazed down at the fools, made the sign of the cross above their bowed heads.

'Get off your bellies you loathsome ticks! I will be properly presented to your master or I'll see your heads on spikes above the gate!' he hissed, smiling serenely at the agitated boy hanging back by the door.

The courtiers crawled backwards, nodding their heads like

lapdogs. They clambered to their feet and half turned to their master, hurrying through the formalities while glancing at the formidable bodyguard the agent had brought with him.

'With my lord's pardon, may we present his sublime highness Monsignor Abandando Briconet of Avignon, Papal Legate and agent of the Holy Inquisition!'

His latest appointment, from Francis I himself, was a matter of the strictest secrecy.

Briconet stepped forward, bowed graciously at his reluctant host. 'My lord Duke. May I begin by offering the sincerest condolences following your tragic loss. Your honoured father was particularly admired by His Majesty Francis I, when they met at Amboise.'

The young Duke looked disconcerted by the well-informed Briconet's unexpectedly ingratiating tone. His callow features arranged themselves into a sullen smile.

'My lord Briconet is too kind.'

'May I also offer my congratulations and the warmest good wishes to you for a long and peaceful reign.'

Gerhard smiled nervously.

Briconet allowed his eyes to slide toward the piled corpses, lying in bloody heaps beside the door.

'Am I right in thinking, my dear lord Duke, that the day has not been without unhappy incident?'

'Unhappy incident indeed!' one of the courtiers piped up, hands clasped to his long face.

'My lord Briconet has obeyed our prayers, arriving in time to nip this hideous rebellion in the bud!'

'Rebellion?' Briconet enquired, astounded.

'It appears . . . my uncle, Baldassare Mounier, had come here intending to relieve me of my inheritance,' the Duke reported, his long neck pulsing and stretching as he prised the words from his throat.

Briconet's hooded eyes widened in alarm.

'He came here . . . to kill his own nephew? What despicable treachery!'

'Thankfully our brave Duke was able to defend himself against his uncle's vicious assaults,' the chancellor reported breathlessly.

'It would certainly appear so,' Briconet allowed.

'Baldassare . . . my uncle . . . fell from the tower,' the Duke reported, lifting his eyes towards the windblown height.

Briconet looked suitably shocked. Perhaps young Gerhard

wasn't the useless sack of goat-piss his agents had reported him to be.

'My troops await your command, my Duke,' he said craftily. 'They will not rest until every last one of your uncle's treacherous bandits is swinging from the gibbet!'

'My heavy heart is gladdened by your selfless offer, my dear Monsignor,' Gerhard whispered.

Briconet just managed to restrain a shout of laughter. 'I must confess I am intrigued by the device you employed to quell this evil outbreak. Some sort of English cannon? A shrimp, I believe it is called.'

'Shrimp? Leonardo's Engine is more of a giant squid, my dear sir,' Gerhard said modestly.

Briconet nodded. 'With more than a suggestion of the wasp about it,' he pointed out.

The Duke frowned.

'I mean to say, my dear Duke, that in stinging those filthy rebels, the device apparently signalled its own doom, just like the wasp.'

'This is but the prototype, an experimental model,' Gerhard said hastily. He was hatefully aware Briconet was already several jumps ahead of him. 'I am sure that should the wise and just government of his sublime majesty Francis I be minded to participate in the project, a fully operational device could be produced in months, if not weeks,' Gerhard said, unsure how far he dared push the black-eyed inquisitor. Briconet pursed his lips.

'You have plans?'

'I have plans, but sadly not to hand at this moment in time.'

'I quite understand your anxiety to preserve the details of your engine's creation, my lord Duke. But perhaps it will intrigue you to know that, in addition to my strictly clerical duties, His Majesty has recently commissioned me to take an interest in rather more secular matters.'

So Briconet was responsible for arms production as well as the ecclesiastical well-being of the nation?

'I didn't know . . . I wasn't aware reports of my engine had reached the ears of the church in Avignon,' Gerhard said guardedly.

'They hadn't. Until now,' Briconet replied, favouring the pale boy with his warmest smile.

69

PART TWO

✦

'The bond of love is one which men,
wretched creatures that they are,
break when it is to their
advantage to do so,'

Machiavelli, *The Prince*

By Roquevaire, near Marseille

✦

Eldritch had recognised the sinister black wagon and the cadaverous features of its despised passenger. Briconet had tugged the flap back just long enough to confer with one of his officers, before ordering the driver forward with a brief twitch of his liver-spotted paw. The Englishman had wondered about putting an arrow between those beetled brows, executing the snake-eyed wretch on first sight. They were safe enough so long as they kept away from the road, melting back into the flourishing fir plantation which had saved them in the first place. The woods were ominously silent, the luxuriously aromatic bed of pine needles cushioning every noise as well as clouding every scent.

He could have strung his bow and nocked an arrow while the serpent gave his orders, slotted an arrow between the rogue's streaked teeth in a blink. But assassinating an agent of the Holy Inquisition would make him a pariah in every corner of every state in Europe.

Abandando Briconet was devilishly well-connected. He would have been forced to find sanctuary with the Turks, if he had followed that particular impulse.

Eldritch cursed his temper, the fiery pride which had brought him and his loyal soldiers to the brink of disaster half a dozen times in the past year alone. He was no better than a murderer now, aye, and a kidnapper to boot, and judging from the rapidity of the pursuit, the French authorities had wasted no time in proclaiming him public enemy, terror of the southern aristocracy!

He crawled back on his belly and found Hobby and his prisoner waiting beside the horses in a small, rocky hollow, fringed with luxurious ferns. The Countess was squatting on a boulder, her elegant chin propped on her palm as she surveyed the horizon from the unfamiliarly cramped bower.

He picked his way back down to his anxious companions,

acknowledging Hobby's concerned glance with a small shrug of his shoulders.

'He's left sentinels along the road, but they've given up searching the woods. They would be lost without a pack of slow dogs to help them, through this lot.'

'That's as may be,' Hobby growled. 'It's how they got on to us so quick, I'd like to know. They never tracked us all the way from the château.'

'Briconet was with them, we know he's no fool. Perhaps he had word from Gueldres that I would be seeking out his long-lost cousin,' Eldritch theorised. He still hadn't quite recovered from the shock of seeing two score and more heavily armed riders bearing down on him. The dreadful, strangulated panic as if he were still in the grip of some waking nightmare. He was no craven, but he liked to imagine he was always one step ahead of his opponents. Eldritch had watched Briconet's driver whip the sweat-caked team off along the coast road, following the rocky shoreline to the east. Was it mere coincidence the inquisitor was heading towards Villefranco, or had Briconet's supernatural gifts enabled him to guess Eldritch's destination from the meagre clues he had left behind?

One thing was certain – his tomfoolery with Charlotte had presented the canny Briconet with the time and opportunity to spring his deadly trap. He had broken his own golden rule, dissipating his energies sniffing after women – and had come within a hair's-breadth of paying with his life. He closed his eyes, trying to squeeze out the lurid images which flashed across his mind, the wicked enticements she suggested with a simple, flickering smile.

She had infected his head and heart, dug her way under his skin as if she were part woman and part rash. Their close escape from Roquevaire had been a timely lesson for him to concentrate on the task in hand – finding and rescuing his sister.

The White Rabbit, he remembered with another inward wince.

'White Rabbit, my dear Monsignor? I am afraid I am unaware of anyone by that name,' Gerhard said casually, taking another chaste sip at his wine. It wouldn't do to cross swords with the shrewd inquisitor while he was in his cups.

Briconet paused over his chicken wing, his gnarled fingers slick with fat. Despite his spare proportions, Briconet had already eaten the best part of a roast duck, a side of beef and half a

74

bronze tureen of fish stew. His assistant and accomplice Maître Sourris had polished off anything his master had inadvertently left. Gerhard had just begun to relax and lower his guard, satisfied the inquisitor did not intend to have them all slaughtered on the spot. Gerhard knew the Papal Legate must be itching to ransack the castle for Montalban's carefully adapted drawings, to secure the innovative and deadly device for his master Francis.

He could have stuck his chin out and flatly refused to divulge any details – Briconet certainly wouldn't have found the drawings without his help. But Gerhard had decided against any delaying tactics. It wouldn't have taken the inquisitor long to persuade him to part with the information he required. Briconet could be remarkably persuasive at times.

Gerhard knew he could never have hoped to manufacture the remarkable organ gun on any sort of scale, certainly not using the Duchy's limited resources. Sooner or later he would have had to take Leonardo's Engine to one of the great powers. He had originally intended to offer the engine to the Empire. The great workshops of Southern Germany could have been set to work turning out a dozen and more full-sized gun carriages every week. The Emperor Elect could have deployed scores of them, blasting the haughty French Gendarmes and their unsuspecting Swiss colleagues to smithereens before they had recognised the dangerous capabilities of the unfamiliar engines. The war-winning device might have sealed his fortune, made his name as the arbiter of all Europe!

But although the Duchy shared a border with the Empire, it was surrounded on three sides by France. Villefranco was trapped between the two, bobbing in the wake left by his embattled neighbours. Up until then Villefranco's sheer insignificance had enabled his poor father to tread a successful path between the contesting empires – now they might have an excellent excuse to invade, if only to deny the opposing party the opportunity of securing the potentially decisive weapon.

Briconet had seen the engine with his own eyes, witnessed the destruction it could wreak on closely ordered formations of troops. It was inevitable he would attempt to pluck the device from beneath the noses of his Imperial counterparts, to carry the crucial plans back to his master Francis.

All that remained for Gerhard was to try and secure the best price possible. And he didn't relish bartering with the dreaded inquisitor.

The Duke had hesitated to come right out with any figures and in the meantime Briconet seemed content to exchange small talk about the comings and goings of his household. He seemed as concerned with the identity of his whores and servants than the whereabouts of the drawings.

'White Rabbit indeed. A nickname and no more, Duke Gerhard. I am told women of this persuasion often use one or more *nommes de chambre*, as it were. We were told she had but lately arrived at Villefranco.'

The rogue certainly was well informed. Gerhard wondered where he got his information from. Which of his closest counsellors, how many of his creeping servants, were taking French pay?

'Well of course I wouldn't know the woman personally,' he countered.

'Perish the thought, my dear Duke.'

'But it occurs to me one of the members of my household might have sent for such a woman. One cannot vouch for the morals of one's staff. An English girl, you say?'

'English indeed. I gather their womenfolk are not generally the most sought-after courtesans.'

'Well, they aren't, as a rule. It's usually as much as you can do to get them to . . . I mean, I have heard tell they are not enthusiastic bed partners, my dear Monsignor,' Gerhard corrected himself, guilty colours rising from his suddenly constricting collar.

Briconet smiled indulgently.

'And of course any sexual activity beyond that necessary for procreation is a sin,' Briconet pointed out. 'So you have heard of such a creature here?' Gerhard nodded cautiously, as if pained by the dreadful confession.

'Lilywhite Lillith, I believe she called herself.'

'Lillith, the White Rabbit are one and the same woman? And she is here, now?'

'She was. I am told she left this very morning, shortly before . . . my uncle arrived.'

Briconet stopped chewing.

Did this spotty-faced jackass imagine he could play the poltroon with him?

'Lillith, I am told, is a very particular courtesan, who pleases herself where she makes her money. I fear she came here expecting me to succumb to her charms, but of course I refused to have anything to do with her. In fact, I sent her on to an acquaintance of mine, Alberto Tarsi, Seigneur of Mont Galliard.'

There didn't seem any harm in dropping the unfortunate Tarsi further in the shit.

Briconet suppressed a shiver of irritation at the mention of the despised name. Tarsi? Was this fool another of that damned rogue's creatures? The inquisitor racked his brains, trying to sieve the vast catalogue of detail he carried in his misshapen head, trying to find some pattern in the chaos he had uncovered. If one looked carefully enough, there was always a pattern. Briconet possessed detailed knowledge of the political and military situation in every state in Europe – even backwaters like Villefranco. He remembered some talk that the former Duke had indeed sent out feelers to Mont Galliard, proposing the betrothal of Prince Gerhard and Tarsi's only daughter Angelica – the girl he had interrogated a few short months before, with a particularly painful lack of success.

Was it possible the two households had maintained some sort of contact in the year since? Could Gerhard be unaware that Tarsi's fortress had been usurped by a band of renegade mercenaries the previous autumn? Mercenaries who were still waiting for the balance of the money he had promised them in order to change their fickle allegiance once again? The more he thought about it, the more Gerhard's simple-minded explanation rang true.

'You have been in contact with Mont Galliard in recent weeks?'

'I can't say as I have. Tarsi keeps himself to himself, and of course he is not exactly . . . his background would not endear him to the established families in the region,' Gerhard explained with creditable snobbery.

'A low-born soldier made good, in point of fact,' Briconet suggested.

Gerhard shrugged indulgently.

'So the woman Lillith left for Mont Galliard this very morning, shortly before your uncle Baldassare arrived with his hired thugs.'

'Precisely.'

'She had arrived, what would you say, earlier this week?'

Why was he so interested in the whore? Fifteen men shot to pieces in the courtyard and yet the inquisitor was more interested in some English bed-pony?

'Oh no. She'd been here longer than that. A month, at least.'

Briconet smiled.

77

She'd fleeced this beardless prick just as she had Milhaud, then set off for pastures new. He very much looked forward to catching up with this Lillith. She was clearly a Succubus, a fornicating demoness who drained a man's energies by night and his purse by day. He had come across many such servants of Satan during his arduous travels about Europe. He could practically taste the smoke as he set the faggots afire around her cloven feet.

'Clearly Villefranco is not the graveyard, the insignificant goat-pen some would have imagined it to be,' Briconet said, his tone hardening.

Gerhard swallowed. 'I ... er ... goat-pen, my dear Monsignor?'

'Oh I don't suggest for a moment that is how an educated man might have looked upon your worthy dukedom. Perish the thought. You have demonstrated Villefranco possesses unlimited potential. An essential stop-over for members of the nobility during their expeditions along our wonderful coastline.'

Gerhard frowned.

Was he suggesting Lilywhite Lillith was an English heiress? An eccentric noblewoman fornicating her way around Europe? She was no more than a moneygrabbing whore same as the rest of them!

'I understand the Countess du Lac is also in the habit of dropping in unannounced?'

'The Countess du Lac?' Judging by the boy's perplexed expression Briconet was fairly sure the bewildered Duke had never heard of the kidnapped woman.

'My informants were obviously mistaken. I was given to believe she was on her way here.'

'I've never heard of her.'

'No matter. Perhaps she had some manner of understanding with your deceased uncle, Baldassare?' Briconet was fishing now, but the youth's agonised responses were as easy to read as an illuminated manuscript.

'My uncle came here ... after my father died,' Gerhard stammered, hopelessly confused by Briconet's crossfire questioning. 'I know nothing of the woman you refer to.'

'The woman I refer to was kidnapped from a *soirée* at the Château Celestine near Marseille,' Briconet snapped. 'It appears her abductor was an Englishman, the brother to the woman you know as Lilywhite Lillith.'

Gerhard looked dumbfounded, his wide, moist mouth hung open. 'Why ... but I told you, she's moved on. Her brother? I never knew she had one!'

'I assure you she does. An absolute scoundrel, a low-born mercenary who has already contrived to worm his way out of our custody through the favour of his unscrupulous patrons.' Not quite true, but good enough to wrong-foot the anxious Duke. Briconet gave a pained smile. 'But no matter. You assure me you have had no contact with the wretch, and your word is good enough for me, my Duke. Perhaps we should turn our attention once again to this newfangled engine of yours. I am intrigued by your descriptions of its powers.'

His skilful probing had driven the inexperienced youngster into a corner, unsettled him well before he had even raised the question of the deadly weapon. Gerhard was hardly in a position to demand a fraction of its worth, given the proximity of the splendid French army. The ambitious boy had overreached himself, imagining he could in some way outwit the French king's agents.

All that remained was to settle a price, sign the agreement, and snatch the remarkable new toy from the silly weakling's grasp.

Eldritch finished explaining his plan and looked up expectantly at his bewildered companions.

'Sir, after all that has befallen us, you surely cannot be serious,' Charlotte snapped in imperious Langue Doc.

'Villefranco? You're goin' after that bastard-whelped wasp of a monk?' Hobby snorted in rather less ornate English. The captain held their stares.

'I'm not expecting you two to go. They would spot you a mile off, Hobby, and I cannot be sure the Countess would not give tongue to her present predicament.' Charlotte raised her dirt-streaked chin in contempt.

'I would not need to advertise your impertinent guilt,' she said coldly. The arrogant Englishman could do with being taken down a peg or two on Monsieur Briconet's well-used rack, but on the other hand, it would be a shame to see the back of such an invigorating lover. He made love to her as if he was trying to saturate his senses, drown between her wantonly spread legs. The sudden, stark image, the depth of feeling for her deadly kidnapper made her belly twitch.

The Countess frowned, furious at her hopelessly divided priorities. He deserved to be punished, yes, but he would be no use to her after Briconet had done his work, turned the scowling rogue into a broken-backed wraith . . .

'I'm not going to stand here arguing with you. From what you

79

have told me my sister might well be in Villefranco. If Briconet discovers her identity as I have done . . . then her life could be in peril.'

Hobby's broad, peasant face creased like parchment as he contemplated the captain's course. Eldritch glowered at his doubtful sergeant at arms.

'I don't have to remind you how we found Mistress Angelica, when *Monsieur* Briconet had finished toying with her,' he said grimly.

Tarsi's headstrong daughter had been implicated in the massacre at the Abbey D'Eleron, and the inquisitor had quite refused to believe her anxious denials. By the time Tarsi had negotiated her return (by giving himself up to the venomous rogue) she had been little more than a bag of bones, her proud spirit wrung from her fearfully scarred body. There was no way on this earth Eldritch was going to stand by while Briconet used his own flesh and blood for his perverted delvings.

'And what are we supposed to do in the meantime?' Hobby enquired, knowing his master's mind was made up.

'Retreat into the wood and wait for me. If I do not return by noon, you had best get yourself back to Marseille as best you can. There are still plenty of English ships in harbour: you can buy passage home with these.'

The gaunt captain tipped a handful of coins from his purse.

'And what do you propose to do with me?' the Countess simmered.

'Hobby will free you when he can, once he is safely abroad a friendly ship.'

There was little more to be said. Eldritch checked over his weapons, tightened his girth and mounted the impatiently prancing stallion.

'I will be back here by noon, or . . . or you will be returning to Marseille without me.'

Charlotte swallowed nervously, hanging on to the rogue's stirrup as if she was some lovestruck twelve-year-old, reluctant to let her new beau tear himself away. For some inexplicable reason, she dreaded the night as she had dreaded no other.

Please God, let this arrogant bastard return.

Eldritch pursed his lips, dug in his heels and urged the stallion up the bank and out of the quiet hollow.

By the Porta Pretoria, Aosta

✦

Alberto Tarsi brought his horse to a halt on the ridge a league or so from the triple-arched Roman gatehouse and studied the familiar town with a mixture of relief and revulsion. Relief because he had managed to reach his destination unopposed by the enemy, revulsion because the quiet, terracotta-tiled town was the headquarters of one of his principal enemies, Eusebius della Stroma, Count of Luningiana.

He had been imprisoned in the rogue's palace the previous winter, standing trial for the crimes Stroma's ally Gueldres had committed. Tarsi had been a soldier all his life, but he had never before felt as isolated, as shorn of friends and favour as he had before the dead eyes of the papal court.

He closed his mind against his insinuating memories, concentrated on the assignment in hand. Tarsi shielded his eyes from the blistering midday sun, squinted through the shimmering heat-haze at the ochre walls. The majority of the town had been laid down in the days of the great Augustus, the walls repaired and extended by his lesser descendants – the long-dead Dukes of Aosta and members of the powerful Challant dynasty.

But the gates were open now, the watch-towers deserted. The wheatfields which ran down the slope towards the east wall were empty, the farmhands finding shade beneath the drooping crowns of the black-boled oaks. Aosta was, for all intents and purposes, asleep.

The soldier sighed, glanced over his shoulder at the dust-smothered host which had hurried up the road from the Imperialist camp at Nus. It wasn't more than a dozen leagues distant, but the unrelenting sunshine had turned the march into a horror of choking dust and stinging sweat.

Tarsi had let them idle away the morning at their ablutions, before ordering the few captains he had left to assemble the men for an immediate descent on the nearby town. Any spy detailed to watch the camp would have relaxed, sought out the cool comfort

81

of the nearest taverna to while away an hour or two with a tart or two on his knee. But Tarsi hadn't allowed his fornicating command any rest. He had force-marched the column out of their quarters, had them eating up the high road despite the excruciating heat of the early afternoon. The men had moaned and cursed, of course, but his unexpected departure would have earned him an hour or two's surprise.

By the looks of it, the fearful pace he had set had been well worth the effort. Stroma hadn't had time to close the gates, let alone order his defences. Tarsi raised his perspective glass and studied the ribbon of road which led away north, towards the cool white pavilions of the Alps. He could see a jumble of carts, knots of men sheathed in dense blankets of white dust.

And somewhere in the midst of that miserable shit-storm, Stroma himself.

Hah! The dog hadn't dared await his coming, let alone contest the road north. He would make his stand further up the narrow valley, in the very gullet of the high pass. Why face a larger force in the open fields, when you could inflict ten times the damage from the sanctuary of a fortress – Tarsi's usurped stronghold of Mont Galliard.

The weary mercenary watched his scouts spur back over the plain, kicking up small tornadoes of brown grit. The riders appeared to have been smothered in threshing-room chaff, their earthy features and robes frosted by the all-pervading dust.

The rolling slopes of the north Italian plain were no strangers to such riders. Huns, Alans, Goths and a rogue's gallery of barbarian tribes had spurred between burning villa and corpse-choked ditch.

But these had come further than the great Eastern tribes. They were Sandy Kerr's Scots, reivers from the bloody border-land with England. Like their despised English colleagues they had been freed from their original contract with Lord Howath by the latter's ill-advised gambling. The Bastard Gueldres had taken over their contract, but it had been declared null and void when his own murderous duplicity had been exposed. The tangle-haired orphans had been facing starvation or banditry, and their chief Alexander Kerr hadn't hesitated to sign on with Tarsi's slowly expanding regiment, taking service alongside English, Italians, Germans, Czechs, Croats and rootless wanderers from all over Europe. Now the reivers scraped a living scouting for Tarsi. It was certainly preferable to a few years of torment in a Venetian galley or an eternity down some Sicilian saltmine.

The two made strange bedfellows. Hardly able to decipher one another's outlandish accents, they communicated with hand signals and frequent reference to Merron Eldritch, who was earning her keep as translator-in-chief. Eldritch's lithe, strikingly handsome sister could speak a little French, a smattering of Italian and – most important of all – she had a working knowledge of Sandy Kerr's fruity, oath-ridden Scots brogue.

Tarsi liked having her nearby. She had such a bold eye, and her thick dark tresses hung halfway down her elegantly tapered back. The old rogue peered back over his shoulder, noting the girl was as usual closely attending his own daughter Angelica.

Ah, Angelica, *figliova mia!*

His heart ached to think of the tortures she had borne, the brutally perverted foreplay which was the hallmark of the Holy Inquisition. Whereas Merron was as full of life as a skittish colt, throwing back her dark head to laugh and joke with her companions, his own flesh and blood had been watered down, wasted by her hideous ordeals on Briconet's bloody table. Before her ordeal Angelica had been very bit as effervescent as the lively-eyed Merron. Now she was sullen and withdrawn, prone to headaches and over-fond of lying on her cot in a darkened room.

He bit his lip bloody, hardly daring to imagine the tortures they had inflicted on that fragile body, how Briconet's screws, pincers and smouldering tapers had inflamed her alabaster skin. In truth, he could hardly look at her without feeling his chest swell up with unbearable pressure, a tide of bile which threatened to explode out of his clenched mouth in some infernal vomit-fit.

He patted the horse's sweating flank, waiting for the Spanish arquebusiers to trudge up the ridge, their coal-black eyes rimmed with dust and silently accusing. Each man carried his cumbersome handgun over his shoulder and a sack of powder and ball about his waist, as well as bits of loot they had picked up on their travels. They had belonged to Captain Isolani, but since his death the previous summer Isadoro Balistado had taken over command.

The rogue was wearing a garishly-cut suit of blue and green quarters, and a rich velvet cap with a tall white feather. Just the thing to cut a dash around the Capitol, or in some Viennese cathouse. Tarsi noted with some satisfaction that the overdressed paladin was as draped in dust as his charges, his jaunty feather beginning to wilt in the heat. The posturing monkey raised his chin in a contemptuous salute as he trotted along past his toiling countrymen, waving them on down the slope under Tarsi's watchful glare. Long files of pikemen followed, trailing their butts in the dust. They were big country boys mostly, German peasants and swarthy farmhands up from the south. Tarsi wondered how they would stand up to the terrifying onset of their Swiss counterparts. He had seen Swiss pikemen sprinting into battle as if the eighteen-foot poles they carried were fishing rods or children's toys. Only the brave (or very foolish) could withstand their shrieking assaults.

Next came two hundred and fifty of Eldritch's archers, grinning despite the heat, their tunics buttoned up as if they were walking barefoot across a glacier. They had unstrung their bows, carrying their precious strings under their marvellously assorted hats. In addition to his war bow, each man carried a sword and long dagger, a small buckler and a large, sausage-shaped provisions sack. The local peasantry had never seen soldiers like them and gawped and whistled as they trudged by, merry as drunkards in a cider orchard. For all their fun and games, though, Tarsi had to admit they hadn't complained about the blistering pace.

No wonder the rogues were so damned red. It looked as if Eldritch had left him a set of lobsters to fight in his place. He had also left his own, elite light horsemen behind. The famed Ride had been reduced to a dusty shadow of its former self, the couple of dozen riders who had survived escorting the guns and wagons at the rear of the column. Tarsi had followed Eldritch's advice and kept the two sets of rival horsemen well apart. If the Scots were in the van, the English horse got rearguard duty. That meant the only place the surly rivals came across each other was in camp. And Tarsi intended to march them so hard they wouldn't have any strength left for internecine feuding once they had bedded down for the night.

These were the elite troopers of Howath's Ride, mounted archers who could turn their hand to throwing a javelin or riding down a broken foe. They had learned their business up in the Borders, riding the length of the great wall the Romans had constructed across Northern Britain. It was strange to think Tarsi's Imperial ancestors might have come up against the Englishmen's across some ancient British hillfort.

Struggling teams of heavy horses dragged his unwieldy supply wagons up the hill. The formidably-built carts creaked and whistled at every turn of the enormous, six-foot wheels, their occupants hanging on to the gunwales as the drivers whipped up their teams. The wagons were covered in stained horse hide, which offered some shade from the relentless weather, but Merron as usual preferred to ride up front beside the curly-haired driver.

Angelica had raised herself from her cot and was peering out between them, a pale wraith between her rosy-cheeked companions. Merron waved, giving him a beaming smile which set Tarsi's heart thumping against his breastplate.

The truth of it was he could forgive her rogue of a brother anything, when his sister commanded smiles like that.

'I was just telling Gelli. We're nearing Aosta.'

'Aosta's not home,' the raw-eyed girl replied, giving her father a weary smile. Tarsi tore his eyes from the gloriously overheating English girl, and encouraged his daughter with a gruff nod.

'Stroma has made a run for the pass, as we anticipated.'

'He hasn't the gall to face you, my lord, not after last winter!' Merron called, straightening her green velvet gown. Tarsi rubbed his eyes. The wretched girl was driving him to distraction, tugging her bodice over her bubies as if she was plying for trade in some backstreet. He wondered if he had done the right thing bringing the girls along, but in truth he had had little alternative other than place the pair of them in a nunnery or somesuch.

And look what happened to the poor innocents at Abbey D'Eleron.

No, Tarsi preferred to have his treasures where he could keep an eye on them, battlefront or no.

The wagon driver touched his cap, nodding enthusiastically at the red-faced commander. What was his name? Ah yes. Hacker. One of Eldritch's more ambitious (not to mention talkative) troopers.

Hacker. In English, to chop up in bits.

The curly-headed rascal seemed to have relished his unofficial role as the girls' guardian, hardly straying from the immense oak wain. He had taken a particular care over Angelica, fetching her meals and offering her a drink from the bottle he kept beneath his seat. He seemed quite devoted to the pitiful creature, finding the patience to forgive her wasted legs and tired arms, her sore throats, headaches and deadly litany of aches and agues.

As he should have done.

Tarsi hardly dared look him straight in the eye, a slight the cheerful driver seemed determined to overlook.

'*Buon giorno, Padrone. Fa molto freddo!*' Hacker announced grandly, gesticulating at the parched countryside.

'Caldo. Freddo's cold, caldo's hot,' Merron corrected him quickly.

Hacker clicked his fingers.

'*Buon giorno. Come sono cortesi, gli Inglese,*' Tarsi snapped back.

The driver looked crestfallen, glaring around to Merron for help. 'What d'e say?'

'No no no. *Parli piu lentamente, per favore,*' she said clearly.

Tarsi smiled. The driver crammed his eyes shut, compressing his lips as he tried to remember the phrase.

'Speak more slowly. Yes.'

'I said, how courteous you English are,' Tarsi told him.

The Englishman sat back on the running board, grinning at his companions.

'William has been learning Italian, and helping me with my English,' Angelica said with the tiniest trace of her former gaiety. Tarsi was convinced the English girl was good for her, bringing her out of the shadows in which Briconet had imprisoned her. He hoped against hope Merron would bring his whole daughter back to him.

As she had brought the quickening pulse of love to his cold, cold heart.

'Excellent. But I don't think he is up to translating our friend Kerr, eh?'

Angelica shrugged, and Tarsi felt a pang of guilt for overruling her.

'You'll need more'n a translator to catch his drift,' Hacker snorted.

The officer in question had spurred up the rise past the Spaniards and reined in beside his chief with a flourish.

The two of them were as diametrically opposed as two members of the same race could be, the one bow-legged and lean from long hard winters on the Border, the other well used to fatty feasts beside a roaring fire, his copper-coloured flesh hanging in generous folds about his large, powerful frame. But another few rides like this one would strip away his excess weight, leave him as fighting fit as he had been a decade and more before.

It was difficult to tell which bit of Kerr's outlandish accoutrements belonged to him and which the horse. His wheezing pony had turned the same shade as its master's rust-coloured plaid. The greasy sheepskin might have been a saddle, or the lower portion of the reiver's filthy costume. All his kit, his hair, his horse's sweat-caked mane, were smothered in grit. The Scot ran his tongue over his teeth and spat on the ground before touching his gauntlet to his temple. But his quick-eyed glare turned the submissive greeting on its head.

Tarsi nodded, cocking his head to catch the scout's broad brogue.

'Yer man's tak'n himself off t'ward yon peaks. Y'ell nivver catch the bugger now.'

Tarsi had seen as much for himself.

'The wee klootie's barely time to pack a bag, half the toon's oot pickin' over his leavings.'

Tarsi turned to Merron, addressed her in quick-fire Italian.

'He wants to know if they've left traps,' she explained. Kerr looked askance at the girl, sister to that blood-curdling rogue Eldritch.

'We have na ridden in to find oot, if that's what you're gettin' at, missy.'

'No traps.'

'Ride on to the Palazzo, make as much noise as you like. We'll make camp in Stroma's gardens, look as if we're settling in for a long stay.'

Merron translated his orders for the scowling Kerr, who eyed her with unconcealed contempt. Merron ignored him.

'But we'll strike camp at midnight, take the north gate towards the pass.'

He unrolled his greasy, calfskin map of the valley, held it out towards his chief scout. 'Here, where the road narrows about the hillock. It's no more than a long bowshot from one wall to the other. That's where we'll entrench ourselves.'

Kerr leaned over his horse's mane to squint at the crudely-rendered terrain. He carried a better picture in his head. The stony gullet of Mont Galliard itself, key to the high pass. Kerr had ridden the length of the awesome gorge the winter before. He knew the ground as well as his mother's grave back in Tullymallock.

'You ride on, secure the hillock. We'll dig in where Captain Eldritch placed his wagons.'

Kerr scowled.

'Aye. Buttoned up safe as a tick in a bedroll while we rode widdershins doon the pass, and got ourselves thrown in a bastle hoose for our trouble!'

'We were no better off in the Palazzo!' Merron cried, her lean cheekbones colouring. Tarsi raised his hand, wearied by their squabbling.

He could have allowed his force some rest, safe behind the walls of Aosta. The ancient Roman fortifications were still formidable enough, at a pinch. But shutting himself into the town would have surrendered the initiative, allowed the enemy to march around the obstacle and continue on down the valley. They might have bypassed his defences, left him to the toiling infantry and heavy guns following along behind the advance guards.

By marching further up the rapidly narrowing valley he would be able to throw a cordon either side of the road, forcing the invading French to make a headlong attack.

It was a dangerous risk, exposing his men to the full fury of an assault, but he had little choice if he was to obey Von Huff's orders.

And if he didn't obey orders, Tarsi didn't get paid.

And if Tarsi didn't get paid, then neither did the men.

And if the men didn't get paid . . . they would be using his testicles as good-luck charms by the end of the week.

By the Castello Villefranco

✦

There was no way closer, let alone inside. The castello's jagged towers seemed to have grown out of the bare rock, crowning the bleak slopes and dominating the uninspiring countryside. Eldritch had hidden himself amongst a cairn of boulders a long bowshot from the fortress, utterly at a loss as to how to gain entrance. He fumed and raged, longing to stride out and challenge the rogues to come forth. The whole enterprise seemed doomed, an aimless exercise which had already cost one life and come within an ace of delivering both himself and his loyal but unimaginative sergeant into the clutches of the fiendish inquisitor Briconet.

The best scheme he had managed to come up with was to hijack an unwary traveller and adopt some unlikely disguise – but he was over six feet tall and broadly built. And only a Muslim's veil could have disguised the scornful menace of his scar-faced stare.

He paced and fretted as the sun passed overhead, acutely aware of the deadline he had agreed with Hobby. He peered at the variously-shaded battlements as if the answer to his prayers would seep out of the mossy stonework and illuminate his best course. There was just one road, a rutted track which switch-backed up the ridge slope from the nearby crossroads. The castello might have been primarily built to decorative rather than functional purpose, but the architect had chosen his ground well, taking full advantage of the barren slopes to dominate the coast road.

A sudden movement startled him from his depressing reverie. The gate had been opened just wide enough for a lone rider, who kicked his way down the path on a sagging mule. The beast's ears flickered as it was immediately enveloped in a swarm of midges. Hardly the sort of transport favoured by Holy Inquisitors, Eldritch thought hotly. No sooner had the rider crossed the threshold than the gate was clanged shut behind him as if the

89

castello had just spat out an unappetising morsel. The ejected individual was wearing a worn leather jerkin bearing some kind of crest. He carried a large canvas sack. Some itinerant shown the door, Eldritch presumed. Or a household servant off on an errand for his master. On a mule? It would be fully dark before he had reached the woods.

The Englishman paused, tugging distractedly at his unshaven chin as he wondered at the rider's identity. Judging by his shambling manner the rogue wasn't planning on going far. A few leagues down the coast road and . . .

Coast road? They had followed the ancient track up from the south, with frequent detours into the surrounding pine woods to avoid fellow travellers and Briconet's baying servants. But they had not come across a single toll gate during their short but eventful journey. The road had been worn out of the bedrock long ages before, known to myth and legend as the Route of Hercules. The Romans had dug it out and drained it, lain broad stone slabs over a bed of sand and gravel to speed their legions from Italy to the Rhône Delta. They had named the route the Via Aurelia. The Duchy of Villefranco was one of half a dozen tiny states which straddled the old route, set up long before to levy the road tolls on behalf of its overlord.

But the castello had been built up on the ridge, a good league from the crossroads – which meant in all likelihood the thoughtful owners would have provided some manner of toll house away from the main castle – and a mule to get to it, no doubt!

Eldritch crouched on all fours, watching the mysterious servant making his way down the barren terraces. Eldritch tracked him, working his way around to the far side of the rocky outcrop. He shielded his eyes against the flaring rays of the sinking sun and took another look at the dusty crossroads.

No wonder he had missed it.

The penny-pinching tax collectors had only provided for the meanest shelter, a narrow stone shrine where travellers left offerings to a Duke rather than the Virgin. The crude structure was no more than a cowpen, its rough structure worn smooth by the punishing gusts of the Mistral and so blending perfectly with its weather-ravaged surroundings.

The captain made up his wandering mind in a moment. He was achieving nothing sitting on his arse, and the direct approach to the castello was out of the question.

He would have to go in by the front door.

He waited until the gatekeeper had completed his careless circuit of the nearest terrace and slipped out over the barren slope, leaving his tethered horse stamping amidst the cairn of boulders. He threaded his way across the loose scree, taking cover in the shallow, rain-washed gullies which had been dug out of the hillside by flash floods. The streambeds took him down the slope towards a tangle of tall grass and dog-roses.

Eldritch worked his way closer, hearing voices now. The mule brayed. Somebody laughed.

Brambles and nettles flourished in what was left of a latrine pit – dug by some previous gatekeeper well downwind of his rocky roost. More recent occupiers had not been as hygiene-conscious as their predecessors, simply stepping outside to relieve themselves against the back walls of their ill-built dugout. The sudden dry stench made the Englishman gag.

The gatekeeper's lodge was surrounded by a drystone wall, long since invaded by vines and dry-leaved creepers. The Via Aurelia – or what little the passing centuries had left of it – ran straight past the gateway. A splintered pine pole had been laid across the road, a brass bell set up in a crude wooden box for honest travellers to ring for attention.

By the time he had worked his way past the stinking back wall, the rider had reached the yard and slid from the mule's back. The rogue was yawning before his shift had even begun. Eldritch could see the feeble glimmer of a lantern behind the leather-curtained doorway. He could barely decipher their mangled dialect.

The mule – well used to its role – stood patiently in the yard, waiting to carry the relieved keeper back up to the fortress with his sack of small coin.

The leather flap was yanked back, and a lean, wide-eyed Frenchman stepped out – berating his colleague for being late, as far as Eldritch could judge. The surly keeper mounted the mule and adjusted his sack. Judging from the easy way the canvas folded over his thigh, it wasn't exactly stuffed with gold.

No matter.

Two minutes later the rider had been knocked out, stripped of his outer garments and jammed in the narrowest fissure Eldritch could find. He'd wake with a blinding headache – and have hell's own job squeezing his way back out. Eldritch tugged the man's leather hat down over his brow and tried to mimic the gate-keeper's weary slouch as the mule picked its way back up the slope towards the merrily lit castello. The evil-smelling jerkin he had borrowed carried a faded emblem, crudely painted fleur-de-lys set within a large golden V. The sack had contained an assortment of unrecognisable coins and a sheet of spider-like jottings. A tally-sheet for the officious collector, Eldritch presumed.

The captain had guessed right, the changing of the gatehouse guard was as routine as the going down of the sun over the cliffs. The great door was opened without a word, the yawning spearman grunting something as the impostor bent his head, kicked the beast into the courtyard. God bless all mules, he would never have a bad word to say about the loyal creatures. The animal made straight for the stables built under the curtain wall to his right. He glanced about the deserted yard, noting Briconet's vast black and scarlet wain, the flags of the Inquisition hanging limply from their poles. A pack of his guards were taking their ease, picking over their suppers beneath the mud-caked hull. They hardly gave him a second glance as the mule made its way to its stall and resumed munching at a pailful of oats.

Eldritch dismounted and looked up and down the deserted stable. A dozen and more horses had been tethered to a rope stretched along one wall, as the stalls were already occupied by the household's own animals. Eldritch presumed they belonged to Briconet's escort. He lifted a blanket from the nearest stall and flung the stinking garment about his shoulders as he made a quick reconnaissance of the yard. A gang of servants were busy in one corner with brushes and buckets, clearing up the mess their butcher appeared to have left behind. What a damned shower, slaughtering their cattle in the public courtyard! He would have imagined several likelier locations for the shambles.

He leaned out of the gloomy alcove, peered up at the imposing mass of the main tower. The old keep was scored with black-eyed lancets. Several larger gunports had been gouged out of the stone to cover the walkways which ran the length of the curtain walls. He presumed his sister's room would be situated somewhere within the formidably-built main tower – if the damned girl had come here at all. He clutched at the splintered woodwork about the stable entrance, remembered the terrible name the wretched French had given her.

White Rabbit.

92

He cringed to think of his own sister, working as a high-class courtesan. An Eldritch wearing the badge of the yellow veil – his dead father would turn in his grave. It was not even as if she were being compelled to behave in this apparently shameless fashion. He hardly dared imagine what he might say to her, should she prove to be within.

Eldritch held his breath, summoning up all his wandering willpowers before stepping out of the stables into the gloomily-lit courtyard. He froze as he heard the sudden commotion, looked up to see a breathless clerk hurl himself down the staircase. The newcomer's momentum almost carried him over the balcony, but he managed to save himself with a despairing lunge at the iron balustrade. Eldritch stepped back into the shadows as the clerk peered around the quiet yard.

Had his clumsy ruse been discovered? Had he been lured into Briconet's trap?

Eldritch squinted around the doorpost, watching the agitated clerk hop from one foot to the other as he peered into every alcove. The lookout was small but smartly turned out, his pale saffron tunic spotted with inks. His wrists, elbows and sleeves had been carefully patched with strips of pale leather. A damned quill-pushing clerk by the look of him, anxiously awaiting the arrival of the day's tolls no doubt. Eldritch cursed and ducked back inside the fragrant stable.

The building was silent save for the quiet munching of the animals. The clerk skipped down the staircase and began to cross the courtyard. Eldritch slowly drew his long knife. Good Christ, he would be throttling half the men in France at this rate.

'Chassebon! Damn you! Where are you off to now?'

Eldritch peered between the rotten timberwork, realised the clerk was not alone. A whole flock of liveried courtiers had appeared on the main landing, followed at a dignified distance by several nonchalant noblemen. He recognised the wizened Briconet, conversing with a pale-faced youngster with a shock of uncombed hair. The youth was gaping about the yard as if he had been led up from the deepest dungeon, nodding his head in miserable agreement with whatever the inquisitor was telling him.

Duke Gerhard, Eldritch presumed. How did the French nobility managed to survive their many and various crises, if all they could breed were lantern-jawed sprats like this?

The clerk paused halfway across the yard, called to heel by his

93

frowning master. The courtier in the long grey gown hurried ahead of his Duke to pinch the nervous clerk by the ear. He hauled him closer to the stable, out of earshot of his distracted master.

'Where are you going in such a hurry?'

'Please sir. Didier's gone missing. I saw him ride up the hill, but he's not reported in!'

'Dolt! What does collecting a few pennies matter now? Do you imagine the Duke will find time to concern himself with a day's tolls?'

'No, master.'

'Very well then. Are the goods loaded?'

'As you bade us.'

'Very well. Get yourself back to my chambers, and be ready with your quills. We've work enough this night. Off with you.'

The clerk scampered back towards the main tower. The guards who had been lounging about Briconet's wagon had jumped to attention as the inquisitor made his way towards them. Briconet snapped instructions and three of the troopers doubled towards the stables.

Eldritch looked right and left, but the stable had been built into the formidable curtain wall. Not even a mouse could have escaped. The second floor had been turned into a hayloft, but some damned rogue had removed the ladder. He backed into the shadows as the soldiers trotted in to close the trap, hiding his knife beneath the dirty blanket. The intruders' eyes adjusted to the half-light. They soon spied him skulking in the corner.

'Here's one of 'em! Oy, Cabbage-Bollocks, get these horses out in the yard or you'll feel my boot up your arse!'

Eldritch bowed his head as the troopers shouldered past, lifting saddles and tack from the straw bales at the end of the crowded block. He clutched the blanket tighter, unhitched the first of their horses from the hanging rope.

'Hurry up yer lanky bleeder. Typical ain't it? I thought we were in for a rest tonight!'

'Not when he'd got his fingers on Gerhard's loot! He'll have her banging away again before you dip yer wick, Henri!'

Eldritch grimaced, his long fingers tensing about the hilt of his dagger. He wished himself invisible as he led the first two horses out into the twilight, under the nose of his sworn enemy Briconet.

Belatavicci hardly noticed him, busy straightening his voluminous sleeves as his master and his distinguished guest arrived beside the stable. The unctuous courtier inclined his head as Briconet and the Duke watched the troopers prepare the wagons for an immediate departure.

'There now Belatavicci. Is our fiendish engine stowed safe?' the inquisitor enquired. Eldritch handed the skittish beasts over to Briconet's guards, who began to tack and saddle them for their night-time journey. He backed into the alcove, lolling his head as if he were simple-minded, the filthy robe hanging about his slumped shoulders. Eldritch cursed their lilting French, desperate to overhear everything which passed between them while sidling into the shadows behind them.

Fiendish engine?

'Even as you ordered, my lord.'

'Your hell-spawned spitfire will be safe enough with us, I assure you,' Briconet leered. 'We'll see what my colleagues in Marseille can make of your mistress, eh?'

The young nobleman was clearly overawed by the inquisitor's menacing bonhomie. He pulled at his nose.

'You are concerned you have sold her too cheaply? In truth, I have been told I drive a hard bargain,' Briconet chuckled. 'But consider this, my dear Duke. You have been of service to His Majesty. Who knows how many men your organ-grinder – or whatever it is you call her – can take on?'

Eldritch drew in his breath, willing his features to stone.

'Of course I am honoured to be of service to His Majesty King Francis. But the . . .' Briconet raised his hand as if pained.

'I shall ensure His Majesty hears of your generous cooperation. Rest assured you and your household will be further rewarded for this most immaculate of conceptions!'

What had the rogues done to her?

'It is not that I do not trust the word of the Holy Inquisitor . . .'

'Perish the thought my dear Duke. Ah, my carriage awaits!'

Eldritch could barely move, transfixed by their beguiling conversation. He ducked beneath the staircase as the rest of Briconet's guards hurried out with their horses. The wagons were dragged about, the steaming teams walked backwards between the traces. Drivers yawned. Bridles rattled.

Gerhard watched dumbly as Briconet clambered up the steps into his enormous black wain.

'Hold your Duchy in the name of your liege lord, Francis I!' Briconet encouraged, making himself comfortable. 'You will be hearing from us very soon, very soon!' He dropped the leather curtain, and the driver clicked his whip over the straining horses.

The enormous, iron-bound wheels grated over the stone pavings as the vast galleon rolled about. Eldritch gritted his teeth, watched the cursed wagon trundle over the yard towards the opened gate. He slipped behind the mesmerised Duke, close enough to slide his blade under the fiend's ribs – send him to hell with his filthy ancestors.

And sentence himself to an immediate and painful death at the hands of his enraged command, the captain thought.

'The wretch! The evil-eyed shit-sifter!'

'A most unbecoming personage, indeed, my lord Duke,' Belatavicci sympathised.

'He was making fun of me all the while, daring me to refuse him!'

'There was in truth little anybody could have done to prevent him.'

'All our work. All my dreams! Fetch Montalban back out of that dungeon you locked him in. There's nothing for us here now!' The courtier paused, stung by the Duke's evident distress.

'But I am sure . . .'

'Do you imagine for a moment Briconet will leave us alone now? He'll be back, sniffing around! We have no choice!' The Duke took the steps three at a time and disappeared into the brooding keep. Belatavicci thought for a moment, and then hurried after him.

The slime-breathing serpents! Selling his sister to the inquisitor as if she were a fresh pullet or a sackful of salt! Eldritch had a good mind to slaughter the entire garrison, emasculate the whole pack! He ground his teeth, determined to overcome the raging tempers which had misled him so many times in the past. Lillith had been bundled inside the wagon, carried off with that imp of hell Briconet.

Think!

He would have to get back to Hobby, organise some sort of ambush before the Papal Legate reached the safety of the city.

Eldritch stroke back to the stable, found the mule had finished its well-deserved supper. He unhitched the docile beast and led it back into the courtyard, glancing about after Gerhard's dozy guards. Thankfully, the jobberknols didn't seem more than half awake. He pulled himself up onto the animal's comfortable broad back and aimed the mule towards the gate, slumping over the saddle as if he too were on the verge of a deep and untroubled sleep. The spearman beside the main door looked up, his idle, peasant's face flaming red from the brazier he had lit to warm his lonely alcove.

'Off again mate?'

'I forgot my tolls,' Eldritch replied in his accented French. The spearman chuckled, shaking his head at the gate-keeper's stupidity. He clicked his heels, urging the mule through the open gate.

But the mule – as well aware of its terms and conditions as any *landsknecht* – steadfastly refused to budge.

'She'll not be happy, breaking her routine,' the cheerful guard commented. Eldritch dug his spurs into the unfeeling beast, cursing the carrion-creature to the uttermost pit of hell. The gate gaped before him. All he had to do was jump off and run.

'She's as stubborn as my damned wife.'

'I didn't know you had a wife.' The spearman was staring at him now, trying to recognise his unfamiliar features in the gathering gloom. Eldritch turned his head, just as the guard's mouth stretched to bawl a warning. He kicked the man backwards. The guard gurgled, staggering back into his alcove. The brazier toppled over. There was a shout from the battlements.

Eldritch jumped down from the mule and sprinted out of the open gate. Briconet's caravan had already reached the lower slopes, heading for the crossroads. More shouts. Eldritch turned to his left and jumped down into the stony ditch which ran around the southern flank of the fortress.

He doubled down the dry bed, hugging the walls for protection against haphazardly-aimed missiles. He could barely see his hand in front of his face now. Eldritch paused, trying to get his bearings. He thanked God he had not wasted his long vigil hidden in the boulders earlier that afternoon. He had a rough idea of the layout of the dark slope, and knew the fastest route back to his waiting horse. The captain gathered his strength, hauled himself up the crumbling bank and dashed for the boulder outcrop, praying to God the animal had remained where he had left it.

There was a shout of triumph from the wall, excited orders were bellowed down to the gate. Eldritch peered over his shoulder and saw a pack of spearmen lope out onto the road. He crossed over a hundred paces ahead of the angry pursuit, making for the stone cairn.

'There he goes!'

'He's on foot! Don't bother with the horses, he won't get that far!'

'Never mind horses, bring torches! He damn near killed Corporal Hulin!'

'Get the bastard!'

Eldritch raced over the tumbled slope, the cursing French hurrying to cut him off.

By Mont Gilbert le Galliard, in the Upper Aosta Valley

◆

The night chills seeped out of the mountain, turning the rocks blue and then black before sealing the high pass in darkness. The officers watching from the windswept eyrie high on the main tower seemed relieved, encouraged by the irresistible black tide which had swallowed the trees, boulders and glimmering snow in turn. The feeble lights thrown out by the fortress barely lit the gallery, let alone the slim bridge which linked Mont Galliard to the breast of the mountain. They could not see the blockhouse which guarded the far side of the delicate span, nor the white-tipped peaks which dwarfed their works as if they were so many children's toys left scattered the length of the valley.

The watchers left cold plumes in the air as the cloudless night ate up the long hours of residual heat in a moment or two. Gradually, their eyes became accustomed to the starlit glimmer, enabling them to pick out the ghostly masks of the mountains. Snowy ridges cut the night sky, clean, blue-white blades taut as bowstrings stretched between the crowning crags. Stroma raised the fur-lined hem of his cloak over his chin as the rime chilled his throat.

'My Lord of Luningiana is invigorated by our mountain air,' Francesco Savvi remarked, his long red moustaches drooping about his mouth. His locotenent Constantin Muhlberg sniggered, raising his hand to wipe his running nose.

Stroma glanced around at the unlikely custodians of the Alpine castle, knowing the rogues wouldn't hesitate to tip him over the walls if there was a bent shilling in it. He had been forced into some scrapes in his time, but selling out to scum like these two made his blood run colder than the torrents roaring in the abyss below. Tarsi's unexpected descent had forced him to run for cover, fleeing Aosta to find shelter with the few so-called friends he had left.

Of course he knew who to blame for his present predicament. Alberto Tarsi was a conniving rogue, a bloody brigand and dirty-minded savage. But he was only doing what came naturally, chasing his opponent from a weak position into an infinitely stronger one. No, although he loathed Tarsi with all his shrivelled heart, the real culprit was his long-term ally the Vicomte D'Toinueill, the bastard son of the Duc de Gueldres.

Stroma had supported him through one daft escapade after another, ruining his own fortune as he aided and abetted Gueldres' fanciful plotting. But Gueldres had gone too far the previous winter – running amok in an abbey, kidnapping a choir and trying to blame his deranged excesses on his old rival Tarsi.

Gueldres had been exposed for the fiend he was, and only a miraculous escape had saved him from a grisly and painfully extended execution. The Vicomte might have escaped with his life, but his few friends had turned their back on him once and for all. The fugitive had been excommunicated by an enraged Vatican and an enormous reward had been offered for his head. Half the manhunters in Europe would be on his trail by now.

The Vicomte had been forced into penniless exile, cast out of all Western Society for his dreadful crimes against church and state. The last Stroma had heard Gueldres had offered his sword to the Turks, and was reported to be busy fighting on their behalf against the resurgent Venetians.

Stroma had suffered torments, losing money and influence as punishment for his long and foolhardy attachment to the Vicomte's cause. The few friends he could claim in Milan and Rome had spurned him for his reckless alliances. His long-running legal dispute with Tarsi over the rights to collect the Aostan valley road tolls had ended in predictable defeat. To add insult to injury the Papal Court which had ruled against him had ordered the Count to find the astronomical costs of the case!

He was a penniless outcast now – he might as well have been exiled with Gueldres. His increasing isolation in northern Italy had left him little choice but to look for new allies over the Alps.

But in truth he did not relish the treachery.

'It gets cold early, this high in the mountains,' he said ruefully, acutely aware of his predicament.

'Cold feet, eh Stroma?' Muhlberg enquired, grinning at his slyly smiling chief. Savvi was a slippery customer, a veteran *Landsknecht* captain who had also tired of dancing to Gueldres' tune. But whereas Stroma had clung on to his ally until the bitter end, Savvi had got out while the going was good, abandoning the Vicomte's cause at the first opportunity.

Tarsi and Gueldres had been so intent on destroying one another they had not seen the black shadow slipping over the mountains in their rear. The sardonic warrior had taken over the fortress they had invested so much blood and money fighting over, walking into the disputed stronghold without firing a shot.

His men hadn't minded the abrupt change of allegiance. One master was as good as another to the scar-faced musketeers and slow-witted pikemen who made up Savvi's black band. So long as they got paid they were happy. They were mercenaries, impure and simple.

'I have learned to avoid counting on the loyalty of hirelings,' Stroma breathed. 'If Tarsi had caught my troops in the open he would have cut them to pieces.'

Muhlberg raised his chin, his peasant eyes twinkling with malice.

'Get yourself some Germans, Count. That rabble of yours, I'm not surprised they wouldn't stand.'

'Are you offering to lead the charge yourself, Muhlberg? I am sure the French will be delighted to see such a legendary commander at the head of their vanguard!'

The tall mercenary's smiled slipped.

'He's just having an innocent jest at your expense, my dear Count,' Savvi said. 'He means nothing by it.'

'Indeed.'

Muhlberg frowned, his boorish features crumpled in contempt. 'Tarsi got the drop on you, chased you out of Aosta!'

'My agents had no opportunity to warn me of his coming.'

'I'd have cut their bastard throats,' Muhlberg snarled.

'I did,' Stroma snapped back.

Savvi grinned. 'Tarsi's quick on his feet, always has been. But moving them a dozen leagues up the valley's not going to do him a lot of good. He's got no more than five or six hundred to hold the place; the French will go round, leave him to rot on the vine.'

'I'm not so sure he will,' Stroma retorted, peering into the dark pass as if he could divine his rival's intentions from the sudden gusts which ruffled their cloaks.

'What, you mean he'll leg it back to Nus and wait for 'em?'

'No. The only way he'll block the gorge is by moving up, towards us.'

'Up?' Muhlberg crowed. 'What, into the open? Down yonder?'

'It's what I'd do in his place. Six hundred men could make a fair showing, dug in across the neck of the valley.'

Savvi sucked his teeth in quiet contemplation as Muhlberg scoffed at Stroma's fanciful strategies.

'That boggard-crew he's hired himself won't stand an hour. English and Scots, a few Spanish and Italians?'

'They did well enough the last time they were here. I hear those Englishmen of his stormed the blockhouse inside an hour,' Stroma replied.

'Pure luck. They got the magazine, blew 'em all sky high before they could make a proper fight of it,' Muhlberg countered.

'A great pity then Seigneur Savvi did not employ the same tactic when he tried to take Mont Galliard last summer!'

Savvi drew a deep breath, his easy smile fading. 'Like he says, a lucky shot. They might have taken the blockhouse, but it didn't do 'em much good, did it?'

'No. Perhaps because the Chevalier Bayard himself arrived, charging them in the rear while they were in the middle of an assault. It is a miracle they managed to hold him off.'

'Only by trickery! And in any case, if you're that taken with the bloody swine, why didn't you go to the trouble of hiring them yourself?' Muhlberg grunted.

'My dear sir, I was merely pointing out the tactical ramifications of our present situation,' Stroma said with feigned innocence. 'It is always good policy to make a full study of your enemy, know his strengths as well as his weaknesses.'

'Indeed. And what of our friends the French? Do you imagine Tarsi will hold the pass? Bayard won't be fooled by a bunch of tricksy English a second time.'

'Who cares whether they hold or not?' Muhlberg growled. 'We've been paid to hold the pass open for them; we've done as much as we need worry about.'

Stroma and Savvi glanced at the truculent soldier.

'It is true we have not been contracted to clear the valley, merely to hold it in Francis' name . . .' Muhlberg nodded at Stroma's laconic assessment. 'However.'

'However,' Savvi echoed.

'We have neither of us been paid in full. We have held our end of the valley – by God, it's not difficult if you're in charge of Mont Galliard. But if Tarsi can bottle the French up here, I cannot imagine they will be happy fulfilling their bargain.'

'What d'you mean? They'll try and trick us out of our fair share?'

'Briconet gave his word,' Savvi snarled, acutely aware of his own *naïveté*. The Papal Legate's word wasn't worth a cup of cold sheep piss.

'Briconet has lots of words. What I mean is this: he has given us a downpayment only. He owes us fifteen thousand livres.'

All Savvi's carefully relaxed mannerisms fell away like spring blossoms after a sharp frost.

'I'd make sure he never filled another contract. A man who can't keep his word in our game is finished, and his damned king with him,' he snarled. Stroma nodded ruefully.

'I am merely playing Devil's advocate, my friends. It is always good policy . . .'

'. . . to bear every option in mind,' Savvi interrupted, irritated by the Count's imaginings.

'Or one's opponents,' Stroma agreed.

'Or one's bastard allies,' Muhlberg concluded.

The three of them lapsed into silence, pondering one another's motives and objectives as the cold night wore on.

For the moment, they were fast friends, allies.

But neither of them trusted the other as far as they could have flung Mont Galliard itself.

Savvi looked up sharply, cocked his red head to the wind as he caught some half-sound in the night.

'What was that?' he asked.

Alexander Kerr, Laird of Tullymallock, was a long way from his home in the High Glens. He might have been the last man on earth, standing beside his snorting horse in the middle of the deadly-dark pass.

His acute senses were alert for every sigh of wind, every snapping fissure beneath his deer-hide shoes. The light boots were as supple as a maiden's skin, and he might have walked across up-turned eggshells without making a sound. Handy gear for dangerous missions such as this, scouting the terrain ahead of the coughing, farting, scratching, jangling, cloth-eared vanguard.

He had taken his best men with him: Duncan of Lochaber, Young Davey, and his own son Angus, who could sense the bats stretching their wings in the vast caverns which undermined the invisible cliff face. Sandy could recall the ground as if he had walked the pass that afternoon and not the previous winter. He remembered the sudden twists and turns, the outcrops, the scree slopes which could send a man tumbling a hundred feet to his death, and alert enemies the other side of the Alps.

He gave a soft whistle. None of them would have seen him raise a hand, not in this darkness. The small patrol froze as their chief gazed at the rearing rock wall.

Slowly, he became aware of the individual peaks, black needlepoints against the deep, deep blue of the night sky. The breeze had turned, deflected by a massive spur of rock to his right. The outflung arm of the mountain was directly opposite Mont Galliard. He waited as his vision adjusted to the subtle changes in light.

The castle's new masters had stripped lanterns and lamps from the once brightly-lit approaches, plunging the causeway into darkness. Kerr snorted softly, wondering how the drastically limited illumination aided the defenders. Perhaps they saw better in the pitch-dark, sitting in their worm-holes watching for intruders, for the furtive messengers who tried to work their way through the gullet of the mountains, avoiding and evading contact with the masters of Mont Galliard.

The Scotsman knew the brittle paperchase would begin in earnest, now the armies were on the march at last. They were rousing themselves like slumbering beasts, each convinced they knew the mind of the other.

And Sandy Kerr's boys were caught up in the middle of it, obliged to fight for foreigners as they would have done for their clans and houses back home. But the war which loomed higher than the mountains, hemming them into a slowly-closing net of fire and sword, was far deadlier than any of the scrapes they might have galloped in and out of back on the Border.

This war between empires would be a clash of Titans in which close-knit squads of men like his would be dwarfed as ants were by rutting stags. A dozen nationalities, a dozen causes, motives, reasons and promises caught up in a firestorm which would engulf half of Europe.

'What is it Sandy?'

'Have ye seen something, father?'

Kerr blinked, squeezed his scarred nose between his thumb and forefinger.

Aye. He'd seen something. The end of the world, if he had reckoned it right.

And his little troop of ants had just walked into the front line.

Tarsi's grumbling, stumbling, cursing legion arrived at the appointed rendezvous in the small hours of the morning, having completed another forced march up the valley from their very temporary quarters in Aosta.

The honest burghers of the old Roman town had been dreading their arrival, emptying their wares from the shops crowded along the Via Anselmo, hiding the silver and plate from the great Gothic cathedral and eating up the last of their eggs and smoked hams before the rotten foreigners made off with it all. Tarsi's dust-caked soldiers had gasped past the alehouses, hurried along by furious captains and shrieking corporals. They had traipsed the length of the town, collapsing in the main square beside the dried-up bed of the river Buthier.

Their throats had been just as dry as the stony streambed, chafed by the stinging grit kicked up by the troops in front. By nightfall, they were so far gone the suspicious townsfolk might have stolen out and murdered them all without fear of resistance, cut their throats and stolen their arms without waking them from their catatonic slumbers. The guns and baggage arrived an hour or two after the last shuffling pikeman, the frantic wagonmasters whipping their drooping teams through the quietly expectant streets. Nerves were stretched as taut as bowstrings by the maddening creak of hundreds of ill-oiled axles.

But it hadn't been Aostan fishmongers with glinting knives who had disturbed the legion's dreamless sleep. Alberto Tarsi had stalked through the living graveyard, kicking the men to their feet as if they had slept a month already.

'On your feet! Fall in, we're moving out!'

The residents, shuttered in safe behind their barricaded doors, imagined it was some trick, a devious attempt to lure them out into the open with their carefully-hoarded valuables. They stayed put, armed to the teeth with hoe and hammer, knife and fork, as their uninvited guests clambered to their feet and dressed their ranks, bewildered by the shouts and flaring torches, exhausted by the debilitating lack of sleep.

They had shuffled the last few leagues like condemned men on the way to galley or gallows, too tired to curse their deranged officers. League after league in pitch darkness, guided only by the uncertain step of the man in front, and those snarling, stinking ape-men from Scotland, the blue-faced barbarians on their terrible, fur-ball ponies.

God only knew where they were leading them. Across the Alps, the Russian Steppes, for all they knew. They were convinced they had been marching for days, even weeks.

Just when the strongest, most determined warrior felt he could go no further, Tarsi ordered a halt. The men collapsed to their knees, crying dry tears of relief. Sergeants hurried back down the columns, dragging men upright, kicking stragglers back into line. The first feeble glints of dawn had stained the sky, but they hardly noticed through half-closed, sleep-caked lids.

'Engineers to the front!'

'Where's the wagons? Get those shovels handed out!'

'We're digging in!'

'Digging in? Digging in? Tell me I'm dreaming!'

'He doesn't mean us, not the bleeding archers.'

'Archers don't bloody dig – how are we supposed to shoot if we're covered in fucking blisters?'

Tarsi turned his horse through the comatose rabble, raising his voice for the first time that long march.

'Everybody lends a hand! I want a six-foot ditch from one side of the valley to the other. A five-foot parapet and solid firesteps that won't crumble the moment a mouse treads on 'em!' he bawled. 'I want emplacements for six cannon, and support trenches dug on each flank! I want swinefeathers out front, cantalopes, mantraps the lot! Captains, you have your orders!'

The reeling pikemen, drunk with dust, blinked in bewilderment. Arquebusiers leaned on their weapons, barely able to understand the furious orders.

Dig in?

Tarsi's diabolical commands were relayed in four languages to the uncomprehending soldiers.

'You heard the man. Fall out, get digging. We're a dozen leagues from ten thousand Frenchmen. What d'you want to do, face 'em in the open?'

'Dig in, in this?' An English archer stamped his foot on the dusty road surface. There wasn't enough soil to fill a food bag. They were being ordered to dig through hundreds of feet of solid bloody rock!

'Don't start your moaning, Teague, lend a hand.'

'Lend a hand?'

'He wants us dug in by dawn, so get your back into it!'

For all his red-faced encouragement, Tarsi knew the ditch he required would never have been completed without the help of Wilfrid Stitchwort. The men were too tired, the valley bedrock too formidable, for anything more than a series of haphazardly-dug scrapes. The French Gendarmes would have tumbled from their horses with laughter to find his command laid out in their own graves, and would not have hesitated to charge right over the top of his cowering drudges. But Tarsi had thought through his dangerous strategy, taken every precaution to ensure his gamble paid off.

Stitchwort was a fireworker, a genius with the black powder. His many experimentations had already cost him several fingers, most of his nose and all of his hair and eyebrows. His flesh was burnt and pitted, scaled by searing explosions of his own making. But his concoctions had also reduced town walls to lumps of fuming pummice, turned formidable gatehouses into leaning ruins. Tarsi had ordered the leathery-faced Englishman to design and assemble rock-breaking bombs, powerful charges which might crack the stones and split the bedrock he knew lay scant inches below the dusty soil.

The grenades had worked exactly as Stitchwort had predicted they would. The men had found out the softer seams and sudden fissures in the bedrock, dug them out to receive the specially-shaped clay pots the fireworker had selected.

It had been almost dawn before the last charge had been thrust into place and the fusecords stretched out behind. No use worrying about being observed now, Tarsi thought, watching the eccentric Englishman fiddle with a handful of waxy fuses.

'What's the matter now?' the Italian had demanded, beside himself with worry Stroma and his gang might risk a sudden charge down the valley.

'I wondered, Seigneur, if you had a light on you?'

The new day dawned slowly, lifting the grey veils from the pass one by one. The officers crowded along Mont Galliard's galleries stared in wonder as the enemy formation was revealed. A loose phalanx a league and a half from their own gate, knots of dusty soldiers standing forlorn beneath limp banners, half-heartedly blocking the narrowing pass.

Muhlberg was hooting with laughter. Savvi was grinning from ear to ear.

Stroma wasn't even smiling.

107

He suspected a trap, some fiendish strategy. Alberto Tarsi might be a thrice damned villain and a bloody minded peasant to boot, but he was no fool when it came to soldiering. He had leapfrogged his legion from Nus to Aosta and now to Mont Galliard – an incredible achievement in itself. But now he seemed to have lost control, riding his horse through the wary ranks as if he were trying to encourage them to charge.

'They'll never budge!' Muhlberg crowed.

'Not in this direction at any rate,' Savvi agreed, running his perspective glass along the rag-tag army.

'It looks as if . . . he's trying to persuade them to dig in,' he said, running the glass this way and that, completely bewildered by Tarsi's suicidal display. 'Muhlie, get the lads kitted up right away. One good charge and we'll drive this pack of shite-hawks right back where they came from.'

'I would suggest we remain where we are, Seigneur Savvi,' Stroma said quietly. 'Tarsi knows this ground, by God, Margaret of Savoy handed it him on a plate! Only a fool would display his men so, and I tell you Tarsi is no fool!'

'Maybe not,' Savvi objected. 'But his men are worthless, rice-munching rabbits! He's marched them up here and they've had enough.'

'That's right! The moment they saw how close he'd brought them they mutinied, look!' Muhlberg seconded.

'Gentlemen, I really think . . .'

The sudden mountain-toppling explosion tore through the bones of the valley, rattling the age-old Alpine fastness like tin cups on a mantelpiece. The breathtaking blast rebounded through their feet, ricocheting from one rearing cliffwall to the other until the defenders were forced to clamp their hands over their ears. An enormous wall of yellow dust flooded toward them, a sandpaper tidal wave which hit each man like a rolled-up blanket. The officers reeled back from the terrible concussion, struck dumb by the terrific, punishing force Tarsi's damned warlocks had released.

By the time the dust had settled, Tarsi's rag-tag army had disappeared – into their fully serviceable trenches.

'Damn his eyes. I'll fill his fucking holes with their bones,' Muhlberg swore, wiping grit from his eyes.

Stroma chuckled, disguising his amusement behind a cough. 'I warned you sirs. Tarsi is not a man to be trifled with. He must have shifted several tons of living rock, using that much powder.'

Muhlberg's grim features were draped in stonedust. 'Well he won't have any left to bang off at us then, will he?'

Savvi had turned his glass to the north, watching the billowing dustcloud settle about the grey outcrops which pocked the ever-narrowing gorge. He could have sworn he had caught the flash of steel amidst the sickening yellow storm. He paused, still as a statue. There was another flash, and another. And then a fistful of pale banners, the silver devices glimmering like angels' wings over the dustcloud host.

'Gentlemen, I think the French might beat us to it.'

Savvi was right: the Chevalier Bayard had arrived at last – fresh from his heroic stand at Mezieres.

By Roquevaire, near Marseille

✦

Truly, God moved in mysterious ways.

Briconet had travelled to the backwater duchy to investigate the murder of a debauched aristocrat. But the trail had led him instead to a war-winning engine of destruction – a human threshing machine which might well tip the delicately-poised balance of power in France's favour.

Briconet sighed heavily and lowered the curtain flap, wearied by the banal coastal scenery. Night was drawing in, the blood-shot splashes of sunlight on the horizon enveloped by steadily advancing clouds. The wagon was moving at speed, turning what little he could see into a grey-green blur. He caught glimpses of sheer cliffs and misty trees – threadbare pinewoods which advanced and then receded from the ancient coastal highway.

The immense, iron-bound wheels were not fitted with springs, and the bemused occupants were being thrown against the upholstery as they careered over every stone and hared into every pothole. Lanterns fixed to the front of the wagon barely lit the strewn track. The driver must have been finding his way by the stars, judging by the nerve-shattering bumps and bangs which rocked the carriage as if it were a frail fishing boat caught in a tempest.

The inquisitor held the door-frame to steady himself against the unsettling passage, wedging himself into the seat beside a chest of his most pressing correspondence. But the Papal Legate hadn't touched the dispatch box, whiling away the journey back to Marseille in quiet contemplation of his astounding coup. He had, by the merest slip of fortune, discovered a potentially decisive weapon being constructed in secret by an ambitious simpleton – the tinpot ruler of what was little more than a border outpost. What was more, young Gerhard had parted with his prize for a derisory sum, having had little choice but to accept Briconet's first offer – a paltry five thousand livres.

Briconet chuckled at his own audacity.

The inquisitor had analysed every word of Gerhard's exasperated explanations, his feeble attempts to pass off the wondrous new war machine as a friend's foolish fancy.

Friends? Gerhard didn't have any! Why, the boy's own uncle had turned up with bloody murder on his mind. The silly boy had certainly been caught with his breeches down. All that nonsense about some eccentric acquaintance of his youth, a brilliant but sadly unstable engineer who had left Gerhard in charge of his precious designs while he 'travelled abroad'.

He couldn't recall where.

And no, he hadn't recalled the fellow's name.

Briconet shook his head at the boy's pitiful attempts to deflect him. Nobody in their right mind would have left Gerhard in charge of their toenail clippings, let alone such a potentially lethal military breakthrough. And as for promising he had been on his way to present the aforementioned designs to the French king . . . well, everybody knew Villefranco had always leaned towards the Empire for protection rather than its western neighbour.

Briconet's unscheduled visit had indeed been little short of divine intervention – Gerhard had been at his mercy. The inquisitor winced inwardly. Perhaps he should have pressed his suit while he had the chance – ensured he had left no stones unturned.

'How far have we come?' he demanded, rousing himself from his reverie for a moment. His clerk Maître Sourris held on to the panelling and peered out of the window, squinting through the feeble light cast by the swinging lantern. He could just make out a cluster of yellow pinpoints on the darkening horizon to the west, the noisome wharfs and rumbustious taverns of Marseille.

'I would say we are over halfway home, my lord.'

'Stop the coach.'

Sourris frowned but relayed the perplexing order to the driver without question. The massive carriage slowed. Sourris felt his empty stomach turn over in wretched sympathy.

'Are we going back, my lord?' he asked, disguising a belch behind his fat fist.

Briconet shook his head, his pitiless features illuminated by the ghastly lantern glow.

'Of course not. It is imperative we get the device to the Royal workshops forthwith. But I am reluctant to let that snivelling worm Gerhard out of my sight. Who knows whether the loathsome little toad has sold the same design to the Empire, or intends to better his bargain the moment we are out of sight?'

'He seemed adamant he had not,' Sourris countered, experienced enough at sifting nuggets of truth from the most elaborate lies. As far as he could tell the boy had been caught completely unawares, his precious prize torn from his grasp before he had quite reckoned its worth.

'Maybe. But he cannot be allowed to change his mind. You and Captain Druchet will return with one quarter of the guards. The Duke must be watched closely, placed under immediate house arrest if necessary. I want the Castello Villefranco sealed off tonight.'

Sourris' busy eyes widened in surprise. Arrest Duke Gerhard? Not even the invincible Briconet had dared to seize a noble of the blood beside his own hearth – plucking him from the bosom of his little empire. The sight of a hundred or more fully armoured Gendarmes might persuade his feckless garrison to give him up quickly enough, but even rat-scuts like them could be expected to bar the door in the face of a mere papal clerk.

'Your pardon, my lord, but would half a dozen men be sufficient to secure the Duke's arrest?'

Briconet's eyes narrowed. 'If we had been more numerous I might have risked securing the castle before we left,' Briconet admitted distractedly. 'It comes to me I may have been over eager to get away with our prize. The five thousand livres I left him might have been money well spent, but it was money destined for those rogues at Mont Galliard.'

Sourris' fleshy features crumpled in dismay at the prospect of such a thankless mission.

'There is no other course. The first priority was to secure the engine, get the components back to safety. Rest assured I will send ample reinforcements to you, the moment we arrive back at headquarters.'

Sourris swallowed. He knew it was no use refusing the mission now. How on earth would he and Druchet impose the master's will on a garrison of troops shut up tight behind six feet of solid wall?

He'd best think of something damned quick.

Night had not saved him, but his long-winded horse had. Eldritch had evaded the pursuit with contemptuous ease, loping across the boulder-strewn slope towards the cairn. He went carefully, anxious to avoid turning his ankle before he reached the quiet sanctuary of the rocks. He ran like an athlete warming up for his race, as if he were intent on stretching his legs after the tedious confinement in the castle. His insolent, lazy gait provoked the pursuing soldiers into furious sprints. One tripped, dropped his spear and skidded down the slope on his chest until a mossy outcrop stopped him dead. They would have stretched his legs for him, and a sight else besides, if his horse had somehow managed to slip its tether and wandered off into the darkness . . .

But the night-black beast had remained where he had left it, snorting and stamping within a closely-cropped ring of grass and lichens. The Villefrancans had gaped in disbelief, closing in on the crown of boulders expecting to corner their deadly quarry, only to see him gallop out the far side on a furiously fit charger.

They had fired a few arrows after the fugitive, hurled the odd spear in defiance, but the Englishman had been swallowed up by the night, drawn up in its protective cloak like some witch's familiar. The cursing soldiers had turned back towards the alerted castle and stamped back up the steep rabbit tracks towards the merrily twinkling lanterns.

And the withering scorn of their sergeant.

Charlotte's anxiety over her lover's extended absence had, through the course of that vile afternoon, turned to raw terror, faded to simmering resentment and finally flared into a righteous fury. Who did this upstart of an Englishman think he was? Toying with her affections as if she were some lapdog to be stroked or discarded on a whim? She might not be rich, her home might have been in hock to the rafters, but by God she deserved better than this!

She glared at Jeremiah Hobby, squatting like some horrid troll beneath the outflung arms of an oak tree. The morose soldier chewed nuts, sucked noisily at his water bottle and raised his leg to release reekingly ripe farts which rebounded about the entire wood. His filthy clothing must have been alive with lice, judging from the time and intense effort he spent scratching, itching and examining. His French was non-existent and his heavily accented English little better. He seemed indifferent to her glimpsed limbs and good looks, responding to her plaintive enquiries with scornful grunts or complete indifference.

She had, in her extremity, even tried to flirt with the rogue, in the hope Eldritch might return to find his loyal champion tupping his carelessly abandoned plunder and box his ears for him. But the gruff sergeant had seemed incapable of differentiating between smouldering suggestion and seething anger. God knew, she had little enough at home to divert her, but was this devilish discomfort any better?

Charlotte had prayed for a knight in shining armour to rescue her from her impecunious existence. To release her from the humiliating straits her fast-evaporating family fortune had reduced her to. Her jewels were nothing but paste – pale imitations of those worn by her so-called friends and her platoon of lacklustre lovers. Her apartments in the fashionable streets of Paris had long since been sold, her country estates shrinking year by year as her debts mounted.

Charlotte had tried to blot out the appalling calamities with wine and song, to fornicate her way into the affections of her rich acquaintances. Surely one of those fat princes, impotent barons or bum-fucking dukes would come to her rescue? Pay her debts and buy her proper jewels, replace her coach horses, rebuild her fine home beside the river?

Ah, she'd seem them come right enough – and go.

She dreaded what would happen to her, if they ever discovered the truth. They would shun her like a leper, once her secret was out. Marie-Charlotte Armonde, Countess du Lac, a penniless whore begging from her friends, adrift on a sea of incalculable debt.

Eldritch, of course, was unaware of her precarious identity. He thought he had stolen a crown jewel, a priceless diamond he could humour and haggle over. She might be virtually destitute, but Charlotte was a sound enough judge of character to recognise her lover's shortcomings just as well as her own.

He was selfish, utterly obsessed with this restless quest to find his sister. But whereas she could admit her own whoredom, Eldritch maintained his harlot of a sister had been held against her will, forced into her highly lucrative career by wicked men and appalling circumstance.

The White Rabbit hadn't been forced into anything. She clearly relished her profession, using men as the flabby nobles used the small coin from their purses. She used sex as an insignificant favour and hadn't hesitated to lie backwards for great statesmen or squinting watchmen. She loved her work as if she were a sexual artist creating masterpieces in living flesh. Why she had seen the legendary *Lapin Blanc* take on half a battalion of French officers – brawling, butter-fingered cadets who imagined themselves the best lovers in Christendom. The dogs had fled with their sore tails between their legs, routed by her insatiable desire.

This was the less than immaculate Madonna, the fallen angel who Eldritch had sworn to rescue! The Countess couldn't make up her mind whether he was an innocent prince among men or a self-deceiving fool with a terminal erection; whether the absurdly intense emotions she felt for the cantankerous Englishman was raw love or undiluted hate.

She closed her eyes, sighing with relief despite herself. Eldritch guided the horse through the trees, the moonlight turning the pocked boughs silver. The deep mulch which lay over the rocky ground smothered the horse's footfalls, allowed the captain to slip through the wood as if he were some night-riding elf-lord.

Charlotte cursed her wayward imaginings. Here he was at last, dismounting with a sigh. He didn't smell a whole lot better than his sergeant, his dark tunic fragrant with human sweat and horse urine.

'Yer back then,' Hobby observed, striding forward to collect the weary stallion's reins. Eldritch rubbed his back, wincing as he stretched his arms. He glanced at the scowling girl leaning against the tree. Charlotte looked away pointedly.

'What's her trouble?'

'She's a spoilt French flibbertigibbet . . .' Hobby growled, lowering his voice so only half the people in France could possibly have overheard his estimation of his prisoner's character. Charlotte snorted, a plume of vapour hanging like a silver question mark.

'She? She is the cat's mother, yes? You forget, monsieur, I speak your language better than you pigs squeal mine!'

Eldritch shrugged resignedly. Hobby raised his eyebrows.

'Did you see Briconet go by?'

'Aye. Like all the fiends of hell were after him.'

'I was too late. He must have caught Lillith at the castle. He had her in the back of the wagon.'

Hobby's rugged face crumpled. Charlotte paused. The White Rabbit a prisoner of Abandando Briconet of Avignon, scourge of all heretics? 'I er . . . didn't know. You said . . .'

Eldritch waved his hand distractedly. 'There was little you could have done against so many of them. Perhaps he will

115

imprison her, hold her back in Marseille in order to entice me into his lair?'

Hobby pondered his captain's assessment.

'Get you to give yourself up, admit you bagged their bare-ballocked duke?' Hobby asked, his eyebrows bristling as stiff as a hedgerow in a hurricane.

Eldritch raised his chin in silent acknowledgment of his own heavy-handedness. The ill-fortune which had brought them to that lonely wood beside the coast road.

Charlotte listened to their gloomy exchange in silence, every fibre of her being vibrating with frustration. 'What has she done, that Briconet could detain her in this way?' she enquired, her blue eyes sparkling with indignation.

'He doesn't need an excuse.'

'Well then . . . perhaps I could be of use, a letter to our King Francis, explaining exactly . . .' Eldritch was shaking his head.

'We either get her out or she will be as dead as that damned Duke of yours,' he snarled. Charlotte was stung by the fierce contempt in his voice. She scowled, clutching at the neck of her sackcloth cloak.

'You think he was my *friend*, monsieur?'

'Women who go about cupping men's balls are generally thought to be on speaking terms,' he said, his eyes glowing with spite.

She was about to answer when Hobby held up his hand, cocking his head to listen to the rustling trees. The captain paused, senses honed as he analysed the mischievously scuttling symphony of night-time noises.

'Horsemen, coming this way,' Hobby hissed.

The Englishmen had strung their bows and doubled through the damp woods, leaving the snarling Countess secured to a tree as if she were some daintily put together packhorse. Eldritch had muttered an apology as he gagged her, ignoring her furious writhings and the fierce kicks she aimed at his shins.

'Mmmmmunnnn!'

The two soldiers worked their way to the edge of the woods, watched the flagging riders spur up a long, exposed slope towards their hiding place. There were no more than seven of them, riding by the glare of a spluttering torch. Eldritch watched and listened as the riders urged their panting horses along the darkened road towards Villefranco. He recognised Briconet's guards, handy looking soldiers in dark livery, their weather-worn hauberks still sporting Briconet's personal emblem, a silver cross on a scarlet and black field. Where were they going in such a hurry, at this time of night?

'D'yer reckon they're out after us?' Hobby enquired.

'They missed us in broad daylight, a whole pack of 'em. I wouldn't have imagined half a dozen of them would bother looking for us in darkness.'

Hobby was about to reply when he heard the dry snap of a twig immediately behind them. They whirled round to see Charlotte – still bound but dragging the bough she had been tied to through the leaf-mould which carpeted the forest floor. The girl leapt aside like a scalded cat, her eyes widening in outrage. Eldritch rose out of the mulch and doubled towards her, his face contorted. The Countess yelped in terror but her warning shout was stifled by the strip of shirt-sleeve Eldritch had tied about her mouth. Equally furious, she swung the broken branch with all her might. Eldritch ducked instinctively but the pine branch clattered over his back and wrapped itself about a tree trunk. A nightjar squawked. Eldritch's momentum upset his balance, and he measured his length on the trampled floor.

Hobby peered from woods to road, electrified by the sudden disturbance behind him. The last rider had heard the noise and reined in, shouting the alarm to his hurrying companions. Hobby cursed, raised his bow and squinted over his wrist to find a target. The Frenchman had turned about, a black shadow on the edge of the sickly yellow pool cast by his friend's torch. Hobby opened his fingers, feeling the great war bow flex in his wrist. The arrow hit the rider in the chest, hurling him from his startled horse as if he had been impaled at full gallop on a gendarme's lance.

The rest were bawling warnings in French, turning in alarm to face the unexpected onslaught. The torch was flung into the woods.

Hobby took three steps backward, already nocking his second arrow. This shot would be trickier.

Eldritch slipped behind the broad bole of a pine tree, covering the sergeant's back.

'Smacked her one, I hope?' Hobby growled, as a shadow slipped past the packed trunks in front of them. They were shouting to wake the dead now, trying to estimate how many fugitives they were facing.

Six against two, in the pitch dark.

Eldritch cursed.

'Did you count how many had crossbows?' the captain hissed.

A bolt hissed between the branches, burying itself in a trunk behind them. Another skittered off a stone and came to rest at their feet.

'They're shouting that we're English,' Eldritch reported, cocking his head to listen to the excited babble from the other side of the trees.

'Bit of a giveaway, an arrow finding its mark in the middle of the bloody night,' Hobby confirmed.

'Go back towards the girl. I'll go right and come in behind them!'

Hobby nodded, crouching down and working his way through the trees, an arrow nocked in case one of the Frenchmen ventured too close. Eldritch could hear one of them cursing as he frantically wound his crossbow. He ducked beneath a bush, squirmed through the mulch on his belly. The crossbowman had turned his back on him, bending over to wind his cumbersome weapon. The ill-oiled mechanism howled like a tortured cat. Eldritch dropped his bow and accelerated towards him, tugging his long knife from his belt. The Frenchman leapt around and managed to deflect the deadly blow, the pair of them rolling over in the darkness. The Frenchman was bawling to his friends, beating Eldritch's blade away with his bare hands. Another rider, somewhat encouraged by the fact they had not been slaughtered in an immediate deluge of arrows, had retrieved the discarded torch and was squinting into the bushes at the frightening kaleidoscope of shadows and shouts. He spotted Eldritch braining his companion with a rock and doubled into the woods after him, drawing his sword as he came. Hobby's second arrow hit him between the eyes. The dead guard stumbled backward with a grunt of astonishment, his flexing fingers releasing the sword. He came to a halt against the trunk of another large tree, a broken bough snagging his armour and holding the dead man upright. The goose-feathered shaft protruded from his cracked forehead.

Sourris peered into the devilish gloom, trying to pick Druchet's men from the tumbling shadows. The captain had remained in the saddle, sword drawn, peering intently after his shouting troopers.

'God damn them!' Druchet was torn between striding into the demon wood or galloping off into the night. Sourris had no such qualms, but hesitated to flee on his own. There might be more of them, waiting just around the corner for him. God damn Briconet and his filthy scheming!

'Calabon! Is that you there?' Druchet shouted, turning his horse as close as he dared to the closely packed trees. His corporal had dismounted, watching the trees with his crossbow. Another rider had closed up, covering their rear. He was muttering encouragements to his dead friends.

'Calabon you swine, can you hear me?' Druchet screamed, his terror eating through the last reserves of his courage.

'Ride,' Sourris suggested. 'We should ride and fetch help!'

'Those are my men in there, you fornicating puppy!' Druchet snarled, beating his horse around with the flat of his sword. The beast reared. An arrow sang overhead, lost in the darkness. Druchet controlled his horse, took one panic-stricken look over his shoulder. There was no saying how many there were of them.

'*Sauve qui peut!* Run! Save yourselves!'

'Hold hard you scoundrels!'

Druchet's pride prevented him from spurring off into the night. He stared at the dark trees, cursing as his horse stumbled into the shallow roadside ditch. He tipped forward, holding on for dear life. He glanced up in time to see a giant tree come alive before his eyes. A massive, needle clad crown hurtled towards him.

One of the raiders had staggered out of the woods, jumping down into the ditch in front of his frightened horse. He had hauled an enormous bough with him, boosting the trunk above his head like some terrible mace. He had swung the massive club before Druchet could move, the terrific blow sending the whinnying horse crashing back on its haunches. The captain was hurled backward, clattering over the roadway. He landed with a spine-shattering crash and lay still, hands twitching.

Sourris almost fell off his horse in terror. He clutched at the beast's reins as it pranced in the middle of the road.

Another figure emerged from the woods, clutching the feebly spluttering torch. Sourris peered at him, recognising the tall helmet and dark hauberk Briconet issued his personal guards.

'*Où est mon cheval?*' the soldier shrieked, clutching his head.

Sourris looked around. The wounded man ducked under the beast's tossing neck and grabbed the clerk's leg. He gave a terrific tug, yanking the startled Frenchman out of the saddle.

The corporal was trying to mount his horse and menace the clubman with his crossbow at the same time. He gave up, discarding the cumbersome weapon to drag himself into the saddle. He didn't wait to settle himself, bawling the beast on as he lay across his back. The two of them cantered off, the exhausted Englishman panting amidst the sudden carnage behind them.

'Bugger,' Hobby commented, hurling the heavy pine bough aside and bending down to lift the dead captain's sword. Eldritch peered through his clouding breath after the survivors.

'Aye. They'll be going after their master,' he panted. The fat clerk was lying in the road, his paws held across his heaving chest as if he would swipe any blow away. Eldritch squinted down at the man's tonsured head, his flabby jowls quivering in fear.

'Monsieur Sourris. We meet again,' Eldritch said in fluent French.

Sourris gave the murdering rogue a nervous smile.

PART THREE

✦

'The Prince who is more afraid
of his own people than of foreign
interference should build fortresses,
but the Prince who fears foreign
interference more than his own
people should forget about them'

Machiavelli, *The Prince*

By the Dora Baltea glacier, near the French border

✦

A Swiss army marched like no other on earth.

For one thing, the men of the cantons – Lucerne, Unterwalden, Basle, Schwyz, Zurich, Uri, Zug and the rest, did without posturing captains and egotistical kings. They had dispensed with the usual peacock-plumed officer corps, the grandly-turned-out suite of generals, dukes, princes and hirelings who preened and paraded beneath a canopy of bright banners at the head of every other army in Europe.

They preferred to elect leaders from the ranks.

Experienced commanders who led their garishly-costumed host from the front, sharing their hardships, enduring the punishing conspiracies of dust and mud, trudging on with a pike over their shoulder despite the extremes of temperature.

And the marked contrast between the men of the cantons and their perpetually squabbling neighbours was not confined to the army's vanguard. The Swiss had pared their bag and baggage to the bare minimum required. They carried just enough staples to get them to the next battle and no more. The fearsome mercenaries who had helped shape European politics for the past century and a half refused to concern themselves with frivolities like food. Their generals preferred to sharpen the troops' appetites for the fighting to follow.

There was always plenty to eat once the battle was won.

Enemy armies loaded themselves down with all sorts of unnecessary ballast. Mobile bakeries and workshops, smithies, laundries, whorehouses and God knew what else. They carried wine by the barrel and biscuit by the ton, squabbled over bitterly salted pork and stinking beef. They hauled water, wine and strong beer over mountain passes, lifted sacks of beans and swinging hams over snow-clogged heights.

No wonder they were lucky if they marched seven or eight

leagues while the lightly burdened Swiss marched ten, twelve, even fifteen leagues in one day.

They were freer, fitter, faster and fresher.

They were not afraid of anything or anyone, each contingent daring its neighbours to greater feats of slaughter and mayhem.

In truth, their battle tactics had never been particularly subtle. The Swiss had never required the services of thoughtful, gifted or opportunist generals to guide them to their victories. They had never bred a Caesar or a Hannibal, an Arthur or a Charlemagne, nor had their junior officers – the cadets and sergeants who had been the backbone of every other army since the Stone Age – ever been called upon to interpret their superiors' plans or react to tactical opportunities. They had no time for subtle deceptions, ambushes, forlorn hopes or flank marches.

The army would normally be divided into three battles: the *nachut*, the *gewaltschaufen* and the *vorhut*. The various cantons represented would squabble over the right to take the vanguard, the privilege of taking the battle to the enemy first. Each battle would advance in echelon, the unit following behind watching the flank and rear of the one in front until the entire force was engaged.

The Swiss relied on the crudest of weapons to demoralise and defeat their opponents. The majority of the lightly-armoured fighters were equipped with eighteen-foot pikes, the remainder an assortment of halberds, crossbows and handguns. But in truth firepower had never been of particular importance to them. Their onrush was practically irresistible, the final, stomach-churning charge delivered at a sprint. There were few troops in Europe who could stand their ground as several thousand bawling Swiss ran in to attack them, their deadly pikes held at shoulder height.

They had become accustomed to quick (though not necessarily bloodless) victories, driving their terrified and bewildered enemies from the field and butchering any unfortunates left behind. The Swiss never took prisoners and couldn't be bothered with the wearisome business of collecting ransom for the nobles they had seized. They saved the last of their energies for looting their victims' camps, helping themselves to what were in effect lavishly equipped storehouses.

In short Swiss pikemen had one aim in life – to conquer or die trying.

The French, on the other hand, had always relied on the shock value of their horsepower, preferring a handful of super-heavy knights to hordes of grumbling infantry. But this summer they had emptied the exchequer to ensure they secured the services of the awesome Swiss. The mountain men had flocked to the colours, filling the loosely affiliated regimental groups which Unkel Von Schwartzer would lead over the Alps on their behalf.

The commander was not yet twenty years old, but he had already fought six pitched battles. He was tall and blond, his features a crude square. His sloping skull and jutting lower lip were evidence of his remote Hapsburg ancestry. His famous father Giebling the Cruel had been killed the year before, leading a pack of halberdiers through a breach in the Spanish fortifications around Niersteiner. Young Unkel had had no difficulty in replacing the gaps left in the ranks, rousing up his followers for another crack at their despised enemy – the German *Landsknechts* who served the Empire in their thousands. The Swiss knew they would earn more in a bloody spring than the rest of the year put together, taking gold, silver, jewels, captured cloth, horses, oxen, cattle and all manner of transportable goods back to their homes in the mountains.

The snow-capped pass of Mont Galliard would be tailor-made for them. Cloud-piercing peaks rearing up from perilous girdles of bare rock. Crevasses which plunged deep into the earth. They could run along scree-lined slopes, nimble as the mountain goats who shared the inhospitable terrain. They could wade through snowdrifts, scale the highest peaks and trot down glaciers, appearing with terrifying effect on flanks or rears their enemies had taken to be secured.

But Alberto Tarsi had no intention of being overawed by the swift-marching Swiss. He had survived several bloody run-ins with them already, and knew that their blunt enthusiasm could be turned to their disadvantage.

The Swiss were stupid, as dumb as rocks. They made it a point of honour to charge home, refusing to vary their tactics for man or God. He had seen two thousand of them fall trying to take an insignificant hilltop in Italy, when a short flank march would have secured higher ground and won the battle without a shot being fired.

Tarsi's fireworker Wilfrid Stitchwort had worked like a demon and saved his men from almost certain destruction. He had used his cunningly crafted powder charges to undermine the valley's bones, blasting a series of pits across the neck of the pass. Shallow fox-scrapes which his weary troops had rapidly expanded into a continuous trench some four feet deep. It made a formidable bulwark which the massed pikemen would be obliged to negotiate before they could punch their way out into the main Aosta Valley. By the time the dust from Stitchwort's fearsome explosions had settled, his men had added a stone and rubble palisade studded with broken pikes and swinefeathers – sharpened stakes they had carried up the valley for that express purpose. He had strewn the ground with caltrops – triangular iron spikes which would cripple horse and man. He had lined the trenches with his Spanish arquebusiers and his English archers. He had ordered the pikemen to break up into small schillitrons of between thirty and fifty men in order to stiffen the long line against the expected attack. To complete his defences Tarsi had place six sows – low-slung medium cannon – between each contingent, completely dominating the narrow approaches.

He had estimated his force would inflict between five hundred and a thousand casualties on any enemy force attempting to rush his position.

The question was whether the Swiss would be prepared to pay such a price to achieve their goal. God knew he had seen them shed more men for less important objectives. If they got over the palisade they would have to fight the mad bastards in the ditch, hand to hand, knife to knife.

And that, in all likelihood, would be the end of Alberto Tarsi's Italian war.

The Chevalier Bayard, immaculate knight of Christ and champion of France, regarded Unkel Von Schwartzer's revolting table manners from behind a heavily scented handkerchief. The bearded rogue ate like a bear just emerged from its hibernation, stuffing meats and jams and great bites of bread down his throat, then washing the barely digested mass down with generous draughts of red wine. Bayard made little attempt to disguise his disgust at the Swiss locotenent's repulsive habits, but Unkel seemed blissfully unaware of the knight's disapproval, demolishing the succulent feast with gusto. He leaned over his fellow diners, grabbing at roast joints, laughing uproariously at every jest, spraying his neighbours with half digested paste.

Bayard felt physically sick at the sight of so much food. He had recently held the town of Mezieres in the face of determined Imperialist attacks, surviving on boiled rat and roast crow for almost two months before the enemy forces had given up and gone home. His skin was loose and jaundice-yellow, hanging like soggy parchment over his weakened frame. His hair had fallen out in clumps, and he had ordered his barber to trim the rest back into a manageable grey wedge.

Von Schwartzer, in contrast, seemed full of all the vigours of outrageous youth. He was broad and well-fleshed; his teeth were white chisels, his eyes alive with malicious curiosity.

He seemed to have picked mongrels for colonels, bandits for captains and the lost tribes of Babylon as footsoldiers. And most of them appeared to have been invited along to the impromptu feast, crawling about the floor to snatch up chewed chicken legs and fat-slimed joints their superiors had hurled away. The rotten crew had turned Bayard's grand pavilion into a pigpen, the torches burning bright on the methane they expelled with every deafening fart.

'Fine food, Bayard,' Unkel drooled, wiping his arm across his glistening mouth. 'But you seem to have misplaced your appetite, eh?'

Bayard gave him a pained smile, wondering at the wisdom of employing such dogs.

'After Mezieres, I can take but bread and water. Until my stomach becomes accustomed to rich foods once more.'

The posturing French bed-faggot, Unkel fumed. He smiled brightly.

'Quite a fight, eh?'

'Indeed.'

Von Schwartzer's moronic grin only slipped once, when Stroma and his ally Savvi arrived at the encampment to discuss their role in the coming campaign. The blond-haired barbarian took his feet from the table, leaning back in his ornately-carved chair as he surveyed Bayard's unwanted guests.

The Chevalier had greeted the newcomers warmly, grasping each man by the arm and leading him to his place at the top table. He welcomed the anxious soldiers in the name of his master, Francis I. Stroma, a past master in cloak and daggerdom, returned similar flowery greetings. His companion Francesco Savvi, nervous in the face of so many mortal enemy Swiss, kept his mouth shut and his eyes open.

'Gentlemen, I am delighted you could accept my invitation to dine,' Bayard began.

'Aye! Squeeze up there, let our noble friends rest their weary legs,' Von Schwartzer growled, making a play of brushing off the empty stool beside his own food-flecked chair. Stroma inclined his head in acknowledgment of this unlooked-for courtesy.

'Of course we all know Count Eusebius della Stroma of Luningiana, rightful master of the valley. And his companion in arms Francesco Savvi, lately declared Seigneur of Mont Galliard.'

Declared by himself, if no one else, Bayard thought darkly, cursing the desperate horse-trading which had obliged him to campaign with such a pack of rogues in the first place.

'To you, gentlemen, I present Locotenent Unkel Von Schwartzer, commander of the Swiss forces presently allied to His Majesty Francis I.'

'I knew your father,' Stroma said curtly.

Savvi muttered something under his breath.

Bayard watched the loathsome bandits square up to one another while simultaneously slumping in their seats. They had been happy enough using their fingers until then, now all of a sudden they had deployed a small arsenal of knives and meat forks.

'Truly, His Majesty has assembled a formidable host for the coming campaign,' Stroma commented by way of preamble, holding up his goblet to one of Bayard's immaculately liveried serving boys.

'I am sure the puny Imperial rearguard which has been left in the valley will not stand above an hour, when they see the force His Majesty has dispatched.'

So he had come after his money, Bayard decided. Well he would get no more, not until that serpent Briconet arrived with the treasury wagons from Marseille.

'You can watch from your precious hidey-hole while we boot them out of the way and march for Milan,' Unkel boasted.

'Truly a hammer to crack a nut,' Stroma simpered, showing his teeth. 'God will make them as young corn to your swords.'

'Pikes,' Unkel corrected.

'We all pray this is so,' Bayard interrupted, anxious to prevent the slanging match from erupting any further. 'Our scouts report Tarsi has returned to Imperial service, digging himself in behind some manner of barricade.'

'It won't save him. We'll have his balls for breakfast,' Unkel crowed.

'I hear your father made a similar vow outside Niersteiner, only the Spanish garrison wouldn't bend over for him.'

Bayard winced. Unkel lowered his glass to the table without spilling any.

'We'll have those bastards on our way home. They'll be happy enough bending over for anyone, once we've finished with them.'

'Giebling's brave death is of course mourned by all,' Bayard said, appalled to find himself obliged to lie for the sake of his master's campaign. If these murderous fishwives started the entire camp would go up in flames. 'The question before us this night is how we are to bring our assignment to the speedy conclusion His Majesty expects.'

Unkel belched. 'I told you. That lizard-ballocked puke-licker won't stand an hour.'

'I think it meet we do not anticipate a bloodless victory, Herr Von Schwartzer,' Bayard snapped, his patience stretched perilously thin by these argumentative ticks. Unkel's thick lips peeled back from his teeth.

'Arseholes!'

'He has dug in six cannon. You'll be marching into a carefully-prepared crossfire,' Bayard countered.

'You can't cook omelettes without breaking a few eggs,' the Swiss said with a shrug, biting into another chicken.

There was little more to be said, as far as he was concerned.

Stroma sighed and leaned closer to the pale Chevalier, tapping him lightly on his mail-clad arm.

'Let him bloody his nose on Tarsi's line, my lord,' he said *sotto voce*.

'They will open a path for your brave Gendarmes and you will carry King Francis' banners all the way to your esteemed cousin Lautrec, defiant in Milan!'

'Indeed.'

'And then of course, your treasurer will be free to settle a few trifling financial details.'

Bayard raised his eyebrows.

'Pardon me for mentioning it at this juncture, but Francis owes us fifteen thousand livres.'

'You will be paid the balance the moment Monsieur Briconet arrives with the treasury carts,' Bayard said coolly.

'Briconet,' Stroma breathed.

'Aye. The very same. He has recently been appointed to the intelligence service, in addition to his pressing clerical duties.'

Bayard was well aware of the dangerous dealings the previous summer, the deadly conspiracies which had been played out in Stroma's palace – just down the valley in Aosta.

'Well, no matter. I am sure you appreciate our predicament, the expenses we have incurred during our recent . . . change of allegiance.'

Bayard understood all too well.

'You will be paid, you have my word on the matter.'

'And your word is worth all the gold in the world, my dear Chevalier. But just so as we understand each other, I feel obliged to point out that if that Swiss bear's ballock tries to march his men past Mont Galliard before we have received payment in full, I regret we shall have no choice other than to open fire at them with every weapon in our possession.'

Stroma delivered his chilling ultimatum with an ingratiating smile.

Bayard glared at the shaven-headed count. 'In other words, the attack cannot be launched until you have your money.'

'The Chevalier Bayard is too kind, grasping our dilemma in a trice!' Stroma beamed.

Bayard shivered, his delicate stomach rebelling at the prospect of dealing with such degenerates.

'I am sure we all understood your position,' he allowed.

Stroma was intending to sit this one out, raking in his twelve silver pieces without committing himself to either party.

The slow dog.

By Rouquevaire, near Marseille

✦

'I ought to cut your throat right here and now!'

Maître Sourris glanced from Eldritch's dagger to Hobby's sword, the gored blades quivering precious inches from his throat.

'Pardon Messieurs, I . . . I only ever obeyed my master Briconet. Your quarrel, just and righteous as it is, is, nevertheless, with him.'

'Stick the bugger, bleed him like a hog,' Hobby leered.

Eldritch grimaced. The French clerk's English had improved dramatically since his capture several moments before. They had hauled the fat Frenchman back under the trees, thrusting him back against the trunk which was supporting his former companion. The soldier's corpse hung from the broken bough, small beads of blood running along the arrow shaft and dripping from the red feathers. Sourris could hardly take his eyes from the grisly reminder of his captors' prowess.

Hobby had managed to catch three of the horses. Two riders had escaped back down the slope. They had looted the bodies of anything of worth, loading one of the spare horses with their hauberks, the French captain's fine sword as well as his soiled banner.

Charlotte had been dragged up alongside the terrified clerk and deposited in the mulch. Hobby had placed his boot in the small of her back while he assisted the captain's interrogation of the prisoner. Eldritch was just about to suggest he let the squirming girl up when the terrified Frenchman found his tongue at last.

'In point of fact, my lord,' Sourris went on, panting in terror, 'it was I who insisted my master investigated the false charges brought against you last summer.'

'You lying toad! You were working for Briconet and passing secrets to Gueldres! How was it he kept himself so well informed of developments in France, eh? You told Gueldres of my regard for my sister and he exploited it to the full!' Eldritch bent closer, his dagger closing to within a hair's breath of the clerk's slick chins. '*In point of fact*,' he went on, 'he cost me my honour.'

'With respect, my lord, your argument is with the Vicomte, not me, his pitiful slave.'

'Slave?' Eldritch recoiled in disgust, reluctant to dirty his blade on such a crawling beetle. The clerk sensed the captain's change of heart, grovelling piteously.

'I give you my word, none of my actions were directed against you or your sister.'

'Perhaps I didn't make myself clear. I was at Villefranco this very afternoon. I heard you talking about her, locked in the back of that damned wagon!'

Sourris frowned.

'When are we talking about, my lord?'

'In the castle, this afternoon, you serpent!'

'Villefranco?'

'Just so,' Eldritch sneered. Sourris thought for a moment.

'You heard my master discussing the . . .'

'Hell spawned harlot was it? Spitfire?'

'You think he was . . . no my lord, no no no!'

Eldritch pressed the blade closer. Sourris shook his head as far as he dared, the flesh quivering.

'He wasn't talking about your sister! She had already left the castle, left for the wars, on my oath sir!'

'Your oath! What are you jabbering about? I heard you talking about her!'

'You heard us talking about . . .' Sourris hesitated, reluctant to divulge his master's latest infatuation.

'Well? What whore did he have in the wagon?' The blade pricked the clerk's flesh, releasing a fat bead of blood.

'Ah! Not a whore, as such, my lord. A spitfire sir, he spoke truly! A gun with a dozen barrels which fire at once, if you'll credit it sir. We saw the men Gerhard had shot down. A devilish weapon in the wrong hands, my lord!'

Eldritch thought for a moment, remembering the shambles in the courtyard. Could that have been the bloody demonstration the maggot was referring to? It would certainly explain Briconet's abrupt decision to abandon the chase.

'A weapon?'

'Is he saying your sister wasn't in the wagon?' Hobby enquired.

'Just so sir! Gerhard swore she had but recently departed for the camps in Northern Italy.'

'Camps? Are you suggesting she's gone to hawk herself about like a common polecat?' Hobby rested his big hand on the captain's arm.

'I don't think . . .'

'She left, she left before we ever got to Villefranco, Gerhard swore it was so!' Sourris cried, tears coursing down his quivering brawn.

Eldritch recognised the bitter truth of the clerk's testimony.

He had missed her once more.

The captain didn't know whether to punch the air or throttle the clerk. At least if she had been Briconet's prisoner he would have had some idea of her whereabouts.

But she was a creature of air and darkness – she had gone.

'And where were you off to in such a hurry, eh? Had your master forgotten something back at the castle?'

Sourris nodded, pitifully eager to please now Eldritch's blade had wavered away from his throat.

'I was sent back to Villefranco, to keep watch on Duke Gerhard. My master anticipated he might wish to absent himself.'

Eldritch raised an eyebrow.

'Because of the gun my lord. My master had persuaded him to part with the prototype, though it was in truth badly damaged by the demonstration in the courtyard.'

'Not as damaged as those poor swine by the wall.'

'No indeed, my lord. My master feared Duke Gerhard might peddle the design elsewhere. He refused to hand over any technical drawings, claiming the designer had taken them with him. We had neither the time nor personnel to search the entire castle.'

'And the moment your master had so much as sniffed this gun's saltpetre, he forgot all about looking for us?'

'He forgets nothing, my lord,' Sourris countered, recovering something of his usual smug confidence. 'He merely felt the gun was of more pressing importance than a couple of . . .'

'English cut-throats, eh?' He held the knife under the clerk's eye.

Sourris swallowed, hiccuping in panic, his confidence evaporating all over again.

These English blew hot and cold as an April afternoon.

'How did he know we had been at the château?' Eldritch demanded.

'Who could have told him?'

'He thought the who . . . the White Rabbit, might possibly have been connected to the murder of the Duke de Milhaud.'

'And that the whore might be my sister, you were going to say.'

'My master had word an Englishwoman was staying at the château as a guest of the Duke. We were watching the roads. He had word of the stolen clothing!' Sourris exclaimed.

And Briconet had knotted these loose ends together, guessed their identity, predicted their possible escape route and been on their trail within hours. Eldritch almost shuddered at the inquisitor's miraculous reasoning.

'And he came this close to catching us all,' he sighed.

Hobby finished tying the rogue's hands and slipped his finger behind the gag he had tied about Sourris' mouth. He tugged at it, his ripe breath making the clerk's eyes water.

'Just making sure you can breath all right. Wouldn't want you to choke, eh?' Sourris' brown eyes came to rest on the girl, lying in the mulch at their feet. She was kicking and scuffing for all she was worth, but bound and gagged securely. Nobody would hear her piteously muffled curses now.

Eldritch hauled the apoplectic Countess to her feet, made a play of brushing the worst of the leaf-mould from her smeared cloak. She glared at him, her moist eyes sparkling with malice over the sopping gag. He eased the wet material from her mouth.

'How dare you leash me like a hawk on your fist! Don't you have any idea who I am?' she gasped, panting with fury.

'You tried to warn your friends. I told you before, they won't hesitate to hang us, the moment we fall into their hands.'

'Good! Though God knows hanging's too good for you! I tell you this, Eldritch. I will get on my knees and beg, beg Briconet to allow me the privilege of playing cat's cradle with your filthy guts!'

'Spoken like a true lady of France,' Eldritch sneered.

Hobby collected the horses, waiting anxiously on his captain's word.

'If this greased weasel is telling the truth, Lillith might be well over the border by now.'

'Aye. And for once I can see some sense in getting after her,' Hobby growled. 'At least old Tarsi ain't goin' to 'ang us right off.'

'Don't you believe it,' Eldritch muttered.

'Refuse him, and I will swear you had no part in these dealings,' Charlotte called, her shapely chin smeared with dirt and slick with the dribble which had escaped from her gag. 'Deliver me to Master Briconet and I will see you paid your weight in coin!'

'My weight! Hah! That's a shit-load of coin!' Hobby joked clumsily.

'If you can't keep quiet I'll replace the gag,' Eldritch warned.

Charlotte gave the captain a withering grin. 'If I were a man, I'd gag you on your own ballock straps!'

Hobby grunted with amusement at the girl's hair-raising threat.

'We waste time. Mount up, we're riding for Villefranco.'

'Villefranco? Back there?'

'What do you suggest, follow a cold trail into Italy? You heard the fat slug. Lillith's off to the wars. That might include any one of half a dozen different nations, let alone towns and cities.'

'And you think Duke Gerhard will set you right. Perhaps she left a forwarding address?' the Countess asked archly. Eldritch smiled sourly.

'He might have some idea which direction she was headed. We might be able to make an enquiry.'

'Your enquiries have already cost the life of my dearest friend!'

'Ah, my lady. You mourned your loss a full half hour,' Eldritch said coldly.

'I hope Gerhard shoots you down on sight, and good riddance!'

'I doubt that lady. Do you imagine Duke Gerhard would be fool enough to shoot down troops belonging to the Holy Inquisition?'

It was almost dawn before the travellers arrived at their destination. Torches and lanterns lit the barren approaches. They could hear men shouting and singing despite the late hour, discordantly competing with the courtyard cockerels. The walls seemed deserted and the flagpole was bare.

Eldritch drew rein on the gravel track which sloped up towards the stronghold, listening to the muffled sounds of celebration.

'Somebody's either broken into it or the garrison's broken into the wine cellar,' the captain observed. Hobby was peering up at the gloomy battlements, torches casting eerie shadows over the deserted walkways.

The gate remained shut.

Eldritch drew his dagger and buried the point in Sourris' paunch. The clerk held his breath, trying to suck his rolled flesh away from the threatening point.

'One word, and I'll empty your guts over the path.' Sourris nodded as the captain leaned over and dragged the gag from his mouth.

'What's all the noise? Did Briconet bribe the garrison?' Sourris shook his head, trying to catch his breath after the punishingly uncomfortable ride up the coast road.

'It is as my master feared, my lord. Gerhard has made his escape, left the few rogues who remain to make sport in his castle.'

'Hobby?'

'I reckon the quill-pusher might have it about right. They're as pissed as Dutchmen, or I'm half frog.'

They sat quietly at the bottom of the slope in Briconet's dread livery. Eldritch wasn't sure the drunken rogues in the castle would care what colours they wore. They didn't sound as if they were in any condition to recognise his devices on their looted hauberks, or the stolen banner Hobby had leaned against his shoulder. There was a terrific crash from within as some massive glasswork impacted with the stone-flagged floor. Eldritch weighed the odds, reckoning whether one of the wine-enfeebled fiends within might have some clue to Lillith's whereabouts. They had already risked everything in this pursuit – they could hardly turn back now.

'We're going up to the gate. Sourris, you'll do the talking, but remember I can speak passable French and I've my knife at your spleen. Shout a warning and you'll be dead before you hit the ground.'

'I understand my lord. What am I to tell them?'

'Exactly what Briconet bid you. That you are here to attend the Duke.'

'But he may already . . .'

'I don't care. Someone within must have some clue as to my sister's destination.'

Hobby glanced at his master but held his tongue.

'I shall try my best, my lord.'

'I am assured you will,' Eldritch said levelly.

The little party spurred on up the slope. Somebody within must have either remained at their post longer than his fellows or refused to drink himself silly. They were challenged before they had fully emerged from the shadowy path.

'Halt! Who goes there?'

'Maître Sourris, assistant to Briconet of Avignon, agent of the Holy Inquisition,' the clerk rasped, his voice lent extra edge by his fear of the wild-hearted Englishman riding at his side.

'Oh ho, back to bother old Piss Pants again eh?'

'Open the gate you dog! Agents of the Inquisition do not exchange banalities with refuse like you!'

'You'd best keep a civil tongue my lardy lad! Or I might stick a bolt or two up your arse! Come into the light where I can see you!'

'Who are you ordering about, offal? Since when does an agent of the Inquisition obey drunken gatekeepers?'

'Not that drunk, my friend, that I couldn't stick one right in your eye!' the disembodied voice came back.

'Ask him where the Duke has gone,' Eldritch hissed.

'Where is your master, Duke Gerhard of Villefranco?'

'Old Piss Pants? He buggered off this evening, left us to it. Took his Grand Council with him. Sergeant Tourain is in charge now!'

'He left a mere sergeant in charge?'

'Oh ho! He left a few others in charge but they didn't relish our company.'

'Where are they?'

'Around and about. Gone off to Marseille,' the guard modified, sobering up a little as he leaned over the battlements and tried to recognise the dread devices on their gear.

'The rogues have slaughtered their own officers,' Hobby hissed.

'Who's that muttering down there with you, eh? Advance and be recognised,' the surly guard challenged.

They had brought more lights now, lit the main lanterns in the gatehouse to illuminate the hillside. Watchful faces flitted at the lancets. Sourris glanced at Eldritch.

'I am Maître Sourris, assistant to Briconet! I was here this very afternoon with my master. Is it possible none within recognise me?'

'Aye, we recognise you. The fat monkey who gobbled all Briconet's leftovers.'

There was a burst of laughter from further along the walls.

Eldritch had heard enough. He raised himself out of his saddle, shaking his fist at the watchers on the walls.

'You know damn fine who we are and what we are about. Either open the gate and get on your knees before us, or I will have my men storm this pukepot and slaughter every last rat!' Eldritch bawled in his strongly accented but plain enough French.

There was a pregnant pause while the cabal on the tower discussed the best course of action.

'Maître Sourris, you say, assistant to Monsieur Briconet of Avignon?'

'Are you going to open this gate or am I to fetch the citizen militia from Marseille?'

'Your pardon sirs. There's been strange folk abroad this day. You must excuse our diligence.'

'Diligence? Get this gate open or I swear you won't see another dawn, diligent or otherwise.'

'We have already been attacked by agents of the enemy! We had to satisfy ourselves as to your identity!'

'The gate!'

'At once, Excellence!'

The massive oak and iron gate divided in two, creaking back on its enormous hinges with a shriek to raise the hackles of every dog in the district. Sourris rode in first, glancing at the guards who staggered out of the guardhouse and at their unconscious colleagues lying in pooled vomit about the courtyard.

The garrison of Villefranco had gone to pieces, its fragile morale shattered by the appalling sequence of events it had witnessed. First, old Baldassare Mounier thrown from the high tower, exploding on the rocks like a sack of tomatoes. Then his bodyguard – handy fighters in full armour – cut down to a man, blown away like chaff by some devilish firework in the back of a cart.

Then an unexpected visit from the ghoulish inquisitor, the dreaded Briconet himself. And as if he wasn't enough to turn turds to water, they had fallen prey that afternoon to some mysterious invader, a black-coated, shape-changing assassin who had apparently come and gone as he pleased about the fortress, unmarked and unchallenged. Duke Gerhard's panic-stricken flight later that same evening had broken their spirit, turned them from soldiers into superstitious, quarrelling fishwives. Gerhard had thrown all his valuables into a wagon, and taken off with his counsellors and personal bodyguard, heading east as if every hound in hell were baying at his heels. The petty captain he had appointed to command in his absence had packed his kit and ridden out shortly afterwards, plunging the garrison into immediate anarchy.

It was little wonder they had felt the need for a few drinks. And now this. The bastard Briconet back once more – or his servants at any rate.

A hiccuping spearman staggered away from his nervously staring companions, straightening his helmet and holding himself upright by clinging on to the nervous clerk's reins. Sourris noticed he had already been involved in some soldier's fight. One eye was black and blue, swollen up so badly he was forced to squint out of the other. The clerk flinched as he caught a blast of the rogue's breath. Strong cider and a few goblets of his master's best brandy, no doubt.

'Corporal Hulin, my lord, and at your service,' the soldier reported, giving the inquisitor a shabby salute.

Sourris said nothing. Eldritch had been forced to drop a few lengths behind in order to negotiate the narrow gateway.

Hulin swung backwards, still hanging on to Sourris' reins. He blinked up at the black fiend riding under the gate. A tall, knife-nosed captain in black . . .

'Here! I know you! You're the bugger . . .'

Eldritch spurred his horse forward, bending over its neck to deal the unfortunate corporal another blistering blow about the head with the hilt of his sword. Hulin flew backwards for the second time that day, crashing into the gatepost, the breath knocked out of him. He slid to the floor, propping himself on his hands and vomiting over the flagstones. Sourris squealed a warning as the lazy garrison gawped on, but the sudden commotion behind him had upset his horse. It reared, flinging the clerk from its back. Sourris landed badly, spreadeagled over an iron horse trough. The rusty sidepanel buckled, releasing a torrent of water which carried the clerk on over the courtyard floor. The astonished guards leapt aside like skittles, shouting and cursing and trying to remember where they had left their weapons. Eldritch charged straight at them, lashing out with his sword. Hobby thundered into the courtyard with the Countess on a leading rein. He used Briconet's despised banner as a lance, jabbing at the loose-jawed crossbowmen who had staggered down the steps beside the opened door. One spearman, braver or drunker than his fellows, managed to upend his weapon and ram the broad steel blade into his horse's flank. The beast collapsed onto its chest, whinnying in agony and kicking out wildly at its grinning butcher. Hobby dropped the banner and sprawled on the stones.

Men were popping out of doors on all sides. Some in mail, some in their underthings, some still smeared with vivid vomit. Hardly any were steady enough to aim a blow, let alone abide an assault led by the fanatical Englishmen. Eldritch had turned his horse towards the stables, protected from missiles fired from above by the elaborate awning he had sheltered beneath earlier in the day. He leapt down in time to meet a bareheaded soldier tripping down the steps with a boar spear. He feinted to one side and then the other, running the bewildered youngster through with one sure thrust to the chest. He shoved his knee into the startled corpse's abdomen and dragged his blade free. It came away in a spluttering arc of warm blood and the youthful soldier collapsed over a bale of straw, puppet limbs twitching.

Eldritch lifted the spear and glanced over his shoulder, relieved to see Hobby had regained his feet and was trying to hold on to Charlotte's furiously rearing horse. The Countess was hanging on to its neck, gagged to prevent her from raising the alarm. The rest of the garrison had fled the slaughter, locking themselves in the guardhouse. Eldritch raced up the steps and paused on the first landing. A crossbowman let off one wild shot and then tried to brain him, swinging his useless weapon like a club. Eldritch ducked down and boosted the man off his unsteady feet, hurling the wretch from the steps. He landed with a spine-jarring crash on the floor below. Another appeared at the main door. Eldritch hurled the boar spear. The heavy shaft struck the man square in the chest, pinning him to the door like a shrike's breakfast. Eldritch was past him before he had stopped breathing, racing into the main building. They wouldn't stand a chance if the garrison was allowed time to organise itself, to surround the courtyard and seal off their escape. He had tricked his way in, now he must cow them into submission, destroy what little fighting spirit they may have possessed.

Such an assault would have been suicide if it had been launched against even reasonably determined troops. But Eldritch knew the stamp of such men. He had seen enough of them that afternoon to know they were idle, indolent backwater skivers. Useless cannon-fodder hardly worth the trouble of pursuing from the field. He paused in an alcove by the main door, peering down the dimly-lit passage towards the great hall. It was in uproar, the bewildered drunken soldiers rushing about like strangled pullets, waiting for somebody to grasp the nettle and bawl an order.

Instead, they heard the murderous, shape-changing, invincible Englishman shouting encouragement to his devilish companions. 'Sergeant Hobby, bring up the rest of our men!'

The poor fools were too shocked and bewildered to wonder why he should have issued such an order in French.

Eldritch had torn the bow from his back, nocked an arrow while he caught his breath. A man in a dirty smock stumbled into the doorway opposite, thinking he would escape through the main entrance. Eldritch put an arrow in his gut, low enough to disable but leave him screaming. The wretch staggered back inside, shrieking in pain as his drinking companions stampeded towards the stairs.

Hobby arrived at his side, his sword notched and bloody.

'Where's the girl?'

'Safe enough. I've barred the gate. She'll not be going far,' the giant observed with misogynistic satisfaction.

'What about Sourris?'

'Broken his back, the lard-bellied bugger.'

'This shower's ready to run. They're holed up in the main hall.'

'How many?'

'Sourris thought about fifty at most. He . . .'

Hobby nodded his head towards the doorway opposite. A bare arm had been thrust through the gap, its owner waving a dirty tablecloth in a frantic gesture of surrender.

'Messieurs! We beg you to spare our lives! Give us quarter! We're unarmed!'

'Unarmed my arse! Throw out all your weapons and come out with your hands on your heads,' Eldritch bawled in French. 'And don't give us any trouble or we'll butcher another score of you!'

Their whirlwind assault had demoralised the defenders, knocked what little fight they had ever possessed out of them in a moment. Eldritch had seen similar fights before, vastly superior forces routed because their hearts had not been in the struggle.

He glanced at his panting sergeant, crouching with his bow nocked and ready. 'If only every siege was as easy as this,' Eldritch remarked drily.

'We'd never get a day's rest,' Hobby observed sourly.

By the Hospice Gilbert le Petit Galliard, on the Alte Vie

◆

The remote hospice had, during its long and turbulent history, been used as a summer hunting lodge by the Dukes of Aosta, a postal relay station and as a hospital for the rich and well to do. Rich pilgrims had once flocked there from the big cities to the south in search of miraculous cures for their chest complaints.

It was believed the crisp mountain air of the high valley was a gift of the Gods, reputedly capable of driving out the blood-flecked sludge and noxious deposits which turned healthy lungs into congested sacks. It was a favoured destination for hundreds of town dwellers – the rich burghers or self-made manufacturers who suffered torments breathing the filthy, fume-filled air which circulated so sluggishly about the narrow alleys where they lived and worked.

Alberto Tarsi knew the hospice well.

He ought to – he had spent several seasons in the high valley, using the remote lodge as a base to hunt fleet-footed ibex and chamois on the high ridges; wolf, deer and wild boar in the pine-scented forests which clung to the lower slopes. He had made painstaking efforts to ingratiate himself with his neighbours further down the valley, hosting expensive hunting trips for his fair-weather friends. He had even gone to the trouble of carting in fresh stocks of game when his ill-tempered guests had slaughtered the aboriginal species. He might just as well have saved himself the money and trouble. Not one of his so-called allies had raised so much as a finger to help, when those black-hearted butchers had seized his home the previous autumn.

That crab-handed turd Savvi had waited until his back was turned to make his sly move, approaching his fortress like a thief in the night while he was fighting for his life before the cursed papal court. He had been moments from the scaffold, about to meet his maker when Savvi and his dirty-fingered crew had exploited his weakness like the vultures they were, swooping in to seize the home he had fought so long to earn and to hold.

The red-haired *Tedeschi* had been there ever since, sleeping in Tarsi's bed, quaffing Tarsi's wine. But the impostor's hold only went so deep. It was typical of the slow-witted Savvi's lack of vision that he had failed to investigate the full extent of his ill-gotten territories. If Savvi had taken the trouble to look at the maps Tarsi had hung in his usurped apartments, he would have noticed the old hunting lodge had been clearly drawn and labelled along with the rest of the tiny realm's assets. Besides the lodge there was a toll-house, an ancient, much-ravaged church with a crooked spire and a small, scrubby village surrounded by olive groves and dusty grazing fit only for braying donkeys and skinny chickens.

Savvi, keenly aware of the stipendiary benefits, had made good and sure he had secured his hold on the toll-house, church and struggling village. But he had failed to connect the far-flung outpost of Le Petit Galliard with his newly won empire. As far as Savvi knew it was some old shack halfway up the hillside, no use to man or beast.

Tarsi could understand if not forgive the impostor's oversight. The lodge was, after all, five leagues or more from the main fortress, at the terminus of the little-used high road – the Alte Vie – which meandered on down the valley. The high road was the back door onto the mountains, a favourite route for hunter and bandit alike. Most travellers kept to the easier roads in the main valley, content to pay the extortionate tolls for the sake of speed and convenience.

Now, Tarsi intended to make Savvi pay for that oversight, incorporating the lodge into his frail defences as a base of operations – and as a final redoubt should all else fail.

The wily Italian hadn't dared to leave the main pass in person, not with several thousand French and cut-throat Swiss lurking beneath the grim towers of Mont Galliard. He had instead sent Alexander Kerr and his wild Scotsmen to scout and clear the high road, ensuring the frail escape route remained open in case his main force needed to leave the pass in a hurry.

The reiver chief had been ordered to escort all their bag and baggage up into the mountains and see it safely secured within the formidably-built lodge. He was then to set about fortifying the place against any sudden assault from the lower valley, turning the lonely hospice into a valuable fortress.

Kerr had been glad enough to accept the assignment. His men were skilled light horsemen and voracious guerrillas, but would be of little use when push came to shove down in Tarsi's trenches. He was content to take his men out of the line, leave the hand-to-hand slog to the idiot Germans and perfidious bloody Sassenachs in Tarsi's command. He didn't give two hoots whether the treacherous wee shites survived the coming onslaught or not.

'These mountains Sandy, they fair tak' ye very breath away,' Davey Dunne commented, urging his nag beside the laird's shaggy-coated pony. Kerr glanced at the scout, the eager boy who had followed him from their hearth at Tullymallock almost a year before. Hard fights and long campaigns had turned boy to man, and he was glad to count him in his tail.

'Aye. My chest feels as if I've taken chill water straight from the burn.'

'And yet the peaks seem sun-glad enough. The glare makes my eyes water.'

Kerr chuckled at his perplexed companion, his narrow imagination quite over-awed by the spectacular Alpine scenery in which they had found themselves – fighting for strangers in strange lands.

'Did ye see he's sent his lassie away wi' us?' his son Angus enquired, his stubbled features raw as boiled leather in the stiff wind.

'Trust ye to mark her,' Davey Dunne chuckled. 'But I would have wagered she was on the skinny side for you Angus!'

Kerr glanced at his son.

Their unintentionally extended expedition had matured him faster than his boyhood companions, turning the brawling boy into a rather brooding adult. He laughed less and drank more, his black eyes following the women as they went to and fro about the camp attending to their chores and menfolk.

There were precious few girls for Angus to set his cap at – apart from the scraggy, knife-wielding whores who had followed the Germans down from their recruiting grounds in the north.

'Aye. I've seen more meat stuck on the point of a dirk.'

'Ye'd not say nay to her lady in waiting, though, eh Angus?'

The boy glanced from the grinning scout to his watchful father, anxious to keep his infatuation from his grievously scarred sire.

'I mean,' Davey corrected himself, 'Lang-ballocks has taken hisself off after his elder sister, so they say.'

Eldritch's absence had been common knowledge for weeks. Kerr raised an eyebrow, caught his son's furtive glance.

'And ye think to make sport with the younger when the man's away after the elder?' the reiver chief enquired with a sour chuckle.

'Och, she's the finest thing I've e'er seen walkin' upright,' Davey observed breezily, still intent on covering his friend's tracks, although Kerr had already marked where his son's affections lay. 'God's truth, she can't help her brother.'

'She's a damned clootie, just like her beanstalk of a brother,' Angus growled. 'Would a man get any peace, keeping such a woman?'

'He might not get much peace,' Davey cried, stifling a laugh. 'But he'd sleep soundly enough after she'd done wi' him!'

Kerr ignored the youngster's banter, concentrating on holding his son's glare.

'Angus, I've n'er been one for drawing pictures as well ye know. Ye'll find their holes quick enough, aye. Second from the back, yer on the right track.'

Davey Dunne barked with laughter at the chief's unexpectedly frank advice.

'But mark me now laddie, and you too Davey. James Eldritch is a shite and a hothead, who'd cut ye balls off wi'out lifting ye kilt.'

'Do we ride in fear o' that bastard whelp of a Pock-Pudding?' Angus asked, as if he had rehearsed the question in his own head a hundred times before.

'I ride in fear o' no man laddie. But I tell ye this. I'd leave his little sister out of my love-plans, if I were ye.'

Angus pursed his lips at this unfamiliar parental guidance, riding in silence for a while.

'Is it true Sandy, his big sister's no more than a common hoor?' the indefatigable scout enquired. 'I've heard it said about the camp as . . .'

'I've heard the scolds, Davey, and knowing a little of Master Eldritch's character, I'd say it was all too likely they are peas o' the same pod. But I'd not want ye repeating the same around the men. If he ever suspected ye minded his business that way, he'd kill ye for the thought alone.'

Angus grunted, anxious to prove he was not afraid of the

upstart Englishman. Why was it his father seemed so impressed with the arrogant bastard? Eldritch had bested him in a fair – or fair enough – fight. Is that why he went in fear of him now?

Kerr watched his son closely.

'Let me tell ye this boys. I've seen hard men and I've seen cold killers in ma time. But Eldritch is all dead and eaten-up inside,' he tapped his closely-quilted hauberk. 'He's more stone than man, and seeing things the way he does, ye cannae put much past him.'

Angus hawked and spat on the rocks.

'Charming,' Angelica commented, sitting back on the bench as the carriage rumbled and bounced along the appalling track. The chill air had stolen her breath, left her lungs wheezing and aching inside her racked chest. Merron smiled, reached over to tug the cloak up about her friend's shoulders. 'Just when you think he might actually begin to behave like a normal human being, he determines on reminding us all what a barbarian he is.'

'James was the same, at his age,' Merron observed, looking out of the slowly moving wagon at the Scots who formed the rearguard. She hadn't known the chief's son longer than a six-month, but he seemed to have grown a foot higher and two feet wider since her brother had carried him into Crow Hole the autumn before.

War and battle seemed to run as strongly in his veins as his beetle-browed father's. Angelica reckoned he was the most handsome man in the camp – with Merron's fanatically loyal brother away on his errands.

In truth, Angelica admired Eldritch's single-minded determination. It was common knowledge the *Transmarini* would have done anything to find (and save) his elder sister. It was less widely acknowledged that Eldritch had actually helped save his enemy Gueldres from the scaffold, simply in the belief the rogue knew something of her whereabouts.

She was not unusual in thinking Eldritch the most arrogantly handsome man on earth. But she knew she had no chance of cornering his fist-clenching affections. Not now.

The butcher Briconet had killed her, back on that blood-engrained table. He had broken her spirit and ruined her body, ravaged what little good looks she had ever possessed. Angelica had always impressed men with her high-spirited enthusiasms, her carefree determination to better their best efforts whether shooting a bow or telling a joke. Her infectious laugh and mischievous smile had lit up her plain features, helped men forget there were prettier women in the house.

But no more.

Worst of all, Angelica was acutely aware of her own state, body and soul. She knew she should try and rebuild herself from within, find some happiness in all this hurt and turmoil. But she seemed to lack the will to recover her former spirit. It danced in and out of her reach, bobbed before her like a fisherman's worm. Not even the effervescent Merron could lift her tormented soul, banish the mind-numbing mood swings which swept over her as regularly as the tides.

'I wish he'd come back,' Merron sighed. 'Your father's about ready to beat him around the camp with a broom handle.'

Her father was about ready to stab his absent captain in the heart, Angelica thought sourly.

'His affairs in France detain him,' she said impassively.

'I don't think he'll ever find her, Lillith, I mean. She would have to want to be found – and I can't imagine her waiting patiently for our dear brother to ride up and throw her over the back of his horse.'

'Then why did you let him go?' Angelica enquired.

'Did you expect me to stop him? Your father could have surrounded him with a hundred pikemen and James would have stolen out between their legs.'

Angelica chuckled, peering up at the white-tipped peaks which cast long shadows over the high road. Maybe he would at that.

She had stayed at the remote hospice once before, but she could only have been seven or eight at the time. Her father had detailed some local shepherds to help them find their destination, far above the clouds.

'If it's as strong as he says it is, why not dig the legion in around it?' Merron enquired. Her friend made herself as comfortable as possible against the jarring ride, gently shook her head.

'He could hold the hospice with a hundred men, but his orders say he has to keep the French out of the lower valley. They would simply march on past, if father retreated up here.'

'Then why *are* we retreating up here?'

'Because father might not be able to fulfil his orders, of course. He needs somewhere to run to, if he can't hold the valley.'

Alberto Tarsi had stared so long at the Swiss lines his eyes had watered, quite spoiling his view of their chaotic encampment.

The enemy forces had set down half a league beyond Mont Galliard, in a wide hollow surrounded on two sides by a tricky, boulder-strewn ridge. He had counted a dozen French banners and half as many Swiss. Their designs tended to be simpler, cruder: bears, bulls or boar's heads, crossed keys or simple crosses. Something even the dimmest-witted pikemen could recognise in the swirling shambles of battle.

Bayard's Gendarmes carried intricately-woven silken master-pieces, glittering gold and silver devices or vast flags portraying biblical events or some saintly miracle. But they would be blasted by shot, torn to shreds and trampled in blood just the same. He had spent hours watching their curious movements, trying to work out what grand strategy they were obeying.

They could not manoeuvre. They could not bring up any more guns without jamming the narrow pass completely. Tarsi racked his brain, trying to remember whether he had ever heard of any sheep trails in the mountains round about, some secret path they might be following even now, ready to attack him from behind. But he had lived in the pass for the best part of ten years. That rogue Savvi might have overlooked the rabbit tracks and snow paths, but he trusted to God that he, Tarsi, hadn't.

So what on God's earth were they waiting for?

Bayard had brought his usual contingent of super-heavy horsemen, immaculately-clad Gendarmes in silver armour, their ornate helmets wafted by the peacock plumes they had secured to the rims. They were armed with long lance and sword, and could be guaranteed to charge straight through most enemy forma-tions.

Most, but not all.

Tarsi had heard tales of Crécy and Agincourt. How the fantastical parades of posturing French nobility had been shot to ruin by massed bowmen in shit-splattered breeks. He would hardly have credited such a victory could be possible, if he hadn't seen Bayard's men routed by the very same tactics outside Mont Galliard the previous summer.

Eldritch's men had shot deliberately short, giving the French a taste of what was to come. Bayard's levies had not relished a second dose, turning their backs and stampeding into the packed ranks of the heavy cavalry following behind. But Eldritch was away in France now, sniffing out his bed-faggot of a sister, and he wasn't sure he could trust his men to fight so well – if at all – without him.

He lowered his perspective glass, biting his lower lip as he tried to imagine what Bayard was about. A sudden charge with all his heavy horse? A massed assault by his degenerate Swiss pikemen? Or perhaps an earth-shattering bombardment?

Whatever Bayard had in mind, he would have imagined the Chevalier would have tried something by now. What the devil was he thinking of, waiting so long?

Prolonging the agony, Tarsi presumed.

The rattle of hoofbeats on the rocky ground brought Tarsi from his tent in a trice, hand on hilt ready to defend himself. His field headquarters had been set up in a disused toll-house, a short walk from the main trenches. His men had toiled for days, gouging out the living rock beneath their feet, burrowing like worms into the bones of the valley. Pikeman, archer and arquebusier alike had lent a blistered hand, digging out deeper and deeper fighting pits. The rock and spoil they had excavated had been tipped over the parapets, raising the walls to five or six feet in height.

But here were riders – a score at least – coming up the pass behind them as he had feared. The intruders arrived from the south in a cloud of yellow grit, having cantered up the toll road from Aosta. Tarsi shielded his eyes, trying to recognise their emblems, as his bodyguard of Spanish sword and buckler men hurried to form a new defence about the squat stone outbuildings. He breathed a heartfelt sigh of relief as he recognised the double-headed eagle motif of the Empire, flapping like a Norse raven above them. Some princeling from Imperial headquarters outside Milan, come to shout a few meaningless orders before hurrying back to the rear, most probably. Tarsi paused, realised the troops were also carrying smaller household devices identical to his own regimental colours, stowed away in his claustrophobic quarters.

He searched their dust-racked faces as the men reined in, but failed to recognise his own chief Mounier. A tall, thin youth dismounted with a grunt, looking about the bustling camp as if he expected to find Turkish carpets and a steaming bath waiting for him. The newcomer spotted Tarsi, standing with his hands on his hips regarding him with weary scorn. The boy strode straight towards him, a pair of cadaverous clerks hurrying at his side, straightening his expensive cloak and whispering advice in his ear. Tarsi thought he recognised one of the men. Belladonna . . . no, Belatavicci. He had come to Mont Galliard the summer before, as part of an embassy from Villefranco. Don't say this strutting turkeycock was . . .

'Ah, Tarsi, there you are!'

The flustered boy came to a halt before him, gave the old soldier a contemptuously brief glance and then peered over his shoulder towards the enemy encampment further down the valley. The sight of so many men and guns within spitting distance seemed to unnerve him further.

'What are you doing here?' the newcomer asked indignantly. 'I expected to find you at Nus, not camped out in the middle of the valley!'

Tarsi took a menacing step closer, thrusting his weather-ravaged features straight into the boy's face.

'And who might you be, riding into my camp without a by-your-leave?' The newcomer stared as Tarsi poked him in the chest with a stubby forefinger.

Belatavicci gave an embarrassed cough and favoured Tarsi with a gap-toothed smile, tugging at his master's sleeve to whisper an urgent introduction.

'My lord Duke,' he cried, straightening up as far as he was able given his habitually hunched stance, 'may I present Seigneur Alberto Tarsi, champion of Margaret of Savoy and former guardian of the high valley, acting commander of your army!'

'Army?' Tarsi snorted. 'Six hundred knaves babbling away in a dozen different languages? If that's an army I'm a . . . Duke, you say?'

'Aye, Duke!'

'My lord Gerhard has but recently inherited the title from the late lamented Lodovico,' the obsequious wraith purred. Tarsi modified his expression slightly, took one step away from his new liege lord. A spoilt brat with a moist eye and a quivering chin? Was this the hairy-palmed spavin who had sent for Angelica's hand in marriage? A visit from a rejected son-in-law was all he needed.

'Ah yes, I understand now. But my lord of Mounier left for Villefranco a fortnight ago. Has he not arrived to offer his sword in person?'

Gerhard smirked.

'My Lord of Mounier is no more,' he said levelly. Belatavicci inclined his head, clearly stricken by grief. Tarsi tensed.

'He lost his footing and fell from the tower,' the Duke went on, as if it was hardly a matter worth discussing.

'Baldassare, fell from a tower?' Tarsi echoed, stung by the unexpected news. Surely they hadn't ridden all that way to jest with him?

'Overcome with grief, he tripped and fell headlong to his death,' Gerhard confirmed, flicking his wrist in careless sympathy. Tarsi frowned, trying to imagine the bull-necked brute overcome by anything or anyone.

'And so of course it falls to me, his only surviving kinsman, to assume command of the men he left behind.'

Tarsi took a moment to realise the idiot youth meant his own men.

'And so I ask again, Seigneur Tarsi, how it is I find you dug in across the valley when all military prudence would suggest you evacuate to the nearest walled town forthwith?'

'Your pardon my lord,' Tarsi retorted. 'But I . . . that is, we, have orders from Imperial general Von Huff himself, orders which supersede those of his respective regimental commanders.'

Gerhard raised his pale eyebrows. He wasn't the coward so many correspondents had gleefully reported him to be, but he hadn't expected to find his wayward troops quite so close to the front line. Or under the apparent control of this ill-mannered brute who hadn't even remembered to bow his head before his master.

'What sort of a fool orders six hundred men to attempt to hold so many without the benefit of walls, gate and ditches?'

'As you see my lord. We have been busy constructing a wall.'

'Of sorts! But why here? Right under the guns of that castle?'

'We are well out of range of their guns, my lord.'

'Oh ho, they've already taken a few potshots, no doubt?'

'No my lord. They are professional soldiers who wouldn't bother wasting the ammunition. I know the range of those cannon because I put them there. Mont Galliard belongs to me and all its culverins and sakers with it, my lord,' Tarsi added as an insolent afterthought.

Gerhard twitched, biting his lip in agitation. He inclined his head as his fawning counsellor whispered into his master's ear.

'Ah yes. That Tarsi, of course. I believe my father sent enquiring after your daughter's hand.'

'Sadly, the match was not considered suitable,' Tarsi said, ready to throttle the swine if he made any disparaging comment about his daughter. Gerhard must have sensed his mood, giving the Italian a cold smile.

'Indeed. Well, I'm here now, perhaps you had better show me your maps, point out your dispositions. To tell the truth, Tarsi, I can't understand why the enemy hasn't already swept down and marched all over your silly little trench.'

Tarsi's generous lips curled back from his teeth, but he modified his expression into a beatific smile. The little runt had it about right, after all.

Why hadn't the bloody Swiss attacked?

By the Castello Villefranco

♦

Jeremiah Hobby found his master with his boots propped up on Duke Gerhard's unmade bed, enjoying a well-earned rest. Eldritch couldn't remember the last time he had slept on so fine a mattress. The sheets were damp and reeked of mould and stale sweat, but a bed was a bed.

'Where's her ladyship?' Hobby enquired, flicking through the paperwork Eldritch had left out on the dresser. It was all in some kind of code that hadn't meant a thing to either of them.

'Helping with the wounded. She says that corporal with the black eye has got a concussion. The other bugger won't last the night, not with an arrow in his bowels.'

Hobby grunted acknowledgment.

'She's still not speaking to you then?'

'I asked her to take a look at Gerhard's papers, but he's either burnt the top copies and left that trash for us to sort through, or his handwriting is worse than yours.'

Like most of the soldiers in Lord Howath's warband, Hobby couldn't read or write. The broad-shouldered sergeant picked up a half-eaten loaf from the dresser and tore himself a chunk.

'What a set of sacks, eh? Two men to storm a castle. They'll make a good song of it, when we get back.'

Eldritch knew full well his sergeant was anxious to finish their mission and get back to the camp – the hard soldier's life he had followed since he was little more than a strapping child. He knew Eldritch had taken him on a wild goose chase halfway around France, in a futile search for his shape-changing sister. They had come close this time, aye, but were no nearer to clipping her wings just yet.

'There's not much to sing about,' Eldritch said modestly. 'Two dozen cravens, too drunk to hold a sword straight. The moment we were indoors I knew we'd take them.'

'Oh aye. I never had any doubt.' Hobby agreed around a mouthful of half-chewed dough. 'You could tell they were pissed as cats just listening to 'em. They've quietened down now though.'

The bewildered garrison had been stripped of their arms and locked in the main hall to cool off. Eldritch had rolled an extra barrel of brandy in for them – to ensure they stayed drunk and therefore pliable. If they sobered up for a moment, they might remember they outnumbered their unexpected guests by twenty and more to two, and try another fall.

Eldritch didn't want any more bloodshed. They had killed and maimed as many enemy soldiers as necessary and no more. Neither of them would ever boast of the triumph. Their two-man attack had been quick and deliberately brutal, calculated to knock the fight out of the Villefrancans rather than kill them.

Serpents like Briconet could say what they liked – the Ride wasn't made up of cold blooded butcherboys.

The morose captain hadn't had time to regret or repent. He had a fortress to secure and a hundred and more hostile inhabitants to worry about. Eldritch had scrutinised the domestic staff, ensuring the surviving soldiers had been carefully segregated from the civilian labourers. He had interrogated the cooks, the stable hands and the old woman who did the laundry, seeking information about his sister. They had all heard of the White Rabbit, marvelling at her rosy cheeks, fine breasts and shapely legs as he sat and seethed. They agreed the girl had left some time the previous morning, but didn't know where she might be headed.

Somewhere towards the wars, was the best they could estimate.

'So what do we do now? Ride on into Italy?' Hobby enquired hopefully.

'I don't know . . . I've been thinking,' Eldritch admitted, stretching his long arms above his head, unusually unsure of himself. 'Maybe we ought to remember our allegiance while we may.'

Hobby looked bewildered. 'What about Lillith?'

'You heard them sergeant, she might be anywhere. Novara, Milan, Turin. Charles might have mobilised one hundred thousand men to fight the French.' Hobby held his tongue, well aware of the point the distracted captain was making. 'Without some further word, we'd spend the rest of our days in idle pursuit. Face facts: the trail's cold.'

The sergeant nodded ruefully. 'So it comes to me it might be meet to make ourselves useful while we may.'

'Go back and find Tarsi, you mean?' Eldritch shook his head. 'We don't need to find Tarsi. Let him come to us.' Eldritch held his hands up. 'We have taken a fortress for him, a fortress which had been about to fall into the hands of the French.'

'But they all say Gerhard's got cold feet and buggered off to join the Emperor-Elect. How can we capture our own side's castle?'

'Briconet would have been here long before Imperial head-quarters could have organised a relief force. At this moment, we're the only two men between him and their outposts further along the coast.'

Hobby had no grasp of their geographic or military position.

'So we stay here, and stop Briconet getting in. Just the two of us.'

'Briconet's no soldier. And all the best troops are away to the north. You saw the stamp of his men, those fools coming after us with crossbows. We've arms enough to keep them busy for a few days.'

Hobby looked bemused by the captain's strategy.

'But we ambushed them. Briconet would be laying siege to us. And two men can't hold half a mile of walls, no matter what arms they've left behind,' the big man observed doubtfully. Eldritch stroked his chin, his darkly handsome features creasing in concern.

'No, that's true enough,' he admitted. Hobby sighed. 'So one of us,' Eldritch went on, 'is going to have to go and fetch Tarsi.'

'Fetch him from Nus? That must be fifty leagues and more!' Hobby guessed wildly.

'Around that. But without siege guns, Briconet will never get in here. Given a good garrison, I'd hold this place for weeks!'

'But we haven't got a good garrison: there's me and you and what's her face . . .'

'Charlotte, Countess du Lac.'

The Englishmen looked up, startled by her sudden appearance in the doorway. Eldritch lifted his boots from the bed and scratched his buttocks, glad to see she had returned of her own accord.

'How are they?' he enquired awkwardly. The Countess had borrowed apron and gown from the garrison's laundry while she attended the wounded. The worn clothing had been smeared and splattered with blood; her arms were stained red to the elbow. Her youthful features were shiny with fatigue, pinched in anger and disgust.

'The man you shot died just now. Corporal Hulin, well.'

Eldritch looked up as the bandaged Frenchman stepped out from behind his lover, a loaded crossbow cradled in his arms. Another soldier moved to their left and another to their right. Both had armed themselves with arquebuses, the spluttering match cords filling the Duke's apartment with the bitter incense of war.

Eldritch was too astonished to move. Hobby was still chewing his bread, hardly aware the tables had been so completely and utterly turned.

The Frenchmen advanced into the room warily, weapons held at the ready. More followed, weighed down in mail and breastplates and bits of armour they had recovered from the lower floors of the castle. The Countess grinned, her blue eyes glittering with triumph and spite.

'So, the mighty Lord Eldritch, caught with his breeks about his ankles.'

Eldritch could feel his cheeks flushing in mortification.

He could hardly believe it.

She had betrayed him!

'Don't even trouble to think about jumping for your sword,' she sneered, stepping forward nimbly to lift the baldrick and blade in question from the end of the bed. 'And you, you great oaf, unhitch your sword and throw it down.'

'Me?'

'Aye, you,' the Countess snapped. Eldritch jumped to his feet, straight into a hedge of sword blades and spear points. The crossbowmen squinted down their weapons as if he were a stag on some distant hillside. The arquebusiers raised their clumsy weapons, hands cocked about their awkwardly-shaped triggers. Their glowing match sizzled and spluttered above the black pans of powder.

'You let this rabble back out?'

'I did! That chicken-witted oaf left the keys on the table!' she cried, practically drooling with indignation. 'Did you think you could hurl me about like a sack of refuse, stamp me into the dirt and expect me to trot along behind you like some lapdog? Have you no idea who I am?' she asked, as incredulous as ever.

Eldritch tried to hold her eye, cursing his own careless arrogance. He had hardly given the girl's loyalty a second thought, assuming their love-making had tied their destinies together – despite their differences on the road. She had tried to alert their enemies: what had she expected them to do, slap her wrist?

His brain reeled. Words and phrases evaporating as he stood forlorn before her. Stripped of his weapons, at her mercy.

'Kill the English bastards,' the corporal urged out of the side of his mouth.

'No! I told you. We take the castle in the name of King Francis, we erase the dishonour you have done to his cause. But we keep these two for Briconet!'

Hobby recognised the dreaded name, glanced at his captain.

'Aye, let the stormcrows hang him out to dry!'

The rejuvenated garrison seemed split on what to do with their prisoners. Charlotte glared at them, grasped at the vengeful corporal's tunic sleeve.

'We send word to Briconet, declare for the king. He'll take these murdering rogues off your hands!'

The corporal seemed reluctant to let the terrifying killers live a moment longer, dreading the captain's black-eyed stare.

'Charlotte, I meant no harm to you,' Eldritch hissed, the full magnitude of the disaster beginning to sink in. 'You wouldn't, you couldn't stand by and let . . .'

'Silence! You murdered my fiancé, the Duke de Milhaud. You kidnapped me and carried me all the way from Marseille. Now you expect me to pardon your crimes, turn my back on your filthy banditry?' Her livid features had paled, but her tautly-stretched skin seemed lit from within.

Her eyes burned with feverish hatred.

'Fiancé? Charlotte,' Eldritch exclaimed, his bowels turned to ice by her barely restrained fury. 'I meant . . .'

'You meant? You mean nothing! Take them away, throw them in the *oubliette*!'

Hobby backed against the wall, disliking the sound of their destination. The *oubliette* was no more than a scrape dug in the deepest dungeon, a narrow coffin with rusty bars, barely big enough in which to crouch upright.

'Get 'em out of it!' The two Englishmen were surrounded, menaced by gleaming blades. Resistance would have meant instant death.

157

'For the sake of Christ, Charlotte,' Eldritch snarled. 'What did you want from me?'

'What do I want from you? Hah! You think about that, while you're holed up with that stinking brute of a sergeant! Get them out of my sight, and send your messengers to me, right away!'

The soldiers, well used to dreary service under lacklustre lords, had relished the girl's energy, and reacted to her blood-curdling encouragements like gasping flowers after a drought.

'At once, Countess!'

She stood aside as her new centurions bundled the protesting English out of the room – kicking and punching the dumb-founded strangers down the stairs.

'Charlotte, for pity's sake!' Eldritch yodelled, his anguished shout rebounding about the tower.

The Countess had given them new belief, inspiring their dormant energies turning beaten curs to warriors.

She had begun quietly enough, moving between the wounded men in the main hall, holding a hissing lantern over their gaping wounds. They had hardly dared catch her eye, as she stitched cuts and doused dry blows with vinegar and mustard poultices. The fit men had backed off, ashamed they had surrendered themselves before they had shed so much as a drop of their own blood.

And then she had become bolder, stalking in and out of their cowering ranks. The grubby slip of a girl had turned on them, scorning their pitiful efforts to defend their master's castle. She had deliberately humiliated every man by invoking the memory of their slaughtered friends. She had spat on the floor, indignantly enquiring how they would have the gall to look a true man in the eye ever again.

The sharp-tongued Countess warned them there was but one way they might erase their ignominious record, to save their questionable manhood. By rising from their pit of drunken despondency and striking back at their arrogant captors.

She had loosened bonds and unlocked doors, shown the blinking prisoners to the chapel where Hobby had so carelessly stowed their arms. They had followed her as if she were a talisman come to life, a magical maiden who would protect them from all hurts. She had barely been able to hold them back, as they crept up the stairs after their unsuspecting guests.

The sudden hubbub died down as the prisoners were frog-marched across the courtyard towards the dungeons. Pale corpses had been draped on carts ready for burial. Wailing womenfolk and screeching children threw dung and brandished sticks as the escort hurried the culprits towards the temporary sanctuary of the south tower.

The Countess sighed, her breath hanging in a silvery veil before her. Her heart was racing, cold fingers trembling.

She had shown *Monsieur* Eldritch; she had taught the knave a lesson he would never forget. Nobody had ever made the mistake of taking the Countess du Lac for granted. Treading on her back as if she were a scullery maid busy over a courtyard step!

The messengers hurried up the steps, hardly daring to approach the furiously pacing noblewoman. They fell to one knee as if she were the Queen Mother, lowering their heads.

'Up on your feet, fools! You've a hard ride this night.'

Abandando Briconet was well used to smoking braziers and unearthly shrieks, but the din His Majesty's blacksmiths were making was quite beyond his experience. He stood beside the door of the vast armoury, choking on the sulphurous smokes belching from the busy forges. The heat and noise were indescribable. Most of the older hands had long since lost their hearing and moved about the hellish arena without being unduly troubled by the earth-shattering thump of the hammers or the thumbscrew screech of tortured metal. Iron bars were clattered and shaped, held up to experienced eyes before being laid back on anvils and clattered again. Sword blades glowing cherry red were plunged into barrels of filthy water, turning the tortured steel the darkest blue.

Steam billowed, smoke belched. Men sweated.

But still Briconet was intent on staying, overseeing the rebirth of Duke Gerhard's deadly engine.

The Royal Armouries had already been placed on full alert, beating out gun barrels large and small, hammering ploughshares to spearheads to supply the vast forces Francis was about to dispatch into Italy. Extra hands had been taken on to help haul charcoal and pig iron up from the dockside warehouses. Hundreds more were busy loading newly-minted weapons onto the wagons waiting patiently in the courtyard below. Fifty grindstones were in constant use, turning dull edges into biting blades.

The vast arsenal resembled a termite mound, illuminated by the ghastly glare of furnace and brazier. Spouts of sparks danced and died in the charged air, the throat-rasping winds which scoured the monstrous hall like the breath of hell itself. A thousand and more lost souls wandered in the half-light, hauling, chaining, pouring, beating, grinding and hammering.

An endless crescendo to turn the mildest man to a gibbering ruin. Briconet covered his ears against the appalling clamour, a sickly smile stretching his thin face.

'We have the final drawings to hand, my lord,' Armand du Galliano, the King's master gunner, cupped his mouth and roared. 'Our engineers have broken the prototype down into the constituent parts, and are quite confident they can rebuild the engine.'

'What?'

The exasperated gunner drew the inquisitor towards the door, nodding his soot-smeared head to excuse his untoward behaviour. Laying hands on an agent of the Inquisition?

'Ah, that's better. It's hotter than the pits of hell in there!'

'Indeed!' Briconet cried, exultant in the face of such raw energy. The King's workshops had reminded him of Pompei, all their puny human endeavour dwarfed by the invincible power of Vesuvius. Only this time the fearsome forces had been harnessed by man's ingenuity . . .

'I was just saying, my lord, the designs ought to be ready for you by noon tomorrow.'

'Designs? All you give me is paper and crayon! You have sketched the designs well enough, du Galliano. I want the engine ready by noon, not a set of pretty pictures!'

The master-gunner blinked, unused to being addressed by cackling gnomes in dirt-stained robes.

'You saw my credentials, du Galliano. This project is a matter of the utmost importance to His Majesty. Either your people will roll out the wagon at noon tomorrow in time for my departure for the east, or your head will be rolling in the sawdust! Do we understand one another?'

'Of course my lord. Tomorrow at noon.'

The mud-splattered messenger stared at the floor while the inquisitor scanned the brief dispatch he had carried from Villefranco. He had been ushered into Briconet's quarters not far from the Royal Armoury, a gloomy, damp-smelling cell illuminated by a guttering candle. The inquisitor frowned, held the note closer to the flickering flame.

'What? The Countess sends word . . . what of Sourris? What word of Captain Druchet?'

The messenger looked blank, his lower lip trembling in the presence of the dreaded agent.

'Did they not return to Villefranco under my flag?'

'No my lord. That is . . . Yes, they did have a flag. There was one other with them, a rather short, tubby man with . . .'

'A fat man in a plain robe, bearing my arms?'

'Just so my lord. But he fell off his horse, when the Englishmen attacked us.'

'Englishmen?'

'A score of them my lord. They made the fat man talk for them, tricked their way past our guards and into the courtyard.'

'Where you fought them to a standstill and imprisoned the survivors?' Briconet read.

'In the name of the King, my lord.'

The inquisitor blinked in bewilderment, as utterly perplexed as he had ever been in his long, arid life. What on earth was going on at Villefranco? The half-forgotten backwater seemed to have acquired some bizarre life of its own in recent days. The insignificant Duchy had become the hub of an entire universe of intrigue and outrage. Every stone they turned had revealed some unexpected secret, another puzzling stitch in a sinister tapestry of murder and deception.

'My assistant Sourris, you say he arrived with these English?'

'We would never have let them past the gate otherwise, my lord.'

'And no sign of his escort? I sent six good men with him!'

'Most likely done in by the English, my lord. We had a terrible time . . .'

'No doubt! And the Countess . . . how did she manage to escape their diabolical clutches?'

'She . . . er . . . must have freed herself, my lord. I don't exactly know the whys and wherefores of how she got there.'

'But she has them . . . under lock and key?'

'Just the two of them, my lord. We killed the rest.'

Briconet raised his gleaming eye from the note, electrified by the unanticipated development. His old enemy, that scowling knave Eldritch, imprisoned not thirty leagues from his own headquarters! What had he been playing at, leaving such a trail of blood and destruction across Southern France? The rogue had left clear tokens a blind man could have followed.

'And Duke Gerhard has fled, crossed the border into Italy?'

'He had left before the English launched their attack, my lord,' the messenger confirmed.

Briconet tugged his meagre lip, trying to pick some sense from the anarchy the kidnapped Countess reported.

According to the astonishly clear-headed Countess, this fiend Eldritch had travelled to France to confront the Duke de Milhaud, whom he believed to have seduced his sister Lillith.

This was sound intelligence. Eldritch had never made any secret of his determination to track down the wayward girl.

But the rest of her letter was a tissue of half-truth or outright lie. She claimed the two of them had fought a duel and that Eldritch had killed him. But Briconet had already concluded Milhaud had been stark naked at the time of his death, killed by a dry blow to the back of the head rather than the sword thrust to the chest one would have anticipated.

She claimed Eldritch had kidnapped her and ridden off into the night. And yet the landlord of the inn at Roquevaire had told him he had assumed the pair of them had been man and wife!

Her memory must have played tricks on her because she had not mentioned how she came to escape their clutches in time to organise the resistance at the Castello Villefranco.

The wretched brat was lying through her teeth, no matter what allegiance she claimed to have remembered now.

'The Countess holds two prisoners, and the rest are dead?'

'Assuredly, my lord.'

'And she holds Villefranco in the name of His Majesty King Francis?'

'Until relieved, my lord.'

'Then we will relieve her, just as soon as my forces are readied for the march!'

Briconet dismissed the messenger and unrolled his map.

He stared at the faded contours and jagged borderlines, trying to decide how these latest developments fitted the equally complex puzzle he had uncovered.

The candle had flickered and died long before the inquisitor had come to any conclusion.

By the Castello Villefranco

✦

In normal circumstances the prisoners packed into the main dungeon would have been using the *oubliette* as a latrine, urinating over the unfortunate occupants rather than fouling their own cell. It was not as if the poor wretches locked up in the barred coffin beneath their feet would ever emerge to take issue with them. Once sealed inside the *oubliette* the only way out was in a sack – and only then when the reek of decomposing flesh had become too much for the turnkeys whose duties took them into the deepest dungeons.

The hellish pit – no more than a yard deep by six feet or so long – was cramped enough for averagely-built prisoners. But Eldritch was well over six feet in height and his grumbling sergeant considerably larger again. They were packed in the filthy hole like rats in a sack, hardly able to scratch the lice which swarmed over their torn clothing without doing each other an injury. Hobby had curled himself up as best he could, his vast bulk pressed against one mouldy wall and his legs tucked in behind his captain's back. Eldritch was crouching with his knees drawn up into his chest, a demon foetus up to his ears in evil-smelling slime.

The Villefrancans had delighted in thrusting them down into the pit, kicking them in the head and stamping on their out-stretched fingers as the two of them fought to escape the barbarous hole. They had finally beaten the Englishmen into the reeking coffin and slammed the gate down on top of them. The heavy brass lock was covered in a film of verdigris, but the elderly mechanism was effective enough. Eldritch had tried to pick it using a bone fragment he had fished from the human refuse which lined the cell, but the ancient lock had not yielded to his clumsy tinkering. He had given up in disgust, his stomach heaving at the appalling stench of death and decay his furious excavations had disturbed.

Previous occupants had scratched their names in the stone-work or kept primitive calendars of their last days. Crude five-bar gates marked their tormented sentences. None of them seemed to have counted much beyond a week or two. That was no surprise, Eldritch reflected bitterly. Although prisoners could scrounge scraps from the fortunates imprisoned in the cell above and suck moisture from the slimy walls, few could endure the terrible punishment for long. The long-forgotten inhabitants had simply curled up in the filth and died.

'The fornicating mare. The hell-spawned frog-bitch. The cheating whore. The leprous merkin . . .'

Hobby's litany of abuse had gone on for an hour or more and he had not repeated himself once. Eldritch didn't need to be told who the sergeant was talking about.

But there was nobody there to hear his furious insults, to finish him off with a quick spear-thrust through the bars. The dungeon above was empty apart from the scurrying, hurrying rats. They seemed to be able to find food enough in the squalor. Even the young squealers were the size of the average household cat. Eldritch had been forced to let go of the bars for fear of being bitten by the teeming vermin.

'Good Christ, what were we thinking of, breaking in to this shit-pit?' Hobby asked for the hundredth time. 'We should have cut the bastards down while we had the chance. Come back and fight, you puke-fucks, you shag-arses!' Hobby yelled.

Eldritch closed his eyes, his body racked with cramps, his mind in a black turmoil of anger and despair. He had never felt such all-encompassing, soul-swallowing terror, not even in the bloodiest battle back on the borders.

He stared at the bone-white scratches in the walls, the futile echoes of long-dead occupants. Maybe in a hundred years' time some sorry bastard would be reading his name off the wall, wondering who on earth he was, what appalling atrocity he had committed to deserve such a cruel death.

For surely this was a short-cut to hell itself.

'I'll wring her scrawny neck, I'll twist her guts out, I'll rip her eyes out and piss in the sockets!'

'For the sake of Holy Christ, Hobby, will you stow that moaning and let me think?' Eldritch exclaimed, goaded beyond endurance by the giant's monotonous complaints. 'You can call her all the names under the sun, but it's our fault she acted as she did!'

'Ours? Yours maybe!'

'Mine then! I dragged her along, I should have . . .'

'You should have cut the little polecat's throat!'

'Well maybe I should at that,' Eldritch breathed, trying to calm his tormented nerves. 'But we're not dead yet, and I doubt if Briconet will miss a chance to toy with us a little further.'

'Ah, so I'm to look on the bright side! A couple of hours answering the inquisitor's questions, it'll be a light relief after this!'

'They'll have to let us out if he wants to get his hands on us. That's when we'll make our move!'

'Move? I'll be lucky if I ever move again,' Hobby wailed. Eldritch was stung to hear the fearless giant on the verge of blubbering. He lashed out in mortification, jabbing and pounding at the trapped sergeant as he lay cramped and helpless beside him.

'Ah! Get off! Stop thrashing, damn you, or I'll wring your neck!'

Eldritch subsided, panting hoarsely in the filthy, stinking cell. He rubbed his fists into his eyes, biting his lip so hard a trickle of blood ran into his snot-plastered stubble.

'We'll get another chance. They couldn't leave us here if they wanted to,' he rasped, praying to God it was true.

The Countess managed to endure the torment of their dreadful imprisonment for six hours.

Six miserable, lonely hours which seemed to drag like dog days as she paced to and fro in Duke Gerhard's ransacked apartment, as alone as she had ever been in her short and vacuous existence. She had been itching to punish the upstart English the same as the rest of them. She had relished the prospect of listening to them beg for their lives. But the harsh reality of their imprisonment had slowly drained her anger.

They had not grovelled, they had fought like tigers in a trap. She had winced as her newly-inspired garrison beat and kicked the intruders into the *oubliette*, prodding them down into the pit with the butts of their weapons. Charlotte had hurried back to the main keep, terrified their incredulous screeching would turn her head once more. She had not trusted herself to remain in the south tower.

Corporal Hulin had assured her they would come to no further harm. 'Let them lie there and rot. Not even that shape-changing demon can squeeze himself out of that pass,' the heavily bandaged soldier had leered.

She hoped the guards would let them alone. The Countess had only taken one quick peek at their prison before the fearsome stink had driven her back into the passage with her sleeve over her mouth. The girl shivered, bit at her thumbnail as she imagined their ghastly torment. The wind whistled about the old castle, finding out the little kinks and cracks in the stonework. The lamps flickered in the sudden draughts.

Charlotte took a deep breath and stalked towards the door.

Enough was enough.

Hulin was a short, squat soldier with dark, cropped hair sprinkled with grey. An old retainer, well used to garrison duty in the backwater Duchy and furious his gentle existence had been so violently interrupted. Eldritch had knocked him down twice, left him with a splitting headache, missing teeth and a faceful of ugly, wine-coloured bruises. The young lass had smelled nice, leaning over as she bandaged his wounds. If he'd stuck his tongue out he could have licked the sweet sweat off her bubbies, pressed up and out by the constricting bodice.

But she was a lady, a Countess, he reckoned.

And it didn't do to go making sport with gentlewomen, not even when the whole world had been turned upside down.

Aye, the old master had snuffed out and the younger had buggered off somewheres – but they would be back, sure as eggs was eggs. Them or some other smarmy swine in fancy armour. She had already sent riders to Marseille, so the stormcrows wouldn't be away long. He'd better mind his manners, or he'd end up in the *oubliette* alongside those butchering English bastards.

In the meantime the corporal intended to make the most of his opportunity, his chance to take charge of the castle he had served so faithfully, so long.

He certainly looked the part. Hulin had found fine new clothes in the looted apartments up in the main tower, rich velvets and fur-trimmed cloaks which weighed his arms down like sheets of lead torn from a church roof. He had lifted ornate swords from the armoury and struck poses before an ancient, flyblown looking glass in the Duke's chamber. He had drunk their wine and eaten his fill – and no stroppy mare of a countess was going to tell him how to run affairs now.

'You want to have a word with them?' Hulin crowed, glancing over his shoulder at the bemused soldiers who shared his vigil.

The watchers were sprawled around a flaming brazier in the guardhouse, hardly bothering to take more than the occasional glance out over the battlements.

The Countess du Lac raised her grubby chin, a fine young chicken even if her linen had been borrowed from the garrison wash-house. 'Has that dry blow affected your hearing, Corporal? It is essential I interrogate those rogues forthwith. It is obvious they weren't acting alone.'

Hulin fingered his jaw.

'We've seen no sign of their friends,' he remarked. 'And besides, Briconet'll have it all out of them in a moment or two.'

'Well that's as maybe. But I command here, not you.'

It was an outright challenge.

The corporal bristled, squaring his shoulders beneath his smart new tunic as he wondered whether he dared call her bluff. His competence had been called into question by a mere strip of a girl. What was he going to do about it?

'Oh yes?' he growled.

'And as such,' she went brazenly on, 'I will have to explain how it was these Englishmen took the fortress from its loyal garrison. Remind me how many of them perished in the assault. A hundred, fifty, a dozen? Perhaps you would like to explain the details to Monsieur Briconet yourself?' the Countess enquired sweetly. Hulin's bruised eye twitched as he contemplated this unpleasant scenario.

'No, my lady. You're in charge,' he growled.

'Excellent. Now open the door.'

Eldritch heard the nerve-rasping squeal as the heavy door was thrust back over the matted straw. A triangle of yellow light illuminated their dreary prison, turning the seeping slime on the walls from black to emerald green. They shielded their eyes as the turnkeys stamped into the dungeon, raising their lamps to check on their iron-jawed trap. Eldritch squinted through the gleaming bars, watched the dim figures make way for the girl. She was clutching a scented handkerchief to her pretty nose to keep the worst of the reek away. Her features were pinched, shining unhealthily in the eerie half-light.

'Charlotte. Thank God!' he cried, hoarse with relief.

'Don't get your hopes up you murdering ape! You're not going' nowhere save down!'

167

The guard's leering comrades guffawed, their ugly laughter rebounding around the dank cell.

'Have the captain brought out and chained to the wall. I can't talk to him crouched down there,' the Countess snapped, her imperious tone smothered somewhat by her handkerchief.

'Open it?'

'Surely he's not going to get past you a second time?' she retorted, removing her gag for a moment, but swiftly replacing it as the stench overwhelmed its feeble fragrance. The girl heaved, holding on to the grinning corporal's arm. Hulin smirked.

'Go ahead. He'll not get far, even if we stood aside and gave him a head start!'

'Cooped up in there, he'll be lucky if he can raise an eyebrow!'

Eldritch watched the guards bend down and wrestle with the heavy lock. A bandy-legged brute in a tasselled tunic seemed to have the key ring attached to his belt. The little corporal bent down and lifted the heavy grille, flung it back with a curse. Eldritch straightened up with a wince, his cramped limbs turned to burning jelly by his fearful confinement.

'Steady now!'

'Watch him, he's quicker than a striking snake!'

Spearpoints and swordblades glinted under his nose. He felt himself being hauled from the cage and laid out on the straw like an eel wriggling free from a crab-pot. He worked his shrieking muscles, ignoring the ferocious smells which rose from the filthy carpet of straw he disturbed.

'That's it matey, stretch 'em while you can! Briconet knows a few tricks for easing aching joints, eh Peppin?'

They got hold of his damp jerkin and hauled him over the straw. The corporal almost dragged his arm out of his socket as he clamped a manacle about his wrist, tugged on the chain to ensure the captain was secure.

'There you are m'lady. Trussed up like a tender pullet, just for you.' He gave the Englishman a spiteful back-heel.

Eldritch cursed, blinking in the hurtful lantern light as he tried to pick Charlotte's familiar features out from the gloomy corner into which she had retreated. The turnkey lifted the grille and threw it back in place over the grimly staring sergeant. Hobby took the opportunity to stretch his legs a little, but his shoulders were still brushing the rim either side of the narrow pit.

'It is well. Leave us.'

'I don't know whether . . .'

'Leave us! Do you imagine I am going to discuss matters of national import before scoundrels like you? Pray to God I don't decide to tell Briconet all about your craven trickery!'

Hulin paused, stung by the rebuke and acutely unsure of himself. He was used to taking orders, not deciding their worth for himself.

'We'll be at the door, in case he gives you any trouble.'

'He won't.'

He lay there for long moments, his back arched, long legs cramped by agonising bouts of pins and needles. He worked his shoulder muscles, barely able to talk as he gasped and grimaced.

'The *oubliette* seems to have reminded you of your manners, at least,' she scolded, pacing the cell just out of the captain's reach.

'It would make the devil himself mend his ways,' Eldritch agreed, rubbing the circulation back into his calf muscles.

'And you. Has it mended your ways?'

'Of course,' Eldritch rasped. 'I see now . . . I see I was wrong. To bind you.'

'Bind me, gag me, hurl me in the mud. That ape you call sergeant stood on my back!'

'I know all that was done to you and I'm sorry for it. I was sorry at the time and I'm doubly sorry now.'

'I thought perhaps you might be,' Charlotte sneered.

'But the truth of it . . . Charlotte you must remember why I came here. Why I left the regiment and came to France, an enemy state.'

Charlotte paused, still furious but fascinated by his sudden confession. She doubted she had heard him utter so many words at once.

'I came here to find my sister.'

'Ah, *Le Lapin Blanc!* I was wondering when she would raise her head again! You mean to use her existence as an excuse for your own foul behaviour, is that it? How many people have you killed so far, searching for this fornicating bitch of a sister of yours, eh? Milhaud was a fool and a drunk to boot, but you killed him with no more thought than you would thumb out a bedlouse! How many died so you could get in here? Three, four, ten? How many more are going to have to die before you and dearest Lillith are united in each other's arms once more?'

Eldritch lay beside the dripping wall, listening to the fearsome tirade in appalled silence.

'Well? These men might well be cowards and cravens in your eyes. They didn't rush to their arms and fight to the death as you would have done, no doubt. You despise mere mortals, don't you James? You make no secret of your utter contempt for such pitiful specimens.'

Eldritch squirmed, his body racked by cramps and his soul exposed to the full force of her righteous scorn.

'I did what I had to do, no more.'

'For what? For Lillith? I doubt she'd take time out from her schedule to come down and visit you. The sister you think so much of seems remarkably reluctant to stay and greet you, her dutiful brother!'

'She follows a dark path. It is up to me to bring her back from the wilderness in which she walks.'

'She's a money-grubbing whore! She takes a stone from strangers for a few silver pieces. Can you not see the truth of it? She enjoys it, damn you, haven't you worked that out for yourself?' Charlotte sobbed, furious to find herself crying with fury and frustration.

Eldritch subsided, helpless on his straw pallet, chained like an arthritic, slow dog to the running wall.

'You pursue her as if she's some innocent virgin. But she lives her own life without reference to you. And by Christ above, I can't bring myself to blame her.' She stalked up to the prone captain, staring down at his suddenly pale features. 'If you treated her like you treated me on the road back there, is it any wonder she flees, runs away to strangers rather than endure your scowls? She's only human, after all. It must be awful for her, a promiscuous Guinevere, trying to please a perfect Galahad like you!'

'Father wouldn't tell her,' Eldritch blurted, his jaw locked in mortification as she wrung an explanation from his constricted throat. Charlotte realised with an odd sense of satisfaction she was in all probability the first person he had ever confided in.

'. . . somebody had to take responsibility for her behaviour. She killed him; she killed our father with her fornicating antics!' Eldritch cried. Charlotte pounced, crouching down beside him and grasping a hank of his wet hair.

'If he was as stiff-necked as you that comes as no surprise! I like this Lillith. She's a free spirit, living her life without reference to self-righteous men like you and your father. God speed her, I say!'

'I cannot allow her to ruin herself. What would you have me do, wash my hands of her for ever? Try and forget she was ever my sister?'

'You cannot allow her to live, that's the trouble. You will not accept that she has made her own choices, picked her own path. What will you do, throw her in a nunnery, lock her into a chastity belt and watch her pine her years away?'

'I'll reason with her.'

'Like you reasoned with me. Cuff, bang! You're no more understanding than that reptile Briconet!'

'I will never harm her,' the captain breathed, his throat aching, eyes smarting.

'Maybe not directly.'

'I will explain . . . as I explain to you now. I will tell her how much I love her.'

'Your love is scrap steel and pig iron! I'd call it stubborn.'

'No. I love her, I love Lillith as I have come to love you.'

'Hah! I turn the tables on you, lock you in the *oubliette* and suddenly I am the woman of your dreams!' The Countess shot to her feet, gave an ironic pirouette on the matted straw.

'I have never met anyone like you.'

'But am I so different from your sister? You blame her for all your ills, despise her lifestyle and turn your head away from her love affairs, but the moment you saw me – in much the same circumstances your sister found herself in – you were over me like a rash, between my legs before we had introduced ourselves! There, you damned hypocrite! You were as hard as a rock just looking at me! What did you tell your ape-friend, that I had raped you in the flowerbeds? Seduced you from your blameless quest?'

She took three quick steps to the edge of the pit and glared down at the silent sergeant, addressing the helpless prisoner in heavily accented English.

'He was in me to the, how you say, to the hilt, within ten minutes. Your precious captain fucked me three times before the moon had gone down, what d'you say to that, eh?'

'He's a man, not a monk. I daresay some find slender hips and flat chests to their liking. Me, I like women with a little more meat on 'em!' Hobby replied with a leer.

Charlotte caught her breath.

'Or a little curly tail, no doubt.' The Countess honked, wiggling her forefinger suggestively. Hobby subsided, staring at the dirty wall of his cramped cell.

171

Eldritch swallowed hard, appalled to think the grumbling sergeant had overheard his broken-spirited confession and, worse, that he appeared intent on getting the both of them flayed alive.

He had been reduced to tears of frustrated rage by a girl younger than Merron. He didn't know whether to grovel in shame or try and bite her ankles in rage.

'Charlotte. Please listen to me. I never meant to harm or humiliate you. But we could not afford to be caught on the road – that is why we killed Briconet's men. The thought Lillith might be here . . . or that some servant might have a clue to her whereabouts, drove me to attack the castle. I make no other apology than that. All I would say is, release the sergeant. You have no argument with him.'

'Release him? Has the rank air affected your brain, captain? I'm going to give the pair of you to Briconet,' she announced menacingly. 'You have allowed yourself to believe I am some fantastically rich heiress, squandering her allowance before she comes into her fortune. But in truth I have nothing but the rags I stand in. Briconet will reward my enterprise, of that I have no doubt. As for your dutiful devotion, I have no need of it. There are dogs aplenty in the kennels!'

She turned, rapped on the door, and strode out into the passage with the captain's hoarse pleas ringing in her ears. Hulin peered in at the demoralised Englishman, leering in satisfaction.

Eldritch lay in the straw, hardly able to lift a finger through sudden, paralysing fatigue. He had said more than he had intended, more than he ever imagined he would ever have confided in a virtual stranger.

At least she hadn't ordered him back into the *oubliette*. He had remained chained to the wall where she had left him while Hobby cussed and grumbled from the hell-hole.

'Well all your fancy love talk didn't get us far,' the sergeant growled. 'You should have asked her to marry you!'

'I did my best, damn your eyes. You heard me.'

'Aye. Warbling like a songbird in a sling.'

'You think I ought to have taken a lesson from you, told her she was a flat-chested polecat?'

'I'll not give these shits the satisfaction of seeing me squirm. Let that prick Briconet poke and prod all he cares!'

The sergeant's hollow boast seemed to sober the pair of them. They relapsed into an awkward silence, each man examining his own conscience.

They had lost all track of time, lost in swirling fogs of self-inflicted misery. Eldritch guessed it must have been an hour or two later when the irrepressible Hulin returned, sticking his bandaged head around the door to tell them his honour Abandando Briconet of Avignon was at the gate.

'We've stoked up the braziers especially for you, to get all his tools nice and hot. They say a strong man can hold out for ten minutes or more before they confess to anything he suggests. I wager he'll have anything he wants from you within two. Two minutes of sheer, bloody hell on earth.'

He laughed and slammed the door once more.

By the French camp,
before Mont Galliard

It was well known that Pierre du Terrail, *Le Chevalier sans peur et sans reproche*, possessed the patience of ten mortal men. His blessing was doubly fortunate – patience was proving as valuable as gold in the high valley that autumn.

The sadly wasted knight stood on the bluff overlooking the approaches to Mont Galliard, the formidable bastion which had become such a thorn in his side. The fortress seemed to grow out of the mountain, reminding him of a faery tower in some fabled realm. It seemed to Bayard as remote as the Crusader castles of Outremer, as impossible a goal as Camelot itself. It was ironic to remember the breathtaking fortress had been overrun by such scoundrels, inhabited by the scum of Europe.

The grim walls had been blended so well with the living rock it was difficult to pinpoint whether man or nature had shaped the soaring arches and fluted columns. The smoothly-worked stone was as sheer as glass in the midday sunshine. Ragged banners fluttered from the battlements. Light flashed on armour and helmet as the otherwise invisible guards paced the walls, back and forth, ever vigilant. Stroma and Savvi were evidently maintaining their watch on the pass as they had sworn they would.

That came as no surprise. Bayard would have been astonished if they had allowed such an opportunity to go by. They held all the cards – Mont Galliard possessed more than enough guns to tear any invading force in half, even if the murderous blockhouse which had guarded the stone bridge had been demolished during the hard fighting the previous summer. They had grasped their chance to improve on their existing bargain, extorting even more money from the French invaders. Bayard had sent a dozen messengers to Grenoble, Avignon and Marseille, seeking news of the absent Briconet and urging him to make haste with the missing treasure. But until the repulsive inquisitor arrived there was precious little he could do to advance his master's cause. The small amount of coin he carried with him would see to the immediate needs of his own troops, but it would not satisfy the blood-gorged parasites who swarmed over Mont Galliard.

Unkel Von Schwartzer crawled from his tent at the crack of noon, yawning and farting as he joined the sickly knight on his daily constitutional about the lines. The uneasily allied forces had camped behind a horseshoe-shaped ridge, throwing up a patch-work city of stained canvas and snapping colours. Smoke from a hundred cooking fires twined around stands of pikes. Horses and mules had been roped out along the perimeters. They were whinnying and stamping as their grooms hurried along with buckets of feed and sacks of precious water. Latrines had been excavated from the rocky ground, and were already doing a brisk business. The rich southern food had evidently disagreed with some of Von Schwartzer's Swiss.

Bayard, peering back over the sea of tents and flapping washing, deliberately avoided looking at their reeking ablutions. But he could sense the troops' uneasiness, their impatience at the unexpected standoff. They had thought to be enjoying them-selves in Milan by now, living off the long-accumulated fat of the Lombard plain. Instead they had been plugged up in the high valley like a genie in a bottle.

The Flaxen-haired locotenent spat on the bare rock, disgusted at the enforced inactivity. 'We ought to attack, right now. Assault them while their gunners have the sun in their eyes.'

'Taking Mont Galliard would cost us two thousand men. Storming Tarsi's position perhaps a thousand more. That would leave us approximately two thousand reinforcements for Lautrec,' Bayard said levelly. 'In other words, our army would be unable to strengthen the garrison of Milan as we have been ordered. We would, in all probability, find ourselves cut off and exterminated by superior enemy forces.'

Von Schwartzer made a face behind the saintly chevalier's back. 'My men travel light, Bayard. They aren't used to sitting about on their arses.'

That was true enough. The overheating officers had already been forced to break up several brawls. Three knife-wielding rogues had fled to the artillery park, claiming the right of sanctuary under the guns. The provost hadn't dare violate that right. If they had done so the master gunner would have been within his rights to withdraw his pieces from the army and go straight home, taking his fee with him. 'I made do with rat meat and water at Mezieres,' Bayard pointed out, his yellow flesh and weary bones testimony to his own very recent privations. No sooner had the enemy forces lifted the siege than Bayard had been on his way again, Francis I's avenging angel.

'Meaning?'

'Meaning the men will survive well enough on our existing rations. Briconet will be here within a day or two at the most.'

'He'd better. That rat-scut Savvi. Holding us to ransom! Who does that jumped-up sutler think he is, eh? Well he can make hay while the sun shines. We'll have that silver back off him by the winter, or my knob's a cheese!'

'The situation appears to be somewhat fluid,' Bayard agreed, paling at the locotenent's off-colour invective. 'Who can predict how men such as he will serve?'

The Swiss commander overlooked Bayard's thinly-veiled criticism. Everybody knew Bayard was content to fight for the glory of his liege lord rather than a handful of gold. But he was the exception rather than the rule. The rest of them were here for the money – and they didn't get paid by the hour.

'If we wait much longer Tarsi might be reinforced. We can't relieve the Milan garrison with him sitting there. What you see there is a screen, intended to delay rather than defeat us.'

'I wonder if our friend Tarsi knows that?'

'I imagine so. He is no stranger to strategic necessity.'

'*Strategic necessity* would suggest we crack on and finish him, before they can complete their preparations.'

'Indeed. But this operation depends on meeting financial obligations as well as military superiority. You must be paid; Savvi must be paid.'

'And Tarsi there, he must be paid and all,' Von Schwartzer pointed out. The Chevalier seemed to have developed an unhealthy respect for the Italian Has-been.

'Tarsi's arrangements though, are with the Emperor Elect. The fact his men have remained in their positions suggests to me his troops at least have received adequate recompense.'

The Swiss frowned. 'Umm. Well I hope this wretch Briconet hurries up. We can't wait here till Christmas.'

Unknown to the acutely thoughtful Chevalier, Tarsi's financial concerns had indeed been eased by the arrival of a small Imperial supply column which had included several knock-kneed mules loaded down with silver to pay his men.

Von Huff had fulfilled his promise and organised the prompt dispatch of the monies required to secure the services of the far-flung Imperial rearguard.

But every silver cloud can have a rotten lining.

A dust-bracketed carriage had tagged along with the fast-moving column, bringing an important visitor from the distant port of Genoa.

And the tidings Master Algernon Salt carried weren't likely to cheer the hard-headed Italian. By the time the self-confident Englishman had explained his mission, Tarsi wondered whether he had a regiment left to command.

Salt looked easy-going enough. He was tall, only slightly stooped, with a full beard, slow brown eyes and a moist mouth. His clothes were draped with dust and grit from the atrocious roads, but even the unsophisticated Tarsi recognised the richness of his wardrobe, the fashionable cut of his coat. He had been shown into the command post by a bewildered junior officer, who hadn't understood a word of Salt's lengthy explanations. He had nevertheless been impressed by the visitor's quiet, self-assured manner. The Englishman looked around the cramped, cobwebbed quarters while Tarsi and the Duke bickered over the map table, hardly aware of his existence.

Tarsi had finally glanced up from his dispositions, silencing his master's ill-informed outbursts with a flick of his wrist. He had taken an instant dislike to the carefree newcomer, his sunburned nose sensing trouble. Duke Gerhard, who had as much idea of fighting a war as a one-legged hen, gave Salt one dismissive glance and returned his attention to the piled parchments as if he intended to teach himself the art of war in the few hours' respite Bayard had allowed them.

'My lords. Allow me to present myself and my credentials. I am Algernon Salt, a simple messenger from my master Edward Kraven, merchant of Bristol, Lisbon and Calais.'

Tarsi stepped across the chamber and examined the English-man's documentation. This was no simple messenger, whatever the lying rascal maintained.

'Come to sell us your fine port wines and sherries, eh?' Gerhard called from the table.

'No my lords. My master is the salesman, I am merely his mouthpiece.' He lifted a leather satchel from his shoulder and extracted a sheaf of yellowed documents. The Englishman tore the ribbon from the bundle and held up the papers. The sheets had been cut down the middle, the edges serrated like the blade of a woodsman's saw. Tarsi knew what it was – God knew he had seen enough of them to last him several lifetimes.

'This is a contract of indenture between my master Edward Kraven and diverse soldiery known collectively as The Ride, previously indentured to the late Lord Howath, warden of the English Middle March upon the borders with Scotland.'

'Well? What of it?' Gerhard enquired, replacing the maps and striding towards the blandly smiling messenger as if to overawe him with his military bearing.

Salt hardly gave the strutting turkey a second glance.

'Howath's signed his men over to Kraven,' Tarsi said tersely.

Gerhard glared at him. 'So? What of that?'

'So the Englishmen you inspected yesterday, the archers and light horsemen, are now contracted to serve this merchant fellow, not you.'

The Duke opened his mouth, then frowned as the implications began to dawn on him.

'Wait a moment! I was told Howath had signed his men over to the Vicomte d'Toinueill!'

'And so he did my lord Duke. But Gueldres' treachery, trial, subsequent escape from custody and well-deserved excommunication have rendered that document null and void. Under international law, the ownership of the contract reverted to the former contractor, Lord Howath.'

'But you've just said the man's dead!'

'But not before he sold the contract to Master Kraven. Master Kraven is now owner of The Ride.'

'You mean . . . he wants his troops back?'

'Just so my lord. I regret to report that the late peace negotiations in Calais have reached an impasse. England is, in truth, about to declare war on France. The Ride is to be employed at once in the defence of the English Pale.'

Tarsi closed his eyes.

Gerhard gaped.

'Now? It may have escaped your notice, Master Salt, but we are about to be attacked by an already vastly superior force!'

Salt shrugged.

'My master has extensive properties in Calais to think about. With the greatest respect, my lord Duke, he is not minded to let his troops fight your battles before his own. Refusal to surrender the assets in question would, as I have already pointed out, be contrary to international law and be treated as an act of banditry.'

'What?'

'My master would have no choice but to protest in the strongest possible terms to His Majesty Henry VIII of England, who would no doubt be obliged to rethink his current stance *vis-à-vis* the ongoing negotiations, and possibly even review his recent alliances.'

Gerhard spluttered his objections. Tarsi snorted.

'In other words, my lord, you either hand the men over or Salt here is saying the English will break their treaty and join the French against the Empire. That's a little strong, don't you think?'

'I would hesitate to summarise the situation quite so precisely; nevertheless Seigneur Tarsi is correct to promulgate this as an all too possible scenario.'

'Oh my God.' Gerhard blinked in bewilderment, trying to remember how many of his recently-inherited regiment would be affected by the swine's laconic announcement.

'But you're talking what . . . about half the legion! How are we supposed to go on with a couple of hundred peasant pikemen?'

'That is of no concern to me or my master. However . . .'

'What?'

'I have been authorised by my master to enter into any negotiations which might ameliorate the predicament in which you presently find yourself.'

'In other words,' Tarsi observed, 'we hire back our men?'

'You hire Master Kraven's men, to be precise.'

'At what rate?'

'I have a complete list of all officers, sergeants, corporals, troopers and grooms, and their corresponding rates of pay. Master Kraven has taken the liberty of adjusting their fees a little. Good soldiers are hard to come by, what with the war and all.'

'I thought perhaps he might,' Tarsi muttered.

'But you've already said, we've had desertions, casualties and God knows how many deaths. They've been over here a year and more!' Gerhard exclaimed.

Algernon Salt nodded sagely. 'My master anticipated wastage of approximately ten per cent. I trust that figure has not proved to be too optimistic?'

Tarsi gave a grim chuckle. 'No. He has it about right. We've lost about forty-five to fifty of them all told.'

'Well then. All that remains is to agree a price. For all except one.'

'One?'

'My master insists that the senior field officer, Captain James Eldritch, returns to Genoa at once for further assignment.'

Gerhard tossed the papers aside.

'Well I hardly think one damned captain's going to make much difference now,' he snapped, trying to estimate what such a force of men might cost. Ten thousand livres? Fifteen? Twenty? He didn't have that kind of money to waste on a pack of smelly archers! Why, if he cared to cross the Mediterranean, he could hire himself a hundred thousand of the scoundrels. He had heard the princes and kings of Ethiopia and the great empires of Africa were in the habit of chaining their archers up in front of their main armies – obliging them to fight like demons for their miserable lives. Attack from the flank or rear and the poor swine would be mown down like new grain, but there were always plenty more to take their insignificant place.

Tarsi was quietly studying the messenger, wondering why his master Kraven should have made a particular point about Eldritch. He was a good fighter, right enough, but he wasn't the only experienced soldier in Howath's Ride, not by a long shot. Eldritch had mentioned the merchant before, told Tarsi something of his previous dealings with this fabulously rich patron. The kindly philanthropist had taken the younger Eldritch children under his wing when their poor father had died, set the eldest son James up with his first commission – hundreds of miles away on the Scots border.

What other secrets had he kept to himself? Tarsi suspected there might be more to the request than met the eye.

'Why Genoa?'

'That is my master's business, my dear Seigneur Tarsi.'

'Of course. Well I suggest we sit down and study this list, and see if we can't sort something out. How much cash have you brought from home, my lord Duke?' Tarsi enquired.

Gerhard had better dig deep or there wouldn't be much of a battle, he thought grimly. Not even Hannibal himself could have held the pass with a hundred nervous arquebusiers and six score ragged-arsed pikemen.

'I'll get the money, but I'll need time,' Gerhard vowed. 'You know I have designs . . . wondrous weapons which the Imperial high command will insist on commissioning the moment I demonstrate their worth.'

Tarsi sighed. The Duke had babbled on about little else since he arrived. These amazing machines which would turn the whole course of a battle with one multi-barrelled blast. Algernon Salt had retired outside while the worried officers pondered their options.

God knew there weren't many.

They could hear the Englishman's patient tread as he paced back and forth outside the stuffy command post, stretching his legs in the late-afternoon sunshine as if he hadn't a care in the world.

Gerhard was thinking so hard his eyes were watering.

As well as the five thousand livres Briconet had paid him for the prototype of Leonardo's Engine, he had brought along the contents of the Villefrancan treasury – which amounted to another twenty thousand or so. His father had left him considerably more, as well as far-flung lands and estates, but the new Duke had already frittered a large portion of that carefully accumulated inheritance.

He was damned if he was going to hand half of it all over to some grinning ape of an Englishman. He glanced up at Tarsi, his mischievous eyes glistening with malice.

'We could have him done in. The valley is crawling with bandits. We could even blame those rotten Scotchmen of yours!'

Tarsi grimaced. 'Those rotten Scotchmen are his, unless you open your purse to pay their wages!'

'We'll do it then. I've killed bigger men than him.' Tarsi pondered Gerhard's cryptic boasting.

'And damn my reputation for ever? I'll not resort to banditry and murder to save you a few thousand livres,' the older man retorted, reddening. 'He has the law and right on his side. You will either meet his demands, or let the rogues go with him.'

Gerhard bristled. The Italian seemed to have precious little respect for his betters, insisting on treating him like some foolhardy student. He was Duke of Villefranco and *de facto* commander of the Regiment Mounier! It wasn't his fault if two thirds of its effectives now belonged to somebody else.

'Your name, Seigneur Tarsi? Until I arrived at this sheep-speckled dung-heap I hadn't even heard of you!'

Tarsi showed his teeth. 'You are in command, my Duke. If you wish to relieve me of my post I will ride directly to General Von Huff and explain how you propose to do without my services.'

Damn the brute, Gerhard thought.

'I am sure General Von Huff would prefer you remained at the front where your unquestioned experience will be worth hundreds of soldiers,' he observed testily. 'If anybody goes to headquarters, it ought to be me. It is essential my designs are handed over to the Emperor Elect's workshops.'

Tarsi had little time for Gerhard's wonder weapons. He had no interest in fantastical exploding carts and multiple-barrelled guns. They needed soldiers and they needed hard cash to pay them, not a set of pitiful pipe-dreams.

Gerhard caught the Italian's impatient frown.

'You may scoff, Tarsi, but I tell you my man Montalban has built a battle-winning weapon. I saw a score of men turned to confetti in one salvo. This weapon will transform modern warfare. Briconet himself could hardly believe . . .'

Gerhard stopped himself just in time.

'Briconet could hardly believe what?'

'Briconet would have given his right arm to possess such a device.'

'Briconet would have cut off your right arm to get it, if it's half as effective as you claim.'

'We're not getting anywhere arguing,' Gerhard said, shrill with frustrated rage. 'It is imperative that I deliver the designs to Imperial headquarters. The battle here, why it's no more than a sideshow, if you want to know!' he exclaimed.

'Then you're going to run out on us?' Tarsi growled.

'The Dukes of Villefranco do not run,' he cried.

They slither, flap and crawl on their bellies, Tarsi fumed.

'There are more ways to win a war other than allowing yourself to be slaughtered. I'll meet Salt halfway, make a down-payment on his master's precious troops. We'll march straight back to Aosta and dig ourselves in, while I take the cavalry on to Imperial headquarters.'

Tarsi gave him a ghastly grin. 'Von Huff's orders are to hold the pass. He'll hang the pair of us if we let the French stroll into the valley without a shot being fired!'

'Shots will be fired, but not here. All we need is time to rebuild one of Montalban's designs. I dread to imagine what it would do to a block of Swiss pikemen.'

'I dread to imagine what they'll do to this valley!'

'The valley is no concern to me!' Gerhard exclaimed, his temper beginning to burn through his fear of the stockily-built warrior. 'And in the long term, it's of no concern to the Emperor Elect. One valley more or less is no matter to him. He has to worry about the whole of Europe, not one pitiful little corner! I tell you Tarsi, it is vital we get this design to his engineers, before the French produce an engine of their own!'

Tarsi saw through the weakling's ruse in a moment. He wouldn't be the first fool to pedal some deranged device around the bored courts of Europe. But young Gerhard had stuck his neck out too far if he imagined he could make money playing one side off against the other.

'So Briconet has acquired the design?' he asked casually.

Gerhard saw little point in denial.

'I had no choice,' he grated. 'I was going to transport the finished prototype to Imperial headquarters. But that slippery devil Briconet arrived . . . it all happened so fast!'

The pale youth bit his thin lips, determined to regain his composure. The Italian seemed to have a heart of stone and a mind like a bird trap. 'The first time we used it . . . the engine exploded, the crew were killed as well as all those . . . as well as the bandits who had attacked my castle. We were still clearing up the remains when Briconet rode in. I had no choice. He paid me a few thousand livres and took the wreckage off to Marseille. As soon as he had gone I packed up and rode to find you.'

Tarsi sighed, pinching his broad nose between his thumb and forefinger as he tried to sort the truth from Gerhard's chaff. If Briconet had taken an active interest in the device, it had to be worth something. Briconet might not have been the world's leading authority on artillery, but he knew all about killing.

'It was completely ruined, Tarsi. I swear it. I doubt he'll ever manage to work out the original construction. He was so keen to be off he didn't even search the castle for the original drawings.'

The Italian nodded. 'So this fireworker of yours, this Montalban character, still has the drawings?'

Gerhard nodded. 'Which is why we must be off with them, before they fall in to enemy hands, don't you see?'

'If Briconet has the bits and pieces, you can wager he'll have it working again.'

'Well then, it's vital we produce our own models before the French arrive with hundreds, thousands of the damned things!'

Algernon Salt gave a polite cough from the doorway.

'Your pardon sirs. But I couldn't help overhearing the gist of your conversation as I walked beside your door.'

Tarsi leered dangerously at the suave impostor. Gerhard clenched his fists.

'I can understand your dilemma, my lord Duke, and fully share your concern that this wonder weapon does not fall into the wrong hands.'

Tarsi laid his hand over his sword hilt. 'Do not imagine you are untouchable sir. I spoke true when I told the Duke I would hesitate to beggar my name for a few pieces of silver, but only a fool would toy with me or my men in such a pass.'

Salt looked suitably chastised, holding up his broad hands in mock supplication.

'I assure you my lords, I did not mean to imply any manner of threat. I was merely about to suggest it might be meet to consider this dilemma together, to see if there is some way we can all . . . scratch each other's backs, as it were.'

'What do you mean?'

Salt took another few steps into the gloomy chamber.

'Simply this, my dear Seigneur. Neither you nor the esteemed Duke Gerhard can possibly be in two places at once. If these designs are so vital to the Imperial war effort – and Duke Gerhard and the honoured Papal Legate to Avignon would appear to think they are – then it is indeed essential they are dispatched to the authorities as soon as possible. However,' Salt went on, apparently relishing his theme, 'if you take them on to the Imperial headquarters, you will be obliged to abandon your position here, thus disobeying your battle orders and signing your own death warrants.'

Gerhard winced. Tarsi frowned.

'So what would you propose, Master Salt?'

'A new agreement, a treaty which will bind the three of us together. The merchant house Kraven with the noble houses of Villefranco and that of the esteemed Seigneur Tarsi,' Salt continued with an ingratiating smile.

'Go on.'

'Pardon my unintentional eavesdropping, my dear sirs, but I believe there may be a simple solution to the current conundrum. My lord, the Duke of Villefranco, is justly concerned to ensure his design is not hijacked by the French. His loyalty to the Imperial cause is beyond question, and he naturally wishes to see this wondrous weapon employed on the Emperor Elect's behalf.'

Gerhard smiled weakly. This man could talk the tongues off both Belatavicci and Vitt put together. He had half a mind to call the rascal counsellors in and let them negotiate on his behalf. But the young Duke was beginning to relish this desperate chicanery, the perilous cloak and dagger which made his heart beat that little bit faster. He was clever enough, aye, and man enough, to deal with serpents like Salt and ruffians like Tarsi.

'What do you have in mind?' Tarsi asked wearily. He found this sort of manoeuvring quite repulsive. Give him a burning barricade to storm and he would be happy. Cutting cards with rogues like this made him feel dirty, cheaper than a backstreet whore.

'I will act as the intermediary between yourselves and your headquarters. All modesty aside, I am highly experienced in such delicate negotiations, and have frequently acted on behalf of my master, Edward Kraven. I will undertake to deliver these drawings to the Imperial authorities, where your worthy engineers will no doubt be able to produce working models for an early inspection. I will of course ensure that the Imperialist high command is made aware of your immense contribution to this project, and the loyal service you have rendered the Emperor Elect by ensuring their speedy delivery.'

'We give you the plans?' Gerhard cried.

'And in return, as a token of my goodwill and true faith, you will retain the indentures I have already referred to, and hold this pass as you have been instructed!' Salt allowed himself a triumphant grin.

Gerhard coughed, the muggy surroundings beginning to befuddle his senses.

'We give you the drawings, we keep the men?' Tarsi enquired, trying to spot the catch.

'In a nutshell, yes. Of course my master will receive all pecuniary advantages, if and when the design is accepted.'

Gerhard chuckled. 'In other words, he lets me keep a few hundred hairy-arsed Englishmen, while he gets full credit for my war engine?'

'My master is not an international philanthropist, my lord Duke. He has a business to run. Please excuse his humble messenger, but it seems to me the solution I have suggested is by far your best course of action.'

'And what if Imperial headquarters tell you to go and take a running jump?' the canny Italian enquired.

'Then Master Kraven would be considerably out of pocket. But having heard Duke Gerhard's description of this miraculous engine of war, I am confident I will be able to persuade the Imperial command of the efficacy of his design.'

'You swear you'll tell them where you got it?' Gerhard enquired.

'On my mother's eyes, my lord. The Emperor Elect will be told precisely who he should thank for this tremendous boost to his arsenal.'

'And we keep the men,' Tarsi repeated. Salt picked up the contracts from the table.

'I am empowered to substitute your name at the top of this document.'

'Then do so,' Gerhard snapped, making up his mind at last.

By the Via Aurelia,
on the French frontier

♦

He had travelled hundreds of leagues, browbeating weary engineers and insulting surly soldiers along the way. His path had proved long, dangerous and difficult, but it had also proved to be deeply rewarding. Briconet hadn't hesitated to use all the terror his office inspired to bend weaker wills to his own, dedicating all his energies to the creation of his monstrous, iron child.

Leonardo's Engine. A degenerate artist's careless doodlings turned into deadly reality by the iron will of its true creator, Abandando Briconet of Avignon.

For the glory of God, all power to the Holy Inquisition!

His cause – under long and arduous assault from heretics and devil-worshipping statesmen all over Europe – would be fortified and invigorated by his triumph.

The weapon had been completed that dawn. It had been delivered from the brick-and-steel womb of the Royal Armoury in Marseille, swathed in the bitter smoke which belched from the cherry-red furnaces. Sooty workmen had sweated despite the early morning chill, heaving and hauling the heavy engine out into the courtyard. Briconet had capered with glee as the awesome machine rumbled and clanked over the cobbles, his gnarled fists clenched at his sides. Armand du Galliano had been too exhausted to share his elation. He stood by, wiping the dust and iron filings from his pinched features as the full-sized war machine creaked to a halt, its outlandish shape concealed to some extend by a huge grey tarpaulin.

Leonardo's Engine resembled a set of organ pipes mounted on an outsized steel carriage. The multiple barrels protruded over the armoured skirts at the front of the wagon. Du Galliano had taken the liberty of adding a steel shield to protect the crew from the hideous back-blast. He had redesigned the powder troughs which fed each barrel, adding a simple steel cover to keep out stray sparks, and had provided a set of huge, iron-bound wooden blocks in a bid to control the fearfully anticipated recoil. Other than that he had followed Briconet's instructions to the letter, rebuilding the engine from the tangled wreckage the inquisitor had brought back from Villefranco. His meticulous reconstruction was, however, ten times bigger than Duke Gerhard's puny prototype.

Briconet looked up as a pack of shouting captains double-marched their troops through the gates, the curious spearmen gawping at the peculiar, grey-clad leviathan they had been detailed to guard. Three hundred soldiers formed a hollow square about the vast shape, as if it were some Trojan horse left by the departing Imperialists. Briconet had commandeered a company of local militia and several squads of marines from the fleet to supplement his own meagre escort for the journey.

Wagoners and drivers fussed and shouted as they walked their horses between the traces. No fewer than twenty, tethered in tandem, would be required to drag the monstrous engine into battle.

'All is ready, your reverence.'

'Excellent work. Be assured I will report your efforts at the highest level.'

Du Galliano sighed, giving the delighted inquisitor a weary salute. He hadn't given the slightest indication where he was intending to march. The hump-backed fanatic seemed convinced Southern France was teeming with Imperialist spies and that their route must be kept deadly secret.

They both stepped aside as the drivers cracked their whips. The heavily-muscled carthorses bent their great heads and took the strain, harness creaking as the enormous engine rolled forwards. On its way to war at last.

His mission had been delayed seven crucial days, but Briconet had assured himself the wait had been worthwhile.

It was true that the delicate negotiations he had been entrusted by the French high command were running dangerously behind schedule. Several local commanders were still awaiting their pay and a small but vociferous core of small-fry frontier nobility had yet to be persuaded to declare for France. A host of messengers had turned their horses inside out bearing desperate imprecations from a dozen directions.

Troops were reported to be on the verge of mutiny in Briançon and Draguignan. Mountain chieftains in the Maritime Alps were said to be thinking of going over to the Empire. Unpaid merchants from Toulon to Nice were set to sell their carefully-hoarded supplies to the enemy.

But the holy inquisitor refused to be stampeded by his pressing duties. He was convinced that possession of the radical new weapon rated higher than pandering to a pack of thieving mercenary swineherds. On the evidence he had seen, Leonardo's Engine was worth any number of backsliding soldiers.

He had left the exhausted du Galliano with precise instructions, charging him with simplifying the design, adapting the over-elaborate firing mechanisms for mass production. Never mind these whining cut-throats and their grubby demands for food, pay, arms. They could only think in the short term – how they would survive the next day or two.

Briconet was blessed with grander visions, and possessed the will and single-mindedness to stand by his convictions.

Lesser men might have panicked, rushed about the country trying to do a hundred things at once. Briconet was determined to see the project through. Why, in six months' time France might be able to deploy hundreds of the murderous carts. Entire pike blocks would be mown down like spring grass. Armies would melt away rather than face such a blizzard of shot. They didn't even need to go to the expense of casting cannon-balls. Any old iron would do to load the greedy engine – scrap steel, lengths of chain, nuts and bolts.

The inquisitor smiled to himself. Such a weapon might alter the delicately-poised balance of power in Europe, reduce the Empire to a sulking shadow. Charles wouldn't dare molest French possessions along the Rhine. All of Northern Italy would become a French colony.

And he would be free to extend the Holy Inquisition into new territories, to blaze a trail across lands which the alleged excesses of the past had denied them. All the zealous inquisitor needed now was some manner of demonstration – unquestionable evidence of the war machine's invincibility.

He huddled in his carriage as the heavily-armed convoy began its arduous journey from Marseille. A scowling, shaven-headed gnome hunched up in his drab, oversized robes. His dreaded reputation emptied the countryside all around, the fearful peasants hiding themselves away from his notorious black and red carriage. He ignored the deserted fields and silent villages, concentrating all his formidable intellect on his God-given opportunity to change the very course of history.

The most obvious course would be to march directly to the nearest French army and wait for the enemy to show his face. He would blast their massed formations to the Imperialist hell in which they belonged and earn instant notoriety for his fearsome creation. But the wily Briconet hesitated to pursue such a course.

For one thing, he could not trust their commanders. The ambitious rogues who led Francis' armies would be sure to claim his victories for themselves. His writ did not run to browbeating the powerful nobles who led France's armies. They were first cousins and friends to the King, and did not fear the Holy Inquisition as lesser men did. In truth, soldiers had no great love of men of God, and even less for agents of the Inquisition. They would be reluctant to credit him with such an astonishing discovery. They would bicker and shout amongst themselves, muddying the waters until it would be next to impossible to determine the engine's ancestry. His role would be deliberately overlooked. He would be ignored by the precious clique of senior officers, possibly even silenced forever on some rogue's dirk. Leonardo's Engine would spawn as many fathers as a goat had ticks – and the canny inquisitor was determined to ensure he remained sole guardian of its deadly capabilities.

He squinted at the drab map he had spread over his knees, searching for a solution to the perplexing conundrum. He thrived on such thorns, craved the delicious thrill of international intrigue. They were not far from the French staging posts concentrated around Grenoble, supply bases set up to support descent into Italy.

Briconet smiled to himself as he remembered who had been placed in command of the invasion.

Bayard.

Of course.

The worthy Chevalier had arrived in the south barely a week after his typically heroic defence of Mezieres – his shining star very much in the ascendant. The renowned knight had wasted no time in moving his vanguard south, but his latest dispatches complained that he had been forced to call a halt in the high pass outside Mont Galliard. The great Bayard foiled by a gang of German renegades!

Bayard had sent a stream of urgent messages after Briconet urging him to hurry to the pass, complete his negotiations and end the deadlock. Bayard's last dispatch had warned that he would come after the money himself, if necessary. Briconet blinked, stroking his bony chin as his nimble mind considered and discarded options.

Bayard.

If only he could be persuaded to attend the début performance of Leonardo's Engine! Who would dare question the great Bayard's word? He would be an unimpeachable witness to its awesome promise. He wasn't far away either – kicking his heels in the pass, unable to move until the scum who infested Mont Galliard were bought off. He could write to him at once, apologising profusely for the unavoidable delay in dispatching the money and suggesting – in the humblest possible terms – that Bayard came to collect his money.

But where should he come?

Briconet's fingers twitched over the map. He had already marked one troublesome duchy in red ink as bright as newly-spilled blood.

Villefranco.

The madhouse Duchy was situated midway between Marseille and Mont Galliard. Duke Gerhard's defection appeared to have sparked widespread anarchy – he could manipulate the foolish crew who had stayed behind as if they were a pack of performing dogs. The wayward Countess du Lac – who had already led him on a wild goose chase about the region – seemed to have been caught up in the deadly chaos. She had sent him a truly preposterous letter, claiming she had taken over the castle in the name of His Majesty Francis I. Hogwash. He would deal with that fornicating slut later – once he had demonstrated Leonardo's Engine's capabilities to the immaculate Chevalier!

The inquisitor grinned as he pictured the scene.

Bayard would be present, waiting impatiently to collect his money as Briconet completed his own trifling assignment – accepting the formal surrender of Castello Villefranco. At last, the great gate opens and the sorry garrison comes trooping out under tuck and drum of truce. But hold! What trickery is this? The deranged bandits who have usurped control from its rightful owners have pulled out their cleverly-concealed weapons and attacked the peaceful ambassadors, determined to sell their evil lives dearly.

The mortified inquisitor has no choice but to order his awe-inspiring gun to open fire, cutting the treacherous rogues down by the score!

Briconet's fist crashed against the carriage's faded upholstery. Bang bang bang! A hundred and more assassins and scoundrels are blown away like sand in a tempest!

The Chevalier Bayard is appalled by the gun's appetite for destruction, riding off with his saddlebags stuffed with coin to tell his colleagues of Briconet's historic discovery.

The inquisitor drooled in delighted anticipation as he penned the letter to Bayard. He raised the leather curtain, gestured at the captain who rode alongside the creaking carriage.

'I want half a dozen riders ready to take this message to my lord the Chevalier Bayard outside Mont Galliard. And send word to the guard commander. We are marching for Villefranco at once. Don't sit there gawping, you miserable cabbage, do it!'

'But your reverence, the size of the engine, the horses need changing, we . . .'

'Never mind all that! I want to be in Villefranco tomorrow, not the middle of next week!'

'But sire . . .'

'If the engine is too heavy you must lighten the load! Throw away some of that trash du Galliano has seen fit to weight it down with.'

'The blast plate, the wheel chocks are essential to prevent a repeat of the unfortunate . . .'

'You have my mind on it sir! Those great sleepers he's slung beneath its belly aren't any use to man or beast.'

'I think you'll find the device is intended to reduce the . . .'

'Never mind all that nonsense! He's made the wretched thing far too heavy for practical use! Get rid of those blocks and whip on your horses. Do it sir, or I'll find somebody else who will!'

'At once, your reverence!'

By the Castello Villefranco

◆

What was left of the garrison had hurried to the battlements at the first warning of Briconet's ponderous approach. The dispirited and deeply suspicious Villefrancans watched in appalled silence as the outriding cavalry turned off the coast road to screen the deployment of Briconet's levies. They weren't to know the crossbow, pike and spearmen the inquisitor had marched from Marseille were second-rate troops – poor quality militia and the sweepings of the waterfront. Instead of a few hundred indifferent levies, the inexperienced garrison imagined they were looking at an innumerable host made up of hand-picked fanatics dedicated to the eradication of every village, town and castle on the frontier which dared gainsay the pious servants of the Inquisition. Woe betide them if they didn't immediately lay down their arms and grovel for mercy.

The shambling files came to a halt on the slopes before the Castello Villefranco, swigging the last of their wine or water as Briconet's dreaded baggage train rumbled up the hill and rolled to a halt behind them.

There was the inquisitor's scarlet and black wagon, festooned with the banners of the Inquisition. His emblems were as familiar as the guild signs which swung above their shops – symbols of his own bloody business. The watchers on the wall swore they could hear the tools of Briconet's dreaded trade clatter and bang within, a hellish chorus guaranteed to turn the sternest foe to slobbering knave.

The wagon was surrounded by a host of smaller carts and carriages fitted with horse-hide awnings – the commissariat which would feed and shelter his scratch army. Weary drivers climbed down from their running boards and stretched their legs. Horses tossed their heads as the grooms ran to and fro, watering their weary beasts – but the garrison wasn't interested in their hectic domestic duties.

All eyes had been fixed on the monstrous leviathan grinding up the slope behind Briconet's mobile torture chamber. It reminded the fishermen in the garrison of a great grey crab turned on its back. Its pincers and claws were held erect, but the oddly assorted limbs were partially hidden beneath a tarpaulin. Sheets of weather-stained canvas had been roped about the outlandish superstructure as if to disguise its true shape. The enormous vehicle squealed and shrieked on its iron-bound axles, the curious engine smothered in a dustcloud of stinging yellow grit. The feeble-hearted defenders gaped in disbelief.

'Whatever is it?'

'Christ knows. Knowing that hell-spawned witchfinder, it could be anything.'

'I reckon it's a great brass brazier, especially to render down human bones!' one ghoul called to his drop-jawed comrades.

'It's a gallows I tell you!'

'Gallows be damned. It's a siege engine or somesuch.'

'What does he need a siege engine for? We're never going to bar the gates to his lot!'

'Her ladyship sent for Briconet; there'll be no need for siege-craft now!'

'I'm not fighting Briconet, that's for damned certain!'

'Nor me!'

'You wouldn't take up arms against a pack of novices on their way to vespers!' Charlotte called, striding up behind them. The muttering soldiery opened ranks, avoided her haughty glare.

Charlotted had changed clothes, selecting a fine if somewhat crumpled damask gown from the clutter in Duke Gerhard's abandoned apartments. She had wondered why the young man's quarters should have been strewn with quite so many women's clothes – was he fond of dressing up himself, or had he simply enjoyed stripping them off his bedwarmers? The household servants had fussed around her, washing the grubby marks from her cheeks and picking most of the debris from her hair while she studied her reflection in the pitted looking glass. She knew she had to try and look the part if she was going to maintain her fragile hold on these rabbits.

Charlotte, Duchess of Villefranco, peered over the battlements, watched Briconet's army deploy as if for battle along the lower slopes.

The horse had drawn off to either flank, leaving a large block of fidgeting infantry in the centre. The wagon which had caused such consternation amongst her browbeaten garrison had been parked in the rear, closely guarded by another strong detachment of troops. She could understand Briconet's reluctance to expose his person before he had assessed the current status of the defence, but why should he feel the need to deploy his men as if for an immediate storm? Had he misunderstood her note? Did he imagine she had tried to entice him into some kind of a trap?

She turned to the scowling rascal beside her, his borrowed clothing and badges of rank looking ridiculously out of place on his wiry, undernourished frame. Corporal Hulin had become her evil-smelling shadow as she made her way about the ransacked rooms of the castello, never letting the Countess out of his sight. The shabby runt picked at his swollen eye, peering down at the silent ranks with more than a twinge of concern.

'But you sent word to Briconet that you intended to hand the castle over to him,' he said indignantly. 'Maybe the messenger never reached him; maybe he thinks we're holding the place for Piss-Pants Gerhard or that swineherd Englishman?'

'Of course the messenger got through,' she snapped. 'And you know as well as I, what I told Monsieur Briconet.'

Oh, it was *Monsieur* now, was it?

Hulin ran his tongue over his streaked teeth.

He had peered over her shoulder as she penned that dispatch, but he had been intending to intimidate her rather than interpret her message – like most of his comrades he could neither read or write.

'I urged him to march here with all speed,' she said, puzzled by Briconet's excessive caution. 'And here he is.'

'But not with all his army!' Hulin exclaimed.

He leaned over the battlements, crossed himself with a brief prayer to God as the agent in question poked his shaven head out of the carriage and stepped down to the rocky ground. He was immediately surrounded by heavily-armed guards, who closed ranks about their hunchbacked talisman. Briconet looked as if he expected siege lines and flying bullets rather than an apologetic welcome from a down-at-heel countess.

'Well, he's taking no chances,' Hulin commented, running his sleeve across his nose. 'Are you going out to meet him?'

Charlotte paused, achingly unsure of herself. Surely she had done nothing wrong, offered no offence to the prickly inquisitor. She had, after all, summoned Briconet to receive the abandoned castle on behalf of France.

Her grubby gown puckered in the brisk wind whistling

between the moss-capped battlements. Was it possible Briconet had received word of her earlier dalliances with the Englishman? The dangerous liaison with the quick-tempered captain? Perhaps Briconet had worked out that her bizarre flight from the Château Celestine had not been the straightforward kidnapping he might have imagined.

The Countess steadied herself against the mottled stone. Surely he knew she had tried on several occasions to escape, that she had raised the alarm which had brought Druchet's soldiers charging into the woods? Aye – and led them directly to their deaths.

She dared not imagine what other lies he had been told.

'We'd best send out a flag, invite Monsieur Briconet within,' she decided.

'He doesn't look as if he'll need a second invitation. Looks to me as if he's expecting trouble,' Hulin complained, studying the pale Countess through the corner of his bloodshot eye.

'Why should he? Your late master the Duke has fled. The English bandits who attacked you are safe in the dungeons. We have no reason to expect anything but thanks and courtesies from our esteemed visitor,' she quavered. Hulin frowned, sensing her indecision.

'I'd best order the gates opened, before His Holiness takes offence.' Charlotte's anxiety ate through her resolve.

'No. Wait. If we let him in . . . he gets everything he wants without a word, with no guarantees for our safety or status.'

'Bugger status! We'd best not leave Briconet of Avignon waiting on the threshold like some Egyptian tinker!'

'Why does he parade his men as if he wants to intimidate us?' she cried, clutching his tunic sleeve. Hulin glanced at her long, elegantly tapered but rather soiled fingers. He shrugged.

Whatever Briconet intended, he had succeeded in intimidating him!

'I sent word for him to come and claim a frontier castle in the name of France. He arrives as if he means to take it by force of arms!'

'It's his way,' Hulin protested, alarmed at her sudden change of tune.

'Go quietly. Have the garrison armed and at their battle stations, but tread carefully and beat no drum.'

'What? Take up arms against the Holy Inquisition?' The foolish girl must have been scavenging in the scullery and eaten some mouldy rye bread if she imagined the castle's defenders were going to bar the doors against a brute like Briconet.

'There is something amiss here. You know it as well as I. If we open the gates we sign our own death warrants.'

Hulin had a sneaking suspicion she might be right.

'What do I know? Apart from the fact we'll all be for the high jump, if we don't get that gate open damn quick!'

'Fetch Eldritch up here.'

Hulin's nervous twitch was replaced by a slow smile.

'That's a thought, my lady. We'll dangle the bastard over the wall, prove our loyalty to the Church. French. Villefranco, whatever,' he went on.

The Countess said nothing, her windswept features pinched with concern as she leaned against the wall, her back to their dreaded visitors.

'Do as I tell you. Deploy your men and bring Eldritch to me. At once!'

'The scrawny-titted leech. The putrid oyster! She's left us to rot, I knew it all the while!'

Eldritch slumped against the mouldy wall, his dead arm suspended from a short but accursedly well-forged chain. His sergeant's litany of abuse had diminished somewhat over the last hours. Hobby grunted and retched, turning his vast bulk over and over again in the narrow *oubliette*. He had fidgeted and cursed, trying to prevent his muscles from seizing up completely as he half-crouched, half-lay in the stinking pit. He uttered strings of curses every time the pain became too much for him.

Eldritch kept silent, staring at the running brickwork, his mind swallowed up in a black turmoil. One moment he hated her with all his lean being, the next he was mumbling and praying, imploring the wilful girl to deliver them from their torment. He had lost all idea of time, crouched in the rustling straw. He had got used to the reek of decay, and hardly bothered to swat the giant rats which emerged from the corners to sniff and nibble at his boots.

He had got on his knees and begged her to release them, poured his heart out to her like some milksop knave.

But she hadn't relented. Charlotte had scorned his pitiful appeals, crowing with derision as he grovelled in the filth.

He wished he'd stayed quiet, suffered her dire punishments in dignified silence. Here was a lesson for every man, he thought.

197

Never give a woman the keys to your heart or she'll lock you in a dungeon – whether physical or psychological – for all eternity.

'I'll rip her guts out with my teeth. I'll torch her merkin and make her eat the ashes! She'll rue the day she locked Jeremiah Hobby in a shit-hole like this!' the sergeant raged impotently.

Eldritch cocked his head, thinking he had heard footsteps in the passage outside.

He had. Booted feet, hurrying down the stone tunnel.

They both fell silent as they heard the keys rattle in the lock. Eldritch shut his eyes against the sudden glare as spluttering torches were thrust into their reeking prison. He felt a boot thud into his thigh. Somebody grasped him by the hair, yanking him to his knees.

'On your feet, Englishman. Her ladyship wants you on the battlements. But don't get any cocky ideas, pal. Your friend Briconet's arrived – and he's after your blood.'

'The troops are deployed as per your instructions, your reverence.'

'Excellent,' Briconet acknowledged the militia captain with a careless flick of his wrist.

He shielded his eyes and gazed up at the silent stack of well-dressed stone. The Mounier clan must have bred out all its warriors over the years, left feeble-minded fools to inherit their hard-won Duchy. The fighting men who had built the grim stronghold had chosen the site well. They had incorporated every natural feature into the defences – ridges, gullies and cliffs had been used to strengthen or screen the curtain walls. But he had not come here to fight a battle, no matter what the fearful defenders might be thinking.

The angular grey shape of the Castello Villefranco reared above his motley host, hoarse-throated stormbirds wheeling and calling about its tall towers. The roof tiles were glowing in the last rays of the sun as if they had been made from new bread just removed from the oven. Below them, he could just make out a series of pale smudges along the walls – the anxious faces of the Countess du Lac's mongrelised garrison.

And well might they stare.

Briconet hoped the wretched girl wouldn't spoil his plan by insisting on opening the gates and riding out to greet him in person. It would suit the inquisitor's purpose if she refused to budge, taking offence at his warlike demonstrations.

She would be given every opportunity to rethink her situation when the Chevalier Bayard responded to his urgent summons and arrived there in person to collect his precious silver.

'They've taken up battle stations, your reverence,' the keen-eyed militia captain reported.

Briconet smiled thinly. 'They dare flout the authority of the Holy Inquisition? Surely they are infected with the terrible vice of anarchy, which, as you know, is second only to devilry in the litany of sin.'

'Shall I prepare a flag of truce, summon them to surrender, your reverence?' Captain Valbien enquired.

Briconet shook his shrivelled head, giving the captain an excellent impression of bewildered regret.

'We are but half an hour from sundown. I would hesitate to venture towards those walls during the witching hours. Satan stalks that castle, my dear captain, and not even I, Briconet of Avignon, would choose to face the Prince of Darkness by night.'

'No, your reverence.'

'Wait until sundown, then have the men stand down. Set double guards and we will watch till morning.'

'It will be done.'

The cold walls turned from slate grey to coal-black as the sun sank behind the mountains. Eldritch wiped his shackled wrists across the bridge of his nose. His eyes were stinging in the twilight glare.

'Here he is, my lady. Do you want me to have torches brought up, so Briconet can watch us hang him?' Hulin yanked the chain, dragged the tall Englishman to his knees. Eldritch lost his balance, cracking his head against the wall.

'Hold hard. He's called in his skirmishers, look. I think he means to stay where he is, wait for the morning.'

Hulin bunched the chain about his fist and yanked the cursing captain away from the wall.

'Hear that matey? You're to be spared till the morning.'

'I hear you, butterfly-balls,' Eldritch muttered through clenched teeth.

'Why didn't he come up to the gate? What does he gain by waiting till the morning?' Eldritch started at the sound of Charlotte's voice. She seemed to be moving backward and forward just in front of him. He opened his eyes a crack, discerned a dim shadow beside the starkly silhouetted battlement.

'He's in no hurry. This hound's not going anywhere special,' Hulin called.

'Stand him up. I can't talk to him crouched down between your legs.' Hulin obediently stepped back and dragged Eldritch to his feet.

'Briconet has received my note. I told him Gerhard had fled, and that I intended to hand you and the castle over to him, for the greater glory of France,' the Countess declared, trying to keep the nervous wavering out of her voice.

Her lover stank like a sewer rat's spleen. His face was deathly pale but his neck and ears had erupted in fierce yellow and red blotches. His lower lip was a swollen leech, a trickle of black blood smeared and scabbed over his stubbled jaw. His hands were covered in red marks as if he had been bitten by fleas. Or worse. Charlotte almost retched as she looked imploringly at her barely recognisable lover.

'What are you telling him for? We're going to stretch his English neck over the castle walls, a token for Briconet!' Hulin objected.

'Hold your tongue you snivelling ape! In the absence of any other experienced officers, I will ask Captain Eldritch what he makes of Master Briconet's tactics. Well? Can you see there? He's deployed his entire force as if he comes to lay siege to Villefranco. Why should he do that, when I wrote summoning him here myself?'

Eldritch tilted his head squinting through his slit eyes at the agitated Countess.

'He's not going to give you a straight answer even if he could!' Hulin gave the Englishman a rib-cracking nudge. 'Look, he can barely stand up straight, let alone work out what's in Briconet's head. You might as well ask the cat what it thinks!'

'Hulin, you are free to lay down your arms and march out. Go on. Get out of my sight. Go and snivel to Briconet, if you're so damned frightened of him!'

Hulin swallowed, stung by the girl's furious reaction. He glanced at the fearful soldiers along the wall, the tall captain tottering by his side. The Englishman's long nose was twitching as if he could sense what was passing between them.

'What d'you mean? You want me to go out there, to see Briconet?'

'Go ahead! What are you waiting for, some of your cronies to hold your hand?'

'Watch your mouth, my lady,' Hulin warned.

'Go on! Get out of here! I'd rather share the walls with stout-hearted men than piss-pants boys like you!' Charlotte snarled. Hulin tensed. Eldritch seethed in helpless frustration, his arms shackled, his eyes still smarting from his long confinement in the dark dungeon.

'Thought better of it, eh?'

'You're not getting rid of me as easily as that,' Hulin piped up, his bravado evaporating quicker than the light. The Countess ignored his feeble riposte, guided the Englishman to the wall, hand on his sleeve.

'What's that shape . . . behind Briconet's carriage?' Eldritch asked, squinting out over the battlements at the inquisitor's bustling camp.

'Some sort of siege engine, we think. But I told him the castle was his. Why doesn't he approach?'

'What sort of siege engine? Can you see any guns?'

'Guns? The whole thing's covered in a big sheet.'

'Barrels, cannon barrels?' Eldritch snapped, annoyed by her confusion.

'Well there's something sticking out at the front, but it's not a barrel. Not . . .'

'More than one . . . a dozen barrels lashed together, like organ pipes?'

'What is it?' Charlotte asked, alarmed all over again.

'He's trying to scare us!' Hulin sneered.

'He's rebuilt Gerhard's war engine,' Eldritch decided. 'Sourris said he'd carried the wreckage back to the Royal Armoury in Marseille.'

'The gun that minced old Baldassare's bodyguard, and its crew with it? It was destroyed in the blast. We were picking bits of barrel and lumps of bone out of the walls!' Hulin jeered. 'And besides, that thing's got to be ten times bigger than the . . .' The corporal paused, alarmed at the dreadful implications of this new, outsized engine.

'Briconet came here after me,' Eldritch said.

'And we're going to give you to him, don't you fret yourself!'

'But the moment he heard about that gun he left off hunting us and escorted the wreckage back to the workshops in person. He wouldn't have gone so far out of his way on a whim, for a pile of useless scrap!'

Hulin was losing what little patience he had. Why were they listening to this long-shanked serpent? He'd already butchered

201

half a dozen of his colleagues and richly deserved to be pissing his breeches on the end of a rope.

'Very well,' he drawled. 'Say Briconet's managed to rebuild Gerhard's fart-cannon. He's got no argument with us.' He tapped his chest to represent the garrison rather than its uninvited guests. 'All we have to do is send somebody out with the keys to the castle, bow our heads and do as we're told, just as we always do. You're wrong about Briconet – he's just being cautious. Not everyone's pleased to see the likes of him come calling.'

'I told you to set the watch! If you want to go out of your own accord, that's your business,' the Countess shrilled, sensing her tenuous hold on the scoundrel garrison was wearing dangerously thin. 'You would have us shuffle out with our tails between our legs?'

'No, Briconet would. He's in command here, not you. If you don't send to him soon, we'll march out and leave you and loverboy to it. Briconet's got no cause against simple soldiers like us.' Hulin's speech earned a chorus of approval from his fellow defenders.

'Gerhard ran out because he knew he couldn't trust Briconet. But you reckon you know better?' Eldritch queried, lips drawn back from his teeth.

'Gerhard was a weasel-ballocked stinkfinger afraid of his own farts. He got the drop on his uncle, but he didn't dare cross the Inquisition.' Hulin turned to the Countess, biting her lip as the last rays of the sun slid out to sea.

Eldritch was still trying to clear his misty vision. He rubbed his eyes on his tunic cuff, almost gagged on the reeking sleeve. Over the wall, a string of fiery pearls glimmered and flickered about Briconet's camp. The weary troops seemed intent to getting on with their suppers rather than the delicate negotiations which would deliver the castello into the inquisitor's hands.

'He won't wait all night,' Hulin prompted.

'Look over the wall, Hulin. He's settling down till morning. Whatever he's got in mind for us, he needs daylight to do it.'

'What are you nattering about, "got in mind for us"? Us? He's got no argument with us!' Hulin's patience had snapped at last. 'Pass the word, we're marching out!'

Eldritch swivelled about, peering at the belligerent corporal.

Hulin thrust the captain back, sending the woozy Englishman crashing against the stone. Charlotte grasped at his shackled arms to prevent him from overbalancing.

'You shut your mouth. We're taking you out with us. Briconet knows who his friends are here,' Hulin gave the Countess a significant look.

With luck, Bayard would have received his message by now and be readying himself for the ride south.

The inquisitor was confident he would come. How would he justify refusal? Without Briconet's precious silver he would be unable to pay off Savvi. If Mont Galliard was held against him, Bayard and his dubious allies would be bottled up in the pass, unable to break through to Milan. Briconet smiled to himself, satisfied his admittedly ramshackle plans had begun to solidify. The operation would require careful timing.

First, he must ensure he had completely overawed the garrison, worn the defenders down so they would be ready to instantly obey his every word. He had not approached the castle, nor would he allow any embassy to come to him before he was good and ready. He imagined them, craven rascals locked up behind the formidable defences. True-hearted men would have defied him to do his worst, dared him to come in after them. These mouse-hearted scuts would be stewing in their own juices by now, shivering and dribbling with terror as they prayed for an opportunity to surrender themselves.

Briconet would try and prolong their agony until the Chevalier's banners came within sight, and then send word that the garrison might march out under arms – so long as the castle was handed over without further prevarication.

And then?

Treachery. Confusion. Chaos. Shouts and misheard challenges. Who fired that shot? And all the world would see what Leonardo's Engine was capable of.

Briconet's reverie was interrupted by a loud knock on the carriage door. Sourris would normally have dealt with such pestilential intruders, but his blubberguts of an assistant would be swelling up in a gravepit by now. He scowled, reached over and raised the leather curtain flap, recognising the sallow features of the captain of the guard.

'Your reverence's pardon, but there's something amiss in the castle. They've abandoned the walls and seem to be opening the gate,' Valbien reported. The nervous officer recoiled in shock as Briconet swore himself hoarse. He stood aside as the inquisitor bustled down the steps to see what the commotion was.

'I thought you said they had taken up battle stations, as we expected?'

'And so they had, your reverence. But it seems they had second thoughts.'

'Stand your men to, horse to patrol the flanks. I don't want the damned blabbermouths escaping in the darkness.'

'At once, your reverence.'

Charlotte had realised – somewhat belatedly – that her frail hold over the garrison had snapped. Hulin, the ringleader and unofficial spokesman, had wrested control of the sixty-odd survivors easily enough. He had promised an end to the dangerous deadlock and to hand the accursed pile over to Briconet before it was too late. What had she done? Attempted to persuade them to bolt the doors and man the battlements, hurl arrows and abuse in Briconet's face. She must have lost her mind, to imagine the garrison would have followed such a suicidal battle plan.

The wavering troops had gone over to the corporal like a bitch on heat, forming up neatly in the courtyard despite the striking absence of officers and sergeants to shout, bawl and knock them into their ranks and files. The Countess was caught up in the rush, heart in her mouth as her lover and his bull-necked sergeant were brought out and bundled along by the nervous soldiery. Eldritch and Hobby had been surrounded by Hulin's ruffians, trussed offerings to Briconet's mercy.

By God she had wanted the arrogant swine punished, taught a lesson they would never dare forget. But she had not envisaged abetting their bloody execution. But then again, Eldritch and Hobby were the only credible witnesses to her own role in the affair.

If the inquisitor finished with them quickly, she might have time to concoct some story, a tale to explain her highly dubious behaviour. She was hideously aware who had roused up the garrison against them, turned the drowsy Villefrancans into bitter fighters bent on revenge. But the game was over now. Briconet was not to be denied.

Hulin strode along the ranks with a halberd over his shoulder, giving his comrades a fevered inspection.

'Get a move on! Open the gate! Drummers, slow march! Bernardo, hold that friggin' flag up!'

He took the Countess by the arm, escorting her none too gently toward the gate.

'You dare lay hands on me?'

Hulin yanked her toward him, pressed his mouth to her ear. His breath reeked of garlic and onion.

'I'll let you go when we see Briconet, tug my forelock and yes ma'am with the rest of 'em. But you start pointing the finger at me and I'll tell them all about you and loverboy!'

'What do you mean by that?'

'I may be a corporal but I'm not stupid, my lady. I saw the way you looked at the bastard, got him out of the *oubliette* before he'd shat his breeks!'

The nervous company had rigged up a crude flag of truce and thrust it upon one of the inexperienced youngsters. Bernardo wasn't quite sure whether he had won a great honour or drawn a very short straw. Hulin propelled him towards the opened gate. The boy would lead the way towards Briconet's camp, accompanied by a brace of drummers whose clattering tattoos would warn the besieging force of their mission.

'You don't think he'll think we're attacking?' one of Hulin's old cronies enquired, leaning on his pike.

'What would we want to do that for?'

'I was just askin', that's all.'

'Hulin you numbskull, you don't know what Briconet wants here,' Eldritch snarled. The vengeful defenders kicked and shoved the shouting Englishman back into line, closing about him as if they had taken a blood oath to protect him from all harm.

'Right, throw your chests out you miserable bastards! Prepare to march, march on!'

By the French camp,
near Mont Galliard

◆

Ten days. Ten whole days they had been sat in this wretched pass, chewing stale bread and squabbling over cupfuls of warm water. And now this. It was not to be borne. A lesser man than Bayard might have hewn the nervous messenger in two, torn the dispatches he carried into confetti and danced the ashes into the dirt, cursing Briconet to the uttermost pits of hell. Unkel Von Schwartzer's scouts had warned him of the messenger's dusty arrival, recognising Briconet's distinctive scarlet and black livery amongst the swirling cloud of grit kicked up by his foaming horse.

A dispatch from Briconet could only mean one thing. Money. The bad-tempered *locotenent* came running with his shirt tails tangled between his hairy legs, every grubby inch the peasant he was. He had spent the last two weeks with his feet up, enjoying the last of summer's bounty while the irritable troops quarrelled and capered. Bayard looked up from the inquisitor's unexpected dispatch, his jaundiced features mottled with anger. He was too distracted to notice the Swiss commander's slipshod dress.

'The money?' Von Schwartzer enquired, stepping from one dirty foot to the other as if he were an anxious schoolboy come to retrieve his ball from the Chevalier's orchard.

Bayard screwed the brittle parchment into a ball and threw it across the tent. Von Schwartzer was appalled at the Chevalier's uncharacteristic flash of temper.

'The money is at the Castello Villefranco, on the coast road beyond Nice,' Bayard reported, hoarse with indignation.

'Castello Villefranco . . . well that's not far,' the Swiss argued, trying to recall the region's geography. 'He can have it here, what, the day after tomorrow at the latest!'

'He can't do any such thing,' Bayard snarled. 'He is engaged in besieging "*diverse rebels and traitors*" within the Castello, and deeply regrets he will not be able to complete his mission until the *"evil vipers' nest"* is completely exterminated.'

'Villefranco? That backwater pukepot? What difference will that make to the price of fish?' the half-naked general enquired, scratching his dishevelled hair in bewilderment.

'The difference is this. The war has started and Briconet must earn his share of the glory as well as the rest of us. Villefranco is a sideshow, but its capture might be a feather in his cap, when he comes crowing to His Majesty, seeking to extend his own dubious influence.'

From the mild-mannered Bayard, the implied criticism sounded like a damning accusation.

'You could countermand his orders,' Von Schwartzer suggested.

The thoughtful knight wiped his pale brow. His health had still not recovered from the ordeal at Mezieres. He needed a month's rest and a few good meals, not mind-numbing aggravations like this.

'He suggests, in the humblest possible terms, of course, that I, Pierre du Terrail, Seigneur de Bayard, collect Savvi's money in person.' Bayard spat out each word as if it were a piece of grit which had lodged in his windpipe. Even the ill-mannered Swiss was taken aback by his righteous anger. 'He intends I travel the length of Southern France, delivering money like some Antioch Jew? We will have to ride about the mountains, approach the Duchy from the west! It must be fifty leagues away!'

'A good march,' the Swiss agreed, the first filament of a plan beginning to connect inside his formidable skull.

'An intermediary between one set of scoundrels and another? If he was a soldier and not some ba . . . God-damned cleric, I'd call the rogue out and run him through!'

Von Schwartzer grinned at the Chevalier's ill-considered dismissal. 'He's got a nerve all right. Those Roman bed-faggots are all the same,' he crowed, coughing a wedge of phlegm onto the dusty floor. 'We Swiss have never cared for 'em, if you want to know.'

The Chevalier overlooked the locotenent's heresies.

'I know Briconet,' Bayard said bitterly. 'He'll have some confounded enterprise in mind – the man is a regular Turk when it comes to personal aggrandizement, most ill-befitting a man of the Church.'

Von Schwartzer chuckled at Bayard's striking *naïveté*. The few churchmen he had ever met had cheerfully admitted they had been out for themselves. The higher their rank the greedier the rogues were. The Church was riddled with sinecures and simony – something to do with the size of their hats, the Swiss commander thought.

Bayard shook his head. 'But we're already almost two weeks behind schedule. We ought to have been advancing on Milan by now. His Majesty is relying on us to reinforce the garrison.'

'And so we will,' Von Schwartzer agreed. 'So we will. Once we've paid off that lamprey Savvi, we'll be through the pass and double-march all the way. My boys are rested enough, they'll run all night if we ask 'em!' The locotenent took a sly breath, eyeing the furiously pacing Chevalier. 'He's not one of us, Bayard, he doesn't understand proper military protocol,' he went on, standing on the threshold of Bayard's tent in his underclothes. 'You're a great knight, and I am but a simple soldier. I have not your honour, your reputation, to uphold.' He held his breath a moment. 'Let me go and collect Briconet's money.'

Bayard looked up at the muscle-bound oaf, blinking in astonishment as he finally realised the grinning Swiss was improperly dressed. The tactful knight sensed an outright refusal might upset the prickly locotenent's sense of grievance. They were notoriously prickly people, the Swiss.

'I thank you for your consideration, Von Schwartzer,' he said levely, 'but Briconet is nothing if not specific. "*Be so good as to collect the silver in person*," he writes.' He left out the clause about not trusting anybody else as far as he could throw them, for fear of causing further offence.

'I must either swallow my pride and become Briconet's deputy paymaster, or we sit outside Mont Galliard until the grand inquisitor can finish his business in the south and march to our relief.'

Von Schwartzer gnawed his fleshy lip as he considered the Chevalier's curt reply.

'When are you off then?'

Bayard took his own escort of two hundred immaculately turned-out Gendarmes, leaving Von Schwartzer in command of the bad-tempered camp before Mont Galliard. Bayard did not relish the prospect of handing the unstable Swiss control of six thousand of His Majesty's troops, but he had little choice but to obey Briconet's outrageously high-handed summons. He would either have to collect the cash to bribe Savvi or explain to his liege lord how he was unable to complete even the first stage of his complex and ambitious mission. He had earned high praise for his defence of Mezieres, but was acutely aware how the hideous anticlimax in the Val D'Aosta would be represented at court.

The great Bayard ridiculed and reduced by a gang of renegade *Landsknechts*. He would never again be able to show his face in Paris. His heroics at Mezieres, at Marignano, Tournai, Therouanne and half a hundred barely-remembered battles would be forgotten as the crowing courtiers gleefully reported his abysmal failures outside Mont Galliard. Bayard, *Le Chevalier sans reproche*, humbled by a nest of drunken, money-grabbing rapscallions.

He would swallow his pride.

He would thank Briconet profusely for his commendable attention to the detail of his campaign.

He would collect the silver and stuff it up Savvi's red nose.

And then he would blast the Imperialists all the way back to Sicily, so help him God!

The heavily-armoured Gendarmes had divested themselves of as much equipment as they dared to speed their ride south. They had stripped off their armour and heavy horse bards and left their lances in the camp. Each rider took a sword or mace and a small sack of provisions, enough to see him to the coast and back.

The Chevalier led his lightened knights at a furious pace, retracing their route down the western face of the mountains and arriving back at the tiny village of St Gervais, a French staging post in the foothills of the Alps. They turned, following the high road to Albertville. Bayard increased the pace on the well-made road, leading the white-clad host over the breathtaking heights of the Massif de la Vanoise to St Michel and Modane before heading sharply south at last. Eight hours and a change of horses later, the indestructible Chevalier had negotiated the mighty Monginevro pass and arrived in Briançon, following the course of the hectic river Durance towards Barcellonette on the western flank of the Maritime Alps. He allowed his exhausted riders another halt, before leading the company to Allos, where they turned south once again to follow the river Var as far as Annot. From there, he drove them on to Puget Théniers, crossed the river Tinée and pressed on across the central Maritime Alps to Breil.

They were within sight of the sea at last, having taken a roundabout route of almost one hundred and fifty miles. The journey had already taken the best part of three days. If he had been free to take the short cut through the Alpine passes, he could have saved twenty-four precious hours. The furious Chevalier realised the journey home would be even slower – they would be riding tired horses and leading a string of silver-laden mules. Even if he completed his business with Briconet promptly, he would not be back in camp outside Mont Galliard before the end of the week.

Bayard was ruminating on the distressing delays when the tired column cantered over the moss-encrusted slopes and reined in on the coast road. A brisk wind set cloaks billowing over slumped shoulders. The blowing horses were grey with fatigue, but another few leagues would see them in Villefranco.

'Ride on. We'll be there by nightfall,' Bayard called, his perilously wasted frame racked by the punishing ride. The journey to Villefranco had eaten up what little reserves of stamina he had left.

The smouldering funeral pyre was visible a good two miles off. The castle's tangled timberwork was still burning. Thick, acrid smoke belched from the shattered towers. The defences had been eaten up from the inside, reduced to a bare shell by the dreadful blaze as if the defenders had been intent on slighting the defences for eternity. The Castello Villefranco had been reduced to a blackened skull washed up on the strand – a leaning chimney all that was left of the once proud stronghold. Bayard wiped the flying smuts from his eyes, peering into the smoke-choked twilight as he contemplated the unexpectedly ruinous results of Briconet's thirst for martial fame. The wretched inquisitor hadn't wasted much time earning his precious laurels. He had taken and burnt the valuable frontier stronghold, turned a potential French asset into a crumbling wreck.

The finely-matched towers leaned drunkenly, fine tile roofs warped by the intense flames. The gatehouse had been shattered, the great doors smashed like worm-holed driftwood. The stony ditch which ran the length of the wall facing the sea had been filled with debris – burnt timbers, fallen masonry.

And mummified bodies.

Their skins had been turned black as toffee by the tremendous heat.

The French Gendarmes rode closer, hoofbeats clattering eerily. A flock of gorged crows croaked in protest as they rose from their evening feasting. Bayard tilted his head into the wind as they trotted towards the reeking charnel-house, appalled by the pervading stench of roast flesh. He gazed at the ransacked remains of Briconet's encampment, wondering how he could have allowed such a slaughter.

Villefranco wasn't worth piggeries like this. The insignificant Duchy should have been exchanged over a goblet or two of wine, honour having been satisfied after a short and painless bombardment.

Instead, carnage and chaos. Heaps of men, scorched into fatty scarlet and black stripes by the tremendous heat. It looked to Bayard as if they had been caught in the fiery breath of a rampaging dragon. Great wagons had been rolled on their side, helpless as giant tortoises on some tropical beach. Tents had been torn down, poor washing hanging on slack guy-ropes. Cooking fires had caused minor conflagrations here and there about the camp, burnt through stacks of provisions and reduced piled barrels to sooty rings and loose hoops.

There were bodies everywhere, lying about the camp. Most wore the simple leather jerkins and fustian leggings issued to France's infantry forces. Some locally-raised rabble Briconet must have hounded and cajoled to this glorious slaughter.

Bayard grimaced, imploring the Almighty to grant him the willpower to resist strangling the evil gnome in his own guts.

'My lord Chevalier! The cliff!'

Bayard turned his horse, trotted into the fresh air blowing in from the sea. He took an enormous lungful, reining in beside one of his dusty Gendarmes. The knight had dismounted, holding his weary mount's bridle in one hand as he pointed down the sudden, steep slope.

Bayard stared at the trampled ground, the sparse turf and windblown furze bushes flattened by parallel wheeltracks.

'There, in the gully, my lord!'

Bayard followed the broad tracks to the edge of the cliff. The ground fell away sharply, the crumbling bed dotted with sandmartin holes. The variously-shaded strata seemed to glow in the last rays of the sun – rich terracotta overlaid by layers of hard-baked biscuit.

The deep gully had been partially blocked by the remains of a vast war engine. The oak and iron monster had tipped over on its side, the crazy contraption which had apparently been carried in the spacious hold crushed and bent out of all recognition.

'Organ pipes?' the scout wondered.

'Cannon barrels,' Bayard said, brows furrowed as he squinted at the scrap vehicle. The back end of the mighty engine seemed to have been burnt black, the formidable timbers and iron-bound axles charred and draped with soot. He turned his head, followed the inter-weaving wheeltracks back up the gentle slope towards the wrecked camp.

'It must be some manner of secret weapon, a super-heavy gun of some kind,' Bayard observed. What manner of gun could have obliterated the castle, turned its defenders into human torches? Bayard shivered with apprehension at the ugly possibilities, shuddered at the idea Briconet may have been tinkering with this new engine of mass destruction.

'They fired the device . . . back there, by the main camp,' Bayard theorised, turning his horse to follow the deep ruts in the hard-baked ground.

'And the garrison made a sally, and rolled the device over the cliff?'

'No. They never got that far,' Bayard surmised. 'The gunners must have misjudged their charges. The cannon was blown back by the recoil.' The doubtful knight estimated the distance the outlandish engine had rolled.

'All the way back? God help anybody in the way.'

The bemused Gendarmes walked their horses across the ruined acre, finding more bodies, some of them hewn with swords or spears, others battered about the head in some fiercely-fought hand-to-hand contest.

Bayard dismounted to examine the ground. Judging by the deep indentations, the massive engine had originally been set up to cover the approaches to the castle. Close by, the remains of what must have been a powder cart. A stack of barrels had been reduced to splinters by the back-blast or the wild passage of the wagon. Bayard stooped to examine a trail of evil-smelling slime, wondering if the engine had leaked some devilish propellant over the scarred ground. He spotted a brass fitting, lifted the misshapen talisman from the filth.

It glimmered in his grubby palm.

He turned it over, realised he had discovered a gold ring carrying a twisted emblem – the distinctive crossed keys of St Peter, symbol of the Vatican.

And papal signet rings didn't fall by chance.

Bayard closed his fingers about the appalling omen, stood back from the filthy, partially-scorched smear on the rock.

'Miserator vestri,' he murmured. *May he have mercy on you.*

Alas for Abandando of Avignon.

There was little use in putting a garrison into the place now. Bayard spent half an hour investigating the abandoned camp and detailed a dozen riders to stand guard over the wreckage until he could send aid and gravediggers from Marseille.

Bayard meant to bury the bodies – and the infernal engine with them. The world had killing devices aplenty, without monstrosities like this. The tired company turned their horses and retraced their steps towards the west, following the coast road through the rapidly gathering gloom.

A few leagues further on Bayard's bone-weary riders caught up with the dispirited conquerors of Villefranco. Two or three tattered companies, their pinched features evidence of some recent ordeal. They had been hurrying home with what little they had been able to salvage from the wrecked camp – a handful of carts piled with assorted loot and groaning wounded.

The captain in command was riding at their head, a groom walking alongside to steady him in the saddle. A broad, blood-stained bandage had been tied about his badly fractured skull.

The rogue peered around at the approaching hoofbeats, tilting his head to catch the angry exchanges at the rear of the column. His loyal groom held on to the captain's horse, steadying the nervously stamping beast as the Chevalier spurred past the restless files of dead-eyed spearmen. They seemed grateful enough for the rest, leaning on their weapons as if their legs had turned to straw.

'Who commands here?' Bayard enquired, bringing his panting charger to a halt broadside on to the curiously nodding officer.

'Captain Valbien, your honour,' the dutiful groom shouted, touching his forelock as Bayard's hard-riding escort raised torches to illuminate the bedraggled legion. The French levies gazed back blankly, each man lost in his own hellish netherworld as their angry masters ranted and raved.

But all they could hear were the mad fortissimos of Briconet's gun, echoing about their skulls as if they had been trapped in the bell towers of their village church. The multi-barrelled killing machine Briconet had ordered dragged before Villefranco had splintered half the legions' eardrums. But the demoralised levies counted themselves fortunate when they recalled in ghastly detail the fate of Villefranco's unwary garrison.

'Of the Royal Marseille Militia, my lord.'

'Is he wounded? Can he not speak for himself?'

The worthy ancient cupped his ear.

'What's that? Can he speak? Not now sir, nor never again, after that giant brute butted him down my lord. Went down like a rock, if you get my meaning sir.'

'Where is the Papal Legate? Where are his treasury wagons?' Bayard bawled, leaning over his saddle to address the grinning groom.

'Captain Valbien bid us pack all that secret gear into the carts you see, my lord. He waved his sword at the rascals who said they'd done enough and deserved a share. It's all there my lord, every penny.'

'And what of Briconet?'

'Ah well, as for the inquisitor,' the old rascal shrugged. 'The last we saw of him, he was taking cover behind that hellish engine, ordering the master gunner to open fire. The next we knew,' the groom shouted, 'the whole hillside was covered in smoke, and there was a great clapping bang as if the world had come to an end.'

'You put the garrison to the sword?' Bayard bawled back.

'What's that my lord? Put 'em to the sword? No my lord. No need. Not after that bleedin' cannon finished with em, leastways. When we could stand, we had a look for him, God's truth we did. But the pair of 'em were no more than a smear of jam in the dust. A smear of jam, the pair of 'em.'

By the Castello Villefranco

$\blacklozenge$

'Treachery! They're launching a sortie from the walls!'

No one knew who bawled that first, deadly warning.

No one could see much further than the camp perimeter, the garish light given off by the few dozen spluttering torches they had staked out about their crude bivouacs. The horsemen on the flanks peered and pranced. The levies massed in the centre clung to their weapons as if they were splinters of the True Cross.

'What?'

'Draw your swords, defend yourselves!' The shout went up from the rear. The darkness was pressing in on them from all sides. The mad clatter of the drums raised the hackles on the backs of their necks.

'Watch the flanks, watch your rear! Ambuscade, Have a care!'

'Who's that shouting there?' Valbien demanded, stalking through the nervous ranks.

'Prepare to shoot!'

'Who? Us? Who are we shooting at?'

'I don't like it,' Hobby growled, struggling to free his manacled wrists. The cold iron had worn bloody weals about his wrists, chafed the skin from his knuckles.

'I can't see a damned thing!'

The Englishmen had been hemmed in by Villefrancans, fearful they might try and fight their way free by main force. Eldritch had almost cricked his neck looking round for Charlotte. She must have fallen behind, following the forlorn host as if she were some officer's doxy. Hulin and the boy with the flag had capered off towards the head of the ill-knit column.

'What's all the shouting?'

The prisoners collided with their stumbling guards as the escort came to a ragged halt a few paces behind the vanguard.

'Drum, damn you, don't stop now!' Eldritch recognised Hulin's high-pitched accent. He was squealing like a stuck pig, up at the front of the staggering column. Eldritch was squinting into the gloom, cursing his defective vision. But the night had sunk its teeth into the coast, bitten out their entire world.

'My lords, my lords!' Hulin bawled from the front. 'We come in truce! Damn you, Bernardo, I said drum! We come to surrender ourselves to . . .'

The end came down as swift and apocalyptic as the night. The ragged company had stopped dead and started forward, staggering and shoving one another. The sound of drawn swords had prompted some of the ruffians at the front to draw theirs.

'Treachery! *Sauve qui peut!*'

The shout swept down the files like some dread disease, turning the tightly-packed company into a market-day rabble.

They had barely cleared the gates when the inky-darkness ahead of them erupted with incandescent light. The bright white flash seared their eyes. They imagined they saw red-skinned creatures caper in the bonfire glare. Others glimpsed a strange blue halo like the St Elmo's fire which formed about the masts of storm-tossed ships.

But the momentary flash of igniting gunpowder was immediately swallowed up by a supernova of mind-melting colour. A lurid fireball of scarlet and yellow energy exploded in all directions. The stunned front rankers averted their eyes a split second before they registered the appalling report.

Heaven was torn asunder in a blink, the night sky split from crotch to clouds with an ear-splitting screech louder than a thousand sails ripped up the middle. The shambling crowd felt the shockwave as a chest-crushing ripple, the displaced air knocking them on their heels split seconds before they were massacred by the wall of hurtling, twisting, spinning steel.

Briconet had ordered the master gunner to load the engine's multiple barrels with rusty bolts and broken nails, odd bits of scrap and lengths of chain. He had weighed the charges down with shovelfuls of lead slugs and variously-sized bullets – all the ammunition the overworked engineering sheds back in Marseille had been able to spare him. The Villefrancan deserters were torn to bloody streamers by the bone-punishing tempest. Men were blown sideways, hurled into the air or dashed against the castle walls by the devastating impacts. Limbs turned bloody cartwheels. Heads rolled and bounced over the rocky ground.

Twelve barrels had been discharged as one, the finely milled powder spluttering and snaking along the complex ignition pipes the French engineers had welded across the breeches. A frisson of sparks burned left to right over the top deck and then right to left along the bottom, tiny dancing flames licking at a dozen touch holes and sparking the carefully-packed charges.

The colossal detonation sent the massive engine rearing backwards. Gerhard's destructive prototype had been a child's toy in comparison with the leviathan Briconet had brought into creation.

The inquisitor had clapped his hands to his ears, grinning like a fiend, possessed with manic glee as the confused vanguard was illuminated by the deadly sunburst.

A fraction of a moment later the transfixed force was swatted from the face of the earth. The jolting recoil sent the astonished gun crew flying through the air like scorched rabbits from a blazing warren. Briconet himself was hurled ten feet onto his meagre backside by the vicious back-draught. He levered himself up on his elbows in time to see Leonardo's Engine rear above him, its six-foot-wide, iron-rimmed wheels spinning on their oiled axles. He threw his thin arm across his face as the massive, oak-girded hull crashed down, crushing him like a bedlouse. The sudden, searing impact obliterated his frail body before the shrill scream had left his throat.

Abandando Briconet of Avignon, Papal Legate and holy inquisitor, did not simply die. He was extinguished, vaporised like a moth in a flaming mortar.

The shrieking wheels buckled as the five-ton Goliath sprawled to earth and skidded off down the slope, tangling a guyrope and tugging up a row of patched tents as it careered towards the sea. The iron and oak turtle belly-flopped towards the sanctuary of the open ocean, gouging the thin soil and scrub in its path.

Grooms and camp followers, hangers on and whores had been grouped a little way back from the curious engine, eager to witness its diabolical debut. They scattered as the wagon picked up speed down the slope, slewing sideways into Briconet's scarlet carriage and dealing it a glancing blow which flipped the heavy wagon on its back. An inch-thick steel plate swung free for a moment and then fell away, decapitating a pair of rearing cart horses.

Screams and shockwaves hurled fearsome echoes out over the barren hillside, catapulting the hellish symphony towards the sea.

But Leonardo's Engine didn't get that far.

A sudden gully opened up before the juggernaut, swallowing it whole. The wagon cartwheeled into the ditch, one dumbstruck gunner still holding on to a flailing rope. The cart hit the ground and burst open on the unforgiving bedrock. The screeching puppet impacted with the twisted pipework and fell, back broken like a straw doll.

The astonished survivors gazed at the sudden carnage, the terrible swathe the wagon had cut through their own rear.

And then the screaming started.

From the bloody front, terrified flanks and wrecked camp.

The shell-shocked levies imagined they had been dropped head first into hell.

Hulin's determination to prevent the shadow-fiend and his giant sergeant from escaping saved the invaders' lives – though they were in no condition to acknowledge the fact.

A sheared-off flagpole hurtled past Eldritch's head, a few scorched fragments of the old Duke's battleflag still smouldering on the splintered shaft. The pale gauntlet still attached to the fractured pole was young Bernardo's right hand.

Next moment The Englishmen were hurled backwards, thrown into a cursing ruck of terrified Villefrancans. The men to their front came piling in on top of them, arms and legs flailing in terror. But their escort had been marching near the rear of the column – the dead men shuffling in front had taken the full force of the blast. Eldritch felt his shoulder muscles pop in agony as his manacled arms were crushed beneath him. Two, three, four bodies landed square on his chest; he did not know whether they were alive or dead.

A stomach-churning storm of flesh and entrails rocketed over the prone men's heads, splashing and clattering against the opened doors of the fortress. Discarded weapons and bits of armour ricocheted from wall to wall as the immense force of the explosion lashed the castle approaches. The heaped guards were scoured by flames and hacked in pieces by the whistling debris.

Hobby was kicking and writhing, shouldering stunned guards aside as if they were flying feathers. The report clapped against the walls. The doors were hurled wide open as if they were rusty shutters caught in a storm. Eldritch had just managed to open his mouth, but the deafening blast had set his ear drums ringing. He squirmed, working his head between a dead man's legs and using his strong shoulders to work his way free from the charnel pile.

Charlotte had been hovering at the rear of the column – the shot and steel had eaten their fill by the time they reached her place in the blasted ranks. Terrified soldiers dropped their weapons and took to their heels, shot-deafened survivors staggered off, fell into the ditch which ran the length of the wall. Eldritch blinked through a smouldering blanket of smoke, the sulphurous stink assaulting his reeling senses. The vanguard had been cut down like new corn, the front three ranks pulverised, the next three torn in two, the next hurled backwards without limbs, without heads. The squabbling pack had disintegrated, the lucky few who had escaped injury buried beneath ranks of dead and maimed men.

Men choked. Men shouted. Men cursed.

Eldritch squirmed to his knees, his blood-splattered sergeant rocking backwards and forwards to free his legs from a logjam of bodies. Here and there a dazed survivor picked himself up and staggered back towards the castle. Eldritch's throat was seared by the gusting smoke, his eyes, thankfully, refused to focus on the tangled carnage.

Charlotte dashed forward, hauling her lover from the smoking bodies.

Her gown was splattered with blood and fragmented flesh. Her hair was stiff and steaming, stuck into a scarlet crest like a battle-maddened Spartan.

She was opening her mouth, bawling his name but making no sound Eldritch could hear over the mad pounding in his head. He reacted to her fierce tugs, digging in his heels and propelling himself out of the bloody mass.

Hobby rose from the dead beside him, his torn tunic smeared and scorched, his hair shorn to a smoking grey stubble. He was spitting and cursing, his tongue protruding from cracked lips.

But he was alive.

And so, by some miracle, was Hulin.

He had been nearest the fatal engine, and had been the first to realise Briconet had betrayed them. He had thrown himself down a fraction of a second before the cataclysm, rolling aside as the super-heated tornado lashed his command. Scrap steel had scored his back, legs and buttocks, set his stolen clothing afire. He rolled over and over the hard-baked earth, trying to extinguish the greedy flames.

He leapt to his scalded feet and ran for his life, obeying some deep-seated instinct for survival, knowing the enemy would not allow any survivors to carry tales of the massacre. He weaved through heaps of rag-doll bodies, leapt over barricades of limbless corpses. He skidded on steaming blood and tripped over blue entrails. The smouldering wounds on his back drove him on, faster, faster, before the horsemen rode in to complete the slaughter.

He ran like a hare, racing past the stumbling shadow-men who had survived the barrage. Some had ducked back inside the fortress. Others had run off over the barren hillside. Hulin veered away from the open doors, the dimly glinting lanterns inside the courtyard. For one crazy moment, he remembered his youth, a nativity scene in his local church. The crib and stable, onlooking animals lit by fragrant candles. Hulin accelerated away from the mischievous vision, preferring the stony darkness of the open hillside.

He didn't see the vast shape loom out of the night, knock him flying over the bare bedrock. He sprawled out, cursing, winded, his back still smouldering. Charlotte bent down beside him, got her arms under his chest and hauled him to his knees.

'Hurry, bring him under cover and grab his damned keys!'

Hulin was too stunned to resist, his vision fading as he felt his groin scrape over the rocks. The Countess leaned back, bent her knees and dug in her heels. The smoking corporal slipped through the narrow gap and rolled on the floor. He caught a glimpse of the castle and then the English sergeant shouldered his way through the crack, obliterating the light.

Hulin knew no more.

'We can't stay here!' Eldritch hissed, working his shoulder muscles to try and relieve his agonising cramps. Every joint in his bruised body seemed to have been filled with its own special fire. Pins and needles swarmed over his neck and back like prickly sea anemones. 'For the love of Christ, Charlotte, haven't you found his keys yet?'

The girl paused, her bloody hands busy searching the stunned corporal's kit.

'I deliver you from the *oubliette*, and yet you still forget who you address,' she said heavily.

'What's that? You delivered us? God damn you, I warned you of Briconet's crazy notions!'

'Keep it quiet there, the hillside's lousy with Frenchies,' the sergeant warned, keeping one eye on the slope and another on his scorched uniform. Hobby was still finding and extinguishing fragments of smouldering clothing. Most of his hair had been scorched away, leaving him blinking comically in a mask of streaked soot.

Charlotte sat up crossly, peered over the rim of their feeble hideout. The same quiet cairn of boulders where Eldritch had hidden out half a dozen lifetimes before.

They could hear the French bawling to one another away by the castle. A squad of horsemen had cantered by, whooping and yelling as they pursued the last of the fugitives down the hill, leaning out of the saddle to dispatch the daft rabbits with a single thrust of their spears. A small number of Villefrancans had worked their way along the ditch, emerging on the blindside of the wall. But the enemy horsemen had been dispatched around the far side of the castle, working their way up the ridge to emerge in the rocky gullies which ran down the slope towards the crossroads.

Eldritch doubted any of them would find their freedom. Half dazed by the explosion, shocked by the dreadful memory of fighting their way from a gravepit – they would be easy meat for the whooping pursuit.

Hobby raised his head, followed Charlotte's furious gaze.

The French seemed to be more concerned with looting the dead and chasing shadows to make a proper search. They heard shouts, braying laughter. The deranged joy which signalled survival.

Gloomy reflection would surely follow, when the fire of battle had finally evaporated from their veins.

Eldritch tilted his head, ran his finger into his ear. His hearing had returned, but his temples felt as if they had been lashed with strips of lead, locked in a vice until his skull felt fit to burst. He glanced at the Countess, shivering with shock as she crouched in the rocky crown, a hundred paces from her raucously celebrating countrymen.

Hobby ducked down.

'The horse are coming back.'

Eldritch glanced down at Hulin. They had smothered his bare back in strips of shirt, extinguished his smouldering clothing with handfuls of dirt. He was muttering to himself, his eyelids fluttering, lips moving in spastic rictus.

'We can't stay here,' Hobby repeated. 'Leave that shit be and we'll run for the road. If we get to the cliffs, they'll never find us, not without a pack of hounds to sniff our trail.'

'He can talk their lingo; he might be of use yet,' Eldritch argued. 'Besides, he has the bastard keys to these,' he snarled, rattling his manacles.

'Quiet, you whore's abortion! We're in the . . .'

The faint scrape of chain and the sudden warning must have carried further than they imagined. A squad of diligent Frenchmen turned, attracted to the rocky cairn like iron filings to a magnet.

Hobby chucked grimly, ducking back down behind their questionable cover.

'Over here!' someone shouted. 'There's more of them in that stone circle!'

Eldritch kicked out at the Countess' twitching foot. 'The keys, for the sake of Christ Almighty,' he croaked. Charlotte was electrified by his blunt appeal.

The shouts came closer.

'The keys, damn you, find his keys!'

'I'm looking, God damn you!' She tore at Hulin's rags, yanked at his broad leather belt.

A Frenchman peered through the narrow gap between the leaning boulders. Hobby elbowed the youngster in the face, splitting his nose and sending him reeling back on his cronies.

'They're in there all right!'

'The keys, the keys,' Eldritch was almost puking with terrified rage.

Charlotte tugged on a length of fine chain, pulled the magical talisman from the remains of Hulin's shirt. Eldritch turned his back on her.

'Hurry, hurry!'

'I'm going as fast as I can.'

'Whatever you're thinking of doing missy, you'd best . . .'

A glinting spearpoint was thrust through the gap. A large rock whistled over the cairn and landed a few feet from Eldritch's prone body.

'There!'

Another of Briconet's levies tumbled into the arena, thrusting the bigger Englishman back with his spear. Two more squeezed in after him, followed by their captain. Hobby hurled himself to the left, trapping the youngster's spear against the wall of rock. He kneed the militiaman in the groin, frantic with rage as the French tried to jab at him past their reeling comrade. Eldritch kicked out, knocking another of them aside. The captain dashed forward into the gap, lunged with his sword. The cold blade sliced through Hobby's shirt and bit into his forearm. He cursed, leaned back and butted the advancing officer square on the bridge of his nose. The brave Frenchman was hurled backwards by the brutal blow, his smashed nose squirting blood. Charlotte shrieked as a hot gout splashed her eyes. Eldritch tore himself free and swung the heavy chain around his head. A one-eyed militia-man ran at him, spear clutched to his chest. The chain wrapped about the shaft, wrenching the weapon from his hands. Hobby barged the man into the wall and kicked the piteously screaming captain in the belly for good measure.

'Run, we can't hold them forever,' Eldritch called.

Charlotte frantically wiped her eyes, choking and spitting. Hulin sat up, bewildered by the savage fight. It seemed he had woken up in hell's torture chamber, just as his mother had assured him he would. Eldritch grabbed a broken spear and impaled the last Frenchman against the rock cairn. The militia-man slumped over the stake, black blood spouting between his clenched teeth.

'Run! Over the wall and down the slope!' Eldritch repeated. Charlotte was busy unlocking Hobby's irons. Hulin had prised himself to his feet and was blinking like an owl, stupid with shock.

'Don't stand there gawping, get over the wall, flee!' Eldritch yelled, kicking the half-daft corporal in the seat of his breeches.

Hulin needed no further urging. He hurled himself at the wall, pulled himself up and threw his legs over the rim. The other three were right behind him, squinting into the total darkness of the night.

'Which way?' Charlotte cried. 'Which way do we run?'

By Mont Gilbert le Galliard

✦

The handful of officers who remained greeted Alberto Tarsi's dramatic announcement with subdued dread, casting doubtful glances at their colleagues and praying to God they might have misheard.

No such luck.

'That's right gentlemen, we are going to attack.'

The captain of pikes coughed into his fist. Isadoro Ballistado, the captain of arquebusiers who had assumed control of the Spanish contingent following Captain Isolani's death the previous summer, scratched his louse-infested tunic as he calculated the suicidal odds.

Duke Gerhard, lounging beside the tent flap in his gilt armour, noted their distinct lack of enthusiasm.

'You look somewhat shocked by the prospect of earning your money, gentlemen,' he snapped, coming to the point with commendable speed, if not tact. 'Did you not say yourselves, this waiting is crucifying us?'

The young nobleman looked to Tarsi for confirmation. The wily commander nodded brusquely, reluctant to undermine his superior. They were, after all, in much the same boat.

The Duke was portraying himself as the godly champion of his brutally-invaded, peace-loving Duchy. The despicable French had forced him to flee his home, obliging him to ally himself with the Empire. Like Tarsi, Gerhard's only realistic prospect of returning to his home was in company with the all-conquering Imperial forces. In the meantime Gerhard had decided to assume the role of loyal servant and devoted soldier, hoping Charles would not be too particular whose careers he helped resurrect.

The Duke had transformed himself, packing away his flamboyant court costume in favour of a set of ludicrously ornate Milanese armour. The young knight had buckled on the outsized sword he had pulled from Baldassare's bloody corpse and wore a black and gold cabacette morion at all times.

Tarsi had observed his striking metamorphosis with tight-lipped scorn. He had met Gerhard's type before. Damp-squib soldiers who poked and preened about the camp and became even more of a liability on the battlefield.

Gerhard himself had been annoyed to discover that the men were even less impressed with his martial appearance than the swarthy Seigneur.

Whatever happened to loyalty?

Didn't the dunghill swine realise he had been obliged to flee his home by their common enemy? That he was ready to share their privations, endure the very same hardships? If he hadn't agreed to sell off the designs for Leonardo's Engine they would be going hungry this night, sitting up to their ballocks in bilgewater on some English cog bound for Calais.

Gerhard took off his helmet and ran his hand through his rapidly thinning blond hair. He frowned at the shabby captains who had obeyed the summons to Tarsi's tent, realising that in all probability they would have preferred the uncertain voyage with Master Salt to Tarsi's harebrained shot in the dark.

The Spaniards scowled from one to the other, wondering whether the northern devils were calling their bluff. One could never tell with these cold-bloodied reptiles. At least two dozen malingerers had already taken themselves off, slipping away into the night during their nerve-shattering guard duties in the trenches. Some had crawled out of their holes on their bellies. Others had climbed the sheer cliff faces, worked their way along non-existent ledges in their determination to escape the rat-trap pass. A few were believed to have sneaked into Mont Galliard, and some had deserted directly to the French.

Tarsi knew the excruciating delays were bleeding the legion dry. An all-out attack by several thousand screaming Swiss would be preferable to this damned waiting.

'The Duke and I are in complete agreement about our present predicament. Our solution is simple, gentlemen. If the Swiss won't come to us, we'll carry the fight to them, aye, and ram it down their damned throats!'

Gerhard looked delighted by Tarsi's deferential manner. The Spaniard Ballistado paled. The pike captain blinked like a lark in a trap.

'But we've fewer than six hundred effectives. If we venture over the parapet we'll . . .'

Tarsi waved the captain's objections aside.

'I am not suggesting an all-out attack. But a raid, in force, at night, might give them a surprise and stop our swine from sloping off through sheer boredom,' he insisted with his customary vigour. 'We've plenty of close-quarter weapons, there's your sword and buckler men and at least a score of *dopplesoldners*. Let them earn their double pay for a change.'

'But a few dozens, against thousands?'

'I mean to take at least half the legion, if not three quarters. We know Bayard has been called away somewhere. Von Schwartzer wouldn't take a piss without his say so,' Tarsi embroidered. 'He won't imagine for a moment that we would have the audacity to attack. They've hardly bothered to set sentinels, let alone fortify their camp.'

The Spaniard knew Tarsi's reputation of old. His night raids, forced marches and frequent changes of position had made him a dreaded enemy during his long and hard campaigns on behalf of Margaret of Savoy. He had heard all about Tarsi's skill and daring, but this time the soldiers involved would be his own countrymen, sworn companions all. He was being asked to lead his men out of a carefully entrenched position and attack a vastly superior force in the open.

And in the dangerous chaos of the night, where the best-laid plans had the habit of going sadly awry. If things went ill for them in the Swiss camp, the pass would become their Thermopylae.

'His men are drunkards, night beasts snoring in their filth. We will hit them hard – three parties from three directions. If we can get to Von Schwartzer himself, they'll be a week electing a new leader.'

But Tarsi's fanciful scenarios failed to convince the experienced captains. They shuffled and scratched, picking at their matted beards. None of them had enjoyed a decent shave in days.

'Their numbers won't count, if half of them are asleep and the other half too drunk to find their pikes. We'll be able to withdraw in good order while they're running about like strangled pullets. Duke Gerhard will remain with the rearguard, and cover our retreat.'

The Duke nodded soberly. None of his captains looked particularly reassured by that intelligence.

Tarsi frowned.

'As Duke Gerhard has already pointed out, it is high time we started earning our wages. The Emperor Elect isn't paying us to sit in a trench sunning ourselves.' He glared at his reluctant understudies. 'Von Huff has moved heaven and earth to ensure our back pay was properly settled. I for one would consider it highly dishonourable to take his money and yet forget my duty.'

'There is no question of that,' Ballistado grumbled. 'But if we are going to attack, I would prefer to have evened the odds a little.'

Tarsi smiled.

'Which is why the assault parties will be equipped by my fireworker, Master Stitchwort here.'

The Englishman in question was crouched in a dim corner of the command post, ruminating over the designs of his latest contraption with his new crony Montisso Montalban.

The two of them could barely understand a word the other said, but they had struck up an unlikely partnership, sharing a sandbagged dugout out near the latrines.

Nobody else went within half a league of their reeking den.

They had compared notes and swapped formulae, pooling their ideas to come up with colossal war machines and ever more elaborate siege engines. They had argued over the correct method of grinding the powder – adding and varying the unstable ingredients which made up their deadly compounds. Montalban had learned an enormous amount about the sinister black powder from the eccentric Englishman, whose bizarre appearance seemed ideally suited to his arcane experimentations. Stitchwort never used the mass-produced German powder, preferring to mix his own, extra-special blends.

'Monk's piss, that's what you need. Monks make for the best saltpetre there is. That's why the best powder always comes from mills adjoining monasteries,' he had explained to the bewildered Frenchman.

Stitchwort, an expert when it came to the chemical composition of gunpowder, had until then been stymied by his complete lack of engineering know-how. He needed powerful, well-forged weapons in order to take best advantage of his compounds, but had always been cursed by poor quality workmanship. He had destroyed any number of arquebuses, small-bore cannon and squat bombards during his experiments – the poorly-cast barrels splitting and cracking under the intense pressure released by his extra-strong powder.

The sooty duo had worked together in gleeful secrecy, confidently predicting a whole range of groundbreaking developments.

Montalban's new-found enthusiasm had helped Duke Gerhard forget his own abysmal dabblings with Leonardo's Engine. The naïve youth had been forced to hand over the wrecked prototype to Briconet and had sold the last of the design drawings to that smooth-talking rogue Salt.

But Montalban had promised he would have a new, improved version by the end of the month. The updated model would use Stitchwort's triple-strength powder, which burned brighter and quicker than the 'German night soil' he had used previously. Gerhard had high hopes the latest breakthrough would help him cement his martial reputation, confound the interfering fools who had tried to muscle in on his discoveries.

'Isn't that right sir? You have developed some, how shall we describe them, Little Equalisers, for us to destroy our enemies?'

Stitchwort looked up from his sketchbook, gave the reluctant heroes a gap-toothed grin. His skin had been scorched so many times it resembled a lizard's belly, a series of shiny sequins which changed colour in the flickering torchlight. He had long since lost his eyebrows and much of his hair, burnt off by flash explosions in his mixing bowl.

'Monsieur Montalban and I have come up with some promising devices,' he admitted modestly. 'I think they might give the Swiss a nasty shock or two.'

'Or two thousand,' Ballistado repeated under his breath.

'It's the skirmishers we'll have to watch out for,' Stitchwort went on, easing himself to his feet, his greasy leather hood brushing the ceiling of the command post. He crossed to the crude diagram Tarsi had laid out on the table.

'Pikemen are only any use in formation. I think we can safely presume they don't stay in formation while they sleep, eh?'

The officers ignored his feeble attempt at humour.

'Whereas their arquebusiers and crossbowmen can be in action the moment they wake up.' The Englishman pursed his chapped lips. 'There's not much we can do about the crossbowmen, apart from the obvious, knocking the buggers over the head. But no arquebusier will stand against fire pikes.'

'Fire pikes?'

'Precisely. I have prepared a few dozen for you to lead the assault. Let me assure you, gentlemen, no arquebusier in his right mind is going to stand his ground in the face of two dozen flaming spearpoints.'

Tarsi nodded. That was true enough. One spark from the flaming pikes could ignite his powder – and turn the arquebusier into a human torch.

'So we knock the crossbowmen over the head and drive all their arquebusiers off with the fire pikes. But what about the others? Three thousand fanatical pikemen?' Ballistado enquired.

Stitchwort tilted his head like a blackamoor at prayer. 'A good point, sir. We can expect them to be massed together in clumps of up to a hundred men. So every time they form up, you must let them share one of these out amongst themselves.'

He lifted one of his terracotta flasks from the table and absent-mindedly tossed it to the doubting Spaniard. Ballistado grabbed the heavy flask with an oath, squinted at the crude fuse which had been sealed in the neck with brittle black wax.

'My special blend,' Stitchwort said, raising his non-existent eyebrows in silent encouragment.

Ballistado handed the flask to Tarsi and crossed himself.

Francesco Savvi had been shaken awake in the dead hours of the night, roused from a pleasant dream of tumbling gold and worshipping women. He came to, blinking up at his horse-faced second in command. Constantin Muhlberg, a fighter since he was a child, was not the prettiest sight first thing in the morning. The drowsy whore curled up next to him turned over with a curse, grumbling in her sleep and tugging the soiled bedding over her bared shoulder. Savvi yawned.

'What is it now?'

'Tarsi's moving.'

'Moving out? The spotted toad!' Savvi exclaimed, sitting up as if Muhlberg had tipped a basket of eels into bed with him.

The *Landsknecht* captain showed his teeth.

'Not out, up. The moon's gone down, it's as black as Cleopatra's cunny-fluff out there,' he reported. 'He's taken two thirds of his men out of their trenches, slipped them up the gorge in detachments of about fifty men each.'

Savvi was already tugging on his shirt, nodding his head at the captain's staggering intelligence.

Tarsi must have been sitting in the sun too long, to risk

everything on such a reckless gamble. A night attack on six thousand Swiss? Not even the legendary Tarsi could carry off such a reckless assault.

'They've taken off their boots, tied up all their ironmongery so as not to clang about, but one of the guards spotted them moving between the rocks.'

'Give him a gold piece for his troubles,' Savvi exclaimed, rummaging under the bed for his long leather boots. Muhlberg stood aside, fists clenched in anticipation of a good fight.

They had all been on edge, sitting up there in Tarsi's usurped eerie, watching the lacklustre manoeuvres below.

But the money they had been due for holding the pass open to the French had still not been forthcoming, and their insistence on being paid in full seemed to have brought the war to a spluttering full-stop. Two weeks on and Muhlberg had even suggested waiving the balance, making do on the downpayment Briconet had sent them in order to get on and have a crack at someone. Savvi and Stroma had listened to his heretical suggestion in stunned disbelief.

'We shook hands on twenty thousand livres, and you're ready to make do with five?' Savvi had snorted. 'What kind of nonsense is that?'

'Well at least we won't have to stay cooped up in here, picking fights with one another,' the captain had replied petulantly.

But not even the criminally naïve Muhlberg had anticipated that Tarsi would take a hand once more, marching up the pass to throw down the gauntlet before the impatient Swiss.

Savvi bent down, tugged up his boots and reached for the sword belt hanging from the bedpost.

'Assemble your men, but do it quietly for the sake of Christ! I don't want Tarsi alerted to the fact.'

Muhlberg's long face creased in bewilderment.

'He'll be alerted soon enough, when we pile out of the gate after him!'

'We're not going out of the gate,' Savvi snapped. 'Not until the Swiss have got him by the short and curlies, anyway.'

Muhlberg's lantern-jaw dropped onto his breastplate.

'You're never going to let him walk on by?'

Savvi finished dressing, cast a quick glance at the yawning whore curled up in the bedclothes. A good tough scrap would give him just the rest he needed, after going several rounds with that raven-haired strumpet.

'Of course we are. If we sally out now, we'll have to fight on equal terms. No my lad. We'll charge in when the survivors are running for it, grab our share of the spoils before those shit-finger Swiss get their mitts on it.'

Much as he disliked the sitting about, Muhlberg was sensible enough to see the sense in Savvi's grand strategy.

'I hope Tarsi manages to cut his way out. I'd love to step out in front of him, see the old bastard's face when we cut off his retreat,' he leered.

Savvi nodded.

'Better send someone along and rouse up Stroma. He'll want to see this.'

They had wrapped Stitchwort's powder flasks in cloth and packed them carefully into wicker baskets. Tarsi had detailed two men to carry each basket, in the forlorn hope that they might get the deadly cargo to the Swiss camp without dropping them – and bringing half the mountain down on their heads.

He had chosen to lead the grenadiers himself, with Stitchwort and Montalban tagging along to lend a hand where they could. Between them they had inflicted as much damage on the troubled world as an average-sized volcano, and Tarsi was counting on causing maximum disruption that night.

Ballistado, up at the front with a picked company of *dopple-soldners* and Spanish sword and buckler men, had been right about the terrifying odds they faced. They would need to even those odds if they were to stand a chance of finding their way back down the gorge. It would be up to Tarsi's bomb squads to exploit the chaos of the initial onset – seconding the swordsmen with volleys of grenades and disrupting their arquebusiers with the fire pikes.

The devilish poles were being hauled along by the third party, the steel points tied up with tough leather sacks filled with Greek fire – a sticky, highly combustible compound provided courtesy of Master Stitchwort.

Tarsi paused, looked up at the jagged cliffs which surveyed their feeble enterprise. He hadn't needed the bright moon to guide him – he knew every step of the pass in either direction. He knew the boulder outcrops, the treacherous scree slopes which could slide away beneath a man and warn the Swiss of their approach. He knew secret paths, narrow tracks left by the fleet-footed mountain sheep. He remembered small gaps in the rock walls, short cuts around the brittle ledges which would bring his command within a long stonesthrow of the Swiss camp. Von Schwartzer's men had pitched their tents on the far side of a small knoll towards the head of the pass.

With luck, they would arrive at the foot of the ridge without being observed. But Tarsi knew the direct route – the ancient trade road which wound its way through the valley – would be heavily guarded. He was also aware that he could not hope to climb the gravel-strewn slopes without attracting somebody's attention, however slackly the Swiss watched their perimeter.

The grenadiers ducked out of the sparse cover near the approaches to Mont Galliard, and doubled across a stretch of open ground to the next outcrop. Tarsi threw himself down, peering up at the merrily-lit fortress which dominated the narrow pass. He frowned to think of those rogues Savvi and Stroma, tucked up in his linen, drinking their way through his cellars. He wished for a moment he was leading his men across the causeway, to assault Mont Galliard itself.

Another time, he thought.

Tarsi looked up, recognising the tall, stooping figure of the Englishman making his way through the cowering ranks towards him. His jerkin appeared to be covered in strange growths – an assortment of stoppered bottles and flasks he had tied about his chest with lengths of string and bits of old leather. He looked more like some itinerant clam diver than a properly qualified fireworker.

Stitchwort huddled down beside him, his thin features framed by his old-fashioned leather hood. Tarsi raised his arm, pointed out the slim bridge which linked the fortress to the valley.

'You see the ruined blockhouse? I want a score of archers in there with a good supply of those eggs of yours,' Tarsi whispered. 'It's not like Savvi to risk his neck unnecessarily, but we don't want them sallying out behind us.'

'I can see that might prove less than helpful to the current operation,' the Englishman agreed.

'Wait until the pikes have passed by, then order the grenadiers into position. Tell them to stay out of sight if at all possible. We'll wait for you to rejoin us, before we launch the main assault.'

'All clear my lord,' Stitchwort said crisply. Tarsi winced.

'And for the sake of the Holy Virgin try and keep the noise down,' he hissed.

Stitchwort nodded apologetically, crouching down behind the

cold rock as the Italian adventurer waved his men forward, took a deep breath and slipped away into the night.

Captain Ballistado's advance party had taken the best part of an hour and a half to reach the broken ground at the foot of the bluffs. They dropped to their knees behind what little cover there was – boulders, broken-backed mountain oaks and outcrops of sandpaper-dry furze. The Spaniards among them were armed with studded shields the size of a dinner plate and long, slightly curved swords. The lightly-armoured fighters could wreak havoc against tightly-packed troops, especially if they caught them on an open flank.

Tarsi had divided the recently re-enlisted English archers into four parties – one to remain in the trenches with Gerhard and the other three to accompany each of his assault groups. He knew they were tough and reliable fighters – not even the continued absence of their precious captain Eldritch could undermine their awesome firepower. He had instructed the archers to provide close support to the swordsmen, firing over their heads until they ran out of ammunition – God knew there would be no shortage of targets this night. Once they had exhausted their supply of arrows he had told them to throw whatever came to hand – Stitchwort's grenades, discarded weapons or flaming torches. They could hurl rocks for all he cared – just as long as they kept up a murderous barrage against the far more numerous Swiss. When they had exhausted their missiles they were to draw their swords and wade in, shoulder to shoulder with the rest. He would have preferred to have Eldritch there to coordinate their efforts, but he had no doubt they would play their part as they had the previous summer – helping to rout the legendary Bayard's forces in this very same pass.

Tarsi remembered they had been ordered to shoot short that day, intending to undermine the resolve of Bayard's inexperienced levies without slaughtering too many of them. Tonight they would be killing for real – killing enemies who would have eaten Bayard's levies for breakfast.

Tarsi had sent along two dozen of his heavily-armed *dopplesoldners* to beef up his multinational host. They were, in contrast to the rest, big, brawny warriors from Southern Germany, their tawny beards twisted and plaited so that they hung like tarred ropes over their breastplates. The boastful soldiers carried monstrous two-handed swords fully six foot long, the iron hilts bound with leather worn smooth from constant use. The average man would have been unable to lift the devilish weapons, let alone swing them above his head in a deadly dance of death. The *dopplesoldners* were employed as skirmishers – their serrated blades designed to lop the heads from the enemy's pikes. Once they had shorn the opposing forces down to size, they would wade into the schillitrons of lightly-armed pikemen, slashing great swathes in their compacted ranks.

Only the desperate, deranged or blind drunk would even consider such a suicidal occupation – double pay or no. But Tarsi had never found any particular problem recruiting likely candidates.

The *dopplesoldners* crouched down in a closed circle, whispering hair-raising challenges or boasting of the miracles they would perform on the ridge above. As they talked they tugged straps and tightened belts, adjusted their helmet straps and peeled the sacking covers from their gleaming blades. Ballistado glanced at them, unable to understand much the dumb brutes were saying – not that it would have made an awful lot of sense to anybody outside their particular company.

Dopplesoldners were truly a dying breed.

The wiry captain held up three fingers and pointed to the top of the ridge – a series of jagged shadows a hundred feet above their shallow scrapes. Horst, their bald-headed corporal, nodded his head and tucked his long waxed moustaches under his shirt collar.

'*Klotzen nicht kleckern,*' he growled. His soldiers repeated the untranslatable prayer, easing themselves to their feet and shaking out their cramped muscles as if they were athletes ready for some Olympian challenge.

Ballistado sighed, mouth as dry as the withered oaks which had sheltered his tiny battalion. No way out now – not without losing face in front of these grinning apes. He drew his dagger and spat on the blade, took one last look at the patient assault party and waved his scouts forward.

They were eager enough, mountain fighters from the Basque country wearing rough leather jerkins over baggy-sleeved shirts and strange, conical caps. They had removed their boots to avoid alerting the guards, their calloused feet long inured to the hard going. Ballistado followed them up the slope, picking his way over the flaky soil which crumbled and cracked like over-cooked pastry. The ground was littered with treacherous rocks ready to tumble and roll beneath their feet. Dead roots snaked over the barren ground as if God had charged the trees with holding the frail hillside together.

The scouts had already drawn well ahead, moving swiftly and silently despite stooping over every few steps to check their ground. They would take care of the sentinels on the ridge, give Ballistado's assault party a chance to get in amongst the host camped on the gentler reverse slope.

The Spaniard paused, held his breath for the alert which never came. He could hear the gentle crunch of gravel underfoot, the occasional sharp ping as a stone bounced away into some gully. He looked over his shoulder, squinting to pick out the army of ghosts which had followed him up the slope. Dim figures moved on the periphery of his vision as his men followed half a dozen paths up the ridge.

Please God the Swiss would be too drunk to notice the phantoms, working their way towards them with murder and mayhem flickering behind their half-hooded eyes.

The ridge began to level off.

Ballistado stumbled, steadied himself with his right hand and came face to face with his first corpse of the campaign.

The man's throat had been sawn through, almost severing the head from the body. His blue and yellow striped tunic was glistening with gore, his green hose splattered and torn. The corpse had straggly red hair, plastered over a large, domed skull. The wrinkled forehead and sallow cheeks told the Spaniard the sentinel must have been well into his forties. His opened eyes were pale blue, gazing sightlessly at the heavens. Ballistado realised he was propping himself up in a pool of hissing blood, soaking quickly into the parched dust.

He rose, wiped his hands on his breeches and hurried on.

The Basques were out of sight now, working their way along the reverse slope, finding and throttling the few sentinels the Swiss had bothered to set. Ballistado found three more of them stretched out a hundred paces on, their brightly-striped legs pointing towards the small, hastily-extinguished fire they had been crouched about. He noticed one of them had a hole the size of a thaler in the sole of his lightly-made shoe. They would be little use to man or beast when the ghouls came to strip the corpses in the morning.

The scream, when it came, split the fragile peace of the night, ruptured the soaring heavens with its intensity. Ballistado broke into a run, altering his course to the right to follow the sudden commotion.

He ran past a tumbled cairn of grey boulders and realised he had emerged on the ridge above the garishly-illuminated enemy camp. The enemy camp which filled the broad bowl from rim to rim, a mountain lake of dirty canvas and upturned wagons, fluttering pennants and stacked arms. An inland sea of sleeping Swiss and muttering Frenchmen and snorting horses and growling dogs and laughing women and crying children and shouting officers and screaming wounded.

Ballistado swayed on the precipice, appalled by the sheer extent of the encampment. He took in the grim panorama in a blink.

There were horselines and bakeries, laundries and smithies. There were command tents and magazines and broad, reeking latrine pits. The Basques had worked their way through the outer ring of sentinels posted along the ridge and had fallen on the sleeping men they found washed up around the reverse slope. Latercomers, hangers on and whores. Tinkers and watermen, pie sellers and fisherfolk. Cobblers and needlewomen and mule skinners and itinerant actors. Shepherds and grooms and cattle boys.

The bloody-minded scouts hardly cared where or what they killed. They throttled and stabbed, clubbed and kicked their way towards the main encampment, tearing pikes from the stacks outside every tent and running the points into the bulging, yelling canvas shapes. The first, terrified shout sparked a sudden cacophony of sound – bawled orders and guttural challenges, bloody oaths and piteous whimpers. The Spanish surged down the slope, following the well-trodden path between the latrine pits and fanning out on either side of the canvas city beyond. Enemy troops were tumbling from their bedrolls and crawling from their tents, peering bleary-eyed towards the unanticipated intrusion.

Ballistado kicked at a stack of pikes, the heavy poles crashing down onto a tent and popping the frail shelter like a water blister. Shouts and muffled screams pursued him down the refuse-littered alley. He slashed at guyropes, stabbed at every face he saw, hacked desperately at the ugly canvas shapes which writhed and cursed beneath him. He peered over his shoulder, relieved to see his sword and buckler men had seconded his charge, finishing off the crawling cripples and sleep-drugged Swiss who had managed to pull themselves from their holes.

And behind them came the *dopplesoldners*, striding out with their fire-flecked faces set, beards tied up beneath their jutting chins. They had left the draff to the shouting Spanish, intent on deadlier prey – the Swiss pikemen packed into the narrow valley like mullet in a net. Ballistado fumbled for his horn, blew a short blast to summon the formidable killers after him. Flames leapt into the sky, illuminating the chaos, every flaming, stamping, woodcutting demon.

Swiss horns blared in reply, angry shouts rebounding about the galvanised camp.

Ballistado hauled himself up on a barrel and peered over the frantic encampment, searching out the flamboyant pavilion which would mark the heart of the enemy lair. He found it, a gold and silver marquee draped with battleflags and hung with gorgeous silk curtains. A company of halberdiers had already formed up in front of the headquarters tent, cruelly-spiked blades gleaming in the firelight. Shots were ringing out to left and right. Crossbow bolts whistled overhead and disappeared into the night. He leapt down before one of the ill-aimed missiles smashed his skull, waited for his men to coagulate about him and then led them on, down the throat of the Swiss camp.

'*Sancta Maria!* For God, Empire and Spain!' he bawled, his nervous jitters extinguished by squirts of undiluted adrenaline.

Behind them the *dopplesoldners* had drawn blood at last, a compact arrowhead of black-liveried fighters, their huge swords glinting and flashing in the lurid bonfires the Spanish had ignited. Their battlecry drowned out the screams of the wounded, a terrifying prayer which shook the foundations of the mountains.

'*Hut, dich baur ich komm!*'

Fugitives crawled away on their hands and knees or leapt over tumbled tents. The narrow alleys were jammed with screaming men, trying to find their arms in the rout.

The Swiss did without officers. Sergeants and corporals were virtually unknown – so the sleepy mob found themselves at a distinct disadvantage in those early moments, leaderless in the sudden, swirling, murderous chaos.

Alerted pikemen were left to find their own flags, to follow the rattle of a hundred drums as they tried to face up to the sudden onslaught. They had no idea how many men had attacked them, no clue as to which direction they had come from.

Their sentinels were slaughtered, the ramshackle horde camped on the broken ground around the rim of the vast bowl hacked to pieces or running for their lives.

Ballistado, running at the head of his gleeful killers, thought for a moment they might drive the entire force out of the pass, flush the Swiss down the gorge like rats before a flood.

And then he saw the first of their halberdiers, bearing down the alley toward them. A compact body of a hundred, two hundred, three hundred fully-alerted troops. He swung his sword, he caught his breath.

'*Sancta Maria! Sancta Maria!*'

By The Pass

✦

David had caught Goliath napping and rapped his knuckles, given him a sharp lesson for snoozing around his watchfires – but the Philistine felt no more than a fleabite, turning over in his sleep to crush the impudent louse which had crawled out from his mattress.

That was how Tarsi judged it, peering over the flaming valley from his vantage point on the ridge.

He could see small knots of his attacking troops surrounded by ever-thickening clusters of wasp-striped Swiss. He could see their crude banners flapping above the blazing tents: bears' heads. Bulls' heads. Crossed keys, antelopes and wolves. Each flag had attracted its own swarm of fighters armed with pikes, halberds, crossbows and arquebus. Each swarm was moving with remorseless determination towards one of his grievously isolated death-squads, strung out on the southern perimeter of the camp like pearls tossed into a furnace.

'Move up, move up!' he cried, his throat already hoarse from bawling orders and breathing the choking smoke. The grenadiers had deposited their baskets in the dead ground behind the latrines, the sulphurous stink of their flasks lost in the pervading stench. Stitchwort was distributing the waxed and sealed grenades as if he were handing out sweetmeats at a summer fair – as many as they could carry without dropping them on the rocks.

Tarsi drew his sword and led the pack forward to support the embattled Spaniards. They trotted between the evil-smelling lagoons the Swiss had been busy filling for the best part of three weeks, watching their footing and making sure to keep their fuming matchcords away from their deadly loads. Tarsi struck out at the few fugitives who blundered into his path, sending bewildered Swiss headlong into their own filth. A gaggle of pikemen emerged from an adjoining alley, intent on cutting off the invaders from their single escape route. They held their weapons at high porte across their chests – easier for hurrying from one end of the cluttered battlefield to another but little use in a close-quarter encounter. The Italian ran straight at them, slashing at hands and faces. A ringing blow severed three fingers from one pikeman's fist and cut his weapon in half. The howling devil dropped the useless pike and clutched his hand. Tarsi's vicious backhander caught him on the jaw, the iron hilt knocking out a handful of teeth and sending the wounded man staggering over a sagging tent.

The canny fighter was in his element, surrounded by a horde of awkwardly-armed opponents. He swung his sword, knocked their unwieldy pikes aside with his armoured-plated elbows. The little band was knocked apart, each man struggling with a craftily-armed opponent. Knives sheared off armour and bone. Daggers quivered in eyeballs. Tarsi kicked a bleeding pikeman between the legs, brought his bunched fist down on the back of the man's neck.

'Come on, we're wasting time here!'

He struck out once again, hacking at the backs of another small band of pikemen. One of the Spanish ducked into the lee of a vast wagon, lit the first of his grenades as the downed pikeman's comrades turned and faced the cornered Italian. The flask sailed over their heads, landing in the midst of a dozen bawling Swiss as they crowded forward to get at Tarsi. The old wolf backed off, hacking at the thrusting pike points and grabbing the exposed poles to keep the front rankers off balance. The tangled tents and flailing guyropes prevented them from forming a proper block. They jostled and kicked, breaking up like a shoal of minnows, but shrieking and hooting as they closed in for the kill.

The thunderous blast tore through the tangle of brightly striped legs, cutting their feet from beneath them in a stinking cloud of orange and black smoke. The screaming Swiss tumbled and writhed, clutching ruined knees, gaping groins and squirting thighs. Tarsi was hurled backwards by the blast, his sword skittering beneath the belly of a wagon. More flasks wobbled through the smoke, shattering explosions reducing the Swiss mob to minced meat. A swordsman thrust at Tarsi's chest. He rolled sideways, the blade striking sparks from the stony ground. The French officer followed up with his boot, but Tarsi raised his knees and deflected the savage kick. A Basque leapt over his prostrate body and skewered the captain on a broken pike. Tarsi recovered his sword and hauled himself to his feet.

'Onward! They'll never stand this!' he cried, waving his grenadiers forward over the shattered Swiss rearguard.

They had torn the lower jaw from the snapping beast, rescued the hard-pressed Spanish swordsmen from imminent destruction. The English archers stood just behind the hard-pressed front rank, drawing and shooting with no more concern than if they were on some village green back home. They were aiming high – shooting over the heads of the fighters in front of them to bring their deadly shafts down at murderous, armour-piercing velocities. The Swiss, packed like cattle in the narrow killing field, could only duck their heads and hope the whistling missiles were destined to impale one of their cowering comrades. Arrows clattered against pike shafts, pierced arms and temples. Dead men were carried upright in the crush.

Tarsi found Ballistado at bay against a logjam of overturned carts. Almost half his sword and buckler men had already been piked, clubbed or throttled by the vengeful – and by now wideawake – enemy. The wiry Spaniard was panting hard, blinking to clear the bubbling blood from his right eye.

'How many of those bombs have you brought along, Seigneur?' he asked, grimacing with pain. Tarsi leaned against the overturned wagon, catching his breath for a moment in the frenzied carnage.

'Not enough for this lot.'

'A brisk walk back to our lines might be advised,' Ballistado suggested, well aware of the terrific odds they faced.

More Swiss were pouring into the arena every moment.

Tarsi could see a forest of pikes moving behind a row of still-standing tents to their flank. The Swiss to their front had slashed and trampled themselves an acre of ground in the middle of the camp, assembling the bulk of their pikemen to protect their grandly-appointed command post. A dozen flags had sprouted from the smoke to their right flank. Drums rattled. Shot seared the drifting fogs.

'We'll have to knock a few more down yet,' the Italian argued.

'You hold here, form a skirmish line so the archers and grenadiers can shoot over your heads. Try and keep the path to the latrines open.'

Ballistado, good soldier that he was, didn't argue.

Tarsi studied the enemy movements, trying to gauge the biggest threat to their perilous bridgehead. He raised his weary arm, his steel gauntlet still dripping with Swiss blood.

'They've massed their shot to our right. We'll drive them back with the fire pikes, try and give you some respite.' Tarsi coughed, spat a wad of sooty phlegm over the upturned carcass of the provision wagon.

'Oh, and Ballistado, you won't leave without us, eh?'

The Spaniard frowned, shook his head. Rivulets of blood coursed around his nose, dripped off his chin.

'We'll wait, but a thoughtful guest never outstays his welcome.'

Montalban was yelling obscenities, hurling his bombs with savage glee towards the ever-thickening pack of Swiss. Jagged explosions bracketed their ranks, opened great holes in their formations. Their ragged phalanx writhed, pulled in all directions as mobs of men raced out, too eager to get at their attackers to obey the bawled orders. Stitchwort was ducking and diving, watching for every sudden thrust from the punch-drunk host.

'There's another lot!' He picked another bomb from the diminishing heap at his feet, lit the fuse and lobbed the spluttering bomb into the smoke-clogged sky.

The skirmish line ahead of him was thinning rapidly, swordsmen dropping over the heaped corpses as the enemy crossbowmen found their mark. William Hacker had passed the last of his arrows to Clement Teague – one of the Ride's best archers – and had lent the Spanish a hand with a fabulously ornate halberd. He wielded the pole arm as if he were scything corn, using the various blades, hooks and spikes to stab, pull and hack at his cursing opponents.

'How much longer are they goin' to keep us 'ere?' Teague wanted to know, blinking his eyes against the foul smoke pulsing over the stricken field. He raised his bow and fired blind, sure the shaft would find some target in the great mass of pikemen forming up across the corpse-choked camp.

Corporal Horst stopped a crossbolt in his right eye and fell onto his backside, cursing like a drunken monk. Ballistado's tunic was shaved bare by an arquebus bullet, the lead slug searing his forearm. The survivors closed ranks, their numbers grievously reduced by the advancing enemy. Behind them, the grenadiers drew and threw for their lives, the matchcords wrapped around their fists, red eyes glowing in the gloom.

The archers had been reduced to tugging arrows from corpses.

Others had slung their longbows over their backs and drawn their swords.

'This is worse than Tournai,' one old veteran complained, weighing the unfamiliar blade in his right fist and wishing he'd remembered to have it sharpened before they had left camp.

The tangled wagons and carts formed a barricade of sorts to their left, smashed timbers and shattered shafts presenting the flanking Swiss with a devilish obstacle. Behind the chaotic wagon park, the brimming latrine pits would secure their rear – at least until the Swiss had thought of working their way along the ridge above.

Ballistado thrust the slackers and lightly wounded and yellow-bellies back into line, yelling at them in five languages to hold their ground.

'You men, draw your swords if you've no more arrows,' he bawled, his excitable Spanish failing to get through to the bemused archers.

'Don't worry about those bastards!'

Flank attacks and feints were not popular with Swiss troops. They preferred the simple pleasure of a full-frontal assault. The Spaniard would worry about their line of retreat later.

Where in hell had Tarsi got to with those pikes?

The Italian had sheathed his sword, bent down to help cut the carefully wrapped fire pikes free from their leather bindings. He had a fleeting memory of using one of the wretched devices to get into some half-ruined castle up in the Spanish Netherlands. The wind had been blowing in their faces that day, forcing the sulphurous stench right down their own throats.

The bundles fell open, the burly *dopplesoldners* who had volunteered to carry them barging in to grab one.

'Stand well back from the points. Keep jabbing at their chests, they won't hang about,' Tarsi called over his shoulder, tugging the bindings away and holding up one pike after another. Corporal Horst – his head bandaged with a length of calico torn from a tent – worked his way between the mob with a flaming torch, lighting the outlandish leather buckets which had been filled with Stitchwort's sticky – and highly unstable mixture.

'Greek fire with a little extra spice of my own devising,' as he described it.

Tarsi prised himself to his feet, joints aching after the desperate effort. He had thought he had fought his last battle. Now here he was, a decade and more on, still fighting other people's wars for money.

'Form up, double order!'

He knew their success would depend on advancing on the broadest front possible, rather than relying on the depth of their formation. He didn't want the rear-rankers setting fire to their own men. The rest of the pitifully weak rearguard packed in behind the leaders, coughing and choking on the fuming debris being blown back into their faces. Tarsi brought his own pike to the charge, tilting his head away from the worst of the reeking smoke. He stepped into line as the right-hand marker, one of the Spanish sword and buckler men dropping in just behind his shoulder to prevent some Swiss from spearing his bared chest. A gaggle of English archers – their quivers long since emptied by the furious assault – had decided to use him as their battle mascot, pressing up behind him with swords and handy axes drawn. He recognised the round-faced wagoner, his matted ringlets damped down with sweat and blood.

'Don't tread on any arrows, Seigneur, the lads have run cruel short,' Hacker called cheerily. Tarsi nodded grimly, thankful the apprentice interpreter had decided against trying out his ever-expanding Italian vocabulary.

'Prepare to advance!'

The ragged line moved forward over tangled debris and sprawled bodies, squinting through a shower of fiercely-spitting sparks.

'To your right hands, right wheel!'

Tarsi checked his pace to enable the left-hand man to hurry about, bring the front rank about on its new heading – directly towards a line of advancing arquebusiers who were ducking and weaving through the belching fogs of battle, searching for an open flank to enfilade.

The enemy skirmishers saw the threat – a long line of spluttering spearpoints – and immediately let fly. The ill-aimed shots clipped pikes and whistled off helmets. One of the Englishmen cursed and dropped his sword, fingers pressed about his spouting forearm. Two of the Germans dropped their pikes and toppled into a ditch. The fiery contents spilled over a wrecked tent, sparking an immediate conflagration. The wounded crouched within were turned to fiery torches, tearing their way out of the burning canvas with their flaming claws. Tarsi's men closed up around the blazing obstacle, reformed their ranks and stepped out over the broken ground towards the milling arque-busiers. The Swiss fell back, reloading furiously but terrified of being caught in the storm of smuts and sparks vomiting towards them. They turned and ran for their lives. Pikemen shoved their way through the shattered ranks, brought their own weapons to the charge. The steel tips quivered at shoulder height.

'Charge! Charge!' Tarsi yelled, doubling forward as his own blazing bucket began to erupt with thick black smoke.

Now they had burned down to their molten cores, the cumbersome firepikes would put Tarsi's men at a disadvantage when it came to a straight push. But the Swiss arquebusiers had disrupted the enemy pikemen – they hadn't had time to form a proper front before the screaming Germans had rushed in amongst them. Pikes clattered, broke or flew up in the air as the two bodies of men crashed together. The closely compacted Germans rolled the Swiss back, trampling over the front rankers and spilling into the ill-prepared ranks trying to form up behind them.

The Swiss phalanx, blasted by grenades, hacked by Spanish swordsmen and battle-crazed *dopplesoldners* and pierced again and again by hundreds of deadly (and unfamiliar) arrows, was slowly but surely being forced back towards the huge head-quarters tent, the bawling devils unable to bring their arms to bear against the determined assault.

Ballistado blew his horn, gathered his surviving troopers and brought them in against the faltering flank.

The Swiss formation quivered, a buffalo attacked by a scorpion. Their charge carried the two assault parties deeper into the Swiss vanguard, deeper into a heaving pack of cursing enemies.

Deeper into trouble.

Unkel Von Schwartzer was shaking his head – not because he was concerned the army which he had been left in command of looked in imminent danger of being swept aside – but in grudging admiration of the enemy fighters.

They had left their trenches, worked their way past those rogues in Mont Galliard and come within an ace of achieving a notable victory. He held his arms out, his grooms busy strapping him into his armour. Another stood by with his ornamental halberd, ready to arm his master for the final triumphant charge on the impudent invaders. The locotenent might have lost four or five hundred men in the unexpected assault, but he had plenty more where they came from. They had been itching for a battle, and now it appeared they had one. What a pity that grey-eyed goliard of a Chevalier wasn't there to see it – or share in the glory.

A wounded captain was mumbling his report, staggering from side to side and trying to hold himself straight on a broken pike. He had been standing too close to one of Stitchwort's grenades, and his fine head of hair had been burnt black by the fearsome explosion. He was champing and spitting through parched lips, his speech slurred as he tried to apologise for his sentinels' dismal performance.

'Oo shaid ooshelf, dey wun tack ush,' he mumbled.

Von Schwartzer waved the cretin away.

'You'd best get that gob of yours washed out, Wittgenstein,' he advised, taking the halberd from his groom.

'They got in through the latrines, you reckon?'

'Dash rike. Mush be a thoushand o' em all tole.'

'A thousand? Take a look for yourself man! Tarsi had about six hundred men. Allowing for the fact he probably left a quarter of them as a rearguard, there won't be more than three or four hundred of the buggers down there.'

He strode towards the main body of his pikemen, drawn up in a vast arc about his headquarters tent. Tarsi's thrust might have dislocated a good third of his encampment, but he hadn't got anywhere near the heart he had presumably aimed for.

Any moment now, he would start thinking about retreating. Von Schwartzer narrowed his eyes, studied the blazing panorama. About a thousand of his men were engaged, swaying and staggering under the enemy assaults. But without reserves Tarsi couldn't win. And he hadn't come here to cover himself in glory – the canny Italian wasn't in the business of organising the mass suicide of his men.

'Monzon and Villiers,' he called, waving two of his underemployed understudies forward.

'You take those shit-breeked skirmishers around the wagon park, cut them off from the ridge. The rest of us will hold them from the front. Oh, and take the old bugger alive if possible. It'll be wonderful, meeting up with old acquaintances again.'

By the Hospice Gilbert le Petit Galliard

✦

The Alps crowned the world, the jewel-encrusted, white-gold points spearing the perfect vault of heaven. The finest artists, the greatest painters of the Renaissance, could not have quite captured the sheer grandeur, the perfection of colour and light.

But the girls were heartily sick of the mountain hideaway, tiring of the awesome views and invigorating air. They might just as well have been dispatched to a nunnery, isolated and virtually alone in the remote sanctuary of the hospice. The impatient angels longed to descend to earth once more, to be reconnected to the tempestuous and tumultuous realities Tarsi had hidden them away from.

They kicked their heels, picked over their meagre wardrobes and bickered over trifles while their Scots guardians laboured in the chill mountain air to stiffen the defences.

Kerr's reivers had built up the perimeter wall, reinforced the gate and built an inner bastion – the height of a man – about the weather-ravaged sanctuary. They had barricaded the windows and nailed great planks over the double doors. Kerr had used all his Border ingenuity to turn the steep approaches into a death trap. He had undermined the road foundations, tearing away the crumbling bedrock to create several bottlenecks. His men had climbed the precarious cliff paths, assembled cairns of easily-toppled boulders on every ledge. They had gouged pits in the fierce scrub beside the paths, filling the trenches with sharpened stakes and rusty spearpoints borrowed from the hospice armoury. The ancient lodge was filled with curiosities from the past, worm-eaten weapons and mouldy shields Tarsi had collected during his travels about Europe.

The painstaking work had kept the men busy for days. But the moment the defences were complete the Scots had begun to explore, rummaging about the abandoned outbuildings before venturing into the brooding treasure house itself.

The place was part hunting lodge, part mausoleum and part

mathom-house, filled with all sorts of junk and relics. Kerr had nabbed the principal exhibit for himself, a fine Etruscan helmet worked with tiny, unreadable characters. He had turned a blind eye to his reivers' unauthorised forays. They had helped themselves to fur-trimmed cloaks, taken long swords and ornate, bone-handled daggers down from the fanciful displays on the wall. They had taken an instant liking to the local throwing axe, stuffing their belts with the small but deadly missiles in case they found themselves involved in a close-quarter fight.

The acquisitive Scots had swarmed over Tarsi's dust-shrouded retreat, picking over his large but largely worthless collection of artefacts. They had used the old hunting hall for target practice, knocking an entire menagerie of trophies from the walls. Stuffed heads, broken antlers and glass eyes littered the floors.

Young Davey Dunne tripped on the rolling globes and cracked his head against the fireplace. His colleagues whooped and cheered, carrying some of the more ferocious specimens outside and thrusting them on to spears, decorating the main wall with snarling if somewhat threadbare beasts.

The continual uproar had roused Angelica from her torpor. She had cursed under her breath and sallied down to confront the grinning bandit chief. Angelica warned the leering Scotsman against making sport in her father's hall – however decrepit the abandoned hospice appeared. Kerr had chuckled, but called his men off all the same. As the girl had rightly pointed out, Tarsi wouldn't hesitate to deduct the cost of any damage from Kerr's wages.

He had neglected, however, to return his prized helmet.

That had been hidden away with the rest of his insight – the easily transportable loot which Kerr would use to defray his own expenses. Not even the short-tempered Tarsi could seriously expect him to occupy a deserted country house without a spot of petty pilfering – it would be going against Kerr's nature to resist such easy pickings. The pale wraith returned to the girls' quarters on the upper floor – formerly her father's finest guest room. The chamber was rather colder than she remembered it, the tapestries and hangings which had warmed the bare walls long since reduced by an army of mice.

Merron looked up from her idle needlework. The patched shift wouldn't have passed muster as a floor rag, but they had been obliged to make hems meet as best they could. The bold-eyed English girl had spent most of the morning making running

248

repairs on Angelica's gowns. Her own scarred fingers weren't up to such complex needlework – not since Briconet had practised his diabolical skills on the poor maid. Angelica was deathly pale and short of breath after her acrimonious meeting, the dark smudges beneath her eyes thrown into unhealthy relief.

'I cannot imagine how these Swiss could do any more damage than the Scots,' Merron commented, leaning forward to bite off a dangling thread.

Angelica opened the shutter, gazing bleakly over the frosty rim of the mountains. Merron put down her needlework and poured her friend a glass of goat's milk. The pitcher had been left out on the balcony and the contents were refreshingly cold. Angelica brushed it away.

'Milk makes me sick.'

'You must try and take something,' Merron said patiently. 'Build your strength.'

Angelica muttered something in her own tongue. Merron frowned, put the glass down and laid her hands on the girl's bony shoulders, pushing her gently towards the vacant chair.

'This place,' Angelica said darkly, gripping the coarse-grained table as if she could hold on to their fluctuating destinies through willpower alone. 'We used to come here in the old days, before we lost Mont Galliard.' She gave a brittle laugh. 'I thought it was a gloomy old ruin then. Now . . . now it is all we have.'

She surveyed the bare apartment, the strange patterns in the plasterwork where faded hangings had fallen from their fittings. The flags and banners of the ancient Aostan families which had survived decades of assault from the teeming vermin had been tugged down more recently as saddlecloths and spare plaids. Ancient arms and battle honours could be found draped over the rumps of Kerr's dung-splattered ponies.

'I don't know,' Merron countered, refusing to be cast down by her friend's constant gloom. 'I would be happy enough with it, given time to restore the rooms to their former glory.'

'Time and money, Merry dear,' Angelica corrected. 'And father has preciously little of either commodity.'

Merron frowned at her wilful despondency. It was true she had suffered untold agonies at the hands of the Inquisition the previous summer. But she had survived – an escape very few of Briconet's victims could claim to have shared.

Merron liked to think she would have been grateful for *her* survival – that she would have counted every subsequent day of her life as a blessing from Almighty God. She maintained that she would not have allowed Briconet the satisfaction of knowing he had broken her spirit so completely. But then again, it hadn't been her hands on the inquisitor's table. It hadn't been her fingers Briconet had flayed with such meticulous relish.

Angelica glanced around at the thoughtful English girl, all too aware what she was thinking.

That she ought to snap out of her doldrums, pull her spirit from the abyss. She was beginning to tire of her wretched sincerity, the pity which welled out of those huge hazel eyes every time she looked at her. Angelica tipped the glass this way and that and watched the cold milk stain the rim. Neither of them spoke, lost in rueful contemplation of their lonely exile.

They were startled by a sudden knock. Merron eased herself to her feet and crossed the room, her natural grace evident in the confident swing of her hips, the haughty toss of her hair as she opened the door. Angelica frowned at her charmingly tapered back. A commoner at heart – just like her – but so much more at home, so easily elegant in this man's world of war and wealth-getting.

'Oh, it's you.'

Angelica tilted her head to eavesdrop.

'Aye, it's me.'

It was Angus, Kerr's tongue-tied son. Merron stepped back as the young Scot entered the room, nervously looking about.

'I thought tae bring ye this.'

It was a young ibex, its horned head lolling over the crook of the boy's arm. He was still carrying the crossbow bolt which had killed it.

'I shot it by the back wall of yon croft,' he explained, gruffly nervous and reddening to the roots of his hair. Merron smiled encouragingly.

'Thank you Angus. We've not enjoyed fresh meat since we left Nus.'

Angus tried to prevent his smile spreading too rapidly, but failed miserably. He pulled at his nose, looked awkwardly at the *de facto* mistress of the hospice.

'I thought I'd try and make up, for the damage and distress we caused ye, throwing dirks at yer wall.'

'I hope your aim is as true when the Swiss come calling,' Angelica replied primly. Merron touched the youth's arm to make up for her friend's ill-natured response. Angus jumped as if he had been stung. 'Take it to the kitchens with our thanks. We would be glad to share it with you, at supper.'

Angus was ecstatic, his white teeth glinting in the dappled light lancing between the shutters.

'Is there any news from the pass?' Angelica asked, returning to her usual refrain. Angus shook his head obliviously.

'Niver a word.'

Not a word in three days. Angelica closed her eyes, wondering what had happened. Surely the enemy wouldn't have allowed her father the best part of two weeks to prepare his defences?

Why hadn't they spotted the survivors, running up the rocky approaches as if the hounds of hell were snapping at their heels?

Always presuming there were survivors with a run left in them.

'Dead sheep and cow eyes? These Scots have a peculiar notion of romance,' Angelica chuckled bleakly. Merron bit her lip, annoyed the boy's tender gesture had been thrown in such a callous light.

'He'll be lining a bower for you next, filling it with trinkets for his pretty maid,' Angelica went on, downright jealous now. 'What fine jackdaws father has set to watch over us!'

'Perhaps you wish he had brought you the ibex?'

'Hah. I'd say of the two of them, the ibex smelt slightly sweeter,' Angelica retorted, her former mischievous wit reduced to spiteful ridicule. Merron knew she should bide her tongue, make allowances, but she had had more than enough of her bitter moods, stuck up here in the clouds.

'Better a pretty maid, then a petty maid,' Merron said softly, but loud enough for the Italian girl to catch. Angelica's dark eyes smouldered through her welling tears.

'Petty? Perhaps. Briconet has seen to that.' She jumped to her feet and held up her hands, the shrivelled skin sagging about her crooked finger joints like bloated chicken feet. 'Perhaps you would have me touch his shoulder like so . . .' She deliberately laid her palm on the English girl's shoulder. Merron determined to suppress her involuntary shudder, face to finger with the twisted claw Briconet had left her as a memento of their bloody interview. 'Or run my fingers through his hair?' Angelica eased her hand into Merron's thick tresses, the dark braids shot with chestnut and golden threads.

'Ouch! Now you're hurting!' Merron tugged her head away.

Angelica held a few strands of her copper-coloured hair, angry and appalled that she had hurt her only friend.

Merron looked up at her, her simple heart overflowing with pity. She leaned forward, opened her arms and held the crying girl about the waist, laying her forehead against Angelica's belly.

'It's all right. It'll be all right,' she muttered, wondering if it ever would.

'Ah, he's sweet on her right enough. That'll take the wind from that Sassenach's sails, to find his precious sister walking out wi' Angus Kerr!'

'Merron Kerr, Mistress of Tullymallock!'

'I'd make her mistress o' mine, quick enough.'

'She'd eat you for oatcakes, ye gelded cur!'

The reivers were sitting around their bivouac fires between the main wall and the hospice doors, howling with laughter as they digested the latest intelligence. Young Angus had not only lost his head to the Eldritch wench, but lost his supper and all!

The youth in question was sitting a little way from the fire, clutching his plaid around his throat. He wouldn't have needed any warmth, if he had Merron for company. But the lying hoor had closed the door in his face, given him some half-cocked excuse and gushing apologies about her mistress and her damned headaches. The ibex, however, had remained in the hospice kitchens, shared out by Tarsi's gloating household. Angus cursed his youthful stupidity, wished he had taken his cronies' advice and found a likely wench from among Tarsi's ever-growing tail of camp followers. There were plenty of girls willing to take a stone in the ear for a silver penny or two.

He had half a mind to mount his pony and get back there right away.

He frowned, his youthful lusts gnawing at his innards.

But he didn't want Merron for that.

He hadn't even imagined haughmaganding with her. Well, not as often as he had imagined sitting by a fire with her, or sharing a bowl of wine and sweetmeats, or going hawking with her, or fishing. Or walking by a lake, hand in hand, laughing and chatting as easily as he did with father or Young Davey.

His father was up on the wall, apparently on guard but well within earshot. He could see the hurt in his son's eyes, and the thought his own flesh and blood could be so gullible grieved him deeply. A Kerr marry an Eldritch?

He'd rather clean the latrines with his dead wife's handkerchief. Angus had a good deal to learn yet, he thought ruefully. Many was the Border feud which had been settled with a wedding band, but he would be damned if he would ever agree to such a match.

And what on earth would the wondrous Captain Eldritch think of his son's infatuation? He'd cut his throat as soon as look at him. Kerr remembered their last foray into England way back the previous Spring. Auld Gully – Lord Howath, the master of the English Middle March – had called a Truce Day, invited his Scots neighbours in for a peace conference. But his renegade master of horse had stolen away, crossing the Border to set a trap for Kerr and his reivers when they turned for home.

Eldritch had caught them like mice in a greased bottle, killed half a dozen men with his first shoot. Young Angus had come after them, led the remainder of his household against the English raiders with predictably dire results. Eldritch had captured the youngster alive, but one look in the damned clootie's stone-dead eyes had been enough to convince Kerr he wouldn't have hesitated to cut his throat from ear to ear. The sheer, undiluted determination to succeed – whatever the cost – had quite unnerved him.

Eldritch had broken two centuries of Border tradition without a second thought. He had drawn arms on a Truce Day, smashed the frail laws which had bound their terrifying lifestyles for decades.

He was out on the edge, alone, beyond the pale. A stick-at-nothing killer with chipped flints and crooked nails for flesh and blood and a rancid haggis for a heart.

His sister Merron might feel fairer, might sound sweeter, but she was water drawn from the same well.

Angus would do well to steer clear of the pox-hearted pair of them.

Nobody challenged him, either at the main door or on the steep stair. Young Davey had drawn the duty, but he was sprawled across the bottom step, a looted stonejar hanging from his crooked forefinger. His red-bearded mouth was slack, misshapen teeth standing out from his pink gums like leaning stones in Tullymallock kirkyard. He paused, wondering whether he should give up his harebrained enterprise. If father caught Davey sleeping there, he'd be riding bare-balled for a twelvemonth. Angus gritted his teeth and stepped over his drunken colleague, climbed the staircase to the first landing. He knew where he was going well enough.

He passed gloomily-lit chambers, the few household staff who had remained huddled beneath blankets and old hangings to keep out the fierce mountain chills. Sentinels snoozed, wrapped in their cloaks, the glowing embers between their lazily spread boots turning their features a subdued terracotta.

Angus tiptoed past them and climbed the stairway to the upper storey. His heart was beating like a gypsy's tambourine, his aching breath shallow. Silver vapour lingered. He came to their door, clenching his fists on the threshold, trying to summon up the courage to turn the handle.

And then what? He tried to imagine Merron rising from her couch, opening her arms to draw him within while her pale friend twitched and murmured in her troubled sleep.

The sudden splash startled him from his fevered reverie.

The noise had come from the second door along the barren passage. It had been left ajar, a feeble yellow glimmer illuminating the hallway. He froze, back to the wall, palms spread over the decayed panelling.

He tilted his head, listened again.

A girl's voice rose and fell, her sibilant phrasing accompanied by the gentle splash of water droplets cascading into a wash bowl.

'Company with honesty, is virtue and vice to flee.
Company is good or ill, but every man hath his free will.'

Angus recognised the tune if not the words. He knew without looking around the doorframe it must be Merron. He couldn't imagine the watery wraith singing so sweetly, so blissfully unaware of herself.

'The best I sue, the worst eschew,
my mind shall be, virtue to use.
Vice to refuse, I shall use me.'

Angus was transfixed, his pierced heart overflowing with hunger and longing. He dimly remembered his mother (or it might have been his nurse) singing lullabies over his cot, high in Tullymallock's draughty tower. Merron's voice carried him back there, back to the warm crib his father had lined with wolfpelt and duck-down quilts. He leaned forward, peeping through the gap between the half-open door and the ancient frame.

Sweet Christ above.

The youth held his breath, steadying his jellied legs by hanging on to the peeling plaster.

The girl was standing beside a disembowelled chest, the ransacked drawers hanging out like a hanged man's tongue. Various musty clothing, ancient linen too worn to wear, had been tugged out and discarded. Merron had tidied the top drawer, thrusting the diaphanous rags back inside the chest, but the bitter cold had obliged her to set the belated housework aside and get on with her toilet before she caught a chill.

She had dragged her hair back and tied it up in a band. The mass of springy auburn curls was lit by the single lantern she had carried in from the bedroom. She had loosened the top of her gown, tugged the threadbare green velvet back over her shoulders. The black silk ties were dangling loose over her shift, spotted here and there with water droplets. Merron stopped humming while she leaned over the wide-brimmed bowl to wring out her facecloth. She stood straight, held the bodice away from her skin and ran the damp cloth over her chest, raising her right arm to wash beneath the tightly-fitting garment. She shuddered with cold, her vapourised breath enveloping her in an Elfin shroud as she completed her hasty ablutions.

Angus swooned, his knees buckling and stomach turning over as it had when he rode to his first battle with the Sassenachs. His heartfelt sigh sent a mischievous plume of vapour through the gap in the door.

She must have spied the silver cloud from the corner of her eye, peering around suddenly at the shadowed figure half hidden behind the wall. Her wet arms flew to her chest, wrenching the bodice back about her breasts.

'Who's there? Come out where I can see you,' she scolded, taking a step away from the door.

Angus was dumbstruck, mortified to think she had caught him spying on her like some black-hearted whoremaster.

'It's you Angus, I can hear your breathing,' she called, but not loud enough to wake her sleeping companion.

Angus closed his eyes, and took a step into the light.

Merron held the lantern in one hand and her bodice strings tight in the other, scowling at the miserable wretch as he shuffled on the threshold.

'What are you doing here? How long were you watching me?' she asked crossly, her breastbone glistening with moisture.

'I . . . came to ask . . . to make sure, ye were safe and well,' he stammered, his broad, workmanlike features suffused with hot blood. He stood with his fists clenched, avoiding her probing eye.

'Is this how you care for me, standing at my door like some old hunchback?' She had recovered something of her nerve now, annoyed to think the youngster had watched her improvised bath. 'I would have expected more from you,' she said archly.

Angus paled.

'I wanted to see ye, I wanted to tell ye to ye face,' he croaked, dragging each syllable from his constricted throat. 'I don't care what fatha and the rest o' them say. I love you, Merron Eldritch.'

Merron stared at the awkward youth, her anger evaporating as his bright blue eyes bored into her right shoulder. She blinked, wondering how to conclude their interview without dashing the poor boy's feelings. He had clearly worked himself into a pitch of emotion, just as Angelica had predicted he would.

But her dispirited friend would never have anticipated the youth's brittle honesty, would never have believed him capable of such an open-hearted declaration. She didn't know what to think, let alone say.

Angus visibly relaxed, his set shoulders slumping as he congratulated himself on his courageous approach. As if it didn't matter how she reacted – once he had said his piece.

'I . . . er . . . I am deeply touched, deeply touched,' Merron replied, reddening herself. The one thing she knew for certain was his feelings were not – would never be – reciprocated.

Merron had loved one man – the carefree Spaniard Isolani. But he had been killed saving her life the previous summer. He had shielded her, taken a crossbow bolt between the shoulder blades, a bolt which would have killed her as surely as it had Isolani.

Not even her self-righteous brother James had dared question her feelings for the Spaniard. Her grief as she crouched at his deathbed had been evident enough even for the iron-willed Eldritch.

'D'ye have nothing to say to me in return?' Angus muttered, his broad brogue becoming more pronounced. He had been wrong about nothing else mattering. Now he wanted her to tell him she loved him too. It was inconceivable she could do otherwise.

'I am truly touched to hear you say so, dear Angus, but there are . . .'

The sudden horn blast sent the pair of them jumping out of their skins. Agitated dogs barked in the courtyard. Angry voices rebounded along the frost-rimed defences. Angus' father had found the immense Alpine horn in one of Tarsi's storerooms and had it dragged out onto the wall as an effective early warning device for his widespread garrison. The clarion call rebounded about the mountains, sounding some infernal echo within the old hospice.

Merron, terribly alarmed, stepped forward and peered down the hall.

He raised his arm, preventing her from leaving the chamber.

'They're blowing the alert, something's happened,' she snapped.

'You were about to say something. There are, aye, are what? Reasons, reasons why ye cannae love me as I love you?'

'They've sounded the alarm. You'll be missed, so will I. Another time, perhaps.'

Angus thought a moment and then raised his arm. Merron gathered her skirts and ducked past him. Angelica was standing in the bedroom doorway, looking curiously down the hall. Merron silenced her with a stare and took the steps three at a time.

The hospice had been plunged into instant uproar. The unexpected alarm had roused up the entire household. Soldiers and servants were running this way and that, tripping over piles of weapons and their flickering watchfires as a small company of riders clattered through the narrow gap Sandy Kerr had left in his defences.

'Frundsberg, Frundsberg!' The intruders were bawling the name as if it were some magical talisman which would protect them from the nervous and heavily-armed defenders. Their chief sprang onto the wall, waving his arms above his head.

'Don't shoot!' Kerr bawled. 'They're out from Tarsi!'

The intruders entered the narrow courtyard, reining their steaming beasts to a halt. Reivers dashed forward to grab their bridles while the spearmen menaced the sweat-flecked fugitives.

Merron flew out of the doorway with her bodice strings tangled, her awkward encounter with Angus forgotten. The weary cavalry were panting as hard as their horses, slumped in their saddles like straw men. The ensign carried a silk-fringed gonfallon, the silver and gold device decorated with a large scarlet V. Merron had never seen such a banner.

'They had the password Sandy,' Davey Dunne called, doubling in behind them with a large axe cradled across his chest.

'Aye, I heard.'

Kerr had watched the shadowy riders work their way into his carefully prepared traps and had been about to order his archers to shoot them down when he had heard the magical password echo over the barren approaches. He scrambled down the ladder, dirk drawn, squinting at the lean knight who stood sway-backed and shivering in the courtyard. The newcomer's fancy armour had been badly scratched and dented, his cloak torn.

'Frundsberg, ye say?'

Duke Gerhard of Villefranco looked round, the ghost of a smile stretching his drawn features. He recognised the bow-legged Scotsman by his strange, crab-like gait. Tarsi had been typically blunt when it had come to describing his absent captain of horse.

'A scar-faced imp with a thievish countenance. You can't mistake him.'

He ran the back of his hand across his mouth and examined the smear of bright blood on his elegant chamois glove. He took a deep breath.

'Captain Kerr. Mount your men. Tarsi is surrounded in the pass, he'll never escape without immediate succour,' Gerhard explained in abrupt Italian.

'What's this dandified pock pudding got to say for hisself?' Kerr snarled, turning to his despised rival's sister for a translation.

He loathed having to rely on the bold-eyed mare, but he was out of his depth when it came to arguing the toss with foreigners. Merron hurried forward, struggling to decipher the Duke's laconic greeting.

Kerr raised his scarred chin, studying the chocolate warrior through his slitted grey eyes while she repeated the gist of his instructions.

'March right on 'oot a here, is that right? Tarsi told us to hold the hospice, in case they needed to retreat,' he argued. 'Who might you be anyways?' he enquired, narrowing his foxy eye at the pale intruder.

Duke Gerhard turned on him, concentrating all his youthful authority on convincing the doubting gnome. Merron began to translate his reply in her schoolbook French, but Gerhard had no time for her or him.

'I am Duke Gerhard of Villefranco, your commander in chief,' he said coldly and in passable English. 'And there isn't going to be a retreat, unless we cut him a path out of there.'

They listened in stunned silence. The Duke seemed to relish the sudden attention, throwing out his chest and examining the rent in his robe. 'He stands at bay, with his back to Mont Galliard. If Savvi sallies out behind him, he'll be finished,' the Duke announced.

'Is that a fact?' Kerr growled, disliking the newcomer's grand manner.

'Yes, it is indeed a fact,' Gerhard replied coldly, tiring of the surly curs Tarsi had insisted on recruiting into his doomed legion. When he had a moment he would go through the entire roster and dismiss every man who didn't come up to standard.

Angelica, standing forlorn and forgotten on the threshold, gasped for breath at his alarming dispatch. She made a grab at the doorframe to prevent herself falling.

Gerhard looked over at her, his mobile mouth half smiling as he guessed at her identity. The washed-out rag of a girl must be Tarsi's headstrong daughter. The haughty tomboy who had so insulted his father's marriage brokers the previous summer. Old Duke Lodovico had sent an embassy after her, seeking her hand for his precious, if somewhat mollycoddled, son. The negotiations had broken down over the size of the dowry – not even the financially embarrassed Villefrancans had been desperate enough to accept Tarsi's derisory offer. Gerhard chuckled to himself. My, what a difference twelve months could make to a family's fortune, he thought.

'Well, do we stand here all night discussing the weather, or ride to Tarsi?' he asked archly.

'We'd best ride,' Sandy snarled, sliding his dirk back under his chainmail shirt. 'I'll not have it said we left our people to die alone.'

There. They had swallowed his story just as he had expected they would. The bow-legged tartar with the face like a centurion's boot had accepted his bloody report and seemed intent on galloping to the great Tarsi's rescue – or into oblivion, whichever came first. He could not blame the fox-whiskered fool. He had duped wiser men than Sandy Kerr in his time.

Duke Gerhard had confounded his father, his counsellors, troops, whores, servants and now his disbelieving officers. The moment they made up their minds he was yellower than reptile piss he turned himself bright red. But no sooner had he begun to impress them with his bravado than he paled all over again, his carefully nurtured nerve gnawed through.

He had thought about nothing else, cantering up the steep, rubble-strewn paths from the tumults in the pass. Fleeing the sudden storm which Tarsi's impetuous raid had provoked.

Gerhard had lived a lie. Why should – how could – the leopard change its spots now? He liked to think his shade-changing abilities made him an enigma – helped keep his acquaintances off balance. Every one of them was, after all, a potential enemy.

If he had learned one thing during his punishment of riches back in Villefranco, it was that nobody would ever look out for him, he would needs must look after himself.

His own father had started the rot, trying to stifle his God-given talents through his obsession with moulding the perfect Renaissance son. No Gerhard, not that way!

Lodovico had imagined that shutting the boy away from the rough and tumble of life, locking him in the tower with a pile of ancient texts and some moth-eaten druid for a tutor would turn the lonely, awkward boy into a skilful ambassador, gifted courtier and fair ruler.

In other words, keeping him in virtual isolation half his life in the vain hope he would somehow be able to cope with fluctuating and fickle human nature when he got older.

But the old fool had made a serious miscalculation.

Gerhard was every inch as selfish as his father, and had reacted against his liberal education like an oyster to a twist of lemon.

He thought his aloofness, his cynical detachment from court or cause, left him free to respond to any situation as he, and he alone, saw fit. Surely it was the only path for a true statesman to follow, in this blackguardy, back-stabbing age.

Left on his own, down in the dreary darkness of the trenches, Gerhard's brittle nerve had snapped like a badly tuned viol-string. He had heard the cries and seen the fires, felt the detonating grenades shudder the ancient bedrock of the gorge.

Panic had eaten through his small store of courage, just as the Swiss would surely tear through the defences, the moment they realised Tarsi's carefully staged attack was the last throw of a demented has-been.

Gerhard couldn't be sure what he had seen or what he had imagined. A vast army of images had crowded into his skull. A mass of men, tumbling and rumbling down the narrow gorge like spring floodwater. A filthy, rushing, boiling tide, a black and brown, many-legged monster, its scaly hide mottled with pale eyes and studded with drooping banners.

There were many too many of them, he knew it. Their game was up. Tarsi's minnows had been swallowed up by a shoal of striped perch, lunging out of the shadows with their razor teeth bared. The Swiss pikemen charging through his mind's eye bore no relation to the sleeping giant Tarsi had so confidently predicted.

Gerhard knew in a moment there was no way their pitiful trenches would stem that storm. To stay and fight would have been suicide. He was not ready to stare death in the face just yet.

So he had ordered the retreat, waved his outnumbered rearguard out of their wormholes. He had flogged his horse bloody, taking Tarsi's carefully-planned escape route up the side of the mountain to the remote hospice. Now all he wanted was to send these Scots fools flying, brush the draff aside and ride for the south.

To save himself, lose himself in the rolling wheatfields and sleepy villages which lay just the other side of the mountains. He would find what he was looking for somewhere, an Arcadia fit for a shrewd statesman like him.

The Scots seemed ridiculously eager to play their part aiding and abetting his great escape. He stood in the courtyard, jostled by swarthy barbarians carrying a startling assortment of weapons. Their chief bustled about waving his long arms and urging his puny rearguard into action. Horses were dragged from their stables, spears snatched from leaning racks.

Gerhard ducked out of their way, stepping into an alcove to collect his wits. He leaned back, taking a deep breath.

'Are you hurt my lord?' Gerhard opened his eyes, found himself face to face with their pretty interpreter – armed with a jug of wine and a blood-smeared rag.

'I am sorry?'

'You sighed as if in pain. Were you hurt, my lord?' the dark-haired girl repeated, holding up the bandage as if she could heal his heart with a length of soiled cotton. Her large eyes glistened with life, sparkling in the flaring torchlight. There was a bloody thumbprint on her jaw, evidence she had already treated one of his hard-riding escort. He felt strangely vulnerable, exposed to her penetrating look.

'No I'm not hurt,' he said, light-headed. The girl's enquiring look had quite unnerved him, jolted him from his selfish scheming. The chill air had brought up the colour in her fine neck and brought goose-pimples up on her slender arms. Her breasts were daringly exposed in her loosely secured bodice. He raised his eyes once more, studied her fine face.

The girl seemed somewhat disconcerted by his reaction.

'Are there enough of you, my lord, to save Seigneur Tarsi?' she asked anxiously, offering him the wine jug. He took a swallow, as much to take his mind from her loveliness as to refresh himself.

'There were thousands of them,' he muttered, shuddering at the appalling memory.

Or had it been his overworked imagination? Damn it all, if he could only think straight for a moment without people pestering him.

'But there are but two dozen men left here!' the girl exclaimed, anguished tears springing in her eyes. 'They won't stop hundreds, let alone thousands.' Gerhard gave her a sickly smile, disconcerted by her flashing looks and quick wits. Those eyes, bright and lustrous. Where on earth had they met, Villefranco, Nus?

'Your pardon my lord,' the girl said levelly, modifying her tone as if she had misread his uncomprehending glare as a reprimand. 'But my companion is Seigneur Tarsi's daughter. Both of us have family and friends in the pass.'

Gerhard swallowed, forcing his features into an easy grin.

'I am sure they will be all right. The fires, the darkness . . . one counts every enemy ten times over.'

Maybe even twenty times. She did not look convinced by his feeble reassurances. He had seen that same look of slightly contemptuous accusation before . . . what was the damn girl's name?

'I feel so helpless,' she croaked. 'If James was here. If I was . . .' The interpreter looked away, tears getting the better of her and cutting glistening paths down her grubby cheeks. She held her arm over her eyes, leaning against the alcove wall.

Gerhard stood beside her, a useless waxwork in a tragic tableau. It was as if he had been cast out of their cruel world, sentenced to wander in some all-seeing, all-knowing limbo. Cursed to look down on their frantic doings as if he were some minor god on the foothills of Olympus.

He glimpsed his life, his whole lying existence from cradle to grave. He was momentarily aware of all his pitiful dealings, the feeble pretences, the pathetic self-deceptions and downright cowardice which had carried him to this lofty hospice on the edge of heaven. Gerhard was stricken with shame. He felt an overwhelming urge to comfort her, to tear the poor girl away from her panic-stricken contemplations.

But what could he do? How could he avert the disaster which had engulfed them down in the pass? What good would they do anyone, hurling themselves into the hellish canyon to rejoin the legion of the dead?

His own escort was on its last legs. A dozen weary light cavalry, shrouded in dust riding hobbling horses. A score of panting spearmen, who had been forced to run to keep up with their fearful flight. He had turned his back on his comrades, left them to face the onslaught while he saved his pitiful skin.

He might find that Arcadia, the glorious realm he had dreamt of. But the bitter memory of his craven service would give him no rest. He would rot in living hell, a weak-willed boy forever.

The girl must have noticed his catatonic stare, guessed the true nature of his turmoil. She clutched at his tunic, shook him from his disturbed reverie.

'What is it my lord? You swore there was hope!' she cried.

'There is,' he growled, clenching his fists and trying to control the jitters which had erupted up and down his chill limbs.

'There is always hope.'

Sandy Kerr reined in beside their quiet corner, bent his scarred head to peer into the alcove.

'The men are ready,' he said. Gerhard bit his lip bloody.

'My men will need remounts.'

'There's a few out back.'

'Fetch one for me. I'll lead the way back.'

Kerr shrugged.

'I didna think you were going to give me directions,' he muttered.

By The Pass

✦

The Swiss were fully alerted now, all those who had escaped Tarsi's initial assaults coagulating about their standards, forming an ever-thickening phalanx about the desperate invaders.

They had attacked with arrow and axe, sword and dagger, grenade and fire pike, taking the battle to the very threshold of the Swiss command post before their awesome impetus had begun to falter. The last of them, less than three hundred battered, bruised and panting fighters, stood at bay beside the latrine pits, being forced back over the littered ground by the slowly advancing Swiss.

Another ten yards and they would be up to their necks in liquid filth.

Tarsi pulled himself out of the front rank for a moment, tried to get his bearings amidst the hopeless chaos. The pitifully outnumbered assault party had been pressed back into a corpse-choked neck of rock between the latrine pits and the wagon park. If it hadn't been for those formidable and easily defendable obstacles, the Swiss would have been tugging their boots off by now.

Tarsi waved his sword towards the wounded Spanish captain, standing beside an overturned cart having yet another wound dressed by his muttering groom.

'Ballistado, get your men back along the wagon wall, get them back between those shit pits!' he bawled. The captain lifted his notched sword in acknowledgment and barged his way back between the resting rear-rankers to spread the word among his hard-pressed front line. They were using discarded pikes, halberds and torn colours to prod and jab the Swiss pikemen back, but were suffering grievously on the cunningly-wielded enemy spearpoints.

Not even trained *Landsknechts* could hope to stop a Swiss pikeblock at point – the mountain warriors were too skilled, too well balanced. They laughed and shouted, keeping up the remorseless pressure on the ill-armed survivors. Jabbing and stabbing their eighteen-foot poles as if they were light javelins or simple tribal assegais.

The *dopplesoldners* who might have held up their advance with their deadly two-handed swords were dead or maimed, lying amid the stricken heaps. Tarsi lifted one of the swordsmen from a pile of corpses and dragged his enormous blade from the bowels of a naked Swiss.

'Make a hole,' he growled. The last time he had lifted one of these damn things was at Ravenna. It had damn near crippled him then.

The nimble Spanish fighters closed up, letting the Italian back into the line. He took a pace towards the jabbing spearpoints, swung the sword over his shoulder and brought it around in a whistling arc. Broken pike points clattered down; others were knocked from numbed hands, but a moment later the jagged wooden spikes were probing for him, skittering off his dented armour.

'Back to the latrines!' he bawled.

They were in the shit right enough.

The sudden horn blast echoed out over the embattled camp, splitting what was left of the night. Hundreds of Swiss pikemen, queueing between the brimming latrine pits for their chance to have a crack at the desperately outnumbered invaders, looked over their shoulders and saw a mass of riders silhouetted on the ridge above them. Some cursed. Some crossed themselves.

For here, surely, were demon riders coughed from the bowels of hell itself.

They had never seen such outlandish garb, nor such breath-taking horsemanship. The screaming reivers hurled their ponies down the scree slopes as if intent on breaking the beasts' necks. Some were using small, Tartar bows, firing as they charged with their reins clenched between their teeth. Others were armed with long, wickedly gleaming spears, jabbing at the backs of the bewildered rear-rankers. Even their round bucklers bore a foot-long spike, just right for lashing out at a bewildered Swiss.

The sedge sea of pikemen reeled under the new assault, the bawling soldiers turning and charging their pikes towards the rear.

The riders hurtled through the narrow gaps between the latrine pits, dodging and ducking the thrusting pikepoints. The slow-witted Swiss who hadn't managed to reform themselves were bowled over, knocked into the evil-smelling mire by the screeching fiends.

Horns blew; drums rattled; the few officers the Swiss possessed bawled themselves hoarse trying to bring their unwieldy formations about to face the new onslaught.

The barbarian horsemen were through the obstacles, hurling themselves at the milling pikemen, hacking at bared heads with swords and crude clubs.

They were followed by another squadron of cavalry led by a fantastically armoured knight, slashing and kicking a path through the stubbornly-packed Swiss. A silver and gold gonfallon rose and fell behind him as his ensign beat off an ambitious Frenchman, intent on wresting his banner from his frenzied grip.

Duke Gerhard of Villefranco was absolutely and utterly terrified. He had hardly believed his eyes when Kerr had led the charge down the slope, throwing his puny command against the biggest army poor Gerhard had ever seen.

His mind-numbing fear had proved a boon. He had fallen into some kind of a battle-trance, clicking his heels without thinking and following the Scot's mad charge as if no harm could possibly come to him in the swirling chaos below.

Before he could think twice he had been hemmed in by dirty, shouting, cursing Swiss, clattering and battering at him with their pikes. They had not managed to bring the points down in time to deflect the charge, and were relying on sheer weight of numbers to block his attack. He stared at their filthy faces for what seemed like hours, wondering what he should do next.

And then he struck out, hacking blindly at the upturned features, the hooked noses, the moustaches and beards, the greasy hanks of hair and oddly decorated bonnets.

And in another moment, the grasping, kicking writhing mass had broken apart, the rear-rankers tipped into the nearest pit by the pressure from the front. The pikeblock reared back, drawing in its deadly points like a wounded porcupine.

Their grudging retreat opened a gap in the Swiss line. The terrible pressure Gerhard had felt before him slackened. He spurred on through the milling pikemen, kicking and stabbing at their bewildered backs. His men packed in behind him, forcing a path through to their embattled infantry.

Unkel Von Schwartzer had climbed up on a barrel to watch the slaughter. He had shielded his eyes, squinting over the chaotic field towards the south ridge. And that was when he had spotted the unexpected reinforcements tumble his men aside.

'And who in the name of the Antichrist are they?' he cried, glancing at his astonished regimental commanders. 'How many more rats has Tarsi hidden in the woodwork?' the furious locotenent demanded, beginning to realise Tarsi's gnat-bite attack was causing more harm than he had ever anticipated.

Thank God that limp-wristed crow Bayard wasn't there to nitpick – criticise his woeful watch, question his crude, full-frontal tactics. Now it appeared Tarsi had found a legion of damned cavalry of his own. The last he had heard, Tarsi had sent his few light horsemen to the rear with the wagons!

'Find those rat-fuck arquebusiers of yours, and get back around the ridge,' the mortified commander ordered, flecks of spittle clinging to his bristling beard. 'They're not going forward, they're trying to get out. Close the trap! Don't let the bastards get away!' he shrieked.

He'd have Tarsi's head on a silver platter for this.

Half a league or so down the narrow pass, the terrible cacophony of battle had brought the plaster down from the ceiling, turning the anxious officers into dusty statues.

They rushed out onto the windswept walls of Mont Galliard and gazed in awestruck silence at the luridly-lit sky. The towering cliffs and snow-tipped peaks nearer the head of the valley were suffused with a soft red glow.

What on earth had Tarsi done – ignited some long-dormant volcano? The tumult was out of all proportion to the nuisance attack Savvi had been expecting. Tremendous explosions, hair-raising screaming, the dim clatter of steel on steel – the signs suggested that Tarsi had inflicted a great deal more than nuisance damage on their reluctant allies, the Swiss. Had Tarsi manufactured himself an army, slipped it down the gorge under their noses?

Savvi knew he could not, had not worked such a miracle.

'Maybe the Swiss are teaching him a lesson,' Stroma suggested, smoothing his small, spade-shaped beard.

'I hope they leave some for us,' Muhlberg growled. He turned, gave his gaunt master an imploring look.

'Let me take a few companies down the pass, we'll soon finish them off,' he suggested, wolfishly eager to get to grips with his old rival.

'We stay where we are,' Savvi snapped, drumming his fingers on the stone balustrade.

'What?'

'Pass the word, roll out the culverins. Every man, woman and bloody child to lend a hand with the guns.'

'Guns? Against whom?'

'The Swiss of course. Tarsi can light up the damned sky all he likes, but not even the brave Seigneur can best six thousand Swiss in a straight fight.'

'You mean to shoot him down as he retreats?' Stroma suggested.

'I mean to stop the Swiss, not Tarsi. Once their blood's up they'll come barrelling down that gorge after him, hoping to rush his defences into the bargain.'

'Yes. Well?'

'Well I don't imagine they intend to call a halt to pay us what they owe for the privilege of using our pass,' the renegade chief pointed out, his neat red beard parting about his gleaming teeth.

Muhlberg's lantern-jaw sagged.

'If the Swiss rush the pass, we'll never get our money. Briconet won't pay to shoe Von Schwartzer's horse, once the bugger's bolted into Italy.'

Stroma was nodding his head in anxious agreement.

'Savvi's right. It is essential we stop them before they penetrate the lower valley!'

'Stop them? That might be easier said than done!'

'We either restore the previous standoff, or we wave goodbye to fifteen thousand livres.'

'Standoff? Since when does the Black Legion seek a damned standoff with anyone?' Muhlberg growled.

'Since I took command,' Savvi said icily. 'We agreed a deal. I intend to make sure those cheese-munching morons keep it.'

Muhlberg was undeterred, beating his fist against the lichen-covered balustrade in frustration.

'Well, we roll out the guns and blast the whole bastard pack of 'em back into France,' Muhlberg suggested.

'You donkey-faced whoreson!' Savvi exclaimed. 'Haven't you listened to a word we've said? Tarsi must be allowed back to his lines, to seal the pass and restore the status quo. We'll never see our money otherwise, you lousy goat turd!'

Muhlberg's sloping brow furrowed as he pondered this devilish strategy.

'Ah, I see that now,' he said uncertainly.

'Well if you're so set on a fight, you can take fifty arquebusiers out onto the causeway. If Tarsi has any men left – let them run on by. But as soon as those bollock-brained Swiss try and rush you, open fire.'

Muhlberg grinned, displaying a mouthful of crooked teeth.

'And what if I see Tarsi himself? I can pot him, I suppose.'

Savvi shook his head.

'You shoot Tarsi and his ragtag legion will run all the way to Sicily. No, my friend, if you see Tarsi, give him your sweetest regards and bid him Godspeed to his own lines! Congratulate him on a splendidly daring raid!'

Muhlberg paled at the unthinkable prospect.

'Give him our regards?' he croaked.

'And let him pass, with as many of his rascals as can stand.'

'Or wave goodbye to fifteen thousand livres,' he breathed.

'We'll have another crack at Tarsi soon enough, just as long as he lives out the dawn. If they brush him aside, you can wager your life we'll be next.'

The time had come. They either got out now or died where they stood, a ring of defiant corpses in the shallows of the Swiss shit-pit.

'Ballistado, that's enough! Get your men back through the latrines and up the ridge!' The fearfully wounded Spaniard – bleeding from half a dozen grievous hurts – nodded his head, blinking at the battered Italian through a fine red mist.

Duke Gerhard's cavalry charge had delivered the last of his legion from certain destruction – hemmed in on three sides by slowly-moving blocks of Swiss pikemen. The spirited attack had cut through the frail cordon the Swiss had thrown across their rear, opened a narrow path between the remorseless enemy. Tarsi had thought he was seeing things when he recognised the truculent youngster hacking a path through to the embattled survivors. Gerhard had certainly kept his martial abilities well hidden from the experienced Italian.

Tarsi strode over the writhing wounded, grabbed at the Duke's blood-splattered bridle.

'Well met indeed, my Duke,' he called, tears of relief misting his vision.

Gerhard was panting hoarsely, his pale lips twitching as he stared down at the bruised adventurer. His horse was trembling

269

like a leaf in a gale, every sinew stretched taut beneath its smooth hide.

The pair of them looked ready to bolt in the unexpected aftermath of their mindless charge.

'You saved us once, now you can save us again: turn your men about and hold their skirmishers back. If they establish themselves on the ridge, we'll be shot to pieces before we can get out of here,' Tarsi called, tapping the Duke's jittery knee to attract his wayward attention.

'What's that? My ears are ringing!'

'I said, your horsemen will have to clear the slopes, keep their skirmishers off.'

Gerhard swallowed hard, took a nervous look back over his shoulder. The Swiss skirmishers were running up the ridge like flotsam on a spring tide, bent double as they negotiated the awkward slope. But the enemy pikemen were still a hundred paces off, watching their step as the unwieldy blocks negotiated the cruelly broken ground.

Sandy Kerr trotted up beside his nominal commander, his slick sword laid across his saddle bow. He had wrapped his shabby plaid about his left arm in place of his shield – the long spike stuck fast in some pikeman's temple.

'Ye'd best get them back, they'll not be long closing their trap,' the Scot called in his barely decipherable English. Tarsi nodded.

'I've ordered the retreat!' he called back. Gerhard shivered, horribly aware of the predicament in which he found himself.

He looked as if he had been woken in the midst of some terrible nightmare, only to find the reality was somewhat worse.

'Turn your horses, they'll not dare rush cavalry! We'll work our way back up the ridge and then run for it. They'll never catch us, packed in a pikeblock.'

Gerhard nodded dumbly. His ensign sagged in his saddle, shot in the back by an arquebusier crouching on top of the wall of splintered wagons. Kerr turned his horse and raised his arm, aimed his light latch at the squinting skirmisher. He pulled the trigger arm, sent the steel tipped bolt whistling into the man's chest. Gerhard turned his horse, reached over to prop the wounded man up. The heavy gonfallon fell to the ground, the scorched banner draped over a heap of dead.

Kerr turned his horse, gazing intently at the fearful Duke.

'Ride ye fool, leave ye damned ribbons and ride!' he bawled. The Scot's spit-flecked instruction seemed to wrench the youth from his panic attack. He dug in his heels, propelled the powerful charger towards the glistening causeway between the latrines.

The horsemen needed little persuasion to follow their knight errant. They knew they had one chance to escape the slaughter – by getting their horses to the top of the ridge before the darting skirmishers.

Tarsi watched the tightly-packed mob skitter and slide down the narrow avenue between the onrushing Swiss.

'Face up, face up, follow the horse!' he bawled. He was acutely aware his daring raid had reached a critical point. If he lost control of them for one second they would be swept aside like chaff – demolished by the leviathan pikeblocks manoeuvring to their front and flanks. The moment one of the front rankers turned to run the whole damned pack would lose its nerve, turn and run and try and save their miserable hides.

'Don't look at me you fornicating hogs!' he screeched, striding back towards the hard-pressed front rank.

There was no order, no fiendishly clever order of battle.

This was a simple fight for survival, Germans and English and Spanish alike hacking and jabbing with any weapon that came to hand – swords pulled from dead Swiss, broken pikes wrenched from shattered ribcages. The Swiss heard the shouts, saw the raiders retire towards the latrines. An immense roar went up from their packed ranks, the file leaders lengthening their stride to pursue the doomed enemy towards the burning ridge.

Tarsi held them, his iron will galvanising the stampeding pack into one final, colossal effort. The fearful soldiery gripped their weapons, bared their teeth. The madness passed, their terror bawled down by Tarsi's furious rantings.

'Break that line and you'll all be slaughtered, face up! Hold hard you scum, the cavalry are opening a way for you! Don't look at me you lousy screw, face up!' His desperate shouts reassured them, his battered armour worth a wagonload of holy relics. Tarsi was panting, drawing forgotten reserves of energy from somewhere. Stitchwort and Montalban were yipping and hooting, capering on the edge of the latrines throwing wreckage into the brimming filth.

Tarsi decided the strain had been too much for the eccentric fireworkers – the march hares had clearly lost their minds. Stitchwort tugged off his leather hood, his great domed skull shorn, the fearsome burns which stained his scalp shining brightly in the lurid firelight. He threw the hood into the ditch, bent down and hauled a small barrel in after it. Tarsi grabbed the madman's arm.

'What are you doing? Pick up a sword if you want to save yourself!'

'I'll save you all!' Stitchwort bawled back. 'Throw enough powder in that pit, I'll turn it into Satan's favourite furnace, and roast their souls for 'em!' He wrenched a bandolier of charges from a dead arquebusier and flung the clattering belt into the pit.

'I've still got a pot or two of my special mixture!' He unstopped a jar of sticky brown oil and hurled it at a partly submerged wagon.

Montalban was doing the same, hurling looted powder horns and any other combustibles into the reeking slurry.

Tarsi hardly understood a word the demented warlock was saying, but his actions spoke for themselves. He waved the embattled fighters back another ten paces, opening a sudden gulf between the weary warriors and their screeching enemies. The front ranks closed up as they packed together between the deep latrine pits.

The Swiss drummers and hornblowers were kicking up a hellish racket, trying to inspire the bloody phalanx forward. But the stricken camp was littered with wounded and dead. Tents and wagons blazed, sending clouds of choking smoke over the grim slaughter. Wagons and carts had been turned over, their broken shafts forming devilish hedges. Panicking Swiss found themselves driven forward by the mass at their backs, unable to avoid the obstacles and impaled on the terrible stakes. The tightly packed pikeblocks reeled and pulsed like anemones in a rock pool, tentacles rising and falling about cairns of dead and ditches full of dying.

Tarsi shoved and kicked his survivors back over the frail causeway, the exhausted front-rankers forming a defiant rear-guard. They peered over their shoulders, their desperately stretched nerves seconds away from snapping altogether.

Every sinew, every cell urged them to drop their notched weapons and run, run, run for their lives.

Only Tarsi's gargantuan presence stopped them, held them together.

The biggest, the bravest, the burliest troops formed a desperate crust, a few score facing a multi-coloured tide of furiously charging Swiss.

Tarsi was walking backwards, one eye on the enemy, one on

the furiously imaginative fireworkers. A gang of lightly-wounded tipped an ammunition cart into the pit. An English archer heaved a barrel of cooking oil above his head, sent it flying into the stinking stew. They snatched every bandolier and powder horn they could find. Broken firepikes, the blazing buckets reduced to smouldering sticks, were hurled into the vile lake as likely tinder.

Slowly, infinitely slowly, Tarsi's brave rearguard retired between the choked pits, the survivors funnelled towards the magical sanctuary of the ridge.

'Face up! Eyes front! They're coming!'

Tarsi's warning shout came just in time. A hundred and more Swiss – driven to distraction by the sight of their enemy's well-ordered retreat – had broken away from the enormous main body, sprinting forward with their pikes held at the charge yelling their peculiar oaths. They came on in a ragged mob, without rank or file, their spearpoints bobbing as they leapt over an obstacle course of dead men and wreckage.

Tarsi turned to the capering Englishman, who was lighting torches from a blazing cart. He snatched one of the spluttering wands and turned to wave the last of the rearguard back over the causeway.

'Set it off!'

They turned at bay, Tarsi and his fireworkers holding burning torches above their heads. Screaming Swiss dashed down the narrow neck of ground between the littered pits, funnelled towards the defiant trio.

'Now!'

Blazing torches sailed through the smoke and landed in the pits. Some fizzled, sank without trace in the reeking mire. Others struck gold – igniting the deadly cocktails Stitchwort had ordered thrown into the pits.

The sudden explosion – actually a series of increasingly powerful detonations – stopped the Swiss in their tracks. A dozen were blown into the air like rag dolls. Pieces of wreckage hurtled into the oncoming pikemen, tearing new holes in their long-suffering phalanx. Deadly shards and splinters skewered legs and faces and groins and knees. The hateful detonations were followed by a less deadly but hardly any more pleasant fallout as several tons of scorched excrement came to earth. The shower of stinking sludge brought the shocked Swiss to a cursing halt, the furious pikemen scraping at their beards, running their dirty knuckles into their eyes.

Unkel Von Schwartzer, watching the chaos from his quiet command post, could have wept to see Tarsi's excruciatingly insulting parting shot.

'Where are the skirmishers?' he croaked. 'Why don't they follow up?'

But his officers were away supervising the slaughter. His halberdiers were laughing and giggling to themselves as they realised what had happened – that their brother pikemen had been caught in a tempest of their own shit.

'Who's that laughing there? I'll see you thrown into the pit with 'em, you cock-eyed bastard!'

The cavalry on the ridge had routed the arquebusiers, opened another gap in the slowly closing cordon of skirmishers he had dispatched to the height. Tarsi's warband dragged themselves and their wounded up the stricken slope. They crawled, staggered and hauled their wounded over the broken ground.

By the time the Swiss had mustered their wits to follow, the majority were running down the far side, kicking up a storm of grit as they sprinted back down the gorge.

The Swiss locotenent watched the last of the fugitives disappear over the crest, wondering how on earth he would explain the dismal carnage to Bayard.

By Mont Galliard

✦

The firestorm had saved them, clawed Tarsi's helpless warband from the pits of hell. The tempest which Stitchwort had unleashed looked set to bring the entire mountain down on their heads, bury their bravery beneath a million tons of icy scree. The white-tipped peaks which overlooked the bloody arena had been illuminated by fireballs, the snowy slopes set to melt in the fallout thrown up from the ransacked camp.

But without those terrible detonations and ghastly gouts of flame there would have been no way over the ridge. The devilishly ignited pits had spewed sparks and brought down a filthy rain of smoking excrement. The reeking debris had blinded and choked the pursuing Swiss, allowing their terribly out-numbered tormentors precious moments to reach the temporary sanctuary of the main valley.

'Run, run! Back to the trenches you slow dogs, you hell-hounds!' Tarsi's lung-bursting bellows had barely registered with the shadow legion tottering or crawling over the ridge, blown like chaff in the hot winds gusting down the gorge.

It hardly seemed possible so many of the raiders could have survived the carnage. Limping archers hauled unconscious Spaniards. Bleeding *dopplesoldners* carried their comrades over their shoulders, using their monstrous swords as blood-glutted crutches.

The horsemen who had survived the murderous escape from the latrine pits had pulled their wounded comrades up behind them, dragged swooning troopers over their saddle bows before spurring off after knots of terrified fugitives. Their horses whinnied in fear, legs tottering under impossible loads, backs beaten black by their desperate riders. Not one of them had a decent trot left in them – Duke Gerhard couldn't have spurred away from the carnage if he had wanted to. They staggered and stumbled on the rocks or collapsed in bloody ruin, spilling their screaming cargoes over the stones.

Tarsi and Ballistado were last off the ridge, holding the desperate rearguard together as the last Swiss who had remained in contact were hewn down or hurled back down the ruined slope.

Tarsi needed no further urging, waving the men on down the valley. They leapt between outcrops of boulders and bounced down the scree slopes on their behinds, determined to make their escape while the reeling Swiss gathered their wits in the burning hollow below.

The swiftly moving pikeblocks were still reforming somewhere in the reeking murk they had fled. The leading files quickly worked their way between the smoking latrine pits, burned out geysers in a barren valley. The leaderless mob swarmed and pulsed about their colours, the few officers who remained shouting and shoving their ranks into some kind of order.

Precious moments went by as the furious mass concertinaed through the narrow neck of rock between the smoking obstacles. They rolled up the ridge, horns blowing to summon the pursuit, drums rattling from all points of the shattered camp.

Unkel Von Schwartzer, goaded beyond endurance by the devastating reverses his army had suffered, had forgotten his duty and put aside his responsibilities in order to get to grips with the impudent rogues who had so upset his applecart.

His place was at the rear of the human trident, guiding their three-pronged counter-attack and reorganising shattered platoons of skirmishers. But the headstrong youth was spitting blood, hacking at the heaped corpses in a drooling, maniacal fury. He had kicked and elbowed his way to the front, catching up with the hotheads dragging their pikes up the ridge.

The corpses, helpless and maimed the fleeing enemy had left behind were bludgeoned and skewered, trampled to paste by thousands of feet. The rubble and clutter and smouldering debris they had thrown up to shield their retreat was heaved aside like seaweed driven up a beach by a spring tide.

The Swiss breasted the ridge in full spate, a forest of pikes sprouting from the swirling smoke. They came down the other side, filling ditches, overflowing the gullies, flooding the pits which had delayed their initial onslaught.

They swarmed down the uneven ridge in their hundreds and then thousands, an army of locusts striding out on brightly striped legs. They lengthened their stride over the firmer ground, flowing down the road after the hobbling enemy.

'I want Tarsi's eyes! I want his balls on a silver platter! No prisoners, d'you hear me you mincing clowns, you whore-spawned cravens! No prisoners!' Unkel's frantic shouts galvanised the warriors who led the charge, invigorating their battle-weary limbs.

The race for Tarsi's trenches was on.

Tarsi was panting like a broken bellows, helping to drag a lolling Spaniard through a thicket of furze bushes. He stopped for a second, peering over his shoulder to see the Swiss tide flow down the gorge, filling up the valley behind him. He could feel the earth tremble beneath his blistered feet, ears assaulted by their brazen fanfares.

He knew this valley like his dead wife's eyes.

They were half a league from their trenches – a few hundred yards short of the slim causeway to Mont Galliard. He peered ahead, saw the graceful spires of his former stronghold rear out of the rock ridges. Pale lanterns winked on the lofty balconies, dark flags streamed from the towers.

He staggered on, his mind dulled by numb panic. What if Savvi made a sortie, ventured out of Mont Galliard to block their escape?

It would be over in moments.

Alberto Tarsi gritted his teeth and boosted the unconscious Spaniard onto his broad back. Loaded down like some armour-plated mule, the Italian adventurer stumbled towards the dawn.

Constantin Muhlberg had led fifty of his skirmishers out of the safety of Mont Galliard, gnawing his pendulous lip at the prospect of a good scrap. His men had loped along the narrow bridge behind him, peering down the valley after their wounded quarry. He had turned to wave the sluggards on when the first bombs rained down amongst them. Shocking explosions had bracketed the bridge, razor shards flying through the night. The leaders had been cut down, the staggering survivors picked off by a sudden flurry of arquebus shots and a brittle storm of crossbow bolts. The unexpected bombardment had come from the ruined blockhouse at the end of the causeway. Muhlberg cursed, realising that the slippery Italian had left an ambush party to guard his rear!

A typically Turkish Tarsi trick!

The *Landsknecht* cursed his enemy's intuition – and his own lack of foresight.

Muhlberg's men threw themselves down behind the bridge parapet, aiming their cumbersome weapons at the blockhouse. They kept up a withering fire, forcing the rogues within to keep their heads down as they worked their way along the bridge and took cover in a gully a stonesthrow from the blazing obstacle. Muhlberg gripped his sword, cursing on a mouthful of dust and grit.

He knew this ground well enough – Tarsi had kept him and his men pinned down there the previous spring during their own ill-fated siege of Mont Galliard. He peered at the enemy-held blockhouse, trying to judge how many men Tarsi had dared spare to hold the ruined fort. Not more than a dozen, he would have thought.

'Hold your fire!'

'What's that Muhlie, hold fire? We'll rush 'em before they can reload!' one of his veterans encouraged, crouching in the gully with a double-headed axe.

'You heard Savvi. He said no shooting Tarsi's men,' Muhlberg growled, mortified by the humiliating restriction. 'Spread out, keep your heads down and make ready. You shoot when I say, have you got it, leper ballocks?'

'Make ready? They just killed Joachim and Edzel!'

'Served the bleeders right for being such lanky Thuringian turds,' Muhlberg bawled. 'We're here to shoot Swiss. They don't get past till we get our money. I'll throttle any man who so much as farts at Tarsi's boys, d'you hear me, you dung-munching filth?'

Muhlberg was a plain soldier, about as imaginative as the long-horned sheep which found precarious tracks of their own over the sheer cliff faces. But the slow-witted German's present orders had driven him to distraction. He had never endured such bitter frustrations, squatting in a ditch watching his own sworn enemy's grievously-reduced warband stumble and stagger along the gorge towards them.

Tarsi's fugitives had been alerted by the sudden gunfire, the shrill detonation of Stitchwort's devilish grenades. The leaders had spotted Muhlberg's black legionaires doubling along the ditch on the far side of the killing ground and bawled the alarm to their comrades hurrying along behind. The raiders threw themselves down, seeking out the questionable cover of the scree slopes and boulders which lay strewn beneath the cliffs, directly opposite the hornet's nest.

Muhlberg watched them milling in terrified confusion, uncertain whether to try and rush his forlorn hope or wait for the pursuing Swiss. He gripped his sword, felt the greasy wire wound about the hilt dig into his palm. Every man was urging him to give the order, willing him to open fire on the helpless mob.

But he had his orders.

'Hold your fire! Let them pass! Wait for the Swiss,' he called, casting warning glances along the shallow trench his arquebusiers had occupied.

The bewildered herd packed in beneath the cliff clustered together like frightened children, certain they were being tempted into the deadliest trap of all.

Alberto Tarsi lay the dying Spaniard down on a bed of crumbling stone, barged his way through the muttering crowd – all that was left of his courageous warband. He shielded his eyes, studying Savvi's galling dispositions. He had thrown enough skirmishers into the ditch to pinch out their only escape route, bring enfilading fire down on the stampeding legion. Tarsi heaved himself dry, half choked on smoke and nauseated by the agonising jog down the gorge. He was bone tired, his legs and arms beaten lead, his head a throbbing cauldron of fireworks and pain. The small ambush party he had ordered into the ruined blockhouse had crawled out to join them, excitedly pointing out Savvi's craven dispositions as the commander leaned on a broken pike.

'They worked their way past us, my lord, but they're holding their fire,' a dust-smothered grenadier reported. Tarsi wiped his eyes, blinking to clear his stinging vision and racking his brains to explain such dubious tactics.

Sandy Kerr drew up alongside him, his pony wearing a grey blanket of foam and grit, a beard of blood-flecked foam hanging from its slack and steaming mouth.

'What's the holdup here?' he asked, as indignantly as if he were addressing his old enemy Eldritch. 'The Swiss'll be on us in a moment, if ye stick here,' the bow-legged Tartar warned. Tarsi glanced at his riders – doubled up behind one another and desperate to escape the rapidly closing trap.

'Savvi's got his men in the pass between Mont Galliard and our trenches,' he explained, so stricken with exhaustion he was unable to devise any solution to their dilemma. Kerr peered through the drifting murk at the figures lurking in the ditch. The fiends appeared to be waving them on, daring Tarsi's men to charge. Judas goats in the leather and steel harness of the dreaded Black Legion.

Their leader rose from the hole, raised his hands away from his sword belt and took a cautious step towards them. Tarsi recognised Muhlberg – Savvi's savage locotenent and despicable partner in crime.

'Yes, it's me, Conny Muhlberg of the Black Legion! You'd best get your finger out Tarsi, get back to your trenches while you can. Leave the real fighting to us Germans, as bloody usual!' the red-bearded brawler shouted across the barren arena.

Tarsi gripped the broken pike, wondering if he could hurl it as far as the braggart. But the canny German had remained well out of throwing range, preferring to shout his challenge at the cowering survivors.

'How would you like us, single file? Or close-ordered so you can save your powder, you turd-skinning shit-house!' Tarsi called, his lips peeling back in a contemptuous grimace. Muhlberg grinned at this pleasantry.

'I'd dearly love to stand here passing the time of day with you, Tarsi, but Von Schwartzer's right behind you with the best part of four thousand men. I'd rather be safe indoors, when they come calling.'

'We're not standing in your way, you worm-tongued wolf!'

'Your men won't be harmed. Savvi said so,' the German called, his lantern-jaw set.

'Hah! What are you proposing, a truce, that we work together to stop their invasion? I don't want to appear pedantic, but you're a little late for switching sides this time.'

'A truce with you? I'd rather break bread with the Grand Vizier himself,' Muhlberg snarled. 'But Von Schwartzer's behind with his tolls, and we don't like gatecrashers at Mont Galliard.'

The wily Italian had been lured towards traps before – but something in the German's frowning explanation rang true. The Swiss had bought the swineherds off, bribed the dirty usurpers to open the pass.

But they hadn't paid in full and the punctilious Savvi was insisting they settled their debts before he let them pass. Tarsi felt a grudging admiration for Savvi's black-hearted courage. Only the very strong or the very stupid gave a Swiss army an ultimatum.

'You must think I'm in my dotage,' Tarsi countered. 'We go on and you'll shoot us down like dogs!'

'Don't tempt me, you pizzle-fingered dwarf! If it was up to me I'd slaughter the lot of you and fuck the money!'

'Ah!'

'. . . But Savvi said we're to let you pass.' He cupped his hand about his ear, listened to the dull rumble in the gorge. 'The Swiss are a stonesthrow behind you; they'll trample you into the dirt, dotage or no,' he challenged.

Tarsi peered over his shoulder. The strutting raven was right. The Swiss were rolling down the gorge, their remorseless momentum funnelled by the sheer walls of rock. The bastards would be on them in minutes and they would be slaughtered in seconds.

'Last chance Tarsi! And remember this, you'd be dead and buried if it wasn't for the Black Legion!'

The tall German waved his men out of their trench and back towards the temporary sanctuary of the blockhouse, ready to try his damnedest to bring the Swiss advance to a stuttering halt.

Tarsi dared not hesitate a moment longer. He waved his warband on, hurrying the red-eyed pack towards the questionable safety of their trenches.

Tarsi's bloodied band hurried by as best they could, light-headed with nervous exhaustion and burdened with groaning wounded. They had no cards left to play now, no secret weapon to disrupt the unstoppable avalanche of humanity sweeping down the pass after them. They had barely enough energy to put one foot in front of the other, let alone defend themselves against an enemy invigorated by the brassy scent of revenge.

English, Germans, Spanish and Scots had given their all, fought until their weapons were notched and broken and their heads numb with slaughter. They had choked on foul smoke, squinted through the drifting fog like red-eyed demons venturing from their stony lair. Tarsi watched them hobble and stumble by, knowing in his bones that they could fight no more. The trenches they had dug with such reckless enthusiasm a fortnight before would no more stop the vengeful Swiss than a single sandbag would dam a river in full spate.

He was damned if he was going to rely on Muhlberg to interrupt their punishing onslaught.

There was nothing else to be done – apart from saving his few hundred brave survivors for another day. Tarsi made up his mind in a moment.

'Ballistado! Kerr!' he bawled, his throat hoarse from smoke and shouting, 'Don't stop when you reach the trenches! Take the fork for the high pass!' the exhausted commander called. 'Get your men back to the hospice, it's our only chance of stopping them now!'

The Swiss were snapping at their heels, their leading warriors striding out with pikes at the charge, hell-bent on cornering the lousy rascals who had so disturbed their sleep.

Muhlberg's forlorn hope crouched in the ruins of the block-house, listening in awestruck silence to their rumbling, bawling, cursing approach. Thousands of feet sent an eerie vibration through the rock, their bawled challenges sent flocks of storm-crows flapping from their roosts along the sheer cliffs.

'Hold your fire, steady!' Muhlberg called, nerves stretched taut by the hideous racket. The stink of smouldering match filled his flared nostrils. The skirmishers could pick individual detail from the mass of men – burnished breastplates and gaudy hose, rakishly angled bonnets and bared teeth.

'Fire!'

The puny barrage was immediately drowned out by the roar of Savvi's culverins, rolled out on the walls of Mont Galliard a hundred and fifty paces to their rear. Six heavy cannon belched fire and brimstone, tongues of flame stabbing into the belly of the night. Howling cannonballs tore through the screaming Swiss files, pulverising men and arms and ricocheting up the cliff walls like pebbles tossed into the waves. Tumbling scree obliterated the bewildered pikemen sheltering from the storm under the lee of the cliffs. The sudden broadside brought the Swiss advance to a bloody halt, the phalanx concertinaed in upon itself like a crushed caterpillar speared by a shrike.

Muhlberg's men didn't wait to see the smoke clear. They bolted from their holes and ran for the bridge like black-harnessed hares while the shocked ranks slewed and pulsed in the killing ground behind them. Savvi had ordered his gunners to raise their arms, to fire directly at the leaning rock faces above the invaders' heads. The storm of shot tore huge chunks from the cliff walls, sent tons of icy debris sliding down the slopes, uprooting trees and burying heaps of shot-scorched wounded. By the time the smoke and dust had settled, the Swiss had retired a hundred unsteady paces, utterly bewildered by this latest catastrophe, the revenge they had set their iron hearts on torn from under their noses.

By the Villefrancan border

♦

The bad-tempered soldiers had, as usual, fallen back from the idly riding lovebirds, giving James Eldritch and his spirited Countess the opportunity to settle their differences in private.

Hulin was as resentful of the Englishmen as ever, treating Hobby especially with withering contempt and a stream of Langue Doc invective. The sergeant, bound and bruised on his stolen horse, listened to the Frenchman's scornful commentary with his usual phlegmatic detachment.

'Ah now 'oolin, that's easy for you to say, weasel-breeked shite that ye are.'

The highly-strung corporal would close an eye, picking the odd word from the muscle-bound brute's laconic replies. He was in the habit of accompanying his abuse with a variety of expressive gestures – bared teeth, furious snarls, ugly grimaces.

Hobby, on the other hand, gave as good as he got with a half-smile playing about his permanently downturned mouth – a skill Hulin found intensely infuriating.

Eldritch glanced over his shoulder at his pitiful warband.

Back in England he had commanded Lord Howath's Ride – two score light cavalry well used to cut and thrust warfare such as this.

Now his Ride was more of a Hobble, and they were a long, long way from home.

The party had picked up horses in the woods.

French horses.

Eldritch had led them over the burning slopes away from Villefranco, making skilful use of the gullies he had scouted earlier that eventful week. The militia forces had soon given up on the unequal chase, returning to the main camp before dawn to crow over their magnificent victory with their companions.

The French had, however, sent a small mounted patrol out

284

over the wilderness, beaters searching the rock cairns and furze bushes for the wounded birds Briconet's stupendous salvo might have missed.

Eldritch had spotted them first, making their way along the ridge a league or so behind, hopelessly visible in the slowly advancing dawn. He had hurried them on, taking them deeper into the canyons which scored the coastal plain. He knew the indifferent scouts would not dare bring their horses down into such inhospitable terrain.

But his detour had taken him a good way from the sanctuary of the pinewoods.

The deep fissures had attracted a handful of fellow survivors, red-eyed fugitives from Briconet's cruel massacre. Comrades of bloody circumstance, they were in even worse condition than Hobby and Hulin, cowering in the barren gullies unable to find the willpower to hide themselves any further away from the searchers. They were on their last legs. Their blisters were bleeding, their backs burnt and scored by the terrible blast. They were nursing an ugly assortment of powder burns and blood-caked lacerations and had been immensely relieved to see their old chief Corporal Hulin among their rescuers. They had been less reassured by the questionable company he was keeping, but none of them possessed the energy to drag themselves away from their sooty-faced saviours.

The Countess had soaked her petticoat in spring water and allowed each man a grateful suck on the saturated cotton. The girl was barely recognisable behind her blood and smuts mask, but to the lucky few who had escaped Leonardo's Engine, she was an angel sent from heaven.

The weary party had found the energy for one last effort, leaving the safety of the gully and striking out for the promised land of pines and fir trees which crowned the open slopes to the north.

They hadn't gone halfway before the French patrol returned, picking up their trail in the brittle, noonday sun.

'Come on, get into the trees! They'll slaughter us out here!' Eldritch called. He and Hobby had borrowed swords from dead militiamen, but the rest were hobbling along, unable to defend themselves against a child with a catapult, let alone half a dozen and more riders.

The patrol cantered after them, every step bringing their features into sharper focus. They could hear the Frenchmen hooting and halloing as they spurred their horses towards the desperate survivors.

Eldritch and Hobby loped along behind the panting Villefrancans, casting doubtful glances over their shoulders and urging the wounded men to one last effort. Facing cavalry in the open would mean certain death, and the sure-thought seemed to lend them the energy to complete the desperate sprint half a minute ahead of the whooping pursuit. Eldritch ducked into the trees, a crossbow bolt thudding into the pine trunk a yard from his sweating temple. They threaded their way through the undergrowth, taking great lungfuls of resonant air. They could hear the French cavalry shouting behind them, trying to urge their horses into the dense woods.

Eldritch called a halt, hands on knees to get his breath. He began to tear at his reeking tunic, the garishly made-up Countess wondering what on earth he was up to.

'Hobby, a couple of staves, as quick as you like.'

The sergeant nodded, bending under a sagging tree to begin his search. Eldritch placed his spare bowstring on a log and grabbed at the bare branches, snapping the boughs off as best he could.

Corporal Hulin, racked by cramps and bleeding from a dozen cuts and weeping burns, watched their handiwork with a derisive grimace.

'You left your bows in Villefranco, Captain,' he remarked.

'We don't need warbows to deal with carrion like you, Hulin,' Eldritch replied curtly, tearing the twigs from the first of his improvised arrows.

The Countess realised what he was about, her shoulders sagging in disbelief.

'You cannot be serious. Surely we must run and hide ourselves, deep in the forest,' she cried.

'They'll be after us with those crossbows at any moment. I would suggest you get those wounded men into cover, and find yourself a stout club.'

Hobby returned with two promising staves and used Hulin's dagger to cut notches in the wood. He looked at the captain, busy trimming his own unlikely bow.

'I can hear them!' Charlotte cried, looking up from the exhausted Villefrancans. They were beyond all aid, their pale features pearled with sweat, their trembling limbs incapable of further effort.

Hobby tossed the knife back to Hulin. The corporal caught it in his good hand, nodded grimly.

'Ah, don't you worry about me. I can defend myself, if those weak-kneed rag-arses can't,' he swore, looking around the tumbled glade for some likely cover. Eldritch strung his bow and gave it an experimental pull. The stave creaked alarmingly.

'Hulin, I'll drop the first man through the trees. For the sake of God, you'll grab his weapons.'

The Villefrancan nodded grimly, poised behind a downed tree trunk.

The Countess shrieked, pointed towards the crackling woods.

One of the Frenchmen had dismounted, scouting ahead of his friends, crossbow held across his chest.

He saw the Countess crouched above the bodies, quickly raised his weapon.

Eldritch's improvised arrow hit him on the temple, breaking the skin and knocking him on his behind, but sliding off his sloping skull. The man gave a startled cry, dropping his crossbow and falling over a tangle of roots. Hulin doubled forward, dagger ready. The man was grasping at his wound and staring at his bloody fingers as if he couldn't believe he had survived to tell the tale.

Hulin snatched up his crossbow and hurled himself into the bushes as two more Frenchmen ran forward, swords in their fists. Hulin fired, catching the first man square in the stomach. The Frenchman screamed, dropped his sword to grab at the shuddering bolt.

Hobby let fly, his bow stave snapping with the pressure of his 100lb pull. The blunt stick caught the second man in the throat, snapping his neck. Eldritch doubled forward, watching Hulin dispatch the wounded crossbowman with a stone. Hulin looked up, mouth slack with nervous tension.

'Call them on, in French,' he instructed. 'Tell them we've caught the Countess.'

Hulin nodded, cupped his mouth and bawled the juicy invitation at the shadowed trees. Hobby doubled across the clearing, tossing the useless bow aside. Eldritch discarded his crudely-forged sword and picked up the cavalryman's slightly superior weapon.

'James, come back!' Charlotte hissed as loud as she dared.

Where were the craven rogues going now?

They sneaked off into the bushes, leaving the furious Countess to crouch by the fallen. She peered around her, imagining grinning Frenchmen behind every trunk.

Four wary soldiers emerged from the woods perilously close to Eldritch's hidey-hole, the last three men watching their progress with their crossbows. Eldritch raised his head an inch, peered through the leafy vegetation to locate the dangerously armed enemies. Three crossbows could turn their ambush on its head, see them all skewered on bolts. He began to crawl on his belly as he had done on raids in the Highlands, careful to make no sound which might alert the enemy.

'Manon, Coule! Where've you hidden yourselves?' the leader called, tilting his head to investigate the strange tableau.

Was this some species of harpy, crouching over her victims ready to suck their blood? The officer flicked his sword from side to side as if he were sniffing the air in the too-quiet glade.

The Countess, too frightened to move, sat down on her haunches, utterly exhausted and hardly caring that they had abandoned her. They had taken to the trees to save themselves like the grubby mercenaries they were, left her to the mercy of these hairy apes wearing the livery of the Royal Marseille militia.

Charlotte remembered *them* of old. Chocolate soldiers parading in fancy uniforms, far more experienced at talking wars than they were fighting them.

A young officer looked from the bewildered girl to the scorched Villefrancans lying about her feet, then turned his head to look for his missing soldiers.

'Manon, Coule? Berti, we're over here!' The other three soldiers closed in about him, searching the surrounding trees and eyeing the distressed Countess, red-eyed and virtually naked on the forest floor.

'They brought their whore, look. One of 'em's wives, d'you reckon?'

'You keep your hands to yourself, Pouli. Until we've found her mates.'

'Wash some of that crap off her and . . . what was that?'

The officer looked up, alerted by a gargled scream from the bushes. Another of his crossbowmen backed out of the woods, swinging his weapon from side to side as if surrounded by woad-daubed Gauls.

'Whatever is it? Where are the others?' the young officer strode towards the fearful crossbowman, his dirty, dishevelled livery hanging out from his outsized . . .

Hobby – his bulky body packed into the looted hauberk – swung around and fired the crossbow at point-blank range. The bolt hit the officer high in the chest, lifted him off his feet and flung him down in the fragrant mulch. Hobby tore the ludicrous helmet from his head and hurled it at the next Frenchman, who gave a startled cry and turned to run – straight towards Eldritch, emerging from the trees to menace the surviving Frenchman with a loaded crossbow.

Eldritch and Hulin had worked their way around the glade, locating and killing the woefully inexperienced militiamen, and emerging on the far side of the clearing to cut off their escape.

The French closed in, back to back to face the terrifying woodsmen.

Eldritch stalked closer, raised the crossbow level with the wounded swordsman's dented forehead.

'We've killed your friends and found your horses. Drop your weapons and you'll live, otherwise, make your peace with your maker.'

The Frenchman looked from the gaunt Englishman to his equally murderous companions. They threw their swords down, raised their trembling hands.

Eldritch walked up to the biggest – blood dripping from the cut where Hobby had caught him with the helmet. He gazed into the blinking Frenchman's eyes.

'I kill Frenchmen, mostly for money, but sometimes for sport. Never, ever, chase me across a field unless you've got the balls to finish it.' He tugged the soldier by the scruff of his neck and booted him towards the waiting woods. His terrified companions joined him, sprinting into the welcoming trees as if they had survived an encounter with Satan himself.

'Nice of them to fetch us their horses,' Hobby observed, wiping his blade on Charlotte's sleeve. The girl pulled her arm away, fuming at the pale-skinned devils she had been forced to take up with.

'I thought you'd left me again,' she croaked, close to draining her reservoir of tears.

Eldritch reached down, offered her his hand. The long fingers were smeared with blood. Charlotte thought for a moment, then closed her fingers about the captain's dirty paw. He pulled her upright, steadied her for a moment.

'I'll never leave you again,' he said simply, in English.

She guessed it was as close to a declaration as Eldritch would ever get. By the time Charlotte had registered the comment, he had stalked off to take his pick of their horses.

The enormous effort he had expended, firstly in obtaining their transport and secondly in declaring his undying love for the Countess, had clearly robbed him of his energy and slowed his wits.

He had led the way through the woods in silence, as if they were approaching the borders of Howath's Middle March and not hundreds of leagues from safety in a trackless Alpine forest. Charlotte had been too exhausted to muster any arguments, to press him to expand on his startling revelation. She had been content to close her eyes, lulled by the horse's drowsy gait. It had been another hour or two before her champion had broken the silence.

'What you told me back at Villefranco, about your fortune,' he asked. 'That wasn't the whole truth, was it?'

Charlotte had blinked, wondering if she had heard him right.

'How much of a lie are you hoping I told you?' she asked levelly.

He glanced at her.

'I remember everything which passed between us, back in the dungeons,' he said cryptically.

'As I do.'

'I told you then, and I tell you now, freely, that I love you.'

Charlotte closed her eyes, determined not to be swayed by his awkward approaches.

'But you're just a little concerned I am not quite the Countess of your dreams. You were hoping for a bulging dowry, wondrous castles and huge estates, in short James, a rich living and a soft bed!'

The Englishman raised his heavily-stubbled chin. He hadn't shaved in days and his black beard was stuck with dirt, scabbed with dried blood.

'I do not care whether you are a goosegirl or the Queen of Sheba,' he said flatly. 'If what you said was true, that you have nothing besides your name, then you can have nothing to go back to.'

Charlotte had been taken off guard by his sideways scrutiny. She thought for a moment.

'It was true. I have little but my name. A tumbledown château in somewhat worse state than Villefranco.'

Eldritch straightened his back, nodded brusquely.

'Well then.'

'Yes?'

He raised his eyebrows, shrugged, and clicked his reins.

She glared at his broad back, irritated by his offhand manner. Most men would have dropped to one knee to press their suit, but not her enigmatic Englishman. Eldritch had hardly bothered to investigate her antecedents. Charlotte remembered he had made more detailed enquiries when hiring beds for the night – way back when they had ridden into Rouquevaire.

The Countess glanced back down the winding trail. Hobby and Hulin were bickering as usual, guiding the drooping wounded on leading reins. She spurred her horse back alongside her taciturn lover's.

'Can I presume from your questioning, that you intend to marry me?' she asked, not sure whether she should be amused or annoyed.

Eldritch studied her grubby features for a moment, his black brows furrowed. He seemed more ill-at-ease discussing their domestic arrangements than he had ambushing the unfortunate Frenchmen.

'The moment I am able to finalise my affairs,' he said carefully, 'I shall ask your hand in marriage. It is only right I make amends, for my previous behaviour,' he said testily.

'Amends? For tying me up and standing on me? I thought your spell in the *oubliette* had settled that account?' she said archly, enjoying his momentary scowl.

'Aye. But it was I who took you from your home, from your people, in the first,' he explained, colouring. 'I should have . . . perhaps I should never have come to France,' he concluded. Charlotte tried to catch his darkly flashing eye.

'But if you had not come, how were we to meet? I am not a soldier or a traveller or a merchant like your father,' she went on, determined he would acknowledge his feelings rather than try and ride over them once again.

'And a good many of your countrymen would still be alive,' he pointed out.

'True. But many more will be killed in this war, on both sides of the border – and without your involvement. Where would you be now, if you had not travelled to Marseille? Killing Frenchmen for your paymaster, what's his name, Tarshan?'

'Tarsi.'

'Killing Frenchmen for the Empire, or killing Imperialists for Francis, I cannot imagine it makes much difference to you,' she said scornfully.

'It doesn't,' he admitted. 'But as I told you in Villefranco,' he mentioned the Duchy rather than the precise location of their conversation, 'I only did what I felt necessary, to further my search for Lillith. I believe, I have come to believe, that you are right. Lillith is beyond my help, she would scorn my advice. I can no more drag her back to England than I could drag you around the pinewoods outside the castello.'

Charlotte was impressed – moved – by his awkward speech, but wished to God the cold fish of an Englishman would stop being so terribly formal. Why not cry out he loved her, that he worshipped her, that he would follow her to the ends of the earth and bugger the money? His studied mannerisms, carefully-phrased enquiries and haughty manner undermined the simple love she felt for the tongue-tied captain.

'Damn it all James,' she hissed, leaning over her saddle to grasp the torn sleeve of his tunic. 'Will you look me in the eyes?'

He did.

'And tell me, without any explanations, footnotes or qualifications, that you love me, here, as I am, as you see me now?'

Eldritch gazed at her storm-racked hair, the grubby face she had tried to wash in the bitterly cold springs. Her gown was torn and split up the middle for easy riding, her hands were red, her tapering fingers waxy with grime where she had gripped her reins.

But he could deny her nothing.

'I love you, as you are, as you will be, forever,' he said quickly.

Charlotte looked ahead, noticed the trees had thinned considerably, the fragrant pinewoods which had sheltered them for two days giving way to sweet green meadows and gently rolling foothills. They had reached the northern tip of the forest and were overlooking the broad vales of Southern Savoy. She could see the broad silver ribbon of the river Tanaro, arching gracefully between the outflung spurs. To the north again, the high roads into Italy.

'Well?'

'Well what?' she asked, spurring her horse out of the trees and over the deliciously fresh, breeze-ruffled slope.

Eldritch frowned, waved Hobby and his argumentative companion onward, and spurred after his maddeningly erratic lover.

By Asti, in central Piedmont

◆

The fugitives made good time once they had acquired their horses from the pursuing Frenchmen. Eldritch led his famished troop out of the woods and across the broad but deserted fields towards the River Tanaro, leaving Briconet's half-hearted militiamen far behind. The Englishmen were wearing their dung-smeared tunics, Charlotte the grubby gown she had borrowed from Duke Gerhard's ransacked apartments, the Villefrancan refugees the sooty rags they had escaped in. An inquisitive peasant, peering through his trees at the outlandish company, might have imagined them to be travelling players down on their luck, or a band of thieving bandits on the prowl.

The ill-made knight led them on, fording the broad river. The foaming mountain water invigorated horse and man, speeding their flight into the fertile valleys along the Tanaro. They bypassed pockets of uncertainly allied territory, skirting small principalities and the tiny County of Tenda, criss-crossing the borders of the ancient Marquisate of Saluzzo. Their route had taken them north through increasingly rocky terrain. They avoided the main trade roads, weaving their way through stony, nettle-choked gullies beneath steep, vine-clad hillsides. The lush slopes were topped with little villages, the creamy stone walls glimmering brightly in the still-persuasive sun. Squat church towers supported a soaring sky, but the weary band had deliberately skirted the distantly chiming towns – preferring to avoid any interference from the local authorities if at all possible. Eldritch did not relish explaining his presence to some minor magistrate. None of the party possessed any kind of written authorisation to travel – the letters, credentials and passes Eldritch had carried into France had been lost along with his personal weapons during the tumults back in Villefranco. Without them he was little more than an invading bandit. They made good time following the lush, well-tended valleys from Fossano to Pollenzo. They had risked riding into Alba to buy a little food

– the city valued its free trading statue, and the merchant barons who competed for its wealth didn't mind who bought their wares. They rode on, admiring from a safe distance the lofty stronghold of Castigliole d'Asti. The fairytale castle was perched high on an ochre ridge – its symmetrical towers surely as impregnable as Mont Galliard itself.

By the time they had reached the busier metropolis of Asti, they had felt safe enough to leave the hills and follow the ancient wagon trails, blending in with the dusty caravans and packs of shiftless refugees without raising undue suspicion. There were hundreds of people on the roads, looking for food, work and shelter. Half a dozen shifty-eyed strangers on foaming horses would hardly stand out in such a colourful crowd.

The last of the harvest had been safely gathered in, throwing half the available manpower of Southern Europe out of work for the rapidly approaching winter. The North Italian staples of wheat and rice, olives and fruit had been picked, sorted, stored and transported. Laden wains rumbled from sun-bleached country-side to the teeming towns, legions of idle peasants coughing and cursing in their wake. They had little choice but to join the hungry throngs heading for the cities in search of new employment. Wages had nosedived – the packs of hired hands who had wandered the region helping with the all-important harvest reduced to earning a few pennies where they could.

The dog days of summer were gradually giving way to autumn, but the embattled empires were still locked in mortal combat – unwilling to stand down while there were towns to be stormed and rival armies to be routed. The unusually mild weather had enabled the commanders to extend the campaigning season – and marching armies required their crop of soldiers just as the rich merchants craved grain and salt and hides and cattle. A constant stream of new recruits to replace soldiers lost in battle, carried off by devastating epidemics or deserting to the enemy.

Their gargantuan appetites had spawned a new class of merchants. Pimps of Battle who dealt in men but left the actual fighting to others. These professional procurers preferred to call themselves *kriegsherren* – gentlemen of war – and it would be inconceivable to go to war without reference to them. The *kriegsherren* were virtually untouchable, their sinister role disguised to various extents by a cloak of bribe-bought immunities and artfully-worded international protocols. They travelled from court to court to collect letters of appointment empowering them to raise troops for a specified state or prince, jealously defending a likely new recruiting ground with bands of hired thugs and enforcers.

The roving recruitment parties knew the seasons just as well as the hungry peasants, descending on likely cities or towns to fill the gaps in their contractors' ranks. The canny *provveditore* could hire themselves a company of men in a few hours, setting up their stalls outside the roadside taverns or in the shade of some tree-lined piazza. Hungry farmhands queued to collect a handful of coin, signing on for service with commanders whose legendary names they could hardly pronounce.

A mark on a paper, a pint of rough wine or cider, and another batch of cannon fodder would begin its dispirited shamble towards the battlefront.

So it had been for their forefathers, so it would be for their sons. The overlapping borderlines of Europe were no obstacle to the commissioners – which was fortunate as they had been forced to roam further and further afield in order to fill their quotas, arranging the shipment of so many men as if they were salted sardines or sides of beef. They generally favoured the bigger ports, the teeming and highly cosmopolitan trading centres where no questions were ever asked and highly profitable deals were lubricated by wine, women and sumptuous bribes.

Algernon Salt could not claim to be an expert at this most essential of professions – he preferred to think of himself as a jack of all trades rather than the master of one – but who could say when one would need to add another string to one's bow, to adjust one's schedule in order to exploit some financial opportunity? Salt had left Calais three months previously and had already used his smooth-talking skills to his master's considerable pecuniary advantage. Kraven knew he could be trusted and had given him a wide-ranging commission to trade, deal and barter where he saw fit. He had begun his mission as a simple messenger, charged with bringing the late Lord Howath's warband back from its adventures overseas. But the shrewd servant had quickly realised the potential in Duke Gerhard's engine, potential worthy of the instant investment of his time and his master's money.

Salt had come across hundreds of snot-nosed lordlings like Duke Gerhard of Villefranco. He had at first paid little attention to the youth's enthusiastic descriptions, imagining the wonder weapon he was so excited about was little more than a figment of his over-heating imagination. But when the Duke described how Abandando Briconet had expressed an interest, Salt's alerted ears had started to glow in earnest.

Briconet of Avignon setting aside his intricate doings to secure possession of the silly boy's childish fancy?

He knew at once that the inquisitor must have divined some terrible potential in the design, hurrying back to Marseille with his cartload of scrap. The esteemed inquisitor must have been overcome with excitement in failing to secure the drawings to go with his collection of twisted metal. What had he been thinking of, allowing the boy the freedom to peddle his designs elsewhere?

Gerhard – to give him his due – had snatched his opportunity while he could, and ridden for the border to throw himself on the mercy of the Empire. Salt smiled as he recalled how easily he had relieved the foolish boy of his prize. Gerhard had no real idea of its worth, only a child's enthusiasm for some shiny new toy. The drooling puppy hadn't stood a chance, allowing himself to be manoeuvred into a corner by Salt's irresistible enticements.

His masterful acquisition of Leonardo's Engine had been a commercial triumph – the sort of deal which would make his cronies back in Calais tear their beards in jealousy.

Salt's quick-thinking enterprise had been rewarded at Imperial headquarters outside Milan. He had been fortunate enough to find the army command in buoyant mood, about to launch an all-out attack on the long-suffering French garrison. According to the rumour-mongers about the camp, the French commander Lautrec had been busy digging his own grave, ruling the captured city with a rod of iron and executing any citizen who dared raise his voice against the occupying power.

Salt had bribed one of the headquarters clerks to attract the attention of one of Von Huff's overworked adjutants. An hour later the weary officer had been poring over the design, nodding his head and trying to disguise his own enthusiasm for the extraordinary project. Salt had described how the prototype – sadly obliterated during its début demonstration – had cut down two hundred Villefrancan rebels in one awesome firestorm of shot. He had described in glowing detail how the magnificent weapon didn't even need expensively-cast cannonballs – any old scrap would do: lengths of chain, lumps of pig iron, rusty nuts and bolts. The adjutant's eyes had lit up.

After a round of bad-tempered haggling – which Salt had

always thrived on – the Imperialist officer had retired to consult with the general himself. He returned a short while later with a leather satchel containing Von Huff's final, take it or leave it offer of two thousand lives.

Salt had packed the designs into his portmanteau and bidden the rogue a good day.

The adjutant had gone to five. Salt had tried for eight but finally settled on six. Six thousand livres!

More than enough to fill the fast carrack he had left moored in Genoa. The Crimson Tun's hold was empty – the human cargo it had been intended to carry to Calais remaining with Tarsi. It had occurred to the shrewd negotiator that he could make up the deficiency quickly and cheaply by recruiting a brand new set of knaves on his way back to the busy seaport. He had more than enough coin to replace the troops he had bargained away in the north. He could return to his master with a company of fighting men *and* a handsome profit to go with them! What did it matter if they were highly experienced border raiders or a pack of empty-bellied peasants? Kraven was a businessman, not a soldier – he would leave their training and subsequent employment to somebody else.

The Englishman had set up his stall beneath a cherry tree in the central piazza, a triangular thoroughfare which doubled as a sort of Circus Minimus every autumn. The town hotheads fought to show off their equestrian skills in the annual *palio*, racing their horses around the slippery streets beneath the handsome, caramel-coloured town houses, hordes of screaming townsfolk packed at every window and balcony or waving gonfallons and pennants in their house colours. Every block had been decorated with pretty red and white mosaics, the squat medieval fortifications which studded the old town carrying the swallowtail merlins of the Ghibellines – the party of the Emperor.

Salt had brought along a strong bodyguard – tough English sailors and stevedores from the Calais waterfront. The rogues were leaning against a taverna wall, sheltering from the bright afternoon sunshine and keeping one eye on their master's back as he supervised his multilingual assistants. As well as John Oldbarn's ruffian bodyguards, Salt had hired an elderly, hook-nosed clerk from the nearby Collegiata di San Secondo to keep the paperwork in order and a ragged little street urchin to broadcast his business. The lively orphan's shrill repartee had already attracted a crowd of curious townsfolk – enjoying their afternoon siesta – as well as a more likely crowd of gawping peasants. The men had left their hungry families shivering in the parks and sidestreets while they looked for work.

'See the world!' the boy cried, 'Terrific opportunities for likely lads who can handle a pike! Sign on for service with His Majesty King Hen-er-ery of Eng-e-land!'

Burghers and well-off townsfolk hooted and jeered. What did that fat braggart want here? The filthy peasants were hanging back at a respectful distance, disliking the sound of service so far from the beloved bell towers of their deserted villages.

'How much is he offering then?'

'How far is he going?'

'I'll not fight Turks, they don't spare man, woman or child, so I've heard tell!'

'Sign on and collect your coin now! A jug of wine and a loaf for every man who makes his mark!' the boy called, prompted by his softly-spoken master. 'You'll be there before you've had a chance to clear the wine fumes from your heads.'

'Where?'

'Europe, tell them Europe,' Salt hissed in his workmanlike Italian.

'What part of Europe? Muscovy? Jutland? Spain?'

Salt frowned. He had come here to find a few hundred lousy pikemen for Northern France, not a pack of navigators intent on finding their way to the New World!

'For service in the English Pale, service against our common enemy, the French!'

'There's Frenchies enough in Milan! We'd sooner fight on our doorsteps than away in the north.'

Salt leaned over and whispered in the boy's ear.

'The French won't be here long! Listen lads, the Swiss reinforcements Lautrec was expecting have been held up in the Alps. The Imperialists will be in there before the winter's out, God's truth!'

The orphan's excitable shouts echoed about the triangular piazza, carrying to the distant corners where packs of road-weary travellers were wont to take their rest.

One small group of dust-shrouded wanderers had dropped down to water their horses beside an ornamental trough, throwing refreshing handfuls of cool water over their grit-streaked features. The men looked up, alerted by the outcry across the piazza.

Their leader tilted his head, listening attentively as the obliging boy brought them up to date on developments in the north. Milan about to fall, Lautrec's Swiss reinforcements held up in the Alps?

James Eldritch thought fast.

Could it be Alberto Tarsi had somehow managed to hold up the Swiss advance, fortifying the Aosta valley and delaying their march to Milan? He had hardly dared imagine what they might find, when they finally returned from the anabasis about Southern France. By Christ, they had been away for the best part of three months now. God alone knew what Tarsi's reduced warband had endured during their unexpectedly extended absence.

Eldritch had promised Tarsi to return from Marseille within a fortnight – the Italian must have cursed his stupidity in letting Eldritch go, imagined his wild goose chase had ended in the Englishman's death or craven desertion. Tarsi had never fully trusted him ever since that business with the Bastard Gueldres the previous summer. Now the warband he had so callously left behind might have been surrounded and slaughtered, wiped out in some terrible last stand in the midst of the mountains.

Eldritch cast a quick look at his dozing mistress – blissfully unaware of his belated pang of conscience. Charlotte was beautiful – too beautiful for him to put in to words to her or anybody else. But she was all he had to show for his jaunt, a penniless countess with nothing but a name – and that name would be mud from now on. Eldritch had gone in search of his love-starved sister and found a love-starved lover instead. He had displayed the morals of an alley cat, while trying to convince himself Lillith was incapable of behaving in such a manner. He had pursued her like some living, breathing grail, a holy quest which had carried him over borders and into enemy-held castles. He had lost count of the men who had died in order that he might proclaim his pyrrhic victories. What would Tarsi think of her? Would he ever agree she had been worth his thankless efforts?

'James? What's the matter?'

'It is nothing,' he said shortly.

Sergeant Hobby shielded his eyes, peering across the piazza at the excitable crowd.

'English Pale? Is that what the boy said?' he enquired, wiping his wet face on his sleeve and immediately replacing all the dirt his impromptu ablutions had removed.

Eldritch nodded briskly.

'Aye. They're recruiting them for the north,' he translated. 'He says Milan is about to fall to the Imperialists.' Eldritch reported with a frown. Charlotte studied her gaunt lover for a moment, trying to fathom his sudden mood swing. She sensed it had something to do with her and yet he had been unusually attentive since leaving the woods – coming as close as he ever had to some kind of declaration as to his intentions. But the arrogant knight had only gone so far, subsiding into an awkward silence as they rode into Asti.

Charlotte wiped her face on her sleeve, leaving a swathe across her pinched features. The hard ride from the south had exhausted her, the uncertainty of their situation gnawing away at her brittle store of patience. She tossed her head, the tumbled auburn ringlets dank with water from the trough.

A countess of France, reduced to supping from a cattle-drink. And by God she had been glad of it. She scowled up at her tall and apparently tireless companion, wondering for the hundredth time why she had chosen to remain in his irascible company.

'Well he's certainly doing a brisk business,' she observed sleepily, watching the first – or perhaps the hungriest – peasant farmhand make his way through the throng towards the recruiting officer's laden table.

Eldritch nodded, watching the transactions with interest. The peasants were crowding forward now, jostling to be among the first to sign on with the smugly smiling gentleman.

Were they really destined for the English Pale?

He gazed at the well-appointed officer who was keeping a wary eye on the recruits, ensuring only the fittest men were signed up by his busily scribbling clerk. The chosen soldiers were given coin, a pot of drink and a loaf, and scurried off to share their good fortune with their waiting families.

Eldritch didn't know the successful *provveditore* – he was not one of the gloating hyenas his colleague Tarsi had been forced to deal with earlier that summer – but the observant captain recognised the emblem on his sagging pennants and on the well-worn cloth he had thrown over the table. The rigged ship and entwined anchor was a familiar enough sign to any West Countryman. It was the mark of Edward Kraven, the wealthy and highly ambitious merchant venturer of Bristol. He looked closer, and thought he might even recognise one of the agent's ruffian escort. What was his name now? He was sure he recognised him from Bristol's wharves.

He would have to be sure and disguise himself well, in case the rogue had a better memory than he did. But what on earth was his master doing here, recruiting hungry peasants in a backwater province of Northern Italy?'

The unusually thoughtful Sergeant Hobby lowered his tankard, swilling his wine about the tarnished pewter.

'But the Pale, it's a good as home, captain. Is he saying he'll pay us good money to carry us there?' he enquired.

Eldritch tugged his greasy bonnet over his black locks. 'You seem to forget we've colleagues in the north, with Tarsi.'

'Aye. But we've been away a good while. They might be dead or gone off home themselves by now. And if Milan is . . .'

'It's possible they've done just that,' Eldritch interrupted. 'But I'd not expect you to leave me rotting here on the off-chance. I don't intend to cut and run just yet,' he said stiffly. Hobby knew full well something had been bothering the young hotspur. He'd been chewing his own spleen since they had left Villefranco.

'You seem mighty distracted by the proceedings, for someone who still intends to report back to Seigneur Tarsi,' Hobby said grumpily. Surely the presence of an English trader, willing to take them all the way back to Calais, signalled that their dire run of luck had changed at last? They should never have left Howath's service, that was the truth of the matter.

'I am, on both counts. You see the badge he bears? The ship and anchor's Kraven's sign.'

'Kraven? That stinkfinger tradesman? What's he want with a gang of hairy-arsed Italians?'

'Maybe we ought to try and find out. You stay here, keep an eye on Hulin and the others. I'm going over.'

'He's got guards there, squatting by that wall,' Hobby pointed out.

'I saw them.'

Eldritch fingered his jaw. Two week's growth had turned him from knight errant to lousy knave, wrought havoc with his well-made, fashionable clothing and taken the shine from his long leather boots. Two swords, a dagger, a misshapen bonnet and a rough cloak completed his road-weary wardrobe – he looked every inch the nameless cut-throat. The townsfolk eyed him as he sauntered through the crowd, the wary peasants stepping out of the bandit's path. As far as he knew, wet-behind-the-ears soldier boys were one of the few commodities Kraven had never dealt in. Now it appeared one of his many minions had seized the opportunity to make hay while the sun shone, and join in the frenzied sweep for new cannon fodder. His quick mind scented possibilities.

This might be some far-from-home clerk, keeping his hand in with some sly trading on the side. More likely, though, he was doing what Kraven did best – making the most from every financial opportunity. Edward Kraven shipping soldiers back to Calais?

The last he had heard, King Henry's negotiators, led by the cunning and immensely able Cardinal Wolsey, had been trying to patch up the truce with France, to keep England out of the war set to engulf half of Europe once more. Kraven's sudden interest in acquiring troops would suggest those crucial talks had broken down – that the English armies in the Pale were crying out for new recruits in time for the spring campaigns.

But why Asti?'

Kraven could have raised the troops he needed back home in Bristol, or from Portsmouth, London, Dublin. Why had this smugly smiling stranger come all this way? Who else could he have expected to find here – apart from Lord Howath's well-travelled Ride?

Algernon Salt glanced up at the surly stranger who had barged his way through the patiently queuing peasants. His guards were on their feet in a moment, hands on hilts as they eyed the sneering newcomer. The stranger ignored them, inspecting the paper-strewn table. He turned from the alarmed clerk to his suave master.

'Ye'll take me back wi' ye, t' th Pale then?' Eldritch enquired in his richest north country brogue. Salt had to tilt his head to catch what he said.

'Maybe. You are far from home, Master?'

'Selby. John Selby.'

Salt knew the name was common up on the warring Borders of Scotland. A typical – if unusually well-travelled – rogue, clearly used to selling his sword where he might.

'And you wish to sign on for further adventures a little nearer home.' Eldritch nodded his head, a passable impersonation of arrogance and awkwardness.

'If what ye say is true, that Milan's about to fall, we'll not find much call for our services here,' he admitted gruffly.

'I am assured the Imperialists will be in the city in weeks.'

'I was assured Lautrec would hold on till hell freezes over,' the impostor replied. Salt shook his head.

'He was relying on reinforcements from France. Those men have been turned back in the Alps.'

'Oh aye?'

'Aye.'

Eldritch was itching to ask about Tarsi, but was reluctant to reveal any clue to his true identity.

'Well I'll get home soon enough mysen,' the impostor snapped. 'But if ye've got a new horse for me, I'll be there all the sooner.'

'I'm looking for honest pikemen at the moment; my master has little need of . . . gentlemen such as you,' Salt replied, feigning indifference.

'Ye've brought all yer officers with ye, eh?' Eldritch asked, nodding at the alerted guards squaring up behind Salt's back.

'You claim to have served, as an officer of horse?'

'Aye, I do,' Eldritch said crisply, bending down to peer at the bemused recruiting officer. 'Here, in Milan and down south aways.'

'Well I am sure we could make an exception in your case, Master?'

'Selby,' Eldritch repeated.

'Selby. I am empowered to offer you full pay and board as a petty captain of horse, to serve with His Majesty King Henry's army of France.'

Eldritch tried not to look too eager to sign on. He frowned instead.

'Petty captain? I've me own tail here wi' me now,' he cried, jerking his thumb towards the rest of his party. Salt studied them for a moment.

'And your good lady wife has also travelled with you.'

'She has. I'd not leave the likes of her back in camp,' he said, raising his eyebrows significantly. Salt was momentarily distracted by the bewitching vision, disguising his intense examination of Mistress Selby by sorting through his sheaf of papers. Eldritch wiped his nose on his cloak. Disguising a rapid inspection of the closely written letters. He spotted a list of names including his own and his former colleague Miguel Isolani – the captain of the arquebusiers who had given his life the previous autumn, saving his own sister Merron from a fatally-aimed crossbow bolt.

Salt look up sharply. Eldritch narrowed his eyes.

'It's nae use giving me some wretched parchment to scribble on, I've not the gift,' he lied smoothly.

The messenger flicked his quill, mildly annoyed by the black-guard's sour disposition.

'I've a list of serving officers, you can make your mark at the bottom. Pay and conditions as agreed.'

Salt handed the document over.

Eldritch sighed and took the paper, adopting a bored frown while he quickly scanned the first page.

'As a petty captain mind,' he warned.

It was a complete order of battle of the old warband – a list of the officers, sergeants, corporals and ordinary soldiers known collectively as Lord Howath's Ride Out, or more usually, the Ride. Only Lord Howath's name did not appear at the top of the document – Edward Kraven's did. Had Howath made some kind of deal with the grasping merchant? He also noticed his own name had been underlined in red and marked with a large asterisk.

'Where at the bottom?' Eldritch enquired.

'Beneath the list of senior officers.'

Eldritch's rat-trap mind saw the silver snare dangle in the air before them.

'And how would I know where that is, I've already told ye, I canna read a word!' Salt nodded, pointed out the place with the tip of his quill.

Eldritch took it from him and made his mark.

While he did so he read the neatly inked note at the bottom of the page:

Make sure this one returns to Genoa. Give him his orders separately, when he's secure on ship. And watch your back, Salt, he's faster than a snake. EK.

'What about that new horse. Mine's about ready for the shambles.'

'You can buy yourself a new horse in Calais, Master Selby.'

'The Pale, ye say. As petty captain to whom?'

'To whoever my master sees fit to hire you,' Salt said simply, his eyes as cold and black as the ink in the pot before him.

'Your master being Kraven, out of Bristol?'

Salt raised his eyebrows.

'You are well informed of merchant's arms, for a *simple* soldier,' Salt said levelly.

'A man should always know with whom he's dealing,' Eldritch countered.

'How true. Well then, Edward Kraven it is. His ship lies in harbour in Genoa. I want all aboard before the week is out.'

Eldritch grimaced.

'That's a fair way for knackered horses.'

'The pikemen will be double timing all the way, so think yourself lucky,' Salt told him. 'Besides, I've ridden from the high valleys beyond Aosta to Imperial headquarters outside Milan, and then back down here inside a week.'

Eldritch clenched his fists, electrified by the tantalising titbit. He had been in Aosta? He must have seen Tarsi!

'Not on my damned nosebag you haven't,' he countered. 'And what of my men? Five good horsemen.'

Salt shrugged.

'Pay and board as light horse. I can go no higher.'

'High enough. I accept yer terms. When do we march?'

'Meet us here in the piazza at dawn, with your people. And you'd best make sure those horses of yours get oats and a rub down before we go. We wouldn't want you falling out along the way.'

'It's Kraven's man right enough. I remember him from Bristol, and that brawler of his. If it hadn't been for this damned beard, he would have recognised me and all,' Eldritch reported, the weary journey forgotten.

Why should this Salt character have been given such precise instructions for dealing with him? Separate orders? Secured on ship in Genoa? The last they had heard, the ownership of the Ride had reverted to Howath. What on earth could have persuaded Auld Gully to part with his precious warband a second time?

Eldritch knew the answer well enough, although he hesitated to contemplate his dismal role in that hideous affair. He

305

concluded the old man must either be dead or dying. He pictured his old master lying on his deathbed, signing over his one marketable asset to Kraven. The merchant had made no secret of the fact that he had guessed Eldritch's role in the treacherous games back at Guisnes – and if it was true he had assumed control of the Ride he might be anxious to ensure his dangerous young protégé served at a safe distance.

Eldritch wondered what orders would be awaiting him in Genoa. A one-way ticket to the siege of Cyprus, a suicidal posting to Malta? The others watched him pull at his stubbled jaw in acute anxiety.

Sergeant Hobby sighed.

He would have been prepared to sign on and ship home, worry about his comrades still serving with Tarsi when they were safely aboard and bound for Calais. He would have wagered all he was owed that the rest of the Ride had long since gone their own way, died or deserted. The captain had snapped his head off for suggesting so, but they were all money-grasping swine, when push came to shove.

'Ah well. We'll be off now then?'

'Not yet we won't. I've just signed us on for a twelvemonth.'

Hobby blinked in bewilderment. Charlotte, who had shared the sergeant's enthusiasm for an immediate passage to a new life in Calais, tried to control her excitement at this abrupt about-face.

'I thought you said you wouldn't abandon your men?'

Eldritch waved the puzzled duo back under the shelter of the ancient cherry tree. Hulin and the others waited by the wall, wearily familiar with their new colleagues' constant intrigues.

'Keep your voices down for the love of Christ. And don't call me Eldritch while anybody's about – I'm Master John Selby now, a cut-throat captain out of the Border country.'

'And might I enquire who I am?' Charlotte asked archly, fists on hips.

'You're my wife. The rest of you are my sworn bodyguards.'

Hobby's sun-wrinkled brow furrowed.

'You've changed your tune,' he growled. 'I thought you said you'd not leave our brothers behind?'

'I don't intend to. I signed on to check his credentials, not to earn a passage home.'

'But you've signed us on for the Pale. If we don't turn up now

306

he'll have those slow dogs of his after us.' Hobby jerked his calloused thumb at the squad of bodyguards who had attended Salt's impromptu recruiting session. 'They'll be harder work than half a dozen French militia boys, I can tell you!' the morose Yorkshire man exclaimed.

Eldritch raised his hand. 'He's carrying a complete list of the warband the Bastard Gueldres won from Howath,' Eldritch explained. Hobby tilted his head at his captain's highly elastic recollection of the incident.

The entire army knew Eldritch had set out to fleece his master Howath, to win the warband for himself with a handful of loaded dice. But the wily Vicomte De Toinueill had proved cleverer even than Eldritch, and had scooped the entire pot – officers, sergeants, soldiers and all – from beneath the hawk-eyed captain's nose.

Eldritch had never forgiven nor forgotten it – and nor had Howath.

Eldritch glanced at the sergeant's slow-moving features, waiting in vain for the grizzled veteran to work it out.

'Don't you see? When Gueldres was excommunicated, the ownership of the Ride reverted to Howath. Now it appears he has sold it on to Kraven.'

'Hah! Why should he do that?' Hobby snorted.

'I don't know the why and wherefores of it. But Kraven's sent his man to Italy to collect us. I saw the damned papers. You, me, Stitchwort, Hacker, Teague and the rest.'

Hobby saw no such thing.

'Salt's just come from Aosta, so he'd know whether they were . . .' His gaunt features clouded with guilt, his sore conscience pricking him once again.

'Whether they are already dead and therefore of no further use,' Charlotte interjected. Hobby bristled.

'So what's he doing here? Why isn't he in Nus, or Aosta or somewhere up north?'

'He's come to Asti to find some replacements for us.'

Hobby let out a bark of laughter.

'Replace ten score and more English archers with a pack of bow-legged rice munchers? His master won't be pleased he's struck such a poor bargain, whoever he is!' Hobby observed with uncharacteristic insight.

'But he'll be more concerned with quantity than quality. If he's got a ship in port empty, he'll want it filled damned quick.

English archers or Italian peasants: we're all the same to Kraven,' Eldritch explained.

Merchant ships certainly didn't pay their way tied up in some harbour for weeks on end. Eldritch's father had run a prosperous merchant fleet of his own back in Bristol, so he knew just how critical accurate timetables were to a successful trader.

'Kraven wouldn't ship us all home out of Christian charity, and he's no use for soldiers himself.'

'Well maybe he's just bringing us home for Auld Gully; maybe the old man's paid his expenses?'

Eldritch frowned. He doubted if their former master would ever have any use for them again. He knew he had broken his heart, aiding and abetting in the sudden loss of the old warrior's precious warband – and that he would carry the guilt of that black night's work to the grave.

'Howath had taken to his bed, the last I heard. Just the place for Kraven to trick him into signing us all over to him,' he speculated.

'Edward Kraven's Ride? Pah!'

Eldritch wagged his finger.

'But what if Kraven intends to sell the Ride on? To some unsuspecting ballock-brain of a knight fresh off the boat? Maybe they wouldn't be too choosy as to the quality of their cannon-fodder – until it was too late,' he said, examining and discarding possibilities before poor Hobby could blink.

'You're saying Kraven's sent yonder quill-pusher to Italy to fetch us home, but he's found out we're either dead or gone, so he's thought to hire himself a set of sprats in our place,' Hobby said ponderously.

Eldritch nodded. The first slender threads of a plan were beginning to form in his quick and calculating mind. Hobby knew the look of old.

'What were you thinking then, signing on with them?'

'A ghost company,' the young knight theorised. 'They always make the best cannon-fodder.'

'Ghost company? They look lively enough to me,' Charlotte argued.

'I mean ghost as in shadowy, anonymous, half-forgotten. But the trouble with ghosts is that you never know when or where they're going to crop up next.'

Charlotte glanced enquiringly at Hobby.

308

'Don't ask me, my lady,' the weary veteran said, noisily downing the last of his wine. 'But whatever it is his lordship's got in mind, you can wager I won't like the sound of it one little bit.'

By the Cherry Tree Tavern, Asti

✦

John Oldbarn ducked into the oak-panelled stall and saluted his master, elbows on table as he set about a cold leg of pork and a dish of apple sauce. The Cherry Tree kept an excellent table, the locally produced food was abundant, fresh and excellently prepared, and the road-weary messenger had decided to indulge himself for once.

By God, he had earned it.

Two hundred and fifty strapping farmhands ready for service in the English Pale! A few days' training and they would make passable pikemen. A morning's work would turn peasant ditch-diggers into arquebusiers! They might not be as battleworthy as the warband he had been sent to Italy to collect, but his master Kraven ought to be more than pleased with the bargains his loyal servant had made on his behalf. Oldbarn coughed into his fist to disguise his grievously rumbling belly. The heavily-built sea-man's stomach was churning in anticipation as he caught the enticing aroma of roast meat. They hadn't had time for a decent supper, chasing about the busy little town on their tireless master's business.

The well-fed messenger glanced up at his hungry bodyguard, wiping his greasy fingers on a napkin as he surveyed the dishes set out before him. As well as the pork and apple sauce there was cabbage and bread soup – another local speciality – stuffed duck, guinea fowl with hazelnuts and a bowl of garlic-sweating mush-rooms and succulent truffles.

'You located the party concerned?' Salt enquired, refreshing himself from a jug of fine Barbera wine.

'Wasn't hard, sir. He's camped out in the courtyard of the Torre Comentina, just down the Corso, him and his woman kicking up enough noise to wake the dead.'

Salt nodded.

'It's true the two lovebirds keep somewhat apart from the others. The big feller sits on his own. As to the other three,'

Oldbarn shrugged. 'Shifty buggers, French or just as bad. Same goes for their horseflesh. They're carryin' French brands and the horse livery is Marseille militia. They stole 'em, or I'm a Froglander.'

Salt was not particularly surprised to hear that *Master Selby* had acquired the beasts from their enemies. The rogue had made no bones about his previous experience, readily admitting to all manner of shady activity. The thoughtful messenger had even wondered for a moment if he hadn't come face to face with the legendary James Eldritch himself – the bandit cheat his master had warned him about back in Calais.

'*Faster than a snake*,' his master had warned.

'Mark him well, Salt. Well above average height, eyes like sea coals and a permanent, devil-may-care sneer. Wont to cock his beaver in as fancy a get-up as he can find.'

Master Selby had fitted the bill as far as his black looks were concerned. Salt knew he might well have changed his clothes, gone abroad disguised beneath a ragged soldier's cloak, but surely not even a knave of Eldritch's disrepute could have been so convincing when attempting to fathom the paperwork Salt had tested him with.

The messenger had tried to catch him out several times, but either this Selby fellow was a master of deception or he was telling the whole truth. He certainly hadn't appeared able to read a single word on that warrant. If he had been able to decipher the dispatch he would have noted that Master Eldritch had been marked down for special attention. Kraven wanted the rest of the Ride back in Calais, ready for field service with some well-heeled but inexperienced captain. Eldritch was destined to earn his keep elsewhere. Kraven had admitted he didn't trust the upstart to obey his or anyone else's orders, but the shrewd Salt knew there was more to his master's suspicions than concern over his worthiness to serve.

The truth was that Kraven didn't want the wild-eyed Eldritch anywhere near his rosebud of a wife, his sweet – though no longer virginal – Miranda. Kraven had other ports in mind for the hotspur, somewhere hot.

Like Cyprus.

An army of Turks more numerous than a gifted mathematician could conveniently count was about to descend on the island jewel – and the garrison needed experienced officers to direct its defence.

Algernon Salt knew his master's mind. And, like the thought-ful Kraven, Salt was nothing if not thorough. He had decided to send Oldbarn out to make further inquiries about Master Selby and his suspicious followers. It wouldn't do any harm to check up on them – he had hired the damned pack for twelve months' service in the Pale, whether or not they were who they claimed to be.

Oldbarn rubbed his stomach over his rumbling belly.

'I hung about like you said, stayed within earshot. The little lovebirds spent most of the time arguing. Going at it hammer and tongs, they were. Some of the things he called her, fair made my 'air curl,' the bald-headed sailor exclaimed, removing his woollen cap and wiping his calloused palm over his skull.

Salt helped himself from the steaming plate of truffles and mushrooms, balancing a succulent spoonful under his twitching nose. Oldbarn eyed the delicious feast, but Salt seemed blissfully unaware of his attention.

'And as . . .'

A sudden, ear-piercing shriek jolted the messenger's arm, spilling the spoonful of truffles over the table.

The tavern door slammed violently, rattling the web-encrusted windowpanes behind Salt's head. The messenger sat up with an oath and peered towards the tavern porch. A grubbily-dressed girl had stormed into the drinking den like a ship under full sail, swept past the wine-pooled tables with her nose in the air.

Salt recognised her at once. Mistress Selby, goodwife to the petty captain he had recently hired. He glanced up at Oldbarn, wondered what the rogue was chewing on now.

'That's her isn't it?'

Before the old sweat could reply the tavern door was flung open once more.

'You speckled harlot! A pox on you and your vermin-ridden drawers! There's plenty more where you came from, you gutter-slinking serpent!'

Salt rose from his seat, peered around the oak settle towards the door. Selby held the door open with one hand and hurled an armful of loose clothing at the furiously staring woman. He turned and stormed out of the tavern in a fit of pique, slamming the door behind him.

The astonished patrons gawped at the pale woman, trembling with fury as she stared down at the bedraggled clothing.

The tavern immediately erupted, a powder keg of excited

Italian. Salt dabbed his beard with his napkin, deciding to seize the opportunity to make some investigations of his own.

'You can go on now Oldbarn. Good work. I'll see you under the cherry tree tomorrow morning with the men.'

Oldbarn coughed into his fist once more, nodded dumbly. Salt narrowed his eyes, noticing his bodyguard's stubbled jaw was slick with gravy.

'And what do you imagine you're about, picking through my dirty linen?' Mistress Selby screeched in French, slapping Salt's hands from the grubby laundry. The messenger snatched his fingers back, smiled nervously at the furious damsel.

The girl was remarkably beautiful, even if her perfect features had been tarnished with dirt, sweat and tears. Her hair was a riot of dark auburn and gold, an amber hairband hanging loosely from her inadequately secured tresses.

'A thousand apologies my lady,' he replied in his own faltering French. 'But allow your humble servant to offer his assistance, in this distressing moment,' he offered smoothly.

The girl eyed him, her pale features quivering with emotion.

'You find me momentarily disadvantaged, sir, but certainly not distressed. Oh no, never distressed,' she growled, making the hairs stand up on the back of Salt's well-fleshed neck. He offered her his hand. She glanced at the simple gold rings he wore – the mark of a wealthy but not ostentatious traveller. She modified her expression a little, took his hand with all the grace she could muster.

Salt bowed his head.

'Forgive me madam, but could it be I have the pleasure in addressing Mistress Selby, esteemed wife of the brave petty captain of horse with whom I have recently concluded some trifling matters of business?'

The girl's half-smile vanished at the mere mention of the name.

'Allow me to introduce and present my credentials. I am, madam, Algernon Salt, chief clerk to Edward Kraven, Merchant Venturer of Bristol, Calais and Lisbon, presently engaged upon diverse business here in Italy.'

The girl straightened her gown, returned the courtesy with an embarrassed glance at the wine-enfeebled customers peering out of their stalls.

'I am, sir, Charlotte Selby, wife of that particular petty captain you refer to. But I must confess,' she tilted her dirt-smudged nose

313

a little closer towards Salt's graciously inclined head, 'at this particular moment in time, that role allows me no pleasure sir, no pleasure at all.'

Salt nodded understandingly.

What manner of fool would so insult such a goddess, skin of dirt or no? Salt rapped his knuckles on the nearest stall, jolting the eavesdropping occupants back to their places.

'What are you looking at, apes?' he cried in Italian. 'Mistress, please ignore this rabble, these *compagnacci*! They have the manners of nanny-goats and smell worse!'

The bemused drinkers went back to their tables or resumed their conversations as Salt gathered the last scraps of her clothing under his arm, and escorted her, politely but firmly, towards his table.

'You look pale my dear. The shock, the rudeness . . .' He didn't say whose. 'Allow me to offer you a cup of Barbera, it's really quite delicious. I'm thinking of laying in a couple of barrels on my master's behalf. Are you hungry, my dear, could I offer you some supper?' Salt enquired.

Charlotte had no need to fake her hunger – they hadn't eaten properly in days. She sat down, smiled courteously as the messenger placed guinea fowl, pork and apple sauce before her.

'Now where on earth are those mushrooms?' Salt thought aloud, examining the empty dish beside his gravy-laden plate.

'. . . And the Polish Cardinal said, "No, no, no, I don't care what you say, you'll bite the end off, I know you will."'

Salt threw his head back and roared with laughter. His broad, fleshy face was suffused with good food and warm wine, his beard stuck with fatty droplets from the marvellous feast. Charlotte had demolished every item he had placed before her, picking the flesh from the ravaged carcasses as if she hadn't eaten in years. She had matched him glass for glass, spilling wine down her gown, over the table and into her lap, cackling like a happy hen at Salt's entertaining conversation and swapping off-colour jokes as if she had spent the majority of her short life on the Marseille waterfront.

'And the innkeeper's daughter said, "No, no, no, Monsignor! Honest I won't." And she swung her legs up on the table so he could have a look. "There," she said, "I told you I didn't have any teeth down there!"'

Salt's face had turned blue. He was choking with laughter, gripping the table as he waited for the punchline.

'And the Polish Cardinal lifted her skirts and had a look and said, "I'm not surprised you haven't got any teeth, with gums like that!"'

Salt brayed with laugher, toppled off the bench and sprawled on the floor, almost wetting his breeches with helpless glee. Charlotte laughed, sitting back in her settle and watching the drunken Englishman bend himself double with uncontrollable mirth.

It was several moments before he could regain his seat.

Several moments in which Charlotte tipped most of her wine into Salt's glass.

'There you are Algy, sit up straight and have another drink! I'm about ready for one if you are.'

The messenger sighed, shaking his flushed head at her outrageous tale. 'Ah, I shall have to remember that one, next time I'm at court. You know our King Harry,' he said, trying to disguise a juicy belch, 'he loves a good joke the same as the next man. He's knighted his fools for feebler jests than that,' he said, slapping the table and blinking at the bewitching vision sipping her wine before him.

By Heaven, Selby must be a fool, to turn his back on an uncut jewel such as this! Charlotte was the most exciting woman he had ever come across. She was witty, quick to anger but quicker to smile. And when she laughed! It was as if an angel had fallen from the clouds, and been brought up on the lower deck of the roughest ship afloat!

Salt leaned back against the settle, letting the reeking tavern stabilise slowly. She patted his hand.

'I don't know how to thank you, for rescuing me from that, that, *bestia*!' Charlotte slurred, her eyes glinting with malice. Salt turned his palm over, closed his strong fingers about hers. He gave her the barest squeeze – any more pressure might have been misinterpreted.

'The pleasure was all mine, my dear Charlotte.'

She took a languid look over her shoulder.

'You have taken rooms for the night?' she asked innocently.

Salt swallowed, leaned over the wine-lapped table and lowered his voice to a confidential whisper.

'I have a room. Am I to presume your husband has neglected to provide you with suitable quarters?'

'Suitable quarters? I'm well used to sleeping on the street, beneath hedges, under trees. I assure you sir, I would consider a goat-pen a palace!' Charlotte tensed, her apricot skin stretching over her artfully-defined chestbone. A good painter could do wonders with a chestbone like hers, Salt thought. He looked up, distracted by the beads of sweat on her breasts. He coughed.

'Your husband will presumably be accommodating himself by the fountain, in the Torre Comentina?' he asked casually.

Charlotte gave a bitter laugh, spilling her wine over her bosoms. Salt licked his lips.

'By the fountain? You don't know him sir. I confess there's little I can do to tame him, when there's the drink in him. I know where it leads you see. Brawls and whores, bawds and battle. He won't come round until the morning, and then all he'll want is his breakfast,' she said ruefully.

Salt was scandalised by her heartbreaking plight. He pressed her hand between his own. 'How dare he?'

Charlotte's eyes misted; her faraway look wasn't lost on the suddenly dry-mouthed messenger.

'My dear, I would be obliged if you would take my chamber for this night at least. I will of course seek alternative accommodation,' he said shrewdly. Charlotte held his gaze for a moment.

'Oh there's no need for that. I'm sure the bed will do us both,' she said over the glistening rim of her glass.

Salt smiled, hardly able to believe his good fortune. He wondered about stepping out to warn Oldbarn he was retiring but thought better of it. Oldbarn was happy enough sleeping in the street with that rogue Selby. He jumped to his feet, knocking the last of the Barbera over the floor. He leaned over his seat and dragged out his iron-bound chest, tucked the heavy box under his arm and took the girl's proffered hand.

'Shall we retire?'

Charlotte gave him a foxy smile, tapped the chest with a broken fingernail.

'What's in there, victuals for our midnight feast?' she enquired, twining a tendril of rich honey hair between her fingers. By God, the little minx had already eaten a small horse! Salt took her elbow and manoeuvred her towards the staircase, glancing about the room.

'Miscellaneous papers my dear. Nothing to worry your head about.'

What on earth was Eldritch thinking of? Another few moments and this many-handed goat would have her naked at his mercy! Charlotte smiled coyly, trying to hang on to her flimsy if rather grubby shift.

Salt was squatting above her, calves along her thighs, his greying head bent and his hairy hands busy about her breasts. He reminded her of some infernal dwarf, grubbing out jewels in the River Styx.

She could feel him, hard and hot against her flat belly, the gauzy shift stretched over her cold crotch.

Where was Eldritch???

'What's the matter my dear?' he enquired, apparently as sober as a judge now he had taken deep draughts of the cooler air in his chamber. The shutters had been thrown back, she could see the stars out of the corner of her eye.

He leaned closer.

'Don't you worry about him, my little sticky bud,' he leered. 'He doesn't deserve a woman like you!' He tore her shift, planted a soft kiss on her chestbone, midway between her small, delicately-rounded breasts. Salt had that right, the girl thought distractedly. 'Beautiful.' Another kiss, left nipple. 'Sensual.' Another. Right nipple.

Charlotte twitched.

The old rogue had technique, she thought distractedly – rare enough in an Englishman.

He sat back, working the torn cotton apart with his fingers, tearing the shift from her warm, maddeningly fragrant body.

She closed her eyes and bit her lip.

Crash!!!!!!

'Ye damned clootie, so here y'are!'

The entwined lovers leapt apart at the sudden cry, peering up at the swinging shutters in stark – and all too genuine – terror.

A demon form – no more than a swiftly-moving blur to the electrified lovers – detached itself from the shadows on the balcony like some evil succubus and ducked inside the room. The thin starlight glinted on his blade, flicking wickedly before him.

Salt sat back on his haunches, one hand on his crotch the other grasping for the leather belt he had hung from the bedpost. The intruder's sword flashed and the belt fell to the floor, hewn in two by the deadly blow. The fiend followed up, thrusting the terrified messenger back on the rumpled bedding and holding the blade to Salt's quivering throat.

'One word and I'll cut ye through to the bone,' the intruder growled. Salt blinked in astonishment, recognising Selby's black-fringed features.

Who else would have known where to look for them? His mind raced, his belly churned, his erection quivered in agonised anticipation.

Charlotte squealed, worked her legs free from beneath Salt's painfully spread limbs.

'Ye stay where ye are, ye damned hoor,' Selby hissed. Salt stared up at his furious features, his livid features etched with mad-murder. 'I came back here to find ye out and apologise for my harsh words earlier, and I find ye haughmaganding with this puny wee shite!' Selby accused.

'It's not what you think!' Charlotte replied, shrill with terror. 'I was angry, frightened as to what you'd do. He plied me with drink and dragged me up here!' she accused. Salt felt the cold blade rest on his taut throat.

'Ye did what?' he asked, stunned with righteous anger.

'I did no such thing!' Salt croaked. 'She practically dragged me up here!'

Selby tensed.

'D'ye mean to call my wife a hoor?'

'I . . . I . . . mean there's been a terrible misunderstanding . . . I have money!'

'So you mean to make my wife a hoor and me her pimp, is that it, ye damned serpent?' Selby demanded, his strong northern accent becoming more and more pronounced as he lost his temper.

'I meant no such . . . I mean, I have money with me here . . . spare me and take it all, I implore you. I meant no harm to either of you, as God is my witness.'

Selby leaned closer.

'Buy me off? Have I no honour? What would I do with ye damned money? What's to stop me cutting ye throat and takin' it for mysen?'

Charlotte collected her clothing, holding her torn shift together with white-knuckled fists.

'John, it was nothing, he means nothing to me! By the Holy Mother you're no saint yourself!' she exclaimed.

Selby purred hatred, itching to run the blade across Salt's wretchedly stretched neck.

'For God's sake John, you heard him! He's money, he's goods, take them and spare his life!'

'Spare his life that he might paw another's man's wife?' Selby snarled.

'Algy . . . Master Salt, tell him please,' Charlotte implored. 'Tell him you have money! He's such a wicked, hot-tempered man, terrible angry when the drink's in him!'

Salt was trembling, his naked body swathed in goose-bumps. His penis had softened, hanging flacidly over his hairy belly.

'Is that all ye think of me? To cool my anger with a few coins?'

'It was a silly fling!' Charlotte exclaimed, wringing her hands behind her lover's back. 'We meant nothing by it!'

'I'm a soldier not a banker! This wretched war's lessened me, and ye think to insult me with a handful of silver pieces,' the murderous intruder accused.

'Offer him something, Master Salt. Give him something to appease his anger or I don't know what he'll do!'

'What? He won't take coin,' Salt shrilled. Selby paused, narrowed his eyes.

'I'm your petty captain now, according to those damned papers I made my mark on,' he observed. Salt nodded.

'Ye can write, make the papers say what ye want . . .' he went on.

'Anything!' Salt agreed. 'Anything you wish, if you would spare a miserable sinner's life!'

'Then you could take ye papers, and make me a full captain once more?'

'Captain, Colonel, you name it!'

'And those flea-bitten shites out yonder, you'd make them my men?'

'At once!'

'And hand over coin enough to arm and feed the rogues besides?'

'The least I could do!' Salt exclaimed. 'I have my portmanteau to hand. A few notes and the rogues are yours, with my best wishes and a thousand apologies!'

Selby considered this.

'And the moment you've raised your men, you'd come after me, and break your word,' he accused.

'Never! On my life, sir! Take your men where you will, I will return to my ship, thanking God you found the courage and conviction to spare a miserable sinner. You may rest assured sir, I will forget I ever heard your name!'

'Do spare him John. You take on so, killing folk in cold blood,' Charlotte cried, immensely enjoying her energetic role-play.

Eldritch had performed as if he had been born to the role. A wife-beating bastard's son with an angry eye and quick blade.

She wondered for a moment just how much the Englishman was having to pretend at all.

'Fetch the chest and make your mark, but my wife reads for me, I warn ye,' he ordered, smouldering with anger. He raised the blade from the messenger's jumping throat.

Salt scrambled off the bed and fetched the chest. He placed it on the soiled counterpane and fished in his discarded clothing for the keys.

'If ye've a weapon concealed in there, ye'd best pick it out, left-handed mind,' Master Selby advised. Salt nodded vigorously.

'You're right sir. I keep a bilbo hidden within, in case I am waylaid on the road. But I will pick it out and put it aside as you command.'

Selby nodded, shadowing the nervous messenger as he undid the lock and lifted the steel-girdled lid.

He reached in, lifted the deadly blade out by the hilt. Selby took it from him and slid it into his boot.

'That's better. Now fetch your quills and your ink, and that seal of yours. I want this indenture to stand scrutiny in any court in Europe. Charlotte, damn your eyes, you read what he writes, and God damn you both if you try and trick a simple man!'

Salt had already broken two quills, snapping them in two as he attempted to copy the flowery preamble which prefaced all contracts of indenture. He had sighed and shivered and squinted at the damned rogue as he stalked the chamber, threatening to kill the pair of them one moment and cursing his foul fortunes the next.

He concentrated hard on the documents spread out before him, the convoluted sentences blurred by tears of shame and sheer bloody terror.

The paper he was amending had begun the day as a simple contract of indenture between his master Edward Kraven and several hundred undersigned volunteers. Salt had inserted a new clause near the top of the page, appointing John Selby as field captain to command the men in Kraven's name.

A few flicks of the quivering quill and he had turned the blackmailing rogue into the properly-appointed chief of his newly-raised company. But he dared not argue. Selby was clearly deranged, seething with anger and jealousy, embittered by galling frustrations and imagined slights. A smouldering powder-keg ready to blow up all over the town and definitely not the sort of man a humble messenger would attempt to get the better of in a night-time knife fight.

Salt took Kraven's seal and a stick of red wax from the chest, ready to authenticate the document – no matter how outrageously it had been obtained.

He would worry about the rights and wrongs of the case later – with Selby safely out of sword-range and Oldbarn's ruffian bodyguard packed in tight around him.

He was sweating hard, blinking the beads from his eyes as he finished his amendments and held the wax stick in the candle flame.

Selby was muttering under his breath, lifting various documents from the chest and thrusting them at his feckless wife.

'What's this? More damned trickery? You've more papers than a Venetian's boggard!' he snatched another letter from the sheaf spilled over the bed and ripped the sealed paper open.

'What's this say here?'

Charlotte leaned over his shoulder to read it.

'Orders. A Captain called . . . what's that, Elder-bitch? To report to the commander of the garrison in . . . Nicosia, in Cyprus.'

'Nicosia?' Eldritch roared, forgetting himself. So that double-dealing whoremonger Kraven wanted him five thousand miles out of the way, was that it? He grasped the paper from her hand and screwed it into a ball.

'What do I care where they're sending the rogue? You make your mark, sir, make me a captain! Master Elder-Bitch can go to hell for all I care!' he shouted, pulling more correspondence from the ransacked chest.

'And what's this?'

'A list of ships in harbour in Genoa, with their cargoes and destinations.'

'What do I care for cargo?' Selby screwed the paper into a ball and threw it into the corner of the room. He slipped the other note under his tunic while Salt pored over his indentures.

'And what's this?'

Selby lifted one of Salt's leather pouches from the chest, gave it an investigative shake. They all heard the satisfying clink of coin.

'Pay and provision for a company,' Selby breathed.

Salt swallowed.

So the bastard meant to fleece him of his windfall as well as swindle him out of his hard-won men? The blacksliding knave! He compressed his lips, not daring to utter any objection.

'As we agreed, eh?'

'As agreed,' Salt said hoarsely. He knew he had three more bags in the chest. Selby eyed them wonderingly and then lifted another purse.

'And for the insult to my wife.'

'No insult intended, to you or her,' Salt grated.

Selby lifted the lid on the point of his sword, shut the last two bags within the chest.

Salt held his breath, hardly daring to catch the rogue's eye for fear of being relieved of his last remaining cash. The wax began to melt, a sticky bead falling onto the crumpled bedding.

By God above, Edward Kraven would hear of this!

Salt paused, wondering how he would ever frame his pitiful explanations. How he had come to sign over two hundred and fifty newly-recruited men to a complete stranger. Kraven was no fool, he wouldn't let the matter rest until he had satisfied himself as to the true sequence of events. But hold! Kraven wasn't even aware he had enlisted the men, nor of the small fortune he had collected from Imperial headquarters outside Milan! He wouldn't miss what he hadn't owned! Selby had left him two bags, a handsome enough profit even if he hadn't been able to complete his original mission. He would tell his master the Ride had been wiped out by the French or succumbed to the plague – he didn't imagine too many of them were going to survive their coming encounters in the Aosta alley.

Salt saw a chink of light at the end of his tunnel. If he could only get rid of this madman, he would live to trade another day! He pored over the new contracts, tilted the paper towards the light and dripped the molten wax over the stiff parchment. The meticulous messenger was so intent on authenticating his documentation that he didn't notice Selby wink encouragingly at his blushing wife.

'Hurry up there man!' The newly-appointed captain snarled, giving the naked messenger a tap on the shoulder with the cold steel.

Salt jumped out of his skin, spilling hot wax over his bared genitals. He sat back with a shriek, rubbing the offending wax away with the corner of the sheet.

James Eldritch smiled at his red faced companion. Maybe the two of them ought to launch themselves on a new career as travelling players – he had, after all, earned more from this night's buffoonery than he had in a lifetime's shabby soldiering.

By the Hospice Gilbert le Petit Galliard

✦

The legion had left the valley far below, by-passing their neglected trenches and leaving their meagre possessions in the abandoned wagon park. Some of the chronically tired fugitives had believed they were running out, trying to reach the fastness of Aosta before the Swiss eagles could swoop down the pass and carry them off as if they were eyeless lambs bleating for their mothers.

But Tarsi knew they would never have reached the doubtful sanctuary of the old Roman town. Famished, burdened with wounded and out of ammunition, the legion would have been obliterated like a cockroach under a boot heel.

The warband had reached the crossroads at last.

'The Hospice, it's our only chance! Hurry you dogs, d'you want to die this day?' he called, urging the survivors to one further Herculean effort – a back-breaking climb up the right flank of the mountains. The high road was not popular with casual travellers or well-laden caravans and had subsequently fallen into serious disrepair.

Overhanging cliffs had spewed scree over the rough track, left rills of ankle-breaking obstacles along the entire route. Tarsi's men couldn't have cared if they had been treading barefoot on flaming coals. The track had carried them out of that cursed valley, up towards the sun-racked plateau which ran like a mantelpiece along the length of the valley. The wind-blown terraces were stacked like broken-backed tiles against the rearing walls of the mountains, jagged spurs running away towards the south-west. Here, at last, the terrain grew greener, softer, easier – the high road opening out onto the marvellously remote foothills of the Valtelline.

But Tarsi's heroes were still a dozen leagues short of their giddy destination when the vanguard turned a corner and came face to face with a gaggle of knights leading a company of pikemen at least as numerous as themselves.

The high road was closed.

The new-born sun rose over the rearing cliffs and snow-trimmed ridges, suffusing the chipped peaks in marvellously tranquil morning light and casting a gold and silver shroud over the prodigious host. Grandly advancing rays illuminated the strange company as if it had risen from the page of some fantastically illustrated tale of the crusades, a legion of fondly-remembered heroes returned to earth at last.

Here were Roland and the Cid, Arthur and Lancelot, Charlemagne and Caesar in glittering armour.

And if Tarsi's legion wanted to reach the Hospice, they would have to go through them.

The old soldier had already aged ten years since the dawn.

He was too stunned, too starved of blood, spit and sense to identify the host which had mushroomed out of the rocks before them. What was left of his motley assortment of walking wounded and shadow-soldiers had strayed into a trap, strung out and hatefully exposed on a precarious ledge hundreds of feet above the pass. They might just as well hurl themselves from the craggy heights as attempt to escape now.

'Who on earth are they?' Duke Gerhard enquired, head lolling on his hunched shoulders.

'What does it matter? We're in no fit shape to argue with them.'

Tarsi didn't have to look around to gauge the mood of his men. They had performed miracles the previous night, taking on and damn near beating an experienced enemy who outnumbered them by ten, twenty, thirty to one. He could have asked no more from them. Further fighting was out of the question – a bad-tempered marmot could have torn them all in pieces.

'Well, what are we going to do?' Gerhard squealed, his small store of courage evaporating in a moment.

The callow prince had fought and survived his first battle, fought with sword in hand like the ancestors of old his dead father had so despised. He could hardly describe the sensation, the sheer, masculine pride he had felt in his own prowess. An overpowering rush of self-belief, of self-reliance, of self-importance.

Simply, of self.

Riding away from the battlefield had reminded him of that night back in Villefranco when he had bedded his first woman.

Perhaps there was some psychological connection between making love and fighting for your life? A mystical revelation left over from the Stone Age? Was he the first man to acknowledge this beguiling phenomenon, or was it some unspoken secret he shared with Tarsi, with that bristling rogue Kerr, with the bloody fugitives packed around them, dumbly expecting their officers to save their miserable skins?

Gerhard had finally discovered something in himself he could believe in, something he could be proud of even alongside stiff-necked old turkey-buzzards like Tarsi.

But fortune hadn't smiled on the young Duke long. No sooner had he begun to congratulate himself on his survival, begun to weave the first tales of the part he had played in Tarsi's famed raid, than fortune had returned to tug the rug from beneath his feet.

'We can't run! We can't fight! You must plead for quarter, for God's sake, Tarsi, enough!'

The Italian brawler sighed at the Duke's all-too-sensible advice. He tilted his head, squinting at the strange company who had seized his one remaining asset – the high ridge and ancient hospice of Le Petit Galliard. It hardly mattered who they claimed to serve – the bandits must have seized the one stronghold he had left, torn the last ace from his pack. He dared not even imagine what had become of Angelica and Merron, the innocents he had left behind.

Tarsi closed his mind to such desperate concerns and strode to the front, his notched sword scraping the spoil which pocked the road surface. His men had shambled to a halt, too far gone to give a tinker's cuss who they were facing.

The blockading force came to a ragged halt. A cloud of yellow dust settled about their shoulders, twined around their glittering pikes. A lone rider kicked up a cloud of grit as he peeled away from the waiting ranks, picked his way down the treacherous slope with breathtaking skill.

Tarsi narrowed his eyes, grudgingly acknowledging the stranger's horsemanship. One slip on those rocks and the bastard would have broken his neck in the chasms which bordered the switchbacked track. The dawn-rider looked as if he had been born to it, as if the rearing Alps and tumbling slopes were a small corner of his own, worldwide domain.

Tarsi knew one man who possessed the arrogant composure for such a display.

The rider drew up, lifted his greasy black bonnet and saluted his commanding officer.

'I told you I'd be back,' James Eldritch called.

Five leagues back down the sun-glad pass the doors of Mont Galliard had opened at last. A funereal procession made its ponderous way down the slim approaches, crossing the bridge to the slow, sombre tuck of a drum. Every eye was glued to the corresponding procession approaching with equal caution down the pass.

The rival colour parties came face to face a stonesthrow from the ruined blockhouse, still strewn with corpses and discarded equipment. The drummers gave one final flourish and crossed their sticks over their chests, heralding a long, eerie silence broken only by the energetic snap and crackle of their proudly-flown flags.

Francesco Savvi had selected his richest costume for the occasion, a superbly cut suit of black and red velvet, heavily slashed about the chest and sleeves to show off his gaudily-laced shirt. He had left his trademark lacquered armour back in Mont Galliard, underlining his status as a powerful magnate wealthy enough to leave the sordid business of fighting to others.

Stroma, on the other hand, had been a powerful magnate long enough to develop an acute sense of self-preservation. He put more value on personal safety than appearance, and had worn every scrap of armour he possessed. He had shorn his costume of all vain pretences – removed any sign of rank in a bid to deter hidden snipers. He stood just behind the tall seigneur, helmet strapped securely beneath his jutting jaw. Savvi had ordered Muhlberg to remain in the fortress – he couldn't trust him when it came to delicate negotiations. He had left him instructions to give the Swiss hell if they dared break the nervous truce.

Mercenary bands recognised few rules of war – they couldn't afford to. But parleys had always been subject to the strictest code of conduct, with terrifying punishments meted out to any transgressors. The fact that Savvi had – without any kind of warning – inflicted several hundred casualties on the intruding Swiss was neither here nor there. Unkel Von Schwartzer would have to restrain his notorious temper, put aside his furiously-sworn revenge and negotiate like any other commander, paying punctilious attention to parley protocol.

The young locotenent's mood had not been improved by his

327

own extensive injuries. He had suffered a mild concussion and lost most of his left hand to Savvi's impromptu bombardment. His surgeons had cleaned and dressed the stump as best they could – treatment which would have killed the average man. He had leapt up from the surgeon's table as if he had just had his toenails clipped, ordered his heralds back up to the ominously silent fortress to demand an immediate ceasefire and a full explanation of Savvi's outrageous breach of military etiquette. Allies weren't supposed to open fire on one another without so much as a by-your-leave, *Landscknechts*, Swiss or no!

Savvi, keen to remind Von Schwartzer who was master of the valley, had gladly accepted the invitation to talk.

The rival parties glared at one another for a long moment, their nervous underlings fidgeting throughout the tense standoff. Von Schwartzer couldn't bear the silence any longer. He held up his bloodily-bandaged stump, waved it angrily under his counterpart's beaked nose.

'I'll knock this off what we owe you, shall I?' the bull-necked warrior snarled.

'When you finally decide to pay up, by all means deduct a weregild for your missing hand,' Savvi said coolly.

The furious Swiss was boiling with rage, his throat flaring lobster-red beneath his armoured gorget. Savvi's self-assurance further undermined his small store of patience.

'I don't carry that sort of money, Savvi, as well you know. Bayard's away to Villefranco to fetch it from Briconet.'

Savvi shrugged.

'It's of no concern to me where you find the money. Surely you understood our agreement, it was simple enough!'

Von Schwartzer rolled his eyes.

'I understood.'

'You agreed to pay us twenty thousand livres in return for which we were to open the pass to your forces. You give us a downpayment of five thousand and the next thing we know you're rushing our position,' the tall German accused. 'Correct me if my mathematics is letting me down again, but by my reckoning you owe us fifteen thousand livres.'

'I'll stick 'em right up your tight Teutonic arse one by one,' Von Schwartzer howled, puce with rage. 'You could see damn fine what was happening man! Tarsi raided our camp and we were going after him! Are you telling me he dropped in to pay his fee before he crept up on us?'

'We didn't have any deal with Tarsi. The raid was his business.'

'And you didn't think to warn us he was on his way past you?'

'Why should I? Your security arrangements are not my concern.' Savvi wiped a speck of Swiss spittle from his cheek before mimicking the outraged youngster's yowling. 'Look out Von Schwartzer, Tarsi's on his way! You set guards didn't you?'

'I set guards. And I strangled the few useless bastards Tarsi left me,' the apoplectic commander replied, clenching his remaining fist in frustration.

The drummers and ensigns held their breath, hands hovering about their sheathed swords.

'All right Savvi,' Von Schwartzer breathed. 'You're right. Tarsi caught us napping and he's given us a bloody nose. But why in the name of God did you have to open fire on us, without so much as a squeak of warning? You didn't have to give that order,' he accused.

'Didn't I? Are you seriously suggesting I should have stepped into your path and waved my hands over my head? That I would have succeeded in sending five thousand Swiss fighters trotting back to their camp like a pack of unruly choirboys?'

'We were legitimately pursuing an enemy force. By God Savvi, since when has Tarsi been a friend of yours? You've let him off the hook good and proper. He'll be back in his hole by now, sitting tighter than a fig in a mule's arse!'

'You know as well as I do you would have smashed straight through Tarsi's defences and punched a way through to the main valley. What you would have signally failed to do would have been to stump up the fifteen thousand you owe us. We had no choice but to fire warning shots.'

'Warning shots?' the Swiss snarled. 'I've got two hundred casualties from your guns alone. God alone knows what that prig Bayard's going to make of it,' he blurted. Savvi raised his eyebrows, having already guessed his counterpart's most pressing concern – how on earth he was going to explain the debacle to the wondrous, indestructible Chevalier.

'I don't care what he makes of it. You'll have a few more than two hundred wounded to worry about if you try and push your men past Mont Galliard again.'

Von Schwartzer bristled up like a wounded boar which had just come face to face with its tormentor.

'You wouldn't dare. I'll tear that shit-heap apart brick by fucking brick if necessary,' he snarled.

Savvi shrugged, his blood running colder than the spume-lashed torrent which thundered hundreds of feet below their precarious platform.

'You'll lose your entire army in the process,' he said smoothly. 'I think it would be simpler for all concerned if you went back to your camp, set pen to paper, and . . . GOT HOLD OF OUR FUCKING MONEY, YOU HAIRY-ARSED, BALLOCK-SCRATCHING SHE-APE!'

The insane echo rebounded away down the gorge, setting up a flock of crows waiting patiently for their feasting to begin.

The Swiss delegation returned to the pass ten times faster than it had come, the furiously cursing locotenent striding back to his stranded army swearing eternal damnation on Francesco Savvi, Sick-knob of Mont Galliard, Eusebius Della Stroma, Cunt of Lunigiana and every diseased reptile who had the misfortune to serve them.

His rage was terrible to behold, startling even the hard-bitten pikemen who had survived Tarsi's assault and Savvi's culverins.

They watched in awestruck silence as he ranted and raved, challenging the hotheads to join his forlorn hope – a hand-picked suicide squad to assault the treacherously-held gates of Mont Galliard. The enraged commander was still selecting likely candidates when a mounted messenger galloped down the pass on a heavily-lathered horse. The rogue spurred his panting mount through the press of anxious warriors, seeking out Von Schwartzer beside his shot-tattered banner. He saluted, tugging the urgent dispatches from his satchel and offering them towards the scowling locotenent. Von Schwartzer eyed him, startling the weary messenger with the sheer ferocity of his stare.

'I hope for your sake you're going to tell me Bayard's on his way with a wagonload of coin,' he growled, rolling his eyes alarmingly. The messenger's hand began to tremble, the breeze riffling the sealed bundle he carried.

'I am sent with orders from army headquarters in Chamonix,' the messenger stammered.

'I've no time for your damned orders now. Get those arse-wipe papers from under my nose!' The Frenchman took the orders back, casting doubtful glances at the surly pikemen packed in about his horse. Von Schwartzer sighed, having second thoughts about defying his paymasters – however remote they might be.

'Read them out damn you, and be quick about it.'

The messenger tore the bundle open and unrolled the covering letter. 'To my esteemed comrade in arms, Unkel Von . . .'

'Skip all that cat-puke. Where's the damned money?'

The messenger went on with his message, eyes darting along the flowing French script to get to the point.

'. . . you are cordially invited to rejoin the reserve forces presently concentrating in Chamonix for the . . .'

'Bayard wants us in Chamonix? That's twenty leagues to the north, damn your forked tongue! One more push and we'll be in the damned valley!'

The messenger coughed, white with dread.

'With respect, my lord, the orders are from army headquarters, not the Chevalier Bayard.'

'Do you mean to tell me the immaculate Chevalier is not in Chamonix with our money?'

'His honour the Chevalier Bayard has been ordered to remain in Marseille, and ensure the rebellion in the Alpes Maritime is brought under control.'

'What rebellion?'

'The Duchy of Villefranco has been overrun by agents acting for the Empire. The Chevalier has assumed responsibility for restoring stability to the region.'

'But where's our money? Briconet was supposed to be . . .'

The messenger, somewhat heartened by Von Schwartzer's exasperated enquiries, swallowed nervously. He was, after all, a properly-appointed Royal Herald, bearing writs from King Francis himself. He wasn't some mountain postboy this puce-featured baboon could order about!

'The esteemed brother in Christ, Briconet of Avignon, was slain in the aforementioned disorders,' the messenger went on. 'The Chevalier Bayard has assumed his responsibilities in the region until a suitable replacement can be found.'

'But what about our . . .'

'There will be no more money until you are mustered once again in Chamonix. Your present orders are countermanded, your operations in the Col Galliard will cease forthwith.'

'What?'

The messenger sighed. Did this night-beast plug his ears with sealing wax?

'Your forces are hereby ordered to return to Chamonix to rejoin the reserve army being readied for Marshal Lautrec, who is concentrating in Como with a view to . . .'

'Como? What's he doing in Como?' Von Schwartzer cried.

'Milan fell to the enemy four days ago.'

The Swiss Locotenent was too stunned to speak.

Milan lost? Four days ago? That meant . . .

'You mean to tell me, my men have died in this damned cat-pissing puke-bucket of a gorge for no reason?'

The messenger carefully folded the orders.

'Headquarters only learned of the loss the day before yester-day. We regret we had no opportunity of informing you sooner. If you will excuse me, my lord, I am to return to Chamonix immediately. If you would oblige me with a fresh horse . . .'

'Fresh horse? Take the fucking lot for all I care! That snivelling shit Lautrec, how in hell did he manage to lose Milan?' the hapless locotenent enquired, peering at the accusing faces of his forlorn hope. 'What are you staring at, damn your eyes? I didn't know! I didn't know about Milan!'

His men stared back, their eyes colder than the scree under their boots.

'*I didn't know! You heard him, they didn't tell me!*' he wailed.

By the Hospice Gilbert le Petit Galliard

✦

Alberto Tarsi had never experienced such an overwhelming sense of relief. He was too shattered to question his wayward captain's extended absence, or enquire how on earth he had managed to recruit himself two hundred peasant pikemen.

The ripe observations he had rehearsed a hundred times since Eldritch had ridden out of the camp at Nus three months before had dissolved into the grey fog which threatened to engulf his brain.

He stood in the road, swaying slightly as he stared at the nervous soldiery in dumb bewilderment. The pikemen clutched their weapons and stared back at the battered fugitives, appalled by their unexpected proximity to the battlefront – and the hazardous consequences of their newly-chosen profession.

Eldritch's dark eyes swept over Tarsi's leftovers as he tried to estimate how many of Howath's Ride remained. He realised with a sinking heart that there were dozens of gaps in the ranks – old friends who he would never see or sup with again. Others, bandaged and bloody, were barely recognisable. He ignored Sandy Kerr's ferocious scowl of welcome, nodded at the cheerfully dishevelled William Hacker and caught the eye of the pale youth sitting on his horse just behind Tarsi.

So Duke Gerhard had thrown in his lot with them?

'I told you I would be back,' Eldritch repeated, wondering if the scowling Italian had lost his powers of speech during the all-too-obvious ordeal in the pass.

An ordeal he was acutely aware he had not shared.

'And I've brought reinforcements,' he nodded over his shoulder at the patiently-waiting column.

Tarsi looked along the shuffling ranks his understudy had indicated, recognising them as typical autumn-levy cannon-fodder. But even cannon-fodder had to be paid and equipped.

'We'll march through you, your pikes can guard the rear until we reach the hospice,' Tarsi said curtly. Eldritch nodded, tugged his horse into the lee of a crumbling outcrop as the bedraggled warband hobbled and hurried past the obstacle. Tarsi stood beside him, watching them go. He couldn't muster the strength to shake the rogue's hand, let alone give the sardonic young officer the grateful bearhug he seemed to be expecting.

Tarsi's legion marched past in cruelly quick time.

'Va Via! Front two ranks charge pikes, second to sixth porte pikes! Avanti, avanti!' Eldritch called in his schoolbook Italian. His farmhands shuffled, clattered, pushed and shoved, forming a passable pikeblock completely sealing the bottleneck track. Eldritch breathed a sigh of relief the scoundrels had remembered what little drill he had found time to teach them.

They had marched up from Asti briskly enough. Used to hard toil in dusty fields, the stifling route march had been a pleasant diversion for most of them. They had, after all, been fed, watered and paid out of Salt's generously-donated stipend, equipped from the town magazine with old but still serviceable pikes, swords, shields and daggers. Eldritch was more concerned with how they would behave in battle – God knew it took more than a couple of hours to turn simple farmboys to effective soldiers.

He frowned, turning his reins over his gauntlets as he waited for Tarsi to respond to his miraculous arrival.

'We passed the Hospice on the way up. God be praised your daughter, and my sister, are safe and well,' he said with awkward courtesy.

'What do you want me to do, kiss your hand?' Tarsi growled, taking an unsteady pace down the road after his grievously-reduced band.

'I am sorry. I was imprisoned in Villefranco, there was nothing more I could have done,' Eldritch explained stiffly.

'Villefranco? By whom?' the Duke enquired, spurring his lame charger alongside the intently-staring stranger.

'My Duke, this is the *Transmarini* I told you of, Captain James Eldritch, returned to us at last from his recent furlough.'

'Ah yes, the one whose . . .'

'Exactly he,' Tarsi interrupted, anxious to avoid any unpleasantness while they were so dangerously exposed on the high road. 'Any this, my dear captain, is Duke Gerhard of Villefranco, colonel of the regiment Mounier to which you, sir, now belong,' he went on, fixing the captain with a curiously inscrutable glare. Eldritch inclined his head in modest courtesy at the nobleman he had spied on from the stable, back in Villefranco. It seemed like an age ago, now.

'We heard on the road . . . that is, I thought Kraven had sent word Lord Howath's former warband was to march . . .'

'He came here to Italy in order to summon you all back to Calais, that much is true,' Tarsi interjected, 'but Duke Gerhard *persuaded* him to sell your services on. We all of us serve the Duke now.'

Eldritch was puzzled by Tarsi's manner – he had expected him to be angry, scathing, bitter – but not offhand. He was equally surprised to see the veteran soldier fawning about this pale whippersnapper of a duke. Gerhard, who had already heard of Eldritch's fanatical sense of duty towards his missing sister, took one look at the brute and decided to follow Tarsi's advice, realising it might not be an opportune moment to mention his sister's recent visit to his bedchamber.

By God, you didn't need to be an Egyptian sorceress to recognise the resemblance between the siblings. Both of them possessed flakes of sea coal for eyes, cheekbones which could cut Parma ham and a mass of thick, dark hair, parted down the middle.

He smiled wearily.

'I am delighted to make your acquaintance, my dear sir. Am I to understand you have had some dealings in my Duchy?'

'That can wait until we get the men back to the Hospice. You can see for yourself these men need care, food, rest and shelter,' Tarsi said stiffly. 'You can tell us all about your adventures later.'

The regiment – reinforced by Eldritch's green recruits – had overrun the remote hospice, grateful to find shelter in each corner, every ramshackle shed. They had lain down in dirt, on straw, in steaming dunghills. They had curled up beneath farmyard sacks and in the mouldy stalls out in the stable block – anywhere out of the snapping wind which whisked about the remote heights.

Tarsi, desperate to reorganise his command following their confused descent on the windswept post, barely had time to greet his own daughter. The women had been kept as busy patching up the wounded as he had been cutting them up in the first place. He had clutched Angelica to his bent breastplate, trying to imagine he felt something other than a bottomless store of pity for the waif. Praying to God he might one day recognise this undernourished waxwork as his own flesh and blood – the vivacious tomboy who had once made his life an absolute delight.

In contrast with his own dismally drab daughter, Merron Eldritch had been as excited as a colt in pasture by their longed-for return, capering in glee to see her menfolk safe.

Angelica pulled at his bloody sleeve.

He smiled down at her pale, pinched features as if he were staring at a miniature of his long dead wife.

'We're safe here now, aren't we father?' she asked.

'Safe as houses,' Tarsi encouraged, wishing it were true. If the Swiss negotiated the bottleneck outside Mont Galliard, they would be swarming over the Hospice's improvised defences within the hour. But he knew there was nowhere left for them to run. They would stand – and die – where they were.

'Of course it's safe you ninny!' Merron exclaimed. 'Now Milan has fallen they won't have any call to go . . .'

'Milan has fallen?' Tarsi choked, looking around at his subdued captain for confirmation. Eldritch nodded, more abashed than ever.

'Four days ago. We heard the news before we left Asti, but it's taken this long to get here,' he explained, well aware of the implications of this cruelly-delayed bulletin. Merron nodded excitedly, her massed auburn curls escaping from the flimsy headdress.

'So there won't be any need to hold the road against the enemy reinforcements, that's right isn't it James?' Merron enquired, her bright eyes flickering over her brother's set features. Tarsi's tired heart lurched despite the bitter intelligence. He would have cut off his own hand for the opportunity of snatching the vibrant girl up in his arms, feeling that vital life-force light up his ageing bones.

'*James!?*'

Tarsi glanced about, noticing the surly-looking wench Eldritch had brought along with him was looking askance at the laughing girl, signalling her brooding brother with her eyebrows. Eldritch held her glance, then, more awkwardly than Tarsi would have imagined, smiled shortly at the company.

'My lords, my ladies, may I present Marie Charlotte Armonde, Countess du Lac. The Countess accompanied us during our journey from the Château Celestine to Villefranco in order . . .'

Tarsi blinked at the dishevelled girl, her road-weary gown grey with dust, the hanging hem as tattered as a tinker's cuffs.

'Accompanied?' the ragamuffin gave a brittle chuckle. 'What a quaint way you have with words, James,' she scolded.

'*James!?*' Merron echoed disbelievingly.

Who did this hedgerow hussy think she was talking to, glaring about as if she had just been unrolled from the nearest carpet?

Merron and the rest of them were so startled by the down-trodden noblewoman's familiar tone they quite forgot their tongues – and Tarsi didn't have time for their tiresomely domestic intercourse. He waved his wrist, irritated at the interruption.

'Milan fell four days ago? So where's Lautrec?'

'Retreating eastwards, to Como.'

'Como?' he cried. 'You know what this means?'

Eldritch knew all too well.

'With Milan in our hands, the French would have seen no need in opening new routes over the Western Alps. They would have used one of the bigger passes further to the east.'

He closed his eyes and bowed his head.

They had fought and died for nothing. Their sacrifice – and that of the hard-fighting Swiss – as insignificant as a single snowflake in an avalanche. Tarsi could have choked on the savage irony of it.

'*C'est la guerre,*' Eldritch murmured.

The girls glanced at one another, studied their subdued men-folk, wondering what terrible cloud had descended upon their joyous reunion.

'. . . So you tricked our old friend Salt into signing the company over to you,' Tarsi repeated, faintly bemused by Eldritch's shameless tale of death and double-dealing. The Englishman had given them a carefully edited account of his adventures, bearing in mind his own sister, his commanding officers and his kidnap victim were all present, ready and willing with inter-pretations of their own.

'Lock, stock and barrel. I would have had him sign over the entire Ride, but I didn't imagine Kraven would have allowed me to get away with that,' Eldritch said candidly. Tarsi raised his eyebrows. Duke Gerhard frowned to think the upstart captain would not have hesitated to cheat him out of the greater portion of his hard-bargained regiment.

Tarsi – one step ahead of his scowling superior – hurried to his protégé's defence, pretending to be greatly intrigued by his deceptions. 'And these pikemen of yours, they raised no objection when you stole them from under Salt's nose?'

'I had worried what they might say,' Eldritch admitted. 'But we did have one stroke of good fortune. The sergeant at arms Salt had appointed as a bodyguard happened to be one of my father's old hands, a fellow called Oldbarn. Once I persuaded him who I was, he was able to see our side of the argument and was happy to re-enlist as an Elder Sergeant.'

'I don't imagine your man Hobby was delighted by his rival's promotion.'

Eldritch showed his teeth.

'Hobby and I had a full discussion of his terms and conditions.'

Merron giggled.

Tarsi frowned, disliking the idea of this cosy little English conspiracy. They were good enough fighters, but generally as transparent as a whorehouse window. He liked to think their naïveté made his *Transmarini* trustworthy – the idea his second-in-command was capable of deceptions as subtle as the notoriously slippery Cardinal Wolsey himself rather unnerved him.

'We had authenticated paperwork, signed, sealed and delivered by Algernon Salt himself. Oldbarn was fully justified in bringing his men over to us.' He paused for a moment, raised his sharp chin a notch.

'I can always order them off elsewhere,' he suggested.

'You've done well enough, Captain Eldritch,' Tarsi said breezily. 'Don't you agree, my Duke?'

'What's that? Eh? Oh well, very well, very well indeed,' the distracted Duke replied, nodding his head and smiling winningly at Merron.

The Italian soldier of fortune had never quite convinced himself he could trust his scheming captain. And Eldritch's description of his miraculous, outrageous and occasionally hilarious adventures around Southern France were not likely to rebuild that bond.

At the root of his suspicions were the Englishman's dangerous dalliances with his own mortal enemy, the Vicomte D'Toinueill. Their sinister liaison the previous summer had eaten through Tarsi's store of respect, undermined his growing regard.

Tarsi had never discovered exactly what the two men had agreed, how far Eldritch had intended to assist in the Vicomte's timely flight from custody. He had guessed that the cunning Vicomte had blackmailed the headstrong Englishman, trading his knowledge of Lillith Eldritch's whereabouts in return for the rogue's support during his audacious escape.

It was a credible defence as far as it went – but Tarsi would neither forgive nor forget the fact Eldritch hadn't hesitated to go behind his back, aiding and abetting the escape of his most dangerous and implacable enemy. Eldritch had tried to disguise his role in the affair – Tarsi had caught up with him near the fishponds in Aosta, clutching a fiercely-bleeding knife wound which had required long and painful stitching.

The shining crescent of scar tissue was a brand, a clear warning to his fellows to beware Eldritch's dangerously dual nature. Now he had returned from his adventures about France, trailing a tale so preposterous it made his previous explanations look like the Lord's gospels – and re-aroused all his master's suspicions about his character and his motives.

Was the rogue truly seeking his missing sister, or had he used his murderous ride to further his own aims, laying the foundations of his own mercenary empire? He had listened to Eldritch's dubious tale in disbelief, wondering sometimes whether the Long-Hair was making a fool of him. God damn *il Zazzera* for imagining he could pull the wool over Alberto Tarsi's eyes!

Dukes of France murdered by accidental blows to the head? Castles stormed by two-strong assault parties? Meddling inquisitors distracted by fantastical war machines which were fully capable of blowing entire pikeblocks to atoms? Tarsi had a good mind to throw the lanky devil straight back into the *oubliette* in which he claimed to have languished. The lying snipe had even brought along this travelling player of a countess, to hang some threads of credibility to his ramshackle explanations. But he had not been able to guess her motives any more than he had been able to explain his own grudging admiration for this arrogant knight errant.

Duke Gerhard had listened to Eldritch's bizarre tale in equally bemused silence, uncertain whether to kick over the can of worms which made up his own questionable role in the affair – or pretend he had been a guiltless victim of foul circumstance.

He had murdered kith and kin, turned his coat, sold his soul, cheated, lied and plotted. And all for what – to stand in this mountain hideaway, the few riches with which he had managed to escape loaded into a covered wagon at the mercy of this pack of land-bound pirates. He had been horribly intrigued to hear Eldritch tell of his suspicions as to the White Rabbit's whereabouts and of his foolhardy raid on Villefranco, appalled at the prospect of Eldritch enquiring into his . . .

The Duke started, acutely aware that the desultory conversation had petered out into a frosty silence. He looked up, pierced to the core by the Englishman's most ferocious of glares. Tarsi looked equally startled. He had been so preoccupied with his own doubts he had missed the captain's subtle change of direction, failed to recognise the sudden switch from amusing confession to damning accusation.

Eldritch repeated the question.

'I asked you, my lord Duke, whether my information had been correct. Were you aware my sister Lillith had left the Château Celestine, intending to visit the Castello Villefranco on her way east?'

The question hung in the air like the stink of a spluttering match cord. Gerhard's nostrils dilated. He glanced at Tarsi, who was standing between him and Eldritch, his broad, peasant's face half-turned towards the quailing Duke.

'I . . . I have never heard of her,' Gerhard stammered. 'The information you were given . . . was clearly incorrect.'

He willed himself to hold Eldritch's stare.

'According to the Countess, it was common knowledge in the château that Lillith had departed for Villefranco.' Eldritch's features had turned to ash and stone, his voice a death-rasp from the netherworld.

The hairs on Gerhard's neck bristled, his hands trembled.

'I know now, she has become a common courtesan,' Eldritch could not quite bring himself to say whore. Merron was appalled, blanching at her brother's unholy accusations. 'You will not offend me by confirming her visit, my lord,' Eldritch leered.

Tarsi held up his hand, alarmed at the abrupt about-face.

Their light-hearted discussion had turned ugly in a blink, the sinister deceptions which had lurked below the surface of their doubtful friendship resurfacing like a many-legged sea monster to drag them down once more.

'Even if it were true that your sister had visited Villefranco – and I do not suggest for one moment it was,' he said cautiously, 'The Duke would have been unaware of your relationship to her, and could not, cannot, be blamed for any unintended offence.'

Eldritch's cold eyes swept from the cowering Duke to the soldier's armoured back.

'I knew of no such visit!' Gerhard cried.

'She left Claude to go to you,' the rag-doll Countess accused with a shake of her head, 'although God knows what drove her to such a course.'

Gerhard's watery eyes bulged with terror at her damning observation.

'All I would know, my Duke, is whither she went?'

'*Is* that all, Eldritch? I have already told you what I make of this matter. Duke Gerhard can in no way, shape or form be blamed for what has befallen your sister,' Tarsi said levelly. 'Nobody forced her to go to Marseille; nobody forced her to come to Villefranco. You, on the other hand – and by your own admission – dragged the Countess du Lac from the château and carried her, against her will, to Villefranco. I must declare I see more fault in your behaviour than Duke Gerhard's!'

The nobleman in question nodded, his weak chin wobbling. His frayed nerves were singing like trapped larks, his eyes popping as he followed the deadly interplay. He knew Eldritch's mood was becoming darker by the second – and he hadn't exactly been full of the joys of spring when he had arrived, casting dastardly glances at him as if he were sowing bitter seeds in their puny hearts. Thankfully, Tarsi seemed intent on upholding his superior's reputation, urging the upstart to curb his ill-mannered interrogation.

'Do you imagine the Dukes of Villefranco are in the habit of cavorting with common wh . . . courtesans?' he asked as levelly as he was able.

Tarsi turned between the two men, broad shoulders tensed.

'Nobody is suggesting any such thing. I am persuaded there has been some manner of misunderstanding,' he said.

'I wish there had been, but I am convinced otherwise. I do not seek to lay the blame for my sister's chosen career on any man present. I merely seek to establish her present whereabouts,' Eldritch repeated.

'So you can take off after her once more?' Tarsi scowled. 'I gave you leave to seek her, I wish now I had confined you in camp, the turmoil you have occasioned.'

Eldritch took a deep breath, every nerve in his body tingling with repressed emotion. He was a blink away from striking out – attacking the rogue-shadows who danced and capered in the periphery of his staring vision. He recognised the same blinding rage which had consumed him back at the château, the uncontrollable furies which had brought his iron-hilted sword down with such fatal force on the Duc de Milhaud's unsuspecting neck.

'My dear lady, Angelica, Mistress Eldritch, be so good as to step out for a moment while I confer with these gentlemen,' Tarsi said briskly. The girls picked up their skirts as if to obey but the Countess stood her ground, grubby chin jutting defiantly.

'This has as much to do with me as him,' she shrilled, nodding at the pale-faced Duke and pointing an accusing finger at Eldritch. 'If it hadn't been for his wretched holy quest, I would be back home with my people!'

'You told me you had neither!' Eldritch said scathingly. 'You ought to be grateful, madam, that I was there to deliver you from your debts!'

The Countess growled with rage, sprang forward to claw at the Englishman's tunic in red-nailed frenzy. He held her off, his bemused smirk throwing oil on her flaming temper.

'You arrogant, two-faced bastard! You sang a prettier tune when you were up to your neck in the *oubliette*! I wish to Christ I'd left you there, you walking serpent!'

Merron gawped at the stranger's murderous outburst, wondering what had passed between this spitfire and her equally headstrong brother. If alchemists had possessed the means to harness their passions, they might have turned water to wine, dung to gold!

'Well I've had better billets,' Eldritch admitted, wrapping his arms about the thrashing Countess to stifle her murderous assault.

'So you gave the captain a taste of my dungeons,' Gerhard said foolishly, desperate not to be left behind in the deadly cut-and-thrust but dangerously out of his depth.

'I did, and damn me I'll do it again if he gives me the chance. Rogue, cockspur, rattlepurse, backstabber!'

Merron covered her mouth, appalled by the Countess' bitter invective. Tarsi, goaded beyond endurance by their damned tantrums, took hold of Charlotte's forearm and dragged her aside, frogmarching her across the room to the awestruck girls as if they could somehow disperse her furiously-directed venom. The girls backed off, reluctant to remain within range of her claws and tongue. Eldritch straightened his tunic as coolly as his battered dignity would allow, watching his tormented lover struggle and kick, slowly subside behind the unflinching Italian.

'Out! All of you. Aye, and you too, my Duke, if you please,' Tarsi barked, pointing the Countess at the chamber door, broad features black with barely-restrained rage. Gerhard thought better of contesting the request, and followed Merron and Angelica into the passage.

'How dare you? Don't you know who I am?'

'Get out, God damn you, or I'll haul you back to your Marseille cathouse myself!' Tarsi roared. The Countess wilted, simmered, and stormed out seething, slamming the door behind her.

James Eldritch stepped from one foot to the other as if he were some beardless novice brought before the abbot. He was acutely aware of the precariousness of his position – his status in Regiment Mounier, his impossible quest to redeem his sister's reputation, his own failing fortunes.

'Listen to me, captain, because I do not intend to repeat myself, nor refer to these matters ever again,' Tarsi began, his fist clenched about his sword hilt as if he would prove his point by any means necessary. 'It is true I gave you leave to follow your sister to Marseille. You found her trail and discovered the truth of her unfortunate life. I sympathise, but you said yourself that no man has forced her to it, no man profits from her sweat.'

Eldritch closed his eyes at the dreadful image of his elder sister, gleefully earning her coin. Tarsi paused, waiting for the Englishman's dark eyes to come to a distracted rest on his own.

'You have fulfilled all reasonable obligations. No man could have done more to redeem his sister's honour. But she is gone, James, gone and glad of it. She does not care whether you chase about Europe sniffing her bed linen and I do not imagine for a moment she would obey your strictest instruction to return home. So, I say to you, enough is enough. You must make your choice. In return for your previous service at my side, I am prepared to sign the papers releasing you from your indentures. I will also pay any compensation your master the Duke may demand. In short, James, I will let you go and hear no more of you.'

Eldritch swallowed hard, cursing the foul air in the draughty chamber, buried deep within their remote Hospice hideaway.

'If, on the other hand you mean to remain at my side, share my struggles, you must renounce this wretched quest of yours once and for all, allow your sister to lead her life as you lead yours. I will indulge your reckless fancies no longer.'

'I will make amends,' Eldritch croaked.

'Do so. To me, to your younger sister, to this hellbitch of a Countess you saw fit to drag here with you. I warn you now, there are but two ways you will buy her peace and ensure she remains silent – a garotte or a wedding band.'

Eldritch's moist eyes flared.

'Marry her?'

'Or garotte her. Your choice, but I know which course I should choose.' He pantomimed pulling a cord tight.

'It is, after all, an extraordinarily light sentence for kidnapping a high-ranking French noblewoman, penniless or no.'

'I will,' Eldritch promised, staring at the peeling ceiling.

Tarsi waited, the reservoir of words he had accumulated set to boil out of his compressed mouth.

The question he had hardly dared ask, ever since Aosta.

'But before you renounce your crimes and take your vows as a soldier of God and the Empire, tell me truly. What happened, back in Aosta?'

Eldritch twitched, his lean hand straying to the scar on his jawline. He saw no point in further evasion, told the truth as plainly as he was able.

'You guessed the truth of most of it, I told you what I could. The Bastard Gueldres sent word he knew of Lillith's whereabouts. He would tell me where she had hidden herself, if I helped him escape.'

'The alley, the waiting horses?'

'His agents organised the details,' Eldritch murmured, shame-faced. 'I provided the diversion which enabled him to slip his guards. I wish to God I had followed him, cut him down like a dog!'

'You do now,' Tarsi rasped. 'At the time, I trust you thought you had made a good deal – you were, after all, betraying me.'

'I had no choice!' Eldritch exclaimed. 'If I had known then what I know now, I would have cut off his head and spat down his neck!'

'So he gave you the scar as a keepsake, to disguise your part in his flight?'

'Deeper than I thought he would. I never expected it to fool you.'

344

'It didn't. To tell you the truth, if he had been close enough to give you that, he could have easily finished you there and then.'

'I would have taken him to hell with me.'

'Perhaps.'

'So you knew, all the long?'

'And let you live, as did our esteemed Vicomte.'

Eldritch frowned.

'Why?'

Tarsi chuckled. 'We missed you, back in the pass.'

'I'll ride back directly, if you command it,' Eldritch offered.

'I have already warned you against pointless gestures. Do you know James, you might make a decent soldier one day, if you learn to obey your head rather than your heart.'

'Like you?'

Tarsi chuckled.

'Like me, my friend. Call them in. You'd better give them the good news about your new alliance.'

'She's not much of a dowry,' Eldritch said ruefully.